Women's

Women's Friendships

Women's Friendships

A COLLECTION OF SHORT STORIES

EDITED, WITH AN INTRODUCTION
AND AFTERWORD, BY
SUSAN KOPPELMAN

University of Oklahoma Press : Norman and London

Edited by Susan Koppelman

Images of Women in Fiction: Feminist Perspectives
(Bowling Green, 1972)
Old Maids: Short Stories by Nineteenth Century U.S.
Women Writers (Boston, 1984)
The Other Woman: Stories of Two Women and a Man
(New York, 1984)
Between Mothers and Daughters: Stories Across a Generation
(New York, 1985)
"May Your Days Be Merry and Bright" and Other Christmas
Stories by Women (Detroit, 1988; New York, 1989)
The Signet Classic Book of Southern Short Stories,
with Dorothy Abbott (New York, 1991)
Women's Friendships: A Collection of Short Stories
(Norman, 1991)

Library of Congress Cataloging-in-Publication Data

Women's friendships: a collection of short stories/edited and with an intro-
duction and afterword by Susan Koppelman.
     p.   cm.
   Includes bibliographical references and index.
   ISBN 0-8061-2376-1 (cloth)
   ISBN 0-8061-2386-9 (paperback)
   1. Short stories, American—Women authors.   2. Women—United
States—Fiction.   3. Friendship—Fiction.   I. Koppelman, Susan.
PS647.W6W66   1991
813'.01089287—dc20   91-50303
                                                                    CIP

Permissions acknowledgments are on page 318.

2   3   4   5   6   7   8   9   10   11   12   13   14   15   16   17   18

To those whose friendship
over many years has
sustained and inspired me

Frances Bollotin Koppelman
Ruth Goldman Benjamin
Gail Mascolo Robbins
Emily Toth

What do friends do for each other?
Whatever is necessary and possible so we can
get on with our lives.

What do friends give each other?
Lots of wonderful presents.

You are the wind beneath my wings.

CONTENTS

ix

PREFACE

I think of the work I have been doing for the last nineteen years as literary archaeology: the restoration of women's literary heritage. I am looking for that thing which the creation and possession of a body of literature—written or oral—gives a people, what Carol Christ refers to in her book *Diving Deep and Surfacing*[1] as the sacred dimension of stories. I think that what the Hebrew Scriptures are to the Jews—a source of history, mythology, rituals, instructions for ethical living, legal and governmental guidelines, poems and songs— women's literature is to women.

I confine my research to the stories of the women of one political entity, the United States, because I need to work with a unit I can hope to encompass with some responsible thoroughness. But I wish I could be doing the same work with the stories of all women, in all genres, from all times, in all places, in all languages. I am not working alone in this field, as I was in the beginning; now the work is getting done more quickly. More of us are working on it together, enriching each other's imaginings and intellectual leaps.

I work to help transform our understanding of the literary and real-life history of women. Women's material and emotional history is recorded in our literature. We are finding our literature, immersing ourselves in it, and learning to understand what emerges from it.

I want to make available to lovers of literature, to women (for we have always been the greatest lovers, readers, and writers of literature), the history of the short story as it has been created and developed by women in the United States or territories that became states since the beginnings of the genre here. I want us to have the evidence of that development so that we can decide what we want to make of it. Most of all, I want us to have it because it belongs to us.

When we who are engaged in the great effort to reclaim women's literature share what we are doing, we are participating in a great feminist communal enterprise. This collection of stories is an expression of the loving cooperation and interaction of such a feminist scholarly community.

With this book of short stories about friendships between and among women, I have begun to ask others to work with me. I wanted this book of stories about women who support each other to be created by women, by feminist scholars, who also support each other.

My first collection of stories, *Old Maids* (1984),[2] includes thirteen stories that trace the evolution of nineteenth-century U.S. women writers in their portrayals of unmarried women coping with the pejorative stereotype of "old maid." The changes in those portrayals reflect the changes in the legal, economic, and social status of independent women.

Single women do not often regret the absence of marriage, but sometimes they wish to share their lives with others. Only two of the stories written toward the end of the nineteenth century portray women who are truly happy with their lives. One is the unnamed narrator of Elizabeth Stuart Phelps's story "No. 13." This single woman living in a boarding house creates a caring community of friends out of a household of solitary boarders. The second is Celia, central character in "How Celia Changed Her Mind" by Rose Terry Cook. As the story opens, Celia, a seamstress, thinks that the indignity, ridicule, and isolation imposed on unmarried women is even more painful than the indignities, dissatisfactions, loneliness, overwork, and loss of independence of the married women she observes as she sews in their homes. She marries briefly "just to be a missus" and discovers her error. When her independence is restored by her husband's death, she is appropriately thankful—and celebrates that gratitude by gathering for a Thanksgiving dinner a community of women friends who share her solitary blessedness.

When I introduced that book I didn't realize that not only are the women in the stories represented as moving toward increasing self-esteem vis-à-vis their status as unmarried women, but they are portrayed as participating with increasing pleasure and intentionality in supportive communities of women, in women's friendships. That collection of stories presents women's friendships as phenomena peripheral to central realities in the lives of women. This collection presents those friendships as the central realities in women's lives.

Certain themes appear in women's stories over and over and over. These are the themes of our lives. Sometimes the themes are central to the stories, that is, they are the subjects of the stories. Sometimes the themes are peripheral to the stories, functioning as storytelling devices or narrative strategies. Sometimes they permeate the story and function in both capacities. The theme of women's friendships is among the themes about which women have written the most.

When we read our own literature we discover these themes and, in recognizing their familiarity, we become visible to ourselves and to each other in new ways; we begin to understand how well we know what each other means. We learn how strong we are.

The faith that has guided my research since 1972 on short stories written by women includes the following beliefs: (1) Whatever there is to be written about by women has already been written about by women. We have never been silent! (2) There is no kind of woman who hasn't written her stories and the stories of her people. None of us is missing from literature. (3) If we work diligently and imaginatively we will find all those stories representing our diversity. We can all be found. (4) Once we recover what survives of women's literature and immerse ourselves in it, all of literature will look, feel, seem, and *be* different to us forever. Women's literature will change women's lives. (5) And when our perceptions are so changed by how much of women's literature we have read, we will never again be overwhelmed by patriarchal judgments. Immersion in our literary heritage will free our minds and hearts.

About Choosing the Stories

None of my collections contains all the stories that I wanted to include. There is never enough room. So I have developed some guidelines to help me work within the limits set by the realities of publishing. On the one hand, the guidelines ensure that the stories I choose are representative along a multitude of axes; on the other hand, they help me find the special story that will lead the way into and open up the other stories for the largest and most varied audience as possible; on the third hand they protect me from going crazy from an overdose of freedom.

I never use more than one story by any writer in one collection, although some writers have given us many stories about one theme.

A whole set of my policies deals with stories that "do the same thing." From those that are equally appealing, I will use the earliest one because I am eager to restore our literary history. When similar and equally exciting stories were written by women of the same period, I choose stories that give the greatest illustration of our diversity. When writers who share ethnicity, race, region, period, and other attributes and who have worked in the same subgenre have written similar stories, I use the story by the writer who has left the larger body of short fiction. I do that because I *love* short fiction. Whenever I discover a writer new to me who has written a story that delights me, that reaches to the core of my being, I want to read more by that writer. So I make the choice that will offer the most to readers with hearty appetites, of which I am one.

After I put together a tentative table of contents, permission to use the stories must be secured. Some stories that I would have included are absent because I couldn't afford to pay the permission fee, the copyright owners were unreachable, or the copyright status couldn't be determined in a legally satisfactory manner.

But if those stories had been secured, which ones would I have left out? That's an impossible question for me to answer. I'm asking only because I know that if I don't, someone else will. I'm asking so you'll know I know it's a question begging to be asked, but don't ask me to answer it.

SUSAN KOPPELMAN

St. Louis, Missouri

ACKNOWLEDGMENTS

Many people have been involved in the creation of this book. Naming and properly thanking all of them would take as many pages as the whole rest of the book. It has been the beneficiary of numerous friendship communities sharing wisdom, laughter, tears, and gossip. I apologize in advance to anyone who feels left out of these acknowledgments and also to anyone who is uncomfortable to find her or his name in print. It is a convention to say that I alone am responsible for whatever errors or wrong thinking appears in this book. Far be it from me to violate convention, so consider it said.

For reading the Introduction and Afterword in various stages and making provocative comments, posing important challenges, and asking the right hard questions, I thank my friends Judith Arcana, Glynis Carr, Sally Ann Drucker, Kathy Gentile, Barbara Harman, Mary Navarro, Joanna Russ, and Mary Sims. For editing and reediting the Introduction and Afterword, my friend Betty Burnett has once again been incredibly generous with her professional skills. My gratitude to the women who wrote the headnotes, who have shared their best scholarship and insights, is immeasurable. The story writers deserve the thanks of all of us for recording our lives. We are all indebted to the writers among us. For teaching this collection in manuscript form to the students of English 210, "Female Friendship in Women's Literature," in the Spring of 1990 at Bucknell University, I am obliged to Glynis Carr, and to the students of English 210 for their responses. For discussing and demonstrating women's friendships while we took long walks through many seasons, I thank Ann Bischoff and Barbara Harman. For sharing women's friendships (along with laughter and hearty appetites) at our monthly women's dinners at Hsu's Chinese Restaurant, I am grateful for the contributions to my thinking of Siné Berhanu, Betty Burnett, Janet Cuenca, Kathy Gentile, Barbara Harman, Sheryl Meyering, Ruth Marquis, Nancy Movshin, Adelia Parker, Ella Sachs, Jean Simon, and Carol Snyder.

For nineteen years of discussing these ideas and everything else we care about over the phone, in letters, across dinner tables, and during walks in cities neither of us lives in, for sharing her brilliant and always politically correct thinking, and for being my beloved friend in the most practical, caring, and clever ways, Emily Toth. For eighteen years of endless hours on the phone during which we dissected the patriarchy, kvetched, strategized, thought our books out aloud, and loved each other, Joanna Russ. For providing me with ever vital and inspiring models of womanly friendships in every stage of life, Frances Koppelman. For sharing special friendships with me over many, many years, Phyllis Sutton Andersen, Rhoda Bonovitz Orme-Johnson, Jeanne Ryan, Gail Robbins, Inuka Mwanguzi, and Helen Eisen. For "friendship for an evening," Mabel Stonecipher. For providing me with feminist sisterhood, scholarly support, and divine silliness, all the wonderful women of SKMSI, the best network possible for feminist scholars and writers. For exploring intergenerational friendship with me, my friend and sister writer and cat lover, Mia Consiglio.

My thanks to Maria Duarte, then Executive Director, and Jerilyn M. Fisher, still Administrative Associate of the Midwest Modern Language Association, for their practical support for the several sessions on women's friendships at our annual conferences. They provided a wonderful opportunity for feminist collegiality and scholarly interchange.

For their help with my research at the University City Library, Linda Ballard, Shirley Goldberg, and the whole staff; at the Washington University Olin Library, Rudolph Clay and the reference staff; at the St. Louis Public Library, Erik Stocker, Rare Books, and the staff in the periodical room. For his faith in this book and efforts on its behalf, Tom Radko. For continuing to shepherd this book after Tom left Oklahoma for Nevada, my thanks to Kimberly Wiar. For her scrupulous and sensitive copy editing and her sisterly care of this book, my thanks to Barbara Siegemund-Broka.

For providing the emotional and material circumstances that make all my work since 1980 possible, Dennis Mills. For keeping the computer working despite my technophobia, St. Louis heat and humidity, and cat hair, Nathan Cornillon.

The cats who supervised the work on this book are Pizza, a half-Siamese calico and the mother of them all; Jack, her faithful consort, a black-and-gray mackerel tiger who lived wild until the unnaturally cold December of 1989 coincided with his free choice of free food in the kitchen and warm laps in the living room; and their three sons: three-year-old Raggedy Andy, the cross-eyed, blue-eyed rag doll, two-year-old Squeaker, the long-haired shiny black with a gray mane; and one-year-old Riff Raff IV, the completely orange cat—orange eyes, orange whiskers, orange fur. During the last two months of work on this book, Pizza presented us with four kittens to remind us to take time off and play. Emily and Bruce from that litter have remained permanent members of our household to supervise the proofreading.

SUSAN KOPPELMAN

Introduction

> Let's start by talking about friendship—the warmth, intimacy, affection,
> joy, obligations, need, jealousy, sorrow, sharing, loving, and why we
> want this central experience of our lives affirmed and articulated. Friend-
> ship gives me a lump in the throat. I can hardly talk about it yet I need to
> talk about it, give it structure, so I want to read stories, articles, poems,
> see plays about it to help me put my feelings in order.[1]

I first learned about women's friendships from my mother. When I
was a little girl, my mother spent time with her many friends at our
house and sometimes I would sit under the kitchen table pretending
to play while I listened to them talk. When I began to grow up and
could not fit under the table anymore, sometimes the women let me
sit at the table with them and listen, and sometimes join in the
conversation.

It seemed to me that those women were conducting the most important business in the world as they talked together and that they
were having a whole lot of fun doing it. The warm, reciprocal, nurturing friendship they shared was one of the reasons I wanted to
grow up to be a woman.

Each friendship had a certain rhythm. At different intervals, Ruth
or Freda or Essye or Fannie or Rose or Louise or Anne or Francie or
Fruma or one of the three Lillians or Mollie or Pauline or Sophie or
Mildred or Bea or Ethel or Jessie or Lottie or several of them would
come over. Some came daily for a time and others never came more
often than yearly. They and my mother would gather around the

table, drink coffee, and talk. And whether the visit was a daily one or a yearly one, the conversation always seemed to be a continuation of yesterday's talk.

Sometimes my mom opened a box from one of Cleveland's superb Jewish bakeries—Davis, where they still have great coconut bars (chocolate or white cake rectangles soaked in chocolate syrup and then rolled in fresh shredded coconut), or Lax and Mandel, whose Russian tea biscuits and dobosh torte are not to be equaled! or Ungar's, who made the best ruggelach in town—and put a dish (almost always the pink multi-faceted glass plate that her mother had bought in a dime store—Depression glass, they call it now) of pastry out on the table. Sometimes one of the women brought something good to share. Molly always baked wonderful mandel brot. Sometimes there was just the bare table and coffee cups.

The women would sit and talk, drink coffee and eat. There was always lots of laughing—sometimes explosions of laughter. It seemed that they talked about everything. I remember them talking and laughing about things I didn't understand, sometimes using Yiddish to make sure I didn't understand. They told stories about their lives, their families, and their problems. They compared their experiences, not to compete but to understand.

One woman was widowed suddenly and had to work out the problems of continuing to run a business while the bankers wouldn't lend her money because she was now a woman alone. She saw her sons through their religious education without exposing them to the bitterness she felt about their abandonment by the men in the synagogue father-son club her husband had helped to run. She packed up and drove to Florida on winter vacation with her boys in the back and no "man to handle things." The other women listened to her talk about these problems, made suggestions, and helped her work out solutions. I saw clearly that there was an exchange taking place: she modeled courage and they reciprocated by mirroring for her the vision of a woman who could do what she wanted to do—a woman of *chutzpah, mentschlichkite,* audacity, character.

These women began to be faced with decisions about aging parents they couldn't care for in their own homes. Others grieved about the deaths of their parents. They carried each other through these times, sharing information about nursing homes, doctors, social workers, insurance plans, funeral costs. They listened to each other's grief and visited each other's failing parents. They supported each other through funerals and during the week of *shiva,* carrying in trays of food, bringing extra cups and glasses, serving the mourners, and bringing husbands and sons to make the daily minyans.

I don't remember them ever talking about "doing the right thing," but they always seemed to know what it was and how to do it. There was an ethical consensus among them.

There were new children born to the women in the group and new children meant new problems to solve—allergies, sibling rivalry, reading problems, accidents in swimming pools, on bicycles, and later in cars. More information was exchanged, more car pools formed, more strategies communally developed.

My mother and her friends talked about books they were reading and brought them to exchange; the plays, movies, and newly available television shows they'd seen were discussed. Sharing books was another way of feeding each other.

They recounted stories about organizations they belonged to, the goals they set and campaigns they waged. They belonged to many organizations—the League of Women Voters, temple sisterhoods, PTAs, Hadassah, B'nai B'rith Women, National Council of Jewish Women, Great Books clubs, parents' groups for their children's school bands and orchestras. They played mah-jong, bridge, gin rummy, and canasta, and they planned picnics for and hosted family club meetings. Some were Girl Scout leaders and some worked "in their husband's business" (as it was said in those days)—one was a construction boss in the family contracting business, another ran her husband's dental practice, another kept her traveling salesman husband's accounts. Some of the women had part-time jobs—substitute teaching, preparing income tax returns, cashiering at a local bakery. One woman taught ceramics classes in her basement.

Their lives were filled with family—their birth families, their husband's families, their nuclear families of husband and children, and the families of their siblings. They were also active in community work. They collected for the March of Dimes (this was in the days when polio was still a horrible threat), the Red Cross, cancer research, and trees for Israel. They volunteered at hospitals, at old folks homes, and at refugee resettlement agencies; they read for talking records, staffed booths at fund raisers, sang in choruses, and worked at libraries. They distributed political education material and clerked at polling places. They chauffeured their children to after-school appointments and classes chosen to maximize their health and opportunities in life.

They worked hard in their homes. In those days automatic clothes washers still had hand wringers, the laundry was hung out to dry in the backyard, and everything needed ironing. Neither TV dinners nor their frozen successors had been invented yet so all the food, except for bread, was prepared from scratch. Chicken still had feet at the ends of their legs and shell-less eggs in their bellies. Despite the media's image of the housewife as a carefree consumer, these women recognized that their responsibility for buying food, clothes, and all the other products it took to run a household was real, skilled work. They worked hard to do that job as well and as carefully as they did everything else.

The friends were colleagues in their domesticity. They comparison shopped and told each other about good bargains; they remembered each other's tastes and picked up things for each other when they saw them on sale; they exchanged coupons. Those who could drive and had access to cars picked up those who couldn't.

They were also colleagues in their parenting. I don't know if any of them liked me, but I knew that I was safe with any of them. After my mom returned to a full-time job in my dad's law office, I could have come to any one of her friends, knowing that she would know how to "mommy" me in an emergency. Their children had the same trust in all the mothers, the friends. We children didn't particularly like each other and did not become friends, and no doubt not all the women liked all the children; but my mother's friends were my play family and I feel connected to all of them by her friendships with them the way I feel connected to my relatives by blood.

No matter how busy, how full, how obligated their lives and their time, these women always had time and space for friendship. My mother's friends were not necessarily in the same groups she was in, although all of them belonged to groups; they didn't take the same classes, but almost all of them studied something. They weren't necessarily relatives, although, over the years, there were cousins and *machetonim* (extended in-law family members) among the friends. Some friends lived nearby and some lived far away. Some of the friendships stretched far into my mother's past, all the way to elementary school. Other friends were new—someone recently met in one of the groups or moved into the neighborhood or married into the family.

The friends were always taking care of each other in various ways. Each of the married women represented the kind of knowledge in which her husband specialized, whether vocationally or avocationally. If one had a husband who understood the law, she got his advice for all the friends. If another's had a special skill in carpentry, he installed the extra shelves. If one's son-in-law worked on automobiles, when he gave the word that it was time to winterize the cars all the friends knew to take care of it. They negotiated a reciprocity with whatever was theirs to share, although they almost never exchanged the kinds of material goods that the world of men considers part of the gross national product. They exchanged information. They shared news about lurking dangers and brainstormed strategies for solutions. They recognized honestly what they valued and didn't take for granted the emotional support and strength they gave each other. Their relationships were reciprocal and mutually nurturing, not manipulative, competitive, or exploitative.

In Brownies our leaders, the mothers, taught us to sing in a round, "Make new friends / but keep the old. / One is silver, / the other gold." It was not just a song: it was a lesson in how we ought to live. It was a description of how my mother lives.

As the years have gone by, my mother's group of friends has changed. Some left—they moved, died, or drifted away; and new ones came. Some who had drifted away came back, and the conversation was resumed as easily as if no time had elapsed. As her changing and growing interests led to new patterns in her life, the foregrounding and backgrounding of her friends sometimes reversed. When some of her friends died and their role in her life became vacant, she always found new friends to fill that empty role—in her own, new way. I remember hearing her sometimes say, "So-and-so and I have become friends. We've known each other all our lives and the time has never been quite right for us to be friends, but we always knew the other was there, and possible, and now we know it's time."

From that I learned that potential friendships are like money in a joint certificate of deposit, appreciating all the time. Learning to recognize those potential friendships is a way of learning to take care of yourself, to know what comfort and pleasure there is in life yet to be enjoyed. When the certificate comes due and together you redeem and explore the treasure you have, the pleasure is enhanced by your shared awareness of all the time spent in anticipation of that moment.

Some friendships feel from the beginning as if they have been there forever, but you just hadn't yet noticed. When you notice simultaneously what you have between you, which may be at the very moment you meet for the first time, it is like an affirmation of the good things in life. The good things in life are indeed good, and friendship is one of the best of them.

I learned from my mother that people are and have friends just as they are and have parents, children, siblings, cousins, spouses, in-laws, classmates, and colleagues. Most but not all of the women had husbands; some were still single, some already widowed and, even back in those days, one was divorced. Not all of the married ones had children. But all of the women had friends.

Recalling my mother's friendships and thinking about my own, I see that some friendships were closer than others. Some were deliberately chosen and very special because of a unique rapport, a particular shared characteristic, temperament, interest, or passion; others were cultivated or tolerated because they were convenient. Some friendships evolved slowly, almost accidentally, without more than the most tentative encouragement; some seemed to spring fully developed in an instant. Some were brief and passing, and others have lasted a lifetime. All were important.

From my mother I learned that friendships vary in their degrees of closeness, intensity, and duration. Friendship implies reciprocity and mutuality; if these attributes are not inherent in the relationship, the relationship is something other than a friendship. Friendships are cultivated and maintained, and do not just happen. They have rituals for celebration, comfort, support, working things out, and healing. Through friendships we can see and imagine ourselves at our best. Friendships, rich with laughter and soft with comfort, make life better. Friends feed each other.

I have learned since I left home that some people don't have friends. Some people, whose parents didn't have friends, grew up not knowing that people are supposed to have friends, that we need friends and need to know how to be friends. Of all the sad and lonely kinds of people I know, those without friends are the saddest and the loneliest.

For years I struggled to evolve a formal and politically correct def-

initon of women's friendship. Now I know that that was unnecessary. We all know what our friendships are, how varied and enriching they are, and how barren our lives would be without them.
Women have always cherished friendships with women, and women
writers have always told stories in which women's friendships were
both central and peripheral realities. When they are peripheral, they
are presented elliptically, as if we need only the slightest hint, the
barest sketch, just an outline to fill in the familiar substance of this
reality. When women's friendships are central to a story, it resonates
with the immanence of a sacred story. Women's friendship stories
have all the characteristics of sacred literature—history, mythology,
rituals, allegories of right action, and style. Friendships are about the
most basic values and facts of women's lives.

Each story in this collection represents one or more aspects of the
complex subject of friendships between and among women. The
stories contain many pungent statements about the nature of friendships, aphoristic constructions that can be extracted, separated from
the lives of the characters from which they grow, and remembered
for their simple eloquence. These statements tell us what friendship
is and what it does.

Even more telling are the stories themselves. In these stories, I
find all the kinds of friendships I have known as an observer and
shared in as a participant. The stories portray the life-enhancing,
survival-abetting, reciprocal walks through life that friendships are.
They can illuminate friendship for those who haven't learned how to
be and have friends; they will reflect something of our experiences
for those of us who have been luckier.

I have shared these stories with my friends. Part of all my friendships is shared reading. I hope you will read them, love them, think
of me as your friend because we are sharing these stories, and share
them with your other friends.

Women's Friendships

LYDIA MARIA CHILD

The Neighbour-in-Law

(1846)

*M*Y dear friend, you know not *how* isolated I am. I have had so many removals, in the course of my married life, that my friendships and my social relations have been sadly disturbed thereby; and during the last ten years, my small remaining circle has been constantly diminished by death."[1] Written at age sixty-two to Lucy Osgood, one of the four friends she counted in her "small remaining circle," this poignant letter sounds the keynote of Lydia Maria Child's last thirty years and hints at a central conflict in her life.

Lydia Maria Child (1802–80) and her husband David Lee Child had shared a passionate commitment to the cause of racial justice ever since their marriage in 1828, when they had begun campaigning against the threatened dispossession of Georgia's Cherokee Indians. Both had sacrificed promising careers to join the abolitionist movement in 1831, and together they had paid a heavy price in social ostracism and poverty. A strong supporter of women's rights, David Lee Child had always taken pride in his wife's intellectual achievements. He had fallen in love with her daring novel of interracial marriage, *Hobomok, A Tale of Early Times* (1824), even before meeting her, and he never begrudged her a prominence in antislavery ranks that far outstripped his own. Yet throughout their forty-six-year marriage, he repeatedly pursued utopian schemes and disastrous business ventures that disrupted his wife's "social relations" and forced her into reclusiveness.

At the time of their wedding, Lydia Maria (Francis) Child was enjoying the patronage of Boston's most fashionable elites as the author of two well-received historical novels and the founding editor of the nation's first successful children's magazine, the *Juvenile Miscellany* (1826–34).

It was a triumph she could hardly have dreamed of during her lonely, straitened childhood in the small town of Medford, Massachusetts, where her father Convers Francis owned a family-run bakery that enlisted the labor of his wife Susannah Rand Francis and their five children. Overshadowed by her mother's prolonged illness and death from tuberculosis when Lydia was twelve, the years in Medford were redeemed only by the intellectual companionship of Lydia's elder brother Convers, whom she later credited with having introduced her to literature.[2] Convers's role as a mentor continued into the 1820s, when he took a Unitarian pulpit in Watertown, Massachusetts, and began allying himself with the intellectuals soon to be known as Transcendentalists. In his home Child met such luminaries as Ralph Waldo Emerson, Theodore Parker, Bronson Alcott and his wife Abba May Alcott (an intimate friend Child would nurse through the aftermath of a stillbirth), Margaret Fuller (still a precocious adolescent), and David Lee Child himself.

The Childs' marriage, which dismayed friends aware of the groom's quixotic proclivities, abruptly ended the fairy-tale reign of the "brilliant Miss Francis" over Boston's literary salons. Within months, the staggering debts David Lee Child had accumulated forced the couple to curtail their entertainment expenses by dropping all their acquaintances.[3] Isolation gave way to actual ostracism by her former patrons, once Child published her ground-breaking indictment of slavery and racial prejudice, *An Appeal in Favor of That Class of Americans Called Africans*, in 1833. Perhaps the saddest loss was the friendship of Catharine Maria Sedgwick, who had warmly supported Child as a sister writer, but lacked the "moral *courage*" to continue the association after Child identified herself with a controversial cause.[4]

Simultaneously, however, the Childs' entry into abolitionist ranks allowed them to reconstitute a circle of friends. William Lloyd Garrison; Maria Weston Chapman and her sisters Caroline, Deborah, and Ann Warren Weston; the poet John Greenleaf Whittier; the South Carolina slaveholders' daughters Sarah and Angelina Grimké and Angelina's husband Theodore Dwight Weld; and Weld's rival in oratorical power, the Brahmin Wendell Phillips (converted to abolition by Child's *Appeal*)— all became intimates during the 1830s. Three special friendships with the abolitionists Henrietta Sargent, Ellis Gray Loring and his wife Louisa Gilman Loring, and Francis Shaw and his wife Sarah Blake Sturgis Shaw lasted throughout Child's lifetime, uninterrupted by the acrimonious feuds that split the antislavery camp in the 1840s.

Unfortunately, no sooner had Child emerged from her isolation than David decided to set up a sugar beet farm in Northampton, Massachusetts, with the aim of providing a viable substitute for slave-grown cane sugar. Marked by unremitting domestic drudgery and intellectual starvation, the two years in Northampton severely tried the Childs' marriage. A call from the American Anti-Slavery Society to edit its New York organ, the *National Anti-Slavery Standard,* finally rescued Lydia Maria Child in May 1841, initiating an informal separation that would stretch into more than eight years.

"The Neighbour-in-Law" dates from the sojourn in New York that marks a peak in Child's social relations. While editing the *Standard* and rebuilding her literary career in the years that followed her resignation from the paper in May 1843, Child cultivated an astonishing number of friendships with writers, artists, reformers, ordinary people who shared her interests, fugitive slaves, and a host of unfortunates she helped in various ways. They numbered among them the *New York Tribune's* correspondent Margaret Fuller, whose famous "Conversations" Child had attended in Boston: the poet William Cullen Bryant, editor of the *New York Evening Post,* and his son-in-law, the reformer Parke Godwin; the Norwegian violinist Ole Bull and the Bohemian composer Antony Philip Heinrich, whose concerts and works Child reviewed; the painter William Page; the actress Jeannie Barrett, whom Child rescued from alcoholism and brought back to the stage; the African-Americans Julia Pell and Charity Bowery, memorialized in Child's best-selling series of journalistic sketches, *Letters from New-York* (1843, 1845); a young Spanish victim of wife abuse named Dolores, whom Child unofficially adopted as a daughter; and two women with whom Child kept up a lively correspondence about theological and literary matters: Lucy Osgood, daughter of the Francis family's minister in Medford, and Marianne Devereux Silsbee, wife of the mayor of Salem, Massachusetts. Most relevant to "The Neighbour-in-Law," however, is Child's friendship with the Quaker abolitionists and prison reformers Isaac T. and Hannah Hopper, at whose home she boarded in New York.

The Quaker ethic of nonresistance, embraced by many abolitionists, undergirds the story: the miraculous transformation Mrs. Fairweather succeeds in effecting in Hetty Turnpenny's character illustrates how patience, kindness, and good-humored friendliness can dissolve the defenses of a woman soured by a loveless upbringing, which she is reproducing in her orphaned niece. The theme recurs in a later story titled "The Man that Killed His Neighbours," based on an incident Child related as fact in her 1853 biography of Isaac T. Hopper.

"The Neighbour-in-Law" first appeared in the June 1846 issue of the *Columbian Lady's and Gentleman's Magazine,* for which Child had contracted to write a story a month. Child reprinted it in *Fact and Fiction: A Collection of Stories* (1846), her second volume of short fiction. The other two were *The Coronal. A Collection of Miscellaneous Pieces, Written at Various Times* (1832) and *Autumnal Leaves: Tales and Sketches in Prose and Rhyme* (1857). All have long been out of print, and some of Child's best stories remain uncollected, notably "The Church in the Wilder-

6 · LYDIA MARIA CHILD

ness," which appeared in *The Legendary* (1828); "Slavery's Pleasant Homes," published in the *Liberty Bell* (1843); and the *Atlantic Monthly* trio "Loo Loo," "Willie Wharton," and "Poor Chloe" (1858, 1863, 1866).

In 1849, shaken by the marriage of the Hoppers' son John, with whom she had been carrying on a platonic love affair, Child reunited with her husband, and the next year the two moved back to rural Massachusetts, where they ultimately inherited the tiny farmhouse of the elder Convers Francis. This time the domestic drudgery and isolation Child faced in the little village of Wayland would last until her death in 1880. Nevertheless, she managed to keep writing and working for racial justice. Her story "The Kansas Emigrants" and her stirring letters in defense of John Brown, both published in the *New York Tribune* and given unprecedented circulation, played an important role in mobilizing the Northern public to fight a war against slavery. In 1860–61 Child edited and helped publish and distribute Harriet A. Jacobs's *Incidents in the Life of a Slave Girl,* in the process forming a friendship warm enough for Jacobs to be one of the few overnight guests Child accommodated in a home that lacked even a spare room. Child also maintained a long correspondence with the Massachusetts Senator Charles Sumner, converted to the cause by her 1833 *Appeal,* and nudged him toward more radical positions.

Meanwhile, Child continued to promote aspiring artists, among them the sculptors Harriet Hosmer, Anne Whitney, and Edmonia Lewis and the writer Charlotte Forten (the latter two African-Americans). Fiercely reclusive in her old age, Child resisted the efforts of biographers such as Thomas Wentworth Higginson and literary patrons such as Annie M. Fields and her husband the publisher James T. Fields to extend to her the attentions she so untiringly requested for others. Fittingly, her surviving abolitionist friends Harriet Winslow Sewall, John Greenleaf Whittier, and Wendell Phillips restored her to the public after her death by publishing a selection of her letters, together with a biographical sketch of her extraordinarily productive life.

CAROLYN L. KARCHER

Who blesses others in his daily deeds,
Will find the healing that his spirit needs;
For every flower in others' pathway strewn,
Confers its fragrant beauty on our own.

"So you are going to live in the same building with Hetty Turnpenny," said Mrs. Lane to Mrs. Fairweather, "You will find nobody to envy you. If her temper does not prove too much even for your good-nature, it will surprise all who know her. We lived there a year, and that is as long as anybody ever tried it."

"Poor Hetty!" replied Mrs. Fairweather, "She has had much to harden her. Her mother died too early for her to remember; her father was very severe with her, and the only lover she ever had, borrowed the savings of her years of toil, and spent them in dissipation. But Hetty, notwithstanding her sharp features, and sharper words, certainly has a kind heart. In the midst of her greatest poverty, many were the stockings she knit, and the warm waistcoats she made, for the poor drunken lover, whom she had too much good sense to marry. Then you know she feeds and clothes her brother's orphan child."

"If you call it feeding and clothing," replied Mrs. Lane. "The poor child looks cold, and pinched, and frightened all the time, as if she were chased by the East wind. I used to tell Miss Turnpenny she ought to be ashamed of herself, to keep the poor little thing at work all the time, without one minute to play. If she does but look at the cat, as it runs by the window, Aunt Hetty gives her a rap over the knuckles. I used to tell her she would make the girl just such another sour old crab as herself."

"That must have been very improving to her disposition," replied Mrs. Fairweather, with a good-humoured smile. "But in justice to poor Aunt Hetty, you ought to remember that she had just such a cheerless childhood herself. Flowers grow where there is sunshine."

"I know you think everybody ought to live in the sunshine," rejoined Mrs. Lane; "and it must be confessed that you carry it with you wherever you go. If Miss Turnpenny *has* a heart, I dare say you will find it out, though I never could, and I never heard of any one else that could. All the families within hearing of her tongue call her the neighbour-in-law."

Certainly the prospect was not very encouraging; for the house Mrs. Fairweather proposed to occupy, was not only under the same roof with Miss Turnpenny, but the buildings had one common yard in the rear, and one common space for a garden in front. The very first day she took possession of her new habitation, she called on the neighbour-in-law. Aunt Hetty had taken the precaution to extinguish the fire, lest the new neighbour should want hot water, before her own wood and coal arrived. Her first salutation was, "If you want any cold water, there's a pump across the street; I don't like to have my house slopped all over."

"I am glad you are so tidy, neighbour Turnpenny," replied Mrs. Fairweather; "It is extremely pleasant to have neat neighbours. I will try to keep everything as bright as a new five cent piece, for I see that will please you. I came in merely to say good morning, and to ask if you could spare little Peggy to run up and down stairs for me, while I am getting my furniture in order. I will pay her sixpence an hour."

Aunt Hetty had begun to purse up her mouth for a refusal; but the promise of sixpence an hour relaxed her features at once. Little Peggy sat knitting a stocking very diligently, with a rod lying on the table beside her. She looked up with timid wistfulness, as if the prospect of any change was like a release from prison. When she heard consent given, a bright colour flushed her cheeks. She was evidently of an impressible temperament, for good or evil. "Now mind and behave yourself," said Aunt Hetty; "and see that you keep at work the whole time. If I hear one word of complaint, you know what you'll get when you come home." The rose-colour subsided from Peggy's pale face, and she answered, "Yes, ma'am," very meekly.

In the neighbour's house all went quite otherwise. No switch lay on the table, and instead of, "mind how you do that. If you don't I'll punish you," she heard the gentle words, "There, dear, see how carefully you can carry that up stairs. Why, what a nice handy little girl you are!" Under this enlivening influence, Peggy worked like a bee, and soon began to hum much more agreeably than a bee. Aunt Hetty was always in the habit of saying, "Stop your noise and mind your work." But the new friend patted her on the head, and said, "What a pleasant voice the little girl has. It is like the birds in the fields. By and by, you shall hear my music-box." This opened wide the windows of the poor little shut-up heart, so that the sunshine could stream in, and the birds fly in and out, carolling. The happy child tuned up like a lark, as she tripped lightly up and down stairs, on various household errands. But though she took heed to observe all the directions given her, her head was all the time filled with conjectures what sort of a thing a music-box might be. She was a little afraid the kind lady would forget to show it to her. She kept at work, however, and asked no questions; she only looked very curiously at everything that resembled a box. At last Mrs. Fairweather said, "I think your little feet must be tired, by this time. We will rest awhile, and eat some gingerbread." The child took the offered cake, with a humble little courtesy, and carefully held out her apron to prevent any crumbs from falling on the floor. But suddenly the apron dropped, and the crumbs were all strewn about. "Is that a little bird?" she exclaimed eagerly. "Where is he? Is he in this room?" The new friend smiled, and told her that was the music-box; and after awhile she opened it, and explained what made the sounds. Then she took out a pile of books from one of the baskets of goods, and told Peggy she might look at the pictures, till she called her. The little girl stepped forward eagerly to take them, and then drew back, as if afraid. "What is the matter?" asked Mrs. Fairweather; "I am very willing to trust you with the books. I keep them on purpose to amuse children." Peggy looked down with her finger on her lip, and answered in a constrained voice, "Aunt Turnpenny won't like it if I play." "Don't trouble yourself about that. I will make it all right with Aunt Hetty," replied the friendly one. Thus assured, she gave herself up to the full enjoyment of the picture books; and when she was summoned to her work, she obeyed with a cheerful alacrity that would have astonished her stern relative. When the labours of the day were concluded, Mrs. Fairweather accompanied her home, paid for all the hours she had been absent, and warmly praised her docility and diligence. "It is lucky for her that she behaved so well," replied Aunt Hetty; "if I had heard any complaint, I should have given her a whipping, and sent her to bed without her supper."

Poor little Peggy went to sleep that night with a lighter heart than she had ever felt, since she had been an orphan. Her first thought in the morning was whether the new neighbour would want her service again during the day. Her desire that it should be so, soon became obvious to Aunt Hetty, and excited an undefined jealousy and dislike of a person who so easily made herself beloved. Without exactly acknowledging to herself what were her own motives, she ordered Peggy to gather all the sweepings of the kitchen and court into a small pile, and leave it on the frontier line of her neighbour's premises. Peggy ventured to ask timidly whether the wind would not blow it about, and she received a box on the ear for her impertinence. It chanced that Mrs. Fairweather, quite unintentionally, heard the words and the blow. She gave Aunt Hetty's anger time enough to cool, then stepped out into the court, and after arranging divers little matters, she called aloud to her domestic, "Sally, how came you to leave this pile of dirt here? Didn't I tell you Miss Turnpenny was very neat? Pray make haste and sweep it up. I wouldn't have her see it on any account. I told her I would try to keep everything nice about the premises. She is so particular herself, and it is a comfort to have tidy neighbours." The girl, who had been previously instructed, smiled as she came out with brush and dust-pan, and swept quietly away the pile, that was intended as a declaration of border war.

But another source of annoyance presented itself, which could not so easily be disposed of. Aunt Hetty had a cat, a lean scraggy animal, that looked as if she were often kicked and seldom fed; and Mrs. Fairweather had a fat, frisky little dog, always ready for a caper. He took a distaste to poor poverty-stricken Tab, the first time he saw her; and no coaxing could induce him to alter his opinion. His name was Pink, but he was anything but a pink of behaviour in his neighbourly relations. Poor Tab could never set foot out of doors without being saluted with a growl, and a short sharp bark, that frightened her out of her senses, and made her run into the house, with her fur all on end. If she even ventured to doze a little on her own door step, the enemy was on the watch, and the moment her eyes closed, he would wake her with a bark and a box on the ear, and off he would run. Aunt Hetty vowed she would scald him. It was a burning shame, she said, for folks to keep dogs to worry their neighbours' cats. Mrs. Fairweather invited Tabby to dine, and made much of her, and patiently endeavoured to teach her dog to eat from the same plate. But Pink sturdily resolved he would be scalded first; that he would. He could not have been more obstinate in his opposition, if he and Tab had belonged to different sects in Christianity. While his mistress was patting Tab on the head, and reasoning the point with him, he would at times manifest a degree of indifference, amounting to toleration; but the moment he was left to his own free will, he would give the invited guest a hearty cuff with his paw, and send her home spitting like a small steam engine. Aunt Hetty considered it her own peculiar privilege to cuff the poor animal, and it was too much for her patience to see Pink undertake to assist in making Tab unhappy. On one of these occasions, she rushed into her neighbour's apartments, and faced Mrs. Fairweather, with one hand resting on her hip, and the forefinger of the other making very wrathful gesticulations. "I tell you what, madam, I won't put up with such treatment much longer," she said; "I'll poison that dog; see if I don't; and I shan't wait long, either, I can tell you. What you keep such an impudent little beast for, I don't know, without you do it on purpose to plague your neighbours."

"I am really sorry he behaves so," replied Mrs. Fairweather, mildly. "Poor Tab!"

"Poor Tab!" screamed Miss Turnpenny; "What do you mean by calling her poor? Do you mean to fling it up to me that my cat don't have enough to eat?"

"I didn't think of such a thing," replied Mrs. Fairweather. "I called her poor Tab, because Pink plagues her so, that she has no peace of her life. I agree with you, neighbour Turnpenny; it is *not* right to keep a dog that disturbs the neighbourhood. I am attached to poor little Pink, because he belongs to my son, who has gone to sea. I was in hopes he would soon leave off quarrelling with the cat; but if he won't be neighbourly, I will send him out in the country to board. Sally, will you bring me one of the pies we baked this morning? I should like to have Miss Turnpenny taste of them."

The crabbed neighbour was helped abundantly; and while she was eating the pie, the friendly matron edged in many a kind word concerning little Peggy, whom she praised as a remarkably capable, industrious child.

"I am glad you find her so," rejoined Aunt Hetty: "I should get precious little work out of her, if I didn't keep a switch in sight."

"I manage children pretty much as the man did the donkey," replied Mrs. Fairweather. "Not an inch would the poor beast stir, for all his master's beating and thumping. But a neighbour tied some fresh turnips to a stick, and fastened them so that they swung directly before the donkey's nose, and off he set on a brisk trot, in hopes of overtaking them."

Aunt Hetty, without observing how very closely the comparison applied to her own management of Peggy, said, "That will do very well for folks that have plenty of turnips to spare."

"For the matter of that," answered Mrs. Fairweather, "whips cost something, as well as turnips; and since one makes the donkey stand still, and the other makes him trot, it is easy to decide which is the most economical. But, neighbour Turnpenny, since you like my pies so well, pray take one home with you. I am afraid they will mould before we can eat them up."

Aunt Hetty had come in for a quarrel, and she was astonished to find herself going out with a pie. "Well, Mrs. Fairweather," said she, "you *are* a neighbour. I thank you a thousand times." When she reached her own door, she hesitated for an instant, then turned back, pie in hand, to say, "Neighbour Fairweather, you needn't trouble yourself about sending Pink away. It's natural you should like the little creature, seeing he belongs to your son. I'll try to keep Tab in doors, and perhaps after awhile they will agree better."

"I hope they will," replied the friendly matron: "We will try them awhile longer, and if they persist in quarreling, I will send the dog into the country." Pink, who was sleeping in a chair, stretched himself and gaped. His kind mistress patted him on the head, "Ah, you foolish little beast," said she, "what's the use of plaguing poor Tab?"

"Well, I do say," observed Sally, smiling, "you are a master woman for stopping a quarrel."

"I learned a good lesson when I was a little girl," rejoined Mrs. Fairweather. "One frosty morning, I was looking out of the window into my father's barn-yard, where stood many cows, oxen, and horses, waiting to drink. It was one of those cold snapping mornings, when a slight thing irritates both man and beast. The cattle all stood very still and meek, till one of the cows attempted to turn round. In making the attempt, she happened to hit her next neighbour; whereupon the neighbour kicked and hit another. In five minutes, the whole herd were kicking and hooking each other, with all fury. Some lay sprawling on the ice, others were slipping about, with their hind heels reared in the air. My mother laughed, and said, 'See what comes of kicking when you're hit. Just so I've seen one cross word set a whole family by the ears, some frosty morning.' Afterward, if my brothers or myself were a little irritable, she would say, 'Take care, children. Remember how the fight in the barn-yard began. Never give a kick for a hit, and you will save yourself and others a deal of trouble.'"

That same afternoon, the sunshiny dame stepped into Aunt Hetty's rooms, where she found Peggy sewing, as usual, with the eternal switch on the table beside her. "I am obliged to go to Harlem, on business," said she: "I feel rather lonely without company, and I always like to have a child with me. If you will oblige me by letting Peggy go, I will pay her fare in the omnibus."

"She has her spelling lesson to get before night," replied Aunt Hetty. "I don't approve of young folks going a pleasuring, and neglecting their education."

"Neither do I," rejoined her neighbour; "but I think there is a great deal of education that is not found in books. The fresh air will make

Peggy grow stout and active. I prophesy that she will do great credit to your bringing up." The sugared words, and the remembrance of the sugared pie, touched the soft place in Miss Turnpenny's heart, and she told the astonished Peggy that she might go and put on her best gown and bonnet. The poor child began to think that this new neighbour was certainly one of the good fairies she read about in the picture books. The excursion was enjoyed as only a city child *can* enjoy the country. The world seems such a pleasant place, when the fetters are off, and Nature folds the young heart lovingly on her bosom! A flock of real birds and two living butterflies put the little orphan in a perfect ecstasy. She ran and skipped. One could see that she might be graceful, if she were only free. She pointed to the fields covered with dandelions, and said, "See how pretty! It looks as if the stars had come down to lie on the grass." Ah, our little stinted Peggy has poetry in her, though Aunt Hetty never found it out. Every human soul has the germ of some flowers within, and they would open, if they could only find sunshine and free air to expand in.

Mrs. Fairweather was a practical philosopher, in her own small way. She observed that Miss Turnpenny really liked a pleasant tune; and when Winter came, she tried to persuade her that singing would be excellent for Peggy's lungs, and perhaps keep her from going into a consumption.

"My nephew, James Fairweather, keeps a singing school," said she; "and he says he will teach her gratis. You need not feel under great obligation; for her voice will lead the whole school, and her ear is so quick, it will be no trouble at all to teach her. Perhaps you would go with us sometimes, neighbour Turnpenny? It is very pleasant to hear the children's voices."

The cordage of Aunt Hetty's mouth relaxed into a smile. She accepted the invitation, and was so much pleased, that she went every Sunday evening. The simple tunes, and the sweet young voices, fell like dew on her dried-up heart, and greatly aided the genial influence of her neighbour's example. The rod silently disappeared from the table. If Peggy was disposed to be idle, it was only necessary to say, "When you have finished your work, you may go and ask whether Mrs. Fairweather wants any errands done." Bless me, how the fingers flew! Aunt Hetty had learned to use turnips instead of the cudgel.

When Spring came, Mrs. Fairweather busied herself with planting roses and vines. Miss Turnpenny readily consented that Peggy should help her, and even refused to take any pay from such a good neighbour. But she maintained her own opinion that it was a mere waste of time to cultivate flowers. The cheerful philosopher never disputed the point; but she would sometimes say, "I have no room to plant this rose-bush. Neighbour Turnpenny, would you be willing to let me set it on your side of the yard? It will take very little room, and will need no care." At another time, she would say, "Well, really my ground is too full. Here is a root of Lady's-delight. How bright and pert it looks. It seems a pity to throw it away. If you are willing, I will let Peggy plant it in what she calls her garden. It will grow of itself, without any care, and scatter seeds, that will come up and blossom in all the chinks of the bricks. I love it. It is such a bright good-natured little thing." Thus by degrees, the crabbed maiden found herself surrounded by flowers; and she even declared, of her own accord, that they did look pretty.

One day, when Mrs. Lane called upon Mrs. Fairweather, she found the old weed-grown yard bright and blooming. Tab, quite fat and sleek, was asleep, in the sunshine, with her paw on Pink's neck, and little Peggy was singing at her work, as blithe as a bird.

"How cheerful you look here," said Mrs. Lane. "And so you have really taken the house for another year. Pray, how do you manage to get on with the neighbour-in-law?"

"I find her a very kind, obliging neighbour," replied Mrs. Fairweather.

"Well, this *is* a miracle!" exclaimed Mrs. Lane, "Nobody but you would have undertaken to thaw out Aunt Hetty's heart."

"That is probably the reason why it was never thawed," rejoined her friend. "I always told you, that not having enough of sunshine was what ailed the world. Make people happy, and there will not be half the quarrelling, or a tenth part of the wickedness, there is."

From this gospel of joy preached and practised, nobody derived so much benefit as little Peggy. Her nature, which was fast growing crooked and knotty, under the malign influence of constraint and fear, straightened up, budded and blossomed, in the genial atmosphere of cheerful kindness.

Her affections and faculties were kept in such pleasant exercise, that constant lightness of heart made her almost handsome. The young music-teacher thought her more than almost handsome; for her affectionate soul shone more beamingly on him than on others, and love makes all things beautiful.

When the orphan removed to her pleasant little cottage, on her wedding-day, she threw her arms round the blessed missionary of sunshine, and said, "Ah, thou dear good Aunt, it is thou who hast made my life Fairweather."

ELIZABETH STUART PHELPS

At Bay

(1867)

*I*N "At Bay"[1] Elizabeth Stuart Phelps
(1844–1911) tells us a winning story regarding one feisty young woman
who outmaneuvers her relentless suitor to discredit publicly his claim on
her: she effectively holds "at bay" those who would impugn her integrity. But another quieter, losing story of friendship between two young
women emerges between the lines of the former. As in other fiction by
Phelps, this story documents the losses that women experience living in
patriarchy. Like her literary model Rebecca Harding Davis (1831–1910),
Phelps depicts the spare living conditions available to the working classes,
conditions that were even more unbearable if the worker were a woman.
The two Davis stories to which Sarah, the narrator of "At Bay," refers
forecast concerns of Phelps's story. "Life in the Iron Mills"[2] depicts the
stifling effect of degrading and exhausting mill labor on the creative capacity of a male protagonist; "Paul Blecker"[3] includes a female character
wanting marriage and family as well as achievement—the wholeness of
development available to men. Phelps, in the chapter "Art for Truth's
Sake" in her autobiography *Chapters from a Life* (Houghton Mifflin,
1895), credited "Life in the Iron Mills" as one of two stories that had
crucially influenced her own development as a writer. The early para-
graphs of "At Bay" provide one of her first statements of a literary creed.

Through the characters Martie and Sarah, Phelps also indicates her
stance on women's issues, or, as it was then called, "the woman question." She depicts two ways of responding to patriarchy: Martie's direct
attack, the approach of rights' advocates, and Sarah's indirect process,
the approach of emancipation through self-growth and enabling care for

another. Phelps joins these two ways as part of an integrated process, neither one of which can work without the other. This pluralist stance parallels her essays on women's needs, rights, and wrongs appearing in 1871 in the *Independent,* a Congregational cultural newspaper, and the *Woman's Journal,* a women's rights newspaper edited by Lucy Stone (1818–93). One in particular delineates "that dummy 'the true woman,'" the construct requiring women's sexual purity, religious piety, and domestic submissiveness.

As "At Bay" makes clear, Phelps saw her writing as a sort of pulpit from which to preach her beliefs. Denied this profession by her sex (although born to it through her male ancestry, as two grandfathers, several uncles, and her father were clergymen) she found voice for political, religious, and ethical matters in using her pen. In this choice, she followed her mother and aunts, also writers, but Phelps more forcefully declares her support for women's emancipation than did her foremothers. In 1865, Phelps published two books for young adults, *Up Hill; or, Life in the Factory* and *Mercy Gliddon's Work,* and in 1866, an *Hours at Home* serialization, "Jane Gurley's Story"—all of which depict living conditions for the working poor. The ameliorating condition in each is a mature benefactress who befriends younger women. "At Bay" is transitional in Phelps's work between these apprentice novels and her early serious work, *Hedged In* (1870) and *The Silent Partner* (1871), both focusing on friendships between women of the same age but different social class. Martie's glimpse of "Empress Nell," the daughter of a printshop customer, suggests the opening chapter of *The Silent Partner,* where an upper-class young lady, heroine Perley Kelso, is struck by the great difference between herself and a mill girl she observes from her carriage. But *Hedged In* is closer to "At Bay": its heroine Nixy Trent, like Martie, must withstand social disapproval for being an "unwed mother," a circumstance beyond her control as a woman in patriarchy. And like Sarah, Nixy loses a dear friend to the institution of marriage. In her masterwork *The Story of Avis* (1877) Phelps strenuously critiques the institution of marriage for its stifling effect on women's creativity. In fact, in the mock-heroic *Old Maids' Paradise* (1879), Phelps's heroine Corona wonders what is the good of Paradise (the name of her summer cottage by the sea) if one's friends desert one for marriage! "At Bay" is a very important early expression of themes central to Phelps's writing.[4]

The themes of Phelps's writing emerge from her living. She was born in 1844 Boston to author Elizabeth Stuart Phelps (1815–52) and minister Austin Phelps (1820–90). The family moved when her father received a faculty appointment to the Andover Theological Seminary, where Moses Stuart, her maternal grandfather, also taught. (This is now the campus of Phillips–Andover Academy, which has absorbed Abbott Academy for girls, alma mater of Phelps's mother.) Her mother died when she was eight and she thereafter took on her mother's name; she had been christened Mary Gray after a friend of her mother. She had four brothers, two by her father's third wife; these last two she helped to raise, as *Chapters from a Life* makes clear. Her autobiography also indicates that she knew personally the Massachusetts mill scene. As a young woman, she was distraught at the 1860 Pemberton Mills fire in Lawrence, Massachusetts, which burned many workers to death: "The Tenth of January"[5] was her cry against such negligent mill owners. She also taught Sunday school for mill children, hence two series of books for this audience: four "Tiny" books and the more secular "Gypsy" series. Her close relationships with women during the early part of her career—until roughly the mid-1880s—were her primary source of emotional support. She shared workrooms with her "boon companion," physician Mary Briggs Harris, a Maine woman trained in Boston who died in 1886. The humorous "Old Maids" series and the heroine of *Doctor Zay* (1882) seem to be derived from this companionship. Phelps was a member of the Boston literary salon presided over by Annie Adams Fields, partner in a "Boston marriage" with Maine writer Sarah Orne Jewett. Phelps was also a summer neighbor in Gloucester, Massachusetts, of reformer Mary Bucklin Davenport Claflin, whose husband was a governor and prime mover in the establishment of Boston University as coeducational. Davenport and Phelps were members of a committee charged with establishing there an endowed chair for a woman. The inspirations for Phelps's own literary career were Elizabeth Barrett Browning, especially in her verse novel about a poet, *Aurora Leigh* (1856), and her own mother, whose *The Sunny Side: or, The Country Minister's Wife* (1851) forecast the popularity of Phelps's "Gates" books depicting heaven as utopia. Phelps memorialized her mother's struggles as wife, mother, housekeeper, and author in *The Story of Avis.*

Given the foregoing, the absence of appealing fathers and husbands in her fiction seems a noteworthy comment on her male relatives. Men fare more favorably as brothers or friends. Her own favorite brother, a gifted Smith College professor of moral philosophy, died from his own accidental gunshot in 1883. In 1888, Phelps married a young journalist and son of a professional acquaintance, Herbert Dickinson Ward (1861–1932)—seventeen years her junior, the age of her youngest brothers just leaving the Andover home. Sadly for Phelps the marriage was disappointing. Her best work occurred before the mid-1880s. She died alone in Newton, Massachusetts, and was buried under a tombstone of her own design. She had established herself as a professional author of some fifty-six books—novels, essays, biographies, collections of poems and short stories—and was fully self-supporting throughout her adult life, a source of pride to her. Her fiction and life demonstrate her belief, however, that friendship between women stands "at bay" within patriarchy.

CAROL FARLEY KESSLER

[I had intended to tell the story myself; but the young woman's account is so much more to the point than another could be that I send her MS just as it fell into my hands, only premising that it seems to me worth the reading.—E.]

I will tell you about it as well as I can, since you ask me to; though it frightens me to think of showing it to any one who knows how to write books; and I do hope you will excuse all mistakes, and remember that I can't tell things in a fine way, but only just as they happened. Of course you will not have it printed as it is, but will write it out yourself, and fix it up in some pretty way.

I do not wonder so much at your wanting to make a story out of Martie. It used to seem like a story to me as it went along. I often think when I have finished a novel, or a story in a magazine or newspaper—and I have read a good many this winter that Dan has brought home—that it is strange why the people who make them up can not find something *real* to say. It seems to me as if I knew a good many lives that I could put right into a book, if I only had the words, and make somebody feel glad or sorry, or help them or track them. But then, you know, I don't know any thing about it. I read a story once—it was a good while ago—called "Paul Blecker." I saw in a paper that it was written by a lady who had written something called "Life in the Iron Mills." I never saw that, nor any thing more of hers, and I don't know who she is. I wish I could find her out and thank her for having written that story. It made you feel as if she knew all about you, and were sorry for you; and as if she thought nobody was too poor, or too uneducated, or too worn out with washing-days, and all the things that do not sound a bit grand in books, to be written about. I think of it often now, since I have had the care and worry of the children here at home. It makes me love her, and it makes me respect her—stranger as she is, and so very far above and beyond any thing that I can ever be in this world or another.

To think that I have troubled you with all this, when I ought to have begun at once with Martie!

It is nothing of a story after all, when you come to it; so very simple and short. I suppose it means more to me because she *was* Martie. But I can not help hoping that, after you have altered it all over, so that it is fit to print, it may make somebody think a little about us poor country girls who go into the cities, homesick and unprotected, to find work. Perhaps they could make it a bit easier or safer for us; and then very likely they couldn't. But it does you good—at least it does me—just to *be* thought about. Sometimes I used to see it in a lady's eyes in the street, or in a horse-car—just a look, and she would go, and I would never see her again; but when I was in bed at night I remembered it. I have heard Martie say the same.

You see, one does feel so lonely! I remember just how hard it was, leaving home; and Dan had already found me my place at Inkman, Tipes, & Co.'s, so that the way was smoothed out for me at the beginning better than ever it was for Martie. But all that Dan could do never made it an easy way. I suppose I am one of hundreds like me, who turn to the cities for work; we start all about alike; we end terribly unlike.

You know how large the family is, and that father and Dan, though they were two as industrious and steady men as could be found at Long Meadow, had hard work of it making the two ends meet. In fact, they didn't always meet; and it was when I found that out that I began to think a little for myself at night, when we were in bed and Mary Ann had gone to sleep; Mary Ann always did go to sleep first.

I had been well educated for a farmer's daughter, as we counted education in Long Meadow. They had a hard pull to get me through the High School, for it was after the war had begun, and hard times; but mother was determined I should do it; so I graduated, and read my composition with the rest, and came home for father and Dan to support. Not that I was by any means idle, for I took the heaviest baking and dairy-work right off mother's hands, and helped about the children's sewing. If she could not have got along without me it would have been all very well, and I should have felt, and so would father, that I was fairly contributing to the household expenses. But Mary Ann was growing large enough to help her about the churning after school, and to mend the boys' mittens very well; so I felt as if I should be better away. I respected myself more and I felt happier as soon as I had made up my mind to go.

I always learn a new thing easily. I had no trouble with type-setting after the first week or two, and never repented my decision. It is not so respectable, as the world goes, to work in a printing-office as to teach, and mother wanted me to take the district school. But I had rather go into a factory or do washing than to drudge in a hot school-room for three hundred a year. As to respectability, I told mother I would make my own, independently of my business, or I would go without.

But after all it was a little rough when the time came to say good-by. Mother *would* cry behind her apron, and father coughed, and Dan winked, and the children pulled hold of my dress so, and looked so pink and pretty! Then the old sitting-room and the kitchen, and the cat and the cows, and the horses, and the sunshine through the window-glass, and the dahlias nodding out in the front-yard with the frost on them—why, I don't suppose I could tell you how leaving them seemed like leaving a part of myself, nor how I cried after Dan had put me into the car and given me my check and gone off.

I don't suppose you would care to hear if I did tell you—not about that long, lonesome journey, and how long and lonesome the city seemed when I stepped out into the rattling streets, in the strange noise and hurry and dirt, nor how long and lonesome the time that I must stay in it, shut out from the red maples, and the sky, and the great wide fields of snow, and May-flowers, and clover-smells, and stillness, and sweetness, and home, and mother. I only speak of it because it made me feel, remembering all about it, so sorry for Martie.

I was a great deal more sorry for her than I was for myself, just because she hadn't what I had to brave. The night that she came to our house—I boarded with Mrs. M'Cracken—I thought that she had the most homesick face I ever saw. The room which she had engaged would not be vacant for three days—it was Josie Sewell's, and Josie was going home sick; so Mrs. M'Cracken asked, Would I let her sleep with me for a night or two? I don't generally like to sleep with strangers, but I had the queerest feeling about her, as if I wanted to talk away or kiss away that homesickness out of her face; so I said Yes most willingly. Though, to be sure, it would not have made much difference if I hadn't been willing, for Mrs. M'Cracken scolded so if she did not have her way that the boarders all gave in to her.

I took Martie up stairs with me to take off her bonnet, and she thanked me, but did not say any more, so I came down again. She looked so shy and uncomfortable when she came in to supper that I wished I had waited for her. The table was full too—printers we were almost all of us, except two seamstresses, two machine-girls, and one young stone-mason, David Bent. We used to call him Davie, because he was such a pleasant-spoken fellow, and will to do a good turn for every body. It was a pretty name, and it seemed to suit him, though he was a great stoutly-built man over six feet.

I remember that Job Rice happened to be punctual to supper that night, and that he passed Martie the butter (Mrs. M'Cracken, by-the-way, did manage to get the worst butter that ever I tasted in my life).

Sue Cummings whispered to me, looking over at Martie as we sat down, that she was as homely as a hedge-fence. Now I don't think that any body but Sue would ever have thought of calling Martha Saunders homely. She was not exactly pretty either, but she certainly was prettier, it seemed to me, than Sue. Sue had black hair and bright cheeks too, and was called a very good-looking girl.

Martie was the palest woman that I ever saw, I believe—just cut like a little sad statue out of marble. I never saw a tinge of color in her face but twice in all the years I've known her. Her hair grew low on her forehead, and she had large eyes—they were gray eyes, set far apart. She had large hands, even larger than mine—for she had done rougher work—but white, like her face, and warm. She took up things in a strong, firm way, like a man. I never saw her hold her tea-cup with her little finger sticking out, like Sue. I noticed these things when she sat down opposite me full in the light. It gives me a cold, uncomfortable feeling looking back so far. I wish I had been the only one that noticed; yet not exactly that either, come to think of it.

I went up stairs with her after supper, and helped her put away her things, and presently got up the courage to ask her if she were coming in at Inkman & Tipes's. She said yes; that they had just given her Josie Sewell's place; that she hoped she should not be slow at learning the trade; and was it very hard to understand? I offered to teach her a little at nooning, and she turned her sweet gray eyes on me to thank me in such a way—nobody but Martie ever had such a way. I believe I loved her from that minute.

"You came from the country?" I said by-and-by.

"Yes."

"Far?"

"About twenty miles."

"I wonder if you are as homesick as I was," I said as gently as I knew how. "You have a home, I suppose?"

She was standing by the pine wardrobe, hanging up one of her black dresses. She hung it up and buttoned the wardrobe door, and began to fold her shawl. I thought she was not going to answer me.

"I *had* a home," she said at last.

She began to undress very fast without looking at me, and I felt that I had better not ask her any more questions. I sat up after she was in bed to read a chapter—mother made me promise always to read my chapter—and the light, where I had put it on the washstand, shone down against her face. I was reading somewhere in the genealogies, and it *wasn't* very interesting, and I could not keep my eyes off from her. I have seen little children often since I have been in New York lost in the streets at twilight on a rainy day. Martie's face that night reminded me of them. I wanted to throw down my Bible and comfort her up and cry with her; but I did not dare to.

I hope you will not laugh at me for making so much fuss over a homesick girl—as Sue did. At any rate I believe you would have done just what I did if you had been there. And I'm sure I didn't do very much. I only kissed her, that was all. After I was in bed and the lamp was out, and we had lain still a while, I only stooped over and kissed her softly on both her eyes.

I was afraid she would be angry with me, but I really could not help it. And instead of being angry with me what do you suppose she did? Why, she threw her arms about my neck and broke out crying in the strangest way:

"It's so long," she said, "it's so long since any body kissed me!"

She sobbed the words over and over in her odd, dry way without any tears as if she would never catch her breath; and I was so taken by surprise, and I didn't know what to do, so I just held her there and let her say it over, "It's so long—so long!"

Well, I suppose you know how short a time it takes for girls to get acquainted when they like each other. One hour is just as good as one year. So you will not be surprised nor laugh—I shouldn't wonder if you *did* laugh a little though—to hear that before we went to sleep she knew all about me, and I knew all about her; and I felt almost as much at home with her as I did with Mary Ann. When the time came for her to take Josie's room I wouldn't hear of it, so we arranged with Mrs. M'Cracken to keep her with me.

She told me all about the home that *had* been, and how it was broken up—"buried," she called it now. Her mother had been dead a great many years, and then two little brothers went next—there was consumption, I believe, both sides of the family—and last of all her father. He had been a shoemaker, comfortably off and kind-hearted, and he had sent her to school, and done every thing for her, and been every thing to her. She kept house for him till he was sick; then she used to bind shoes all day and half the night, sitting by his bed and watching to see if he wanted any thing. He had a little laid up, but it soon went for doctor's bills, and so she supported them both and kept him in comforts to the last; and he died while he was kissing her good-night—died with his lips on her cheek.

After that the place grew so lonely to her—and the grave was right in sight every day as she went to work—and she said it seemed as if she *must* get away. But she did not know where to go, and she had nobody to tell her; so she staid on, till one week, all of a sudden, the Corporation failed. They had been crowding on hands at very high wages—eight dollars a week to good workers—running a venture against a rival Company, and, without any warning, the whole thing fell flat, turning five hundred hands out of work.

Martie took the next train for New York. She came in in the dark and cold as I did, only she had not a place provided in which to lay her head, and she did not know a face in all the great, strange city. She wandered about for two or three days trying to find work, and sleeping at a miserable little lodging-house that she came across— a place, she said afterward, to which she felt that no respectable girl ought to go. But what could she do? Money to board at a hotel she had not, and apply to the police she dared not; she said she was afraid that they would arrest her as a vagrant. Martie always had dreadful notions of the police; and so had I for that matter. They act, and I don't know but they must act, so different to a poor girl in a calico dress from what they do to the ladies who want to be helped across the mud in Broadway.

Perhaps there may be a place somewhere in the city where they take care of country girls until they can take care of themselves—I'm sure there ought to be—but if there is, I don't know where; nor did Martie. Dan told me that there is such a place in Boston, under the charge of some Catholic women. I think they must be very good women, and I don't say any thing against them; but I suppose Protestant people must know how much more girls think about saying their prayers and every thing good, when they are homesick and lonely, and how easily they can be turned and guided. I believe that any body who had cared for and been kind to Martie those first few days might have made—why, might have made a Buddhist of her without any trouble at all.

But at last, when she was all worn out and discouraged, she happened to come across Inkman & Tipes; and so Mr. Inkman, who said she looked like a smart girl, took her on trial, and the foreman told her about Josie Sewell and Mrs. M'Cracken, and that was the way she came to me, and—to so much else.

And if I don't hurry I shall never come to it.

The first day—I think it was the very first day—that Martie went to work, Job Rice came up when the foreman was looking the other way, and asked me to introduce him to the new girl. Now I never did like Job Rice—not from the first minute I saw him. I did not know much about him, nor had I any thing against him but his swearing and his face. All the fellows at our table swore though, except Davie Bent, and I shouldn't have thought so much of that but for his face. I can't explain what was the matter with that either, except that I did not like it. So I did not want him to speak to Martie, and I said so. Then he said he would get somebody else to do it, and that I was the rudest and most unreasonable girl he ever had seen at Inkman's. So I thought perhaps it was rude and unreasonable, and I took him over to Martie at the window. I used to blame myself for it afterward; but Martie said that was foolish, for it would have made no difference in the end. He walked home with her that day to dinner.

The next noon she begged me to wait for her; and when we were in the street she walked on so fast that I could hardly keep up. But Job could walk faster than we, and he gained upon us, and fell into step beside her.

"Just what she meant he should do!" said Sue from behind, in her spiteful way. Of course the other girl heard her.

The next day Martie said she wanted to see Mary Bailey about her sack-pattern, so Mary walked the other side. But where there's a will there's a way, they say, and Job Rice's wicked will found ways enough. He would come upon her suddenly as she waited after breakfast for me upon the stairs. He joined us at night, because he said it was too dark for us to come back alone. He waited about after supper when she staid to help Mrs. M'Cracken with the dishes—that went a little way toward her board, and she could not earn much, you know, till she had fairly learned her trade. He went to church whenever Martie did. He went to Sabbath-school just to sit in a class opposite and watch her. He was always asking her at the table to go with him to the theatre, or evening-school, or negro minstrels, or something, till he worried the poor child half sick.

Before long they were the talk of the house, and Sue Cummings did her best to see that they should be. The fact was, that Sue had been used to having things her own way among the boys, and especially with Job Rice, till Martie came.

One night Davie Bent met me and walked home with me. Davie didn't often walk home with me. Just as we came to the slope he asked me—we had been talking about Martie—if this was true that they said about her and Rice? He supposed she *did* like him, didn't she?

I was thinking of something else—some thought of my own that it was silly to waste time over—and I did not say much to Martie when I first went up stairs. Presently I told her what Davie said. She turned just as quick, with a little stamp of her foot.

"And you? What did you say to him?

So I told her what I said: that I knew she didn't like Job, and that he worried and dogged her.

"Well, I should like to tell you something else to tell him. No, I suppose it would make it the worse for me though. I wish Job would let me alone. I *wish* he would let me alone!"

I noticed then how her eyes burned—just like coals at white heat; I never had seen them look so before.

"Martie," said I, beginning to wonder, "what is the matter? What did you wish you could tell Davie? What has happened?"

She was brushing out her hair, and she stopped and threw down her brush with a childish burst of vehemence as if her nerves were strung to their tightest:

"Job Rice told me to-night he wanted to marry me, that's what he did! He might have known what I would say, and he might have known what an insult it was after I've shown him and shown him how hateful he is to me. He said—I wouldn't even tell you what he said. It seems as if I couldn't bear it!"

"You told him?"

"I told him," she said, slowly—"I told him I would rather be cut to pieces inch by inch! Explicit, wasn't it, dear?"

She broke out laughing, but it sounded as if she would much rather cry; and by-and-by she hid her face in the pillows a while, and I shouldn't wonder if she did cry.

"You see he said such things!" she said presently, her voice smothered up in the pillows. "He said such things to me! Father wouldn't have to let him, father wouldn't! Oh, Sarah, Sarah!"

I was very sorry for her, though I had to be sorry without half understanding why. But after that I always felt that Martie was afraid of Job Rice. Sometimes it used to seem as if she let him go with her just to hush up words that were on his lips. One day when he had said something that displeased her, she flashed up a little, and told him before us all that he was a miserable cowardly villain to treat a girl so. I saw him go to his case, set up something quick in type, strike it off on a slip of paper, and toss it over to her. A gust from an open window blew it toward me, and I saw the three words: "*We will see.*"

They did not sound so very dreadful, to be sure; but when Martie read them that curious look, like a lost child, crept all over her face, and never went out of it all day, nor could I kiss it away at night, though I tried as hard as I could.

It was the next week, I believe, that we had our little week's vacation that we had waited for so long. Business was dull just then, and Mr. Inkman was glad to let us off. I took Martie up to Long Meadow with me, and I verily believe that was one of the happiest weeks the poor girl ever spent in her life. Mother took her in as if she had been one of us, and kissed her, and cured her neuralgia, and made her flannel petticoats, and treated her just as she did me; and father used to pat her on the head when she had read the Almanac to him evenings. Pour little Martie! Her eyelids used to tremble a little at that. The children petted her to death, and as for Dan—well, well! poor fellow!—I don't mind telling *you*—I am afraid Dan thought a great deal of Martie; but I saw, and he saw, that it never could be; she would never care for him—in that way, I mean. I could not understand then why, Dan was so good and handsome. Poor Dan! I thought this winter that he might take a fancy to Jinny Coles; at least I hoped so; but he says he does not care to marry just yet, and Jinny calls him an old bachelor, and so do all the Long Meadow girls.

Well, Martie went out with me into the sweet spring days—there seemed to be a great many days to that week—and fed the cows, and looked at the horses, and played with the chickens, and hunted for May-flowers, and filled her carpet-bag with sea-weed moss to carry back; she liked it because it was cool, she said; she used to bury up her face in it and sit thinking.

"Sarah," she said, the night before we went back, "I have felt so *safe* here. Just think if one could feel safe all the time!"

So to-morrow came, and we had to bid goodby to all the sweetness, and dearness, and safety; and the long, lonesome city looked longer and lonesomer than ever.

When we got back, all drabbled and cold and tired, Mrs. M'Cracken met me at the door.

"How do you do, Sarah?" said she, in a very high key. "You'll find your room ready; and you'll better take your bag and run right up, and not stand here lettin' the draught in.—Marthy Saunders, I'm sorry to say I haven't got any room for *you*."

"Not any room for me!"

Martie turned about and looked at her. It was growing dark fast, and the dreary wind blew up from the street against her.

"No, I hain't; and, I'm sorry to say, I never expect to. I'm a respectable widow, *I* am, and this 'ere's a respectable house. I've no place for the likes of you!"

Martie just stood and looked at her—looked at her with her great, wide-open eyes. I don't believe any of those little lost children could have been slower to take in the shameful words.

I must have said something dreadful to Mrs. M'Cracken—I believe I told her she lied; then it occurred to me that that wasn't polite, so I told her I should like to know what she was talking about, and whom she was talking about.

"I'm talkin' about Marthy Saunders," says she; "and I say girls as behaves shameful and loses their virtoous name, and then begs young men to marry 'em, ain't fit company for me, nor my boarders! So, Marthy Saunders, I'll be obleeged to you if you'll jest step out of the way, for it's cold, and I want the door shet!"

Then, for once of the two times, I saw the hot color go shooting all over Martie's face, up to her forehead, down to her neck. It blazed for a minute like a jet of fire, and then died down. I never saw her look so white—I never saw her look so pure and white as she looked when it had gone.

She opened her lips to speak, but Mrs. M'Cracken had slammed the door; slammed it so close upon her that her shawl was caught in the hinge.

The girls were laughing out in the dining-room, where they were playing forfeits with Davie Bent. The light twinkled out warmly through the side-glass, and shown down warmly from our own room where they had just made things ready for me. The dreary wind blew up from the street; the dust whirled about in clouds; two or three people went by in the dark, hurrying home. Poor little Martie!

Dear me! dear me! To think that I can't write about it after all this time without crying!

I broke out into something about Job Rice, and the landlady, and what should we do? And had it all in a jumble of anger and grief and bewilderment; but noticed at last that Martie stood yet, with her shawl shut in the door, perfectly still. I noticed, too, that her hand was lifted solemnly up above her head.

"Martie! Martie! what are you doing?"

"Praying God to settle accounts with him," she said in a very quiet voice; but a voice no more like Martie's than it was like Job's. "Well, Sarah, good-by. You'd better go in."

"He just did it for revenge!" I cried out, sobbing. "Poor Martie! poor Martie! And not a place for you to sleep this night!"

"You'd better go in," she repeated, in the same strange, quiet way. "You will take cold. I suppose I can find a place. At least there's the station-house always for such as us," with a laugh. "Good-night, dear!"

But I never could have let her go in that way all alone; and though she did her best to send me back, I went out with her into the dreary wind to find a shelter for her head. Something in her face, as we passed the streetlamp at the corner, set me to thinking how it must choke and stifle one to walk on gasping in the cruel wind, leaving one's good name further behind at every step. Then I thought of the warm light in our window, and the girls and Davie. Then I thought of the good, strong father—she had often told me how good and strong he was—and of the grave away in the country, and I wondered how he could bear it to be lying there, and she *here*, his only little daughter; and she said he had sheltered her in so with his love. Poor, poor little Martie! Why, I thought till it seemed as if my heart would break for her.

I looked up, I remember, into people's faces as we passed, wondering why there wasn't any body in all the city to help her. I knew there were many good men and women who would have trusted and cared for her, but we did not know where to find them, and Martie was so shy of strangers. I remember how the lamps flitted and whirled, and how bright the shop windows looked, as we walked on, still watching the people, face after face, for one kind look; one kind look would have given me courage to speak. It did seem to me strange that they could *help* noticing us. But nobody did notice, and we did not dare to speak. I went once into a jeweler's, where I saw through the great plate-glass a pleasant-faced gentleman with gray hair, and I asked him could he tell me where a poor girl could get a respectable lodging for the night? He answered very pleasantly that the police would tell me best, and I ran out frightened, and did not try that again.

There were our employers, you say. Yes, but they did not know nor care much about the hands out of working hours. Mr. Inkman was a good sort of man, but he would not be likely to trouble himself that time of night about Martie. Besides, he would probably take Mrs. M'Cracken's word for the truth, and it might cost Martie her place for him to hear the story. As for her Sunday-school teacher, why, she would about as soon have thought of going to the police, for she had never spoken with her except to give her name and answer the Bible-questions. Besides, we did not know where she lived. So Martie must help herself.

We went to boarding-houses till we were tired out. Nobody would take a strange girl in at night. Where had she been last? Mrs. M'Cracken's. Had she a recommendation? No. They were sorry, but the house was full. Good-evening.

I don't suppose they can be exactly blamed; but it seemed hard. Just such a night as that was to Martie has sent many of us poor girls right straight to destruction. It did seem hard.

Pretty soon, worn out and in a sort of desperation, she said that she should go back to the place where she spent her first few days in the city. I thought the police would be better than that; but she said no; what could she do in the hands of the police, with the character that she had brought away with her from the door-steps back there? She would go back to the old place and take her chance. It was safe enough, probably, only she was foolish and fanciful. It would be better than to run the risk of worse. So we went, and they took her in.

I would have staid with her, I could not bear to have her there alone, but she would not listen to it. She said I should not lose my home and my good name with hers. She begged me so for her sake to go back that I had to go. She walked a little way with me till I would let her go no farther. Then I watched her going back alone.

I gave Job Rice a piece of my mind that night, and I stood up for Martie against Mrs. M'Cracken and the girls. But it was of no use. Sue had been before me to echo every word of Job's and a little more. Sue said it was just what she had always expected of her. When I looked at Sue's bold, bad face, and thought of that pure white look of Martie's, I wondered how God could *let* any body believe one against the other. But I suppose, after all, we do our own believing; we can not blame Him for it.

Davie Bent came up to me a minute as I stood apart by the window; Sue and Job had been talking so that I could not stand it.

"Davie," said I, between my teeth, "I hope God *will* 'settle accounts' with him fair and square, for it's a fiendish lie! It's a fiendish lie, Davie!"

He opened his kindly, honest eyes wide on me, and a color like a girl's went over his face.

"Did you think," said he, "*could* you think that I—"

Sue came up just then, in her inquisitive way, and he broke off and went out of the room.

I did not think to tell Martie of this for several days. It occurred to me when I did speak of it, and she looked up, that perhaps she would have liked to hear it before.

"You see, Martie," said I, "it is plain what he was going to say, though he didn't finish his sentence. He believes in you, and I knew he would."

But she shook her head drearily.

"You don't know that. He did not say so. He would have said something quite different. Nobody believes in me. Why should *he*?"

With that she turned away to look into a shop-window and said no more the rest of the way home.

"Davie wouldn't be so mean," I argued. "Davie is true, and fair, and good." But she would not talk about it.

She spent two weeks at that place. I never knew till it was all over, not till long after it was all over, just what she lived through there. How there was a rum-shop on the first-floor; how late the hooting and singing used to last; how she sat up night after night till two or three o'clock, unable to sleep for the noise and fear, and trying to muffle her windows, and the crack under the door, so that she should not hear the words they said and sung.

Her story came to Mr. Inkman's ears, too, soon enough, and there was talk of dismissing her; but it finally blew over; she was a valuable compositor, quick as a thought, and very accurate; and Inkman & Tipes did not care so much as they might have done about the morals of their hands.

But, take it altogether, those two were as miserable weeks as ever a poor girl lived. That lost look, I noticed, settled down into her face, and before they were over became her only look.

One night—it is a little thing to tell, but it hurt me at the time—it chanced that she had to carry proof to some editor—I've forgotten his name, but he was connected with a Magazine which Inkman & Tipes printed. The boy whose business it was to carry proof and copy was sick, and as the errand was right on Martie's way the foreman asked her to attend to it.

The editor was at dinner—she told me about it afterward—and she had to wait for him a few moments in the hall. She was tired and faint, and the jets of gas-light dazzled her. She leaned up against the balusters for support, looking around at the carpeted hall and stairs, and in at the open door of the parlors, where glimpses of mirrors and crimson curtains, of pictures, and books, and flameless, hot coal fires showed through. I knew just how she must have looked, standing there, homeless and outcast, in the midst of it all.

While she was waiting a young girl about her own age—a pretty, delicate creature, with a rich dress and soft, ringed hands—came from somewhere and fluttered into the parlors, looking like a picture cut out against the flameless fires, and fluttered out again, softly humming a tune. Her father met her at the further end of the hall, and Martie, who had shrunk out of sight at the foot of the stairs, heard him say, the words broken up with a laughing kiss:

"Well, Empress Nell! So you insist on dragging your old father out to the concert tonight? The carriage will be punctual, and I hope you will be likewise. Your hair? Oh no, that doesn't need to be frizzed over. You look pretty enough already. Be sure and wrap up warmly, dear; it is a chilly night. Jane, where did you leave the young woman? Is she waiting? Oh yes."

It doesn't seem so much to tell of, but it came over Martie so—this other girl, sheltered in by the light and elegance and warmth and love, so watched and protected, so pleased and petted through her happy days and nights—and she to be shut out into the cold and dark of the streets, shut back into her wretched room, home and help and good name gone—and the grave lying out far away in the night—it came over her so for the minute that she staggered up against the balusters, a sick faintness creeping all over her. I believe she might have had courage to tell the gentleman all about it had he asked her; and I suppose he would have asked her had he thought of it, for she said he had a pleasant face. But he was a busy man and hurried, so he took the proofs and opened the door politely for her, and she went slowly out. He must have been struck by her look, for she heard him say to his pretty daughter as he latched the door,

"That poor girl is very pale. Consumptive, probably. Come, Nell, fly away and get ready!"

At the end of the fortnight Martie had a dress to be cut at little Miss Tripp's. And little Miss Tripp—God bless her for it!—no sooner had questioned the story all out of her than she said: "Martha Saunders, I'll stand by you. You just leave that dreadful place and come board with me."

So Martie went to little Miss Tripp's, and I insisted on her letting me go with her. As to its "hurting my character," which she argued in her dear, unselfish love, I said, as I had said about my respectability, I would make my own or I would go without.

We had been at Miss Tripp's just a week when the most astounding thing happened. Martie came in one night with very bright eyes, and said:

"I am going to be married to Job Rice."

I do not know what I did or said. I am sure I never was so bewildered and confounded in my life.

"We shall be married in three weeks," she said, quietly drawing the curtain and beginning to take down her hair. "That is about as soon as I can get ready. You needn't look so at me, Sarah. Continual dropping wears away the hardest stone, you know. Come, I am tired and want to go to bed."

I don't know what it was, but something in her eyes stopped me from reasoning with her. I tried it once, and after that I gave it up. So, still bewildered and confounded, shocked and worried and grieved, I yielded silently to Martie's plans for this horrible wedding.

I cut out and basted and sewed; I bought patterns and tucked muslin; I went about and looked at her and touched her as if I had been in a nightmare.

Davie Bent had been home to see his mother, and had not heard. The first night that he came back—it was a warm light spring night—he and Martie went to walk. I was sitting at my window thinking about them, when they came home and stopped by the steps a minute to talk. I remember how warm the air was sweeping up against my cheeks, and I remember how Davie's voice sounded so manly and low and still. I did not mean to hear, and I shrank back; but I had caught one word, and I knew—what I ought to have known long before; but it is very hard for us to find things out sometimes.

I did not notice Martie when she first came up; but presently she called me, and turning round I wondered what had happened.

"Sarah," she said. She waited a minute after that, and then I saw for the second and last time the color in her face—sweet, faint color, like a happy child's. It made her very pretty. "Sarah, he *did* believe in me. He told me that he believed in me all through."

"Martie," said I, very low, "he told you something more than that."

"Yes." She turned her head away quickly.

"I wonder what you told him."

"What should I tell him?" said she, turning back in a sharp way. "I have promised to marry Job Rice."

So we neither of us said any more about it.

Martie's wedding-day came on very fast, and we were very busy. She had spent all her money over her little outfit; and she could not have taken more pains over her white muslin dress if she had been going to be Job's very happy wife; I never *could* think that. It did seem to me as if I must stop it, and the nearer the time came the more terrible it seemed. But she never called it terrible. One of the last nights I broke out crying, and asked her if she had not a word to say to me about it.

"No," said she. "Why should I have?"

She had sent a special invitation to Mrs. M'Cracken, and the girls there, and Sue; and, strange as it seemed, they all came. We did not have many weddings, and it gave them something to talk about. We were all there waiting in Miss Tripp's little parlor—waiting in the nightmare it seemed to me—when Martie came in with Job. She did not blush or look shy, as most girls do; she was pretty and white and quiet. I did not see what made her so quiet. There was an odd light in her eyes. It reminded me somehow of a look I have seen in pictures in the eyes of hunted creatures that had been driven till they could be driven no further.

Davie Bent was there, trying to flirt a little with Sue. He was very white. I felt sorry for Davie; sorrier than I did for Martie, or for— well, no matter who!

The minister was a little late, and we were talking when he came in, but hushed up at sight of him. He was a tall, fine-looking gentleman, who treated Miss Tripp and Martie very politely—almost as politely as if they had been rich and educated ladies; and looked around the room with very keen eyes. Martie sent for him because she liked his sermons. She had been to his church several times; she did not go regularly, because it was a grand church, and she did not feel at home there.

Dear me, how I trembled when he began the Marriage Service! And how still the room was! And how that hunted look in Martie's eyes grew and brightened into another look—and that look was stranger yet!

The minister was through with what he had to say to Job; and Job, with his complacent, evil smile, had made his responses; and it came Martie's turn, and you could have heard a pin drop. I remember how solemnly the words sounded:

"Do you take this man who stands beside you to be your wedded husband?"

He waited for her answer, and it came:

"*No! and I never will!*" and she flung off Job's hand as if it had been a serpent, and stood there quivering.

In an instant every thing was in a hubbub. I'm sure I never saw a minister's face look blanker than that minister's face looked.

"Madam," said he, with a low bow, "I consider that you have insulted me, and insulted my profession beyond hope of apology. I wish you good-evening!" and he walked right out of the room.

Miss Tripp screamed; Sue Cummings tried to faint; Job, purple with passion, gasped for breath to speak, and every thing was in an uproar. Above it I saw Martie standing still and triumphant; and above it I was conscious of Davie's face with a sudden light striking it through and through.

Job found his voice at last, and he stood and swore at Martie, oath after oath; I never heard such swearing. She just stood there perfectly still and smiled. Then he turned upon her and raised his hand. I believe, woman though she was, he would have struck her to the floor, but there was a spring at the other end of the room; the girls made way screaming, and Davie just caught her out of Job's reach in his great, strong arms, and held her—held her there, before us all—and she never struggled nor blushed; but the lost look faded out of her face in that minute, and I never saw it again.

So it was all explained now. She had not meant it so much for revenge, though it was revenge enough, and Job deserved it, and I'm glad he had it; but she took it as the only way possible to her to defend herself, and give the lie to his foul slanders. And to think how she had kept it from every human soul, and planned it so well, and done all her sewing, that Davie never suspected the truth till it came; and, stranger than that, that she had never hinted a breath of it to me, and I rooming with her all along! I wonder how many girls could have done it! Nobody need tell me that a woman can't keep a secret again!

She sent for Dr. ———— the next day, and explained to him, before Miss Tripp and me, the whole story. She apologized for the rudeness done to him yesterday; and said that the chief thing that troubled her about the plan was the insult to a clergyman which it involved, but she was driven to it, and she begged his pardon, and hoped he would not judge her harshly. He received her apology kindly, and said he wished that he had known how she had been situated before; he should have been glad to help her if he could in silencing the cruel scandal. I think he believed, when he saw her face, that she spoke simple truth. I think he was a good man.

Well, and so later in the summer there was another wedding-day. It came away from the hot city and Sue's gossipy tongue, and away from Job, who was always vowing vengeance, but has never found his way to wreak it yet. It came with Long Meadow sunlight and flowers, at home, in our little front-parlor—it seemed so strange, you know, that Davie should ever be in my home—and he looked so proud of Martie, and Martie so content with him! I think it was the sweetest, stillest wedding that I ever saw. I think it made me very happy—at least—yes, I think it did. It was so pleasant to know that I never should have to call her Poor Martie any more. Happy little Martie!

By-the-way, you may be sure that we sent for little Miss Tripp to come out, and that she came.

Now, since mother died, and I have been at home keeping house—since there has been so much to do, and I get tired and cry a little sometimes by myself when the children have been naughty or sick—sometimes, when life looks very different from what I used to think it would be—from what I suppose all girls think it will be at some time or other—I believe it does me good—I'm sure it ought to—to think of Davie's wife——

[There were one or two words more, but so blotted and blurred by a large round mark that I struck them out as unintelligible.]

SARAH ORNE JEWETT

Miss Tempy's Watchers

(1888)

*S*ARAH Orne Jewett (1849–1909), foremother of the twentieth-century "woman-identified woman," was born to a prominent and well-educated family in South Berwick, Maine. She was the middle child of three daughters born to Caroline Francis Perry and Theodore Herman Jewett. Her mother was the daughter of a successful doctor in New Hampshire. Jewett's father, a country doctor, was independently wealthy because of an inheritance from his father, a shipbuilder and merchant in the West Indies. Sarah's inheritance of family wealth ensured her the economic freedom to write.

Both parents and her paternal grandmother influenced her intellectual growth and literary tastes. Her mother and her grandmother introduced her to such women writers as Jane Austen, George Eliot, and Mrs. Oliphant. Because of childhood illnesses, Sarah often stayed home from school and traveled with her father on patient rounds. During these outings, Jewett's father taught her the reverence for nature and rural life that appears in her writing. He also encouraged her to read the classics in his library and discussed her writing with her. In Miss Olive Rayne's School and the South Berwick Academy her teachers also encouraged her interest in literature. Jewett, as a youth, kept diaries and notes on her reading. As a result of these early influences, she struggled less than many women do to believe in herself as an artist. She continued throughout her life to read widely—the classics, philosophy, history, religion, and her literary contemporaries in America, England, and France. Some of her favorite writers were Austen, Stowe, Thackery, and Flaubert.

Jewett decided in her teens to write, and not to write "about things" but to "write the things themselves just as they are," as her father had advised her. In 1869 when William Dean Howells, a feminist and prominent editor in search of realism and women authors, accepted her first story for the *Atlantic Monthly,* he saw in her work the American writing he wanted to publish. Howells remained one of Jewett's strongest supporters.

Jewett's "Boston marriage" of thirty years to Annie Adams Fields was a relationship acknowledged by the nineteenth-century literary world, but minimized in the seventy-five years of scholarship between Jewett's death and the advent of feminist scholarship. Annie Fields was the widow of James T. Fields, the prominent Boston publisher of Ticknor and Fields and the editor and publisher of the *Atlantic Monthly.* Annie and James worked to publish women writers and to encourage them to make a living with their art. In 1881, when James Fields died, Sarah and Annie began living together—part of the year in Boston in Fields's home, part of the year in Jewett's Maine home. Jewett and Fields traveled to Europe together several times and met many prominent literary figures. Fields, through her abilities as a hostess, created one of America's most important literary salons. When Jewett moved in with Fields, the salon became a haven for women writers. In this circle of artists Jewett became both the critic and intimate friend of many American writers, most of whom were women. The list includes Celia Thaxter, Harriet Beecher Stowe, Mary E. Wilkins Freeman, Elizabeth Stuart Phelps, Louisa May Alcott, Alice Brown, and Willa Cather. Unfortunately, when Fields edited the 1911 edition of Jewett's letters, Mark Anthony DeWolfe Howe, historian and friend of Fields, convinced her to leave out all the love letters Jewett had written to Fields, letters that began in 1877 and became romantic early in their relationship.

Jewett's first stories appeared under the pseudonyms Alice Eliot or A. C. Eliot in such magazines as the *Atlantic Monthly* and *Riverside Magazine for Young People.* Many of her early stories lack intensity. She writes naively about the happiness of girls in the leisure class, allowing her Christian didacticism, influenced by her Congregationalist youth, to overshadow her art. Much of Jewett's work before the late 1870s examines relationships between females but also reflects an upper-class elitism.

However, Jewett's maturity, her entrance into Swedonborgianism and esoteric spiritualities, her lesbian partnership with Annie Fields, and their involvement with a community of women artists changed Jewett's literary voice in a dramatic way. Her voice becomes one crying in the wilderness for women to protect nature from the destructive forces of masculinist progress, speaking against the oppression of women, and celebrating the bonds of mature women.

Jewett herself said that there is "something transfiguring in the best of friendship"; this was as true of her relationship to Fields as it is of the relationship of the characters in "Miss Tempy's Watchers." This story reflects Jewett's ability to recreate the subtle intimacies between women that lead to those transfiguring experiences of love between women. Jewett knew the importance of showing the power of women's love, as she demonstrated in her now well-known advice to Willa Cather: in regard to the development of one of Cather's male characters, Jewett cautioned Cather not to try to be a man, for "a woman could love her in the same protecting way."

During her lifetime Jewett's contributions to American letters received critical acclaim in a variety of publications such as the *Nation, Cottage Hearth,* and *Revue des Deux Mondes.* One of the most interesting reviews of a Jewett novel, written by feminist writer Alice Brown, was published in *Book Buyer* in 1897. Jewett received an honorary Doctor of Letters from Bowdoin College in 1901. Although her work has continued to receive critical attention, the use of disempowering labels such as "regionalist" and "minor writer" has discouraged her inclusion in American anthologies and curricula and called into question her position in America's male-defined literary tradition. Our new abilities to read her meditative writing for what it is—experimental in narrative voice, plot structure, and subject matter, including role reversals, transvestitism, love between women, the appeal of older women, exploration of unusual mental states, exploitation of nature, women's spirituality, and women's community—will lead us to a greater sense of our own power as women-identified women.

Jewett's works include *Deephaven* (1877), *A Country Doctor* (1884), *A White Heron and Other Stories* (1886), *The Country of the Pointed Firs* (1896), *The Best Stories of Sarah Orne Jewett* (1925, in two volumes, with an introduction by Willa Cather). *The Country of the Pointed Firs and Other Stories,* edited by Mary Ellen Chase in 1896, was reissued in 1981 with an introduction by Marjorie Pryse. Richard Cary edited *Deephaven and Other Stories* in 1966, the *Sarah Orne Jewett Letters* in 1967, and *The Uncollected Short Stories of Sarah Orne Jewett* in 1971. Recent critical studies include Josephine Donovan's *Sarah Orne Jewett* (1980) and *Critical Essays on Sarah Orne Jewett,* edited by Gwen Nagel (1984). "Miss Tempy's Watchers" was first published in the March 1888 issue of the *Atlantic Monthly.*

ABIGAIL KEEGAN

The time of year was April; the place was a small farming town in New Hampshire, remote from any railroad. One by one the lights had been blown out in the scattered houses near Miss Tempy Dent's; but as her neighbors took a last look out-of-doors, their eyes turned with instinctive curiosity toward the old house, where a lamp burned steadily. They gave a little sigh. "Poor Miss Tempy!" said more than one bereft acquaintance; for the good woman lay dead in her north chamber, and the light was a watcher's light. The funeral was set for the next day, at one o'clock.

The watchers were two of the oldest friends, Mrs. Crowe and Sarah Ann Binson. They were sitting in the kitchen, because it seemed less awesome than the unused best room, and they beguiled the long hours by steady conversation. One would think that neither topics nor opinions would hold out, at that rate, all through the long spring night; but there was a certain degree of excitement just then, and the two women had risen to an unusual level of expressiveness and confidence. Each had already told the other more than one fact that she had determined to keep secret; they were again and again tempted into statements that either would have found impossible by daylight. Mrs. Crowe was knitting a blue yarn stocking for her husband; the foot was already so long that it seemed as if she must have forgotten to narrow it at the proper time. Mrs. Crowe knew exactly what she was about, however; she was of a much cooler disposition than Sister Binson, who made futile attempts at some sewing, only to drop her work into her lap whenever the talk was most engaging.

Their faces were interesting,—of the dry, shrewd, quick-witted New England type, with thin hair twisted neatly back out of the way. Mrs. Crowe could look vague and benignant, and Miss Binson was, to quote her neighbors, a little too sharp-set; but the world knew that she had need to be, with the load she must carry of supporting an inefficient widowed sister and six unpromising and unwilling nieces and nephews. The eldest boy was at last placed with a good man to learn the mason's trade. Sarah Ann Binson, for all her sharp, anxious aspect, never defended herself, when her sister whined and fretted. She was told every week of her life that the poor children never would have had to lift a finger if their father had lived, and yet she had kept her steadfast way with the little farm, and patiently taught the young people many useful things, for which, as everybody said, they would live to thank her. However pleasureless her life appeared to outward view, it was brimful of pleasure to herself.

Mrs. Crowe, on the contrary, was well to do, her husband being a rich farmer and an easy-going man. She was a stingy woman, but for all that she looked kindly; and when she gave away anything, or lifted a finger to help anybody, it was thought a great piece of beneficence, and a compliment, indeed, which the recipient accepted with twice as much gratitude as double the gift that came from a poorer and more generous acquaintance. Everybody liked to be on good terms with Mrs. Crowe. Socially she stood much higher than Sarah Ann Binson. They were both old schoolmates and friends of Temperance Dent, who had asked them, one day, not long before she died, if they would not come together and look after the house, and manage everything, when she was gone. She may have had some hope that they might become closer friends in this period of intimate partnership, and that the richer woman might better understand the burdens of the poorer. They had not kept the house the night before; they were too weary with the care of their old friend, whom they had not left until all was over.

There was a brook which ran down the hillside very near the house, and the sound of it was much louder than usual. When there was silence in the kitchen, the busy stream had a strange insistence in its wild voice, as if it tried to make the watchers understand something that related to the past.

"I declare, I can't begin to sorrow for Tempy yet. I am so glad to have her at rest," whispered Mrs. Crowe. "It is strange to set here without her, but I can't make it clear that she has gone. I feel as if she had got easy and dropped off to sleep, and I'm more scared about waking her up than knowing any other feeling."

"Yes," said Sarah Ann, "it's just like that, ain't it? But I tell you we are goin' to miss her worse than we expect. She's helped me through with many a trial, has Temperance. I ain't the only one who says the same, neither."

These words were spoken as if there were a third person listening; somebody beside Mrs. Crowe. The watchers could not rid their minds of the feeling that they were being watched themselves. The spring wind whistled in the window crack, now and then, and buffeted the little house in a gusty way that had a sort of companionable effect. Yet, on the whole, it was a very still night, and the watchers spoke in a half-whisper.

"She was the freest-handed woman that ever I knew," said Mrs. Crowe, decidedly. "According to her means, she gave away more than anybody. I used to tell her 't wa'n't right. I used really to be afraid that she went without too much, for we have a duty to ourselves."

Sister Binson looked up in a half-amused, unconscious way, and then recollected herself.

Mrs. Crowe met her look with a serious face. "It ain't so easy for me to give as it is for some," she said simply, but with an effort which was made possible only by the occasion. "I should like to say, while Tempy is laying here yet in her own house, that she has been a constant lesson to me. Folks are too kind, and shame me with thanks for what I do. I ain't such a generous woman as poor Tempy was, for all she had nothin' to do with, as one may say."

Sarah Binson was much moved at this confession, and was even pained and touched by the unexpected humility. "You have a good many calls on you"—she began, and then left her kind little compliment half finished.

"Yes, yes, but I've got means enough. My disposition's more of a cross to me as I grow older, and I made up my mind this morning that Tempy's example should be my pattern henceforth." She began to knit faster than ever.

" 'T ain't no use to get morbid: that's what Tempy used to say herself," said Sarah Ann, after a minute's silence. "Ain't it strange to say 'used to say'?" and her own voice choked a little. "She never did like to hear folks git goin' about themselves."

" 'T was only because they're apt to do it so as other folks will say 't wasn't so, an' praise 'em up," humbly replied Mrs. Crowe, "and that ain't my object. There wa'n't a child but what Tempy set herself to work to see what she could do to please it. One time my brother's folks had been stopping here in the summer, from Massachusetts. The children was all little, and they broke up a sight of toys, and left 'em when they were going away. Tempy come right up after they rode by, to see if she couldn't help me set the house to rights, and she caught me just as I was going to fling some of the clutter into the stove. I was kind of tired out, starting 'em off in season. 'Oh, give me them!' says she, real pleading; and she wropped 'em up and took 'em home with her when she went, and she mended 'em up and stuck 'em together, and made some young one or other happy with every blessed one. You'd thought I'd done her the biggest favor. 'No thanks to me. I should ha' burnt 'em, Tempy,' says I."

"Some of 'em came to our house, I know," said Miss Binson.

"She'd take a lot o' trouble to please a child, 'stead o' shoving of it out o' the way, like the rest of us when we're drove.

"I can tell you the biggest thing she ever done, and I don't know's there's anybody left but me to tell it. I don't want it forgot," Sarah Binson went on, looking up at the clock to see how the night was going. "It was that pretty-looking Trevor girl, who taught the Corners school, and married so well afterwards, out in New York State. You remember her, I dare say?"

"Certain," said Mrs. Crowe, with an air of interest.

"She was a splendid scholar, folks said, and give the school a great start; but she'd overdone herself getting her education, and working to pay for it, and she all broke down one spring, and Tempy made her come and stop with her a while,—you remember that? Well, she had an uncle, her mother's brother, out in Chicago, who was well off and friendly, and used to write to Lizzie Trevor, and I dare say make her some presents; but he was a lively, driving man, and didn't take time to stop and think about his folks. He hadn't seen her since she was a little girl. Poor Lizzie was so pale and weakly that she just got through the term o' school. She looked as if she was just going straight off in a decline. Tempy, she cosseted her up a while, and then, next thing folks knew, she was tellin' round how Miss Trevor had gone to see her uncle, and meant to visit Niagary Falls on the way, and stop over night. Now I happened to know, in ways I won't dwell on to explain, that the poor girl was in debt for her schoolin' when she come here, and her last quarter's pay had just squared it off at last, and left her without a cent ahead, hardly; but it had fretted her thinking of it, so she paid it all; those might have dunned her that she owed it to. An' I taxed Tempy about the girl's goin' off on such a journey till she owned up, rather'n have Lizzie blamed, that she'd given her sixty dollars, same's if she was rolling in riches, and sent her off to have a good rest and vacation."

"Sixty dollars!" exclaimed Mrs. Crowe. "Tempy only had ninety dollars a year that came in to her; rest of her livin' she got by helpin' about, with what she raised off this little piece o' ground, sand one side an' clay the other. An' how often I've heard her tell, years ago, that she'd rather see Niagary than any other sight in the world!"

The women looked at each other in silence; the magnitude of the generous sacrifice was almost too great for their comprehension.

"She was just poor enough to do that!" declared Mrs. Crowe at last, in an abandonment of feeling. "Say what you may, I feel humbled to the dust," and her companion ventured to say nothing. She never had given away sixty dollars at once, but it was simply because she never had it to give. It came to her very lips to say in explanation, "Tempy was so situated;" but she checked herself in time, for she would not betray her own loyal guarding of a dependent household.

"Folks say a great deal of generosity, and this one's being public-sperited, and that one free-handed about giving," said Mrs. Crowe, who was a little nervous in the silence. "I suppose we can't tell the sorrow it would be to some folks not to give, same's 't would be to me not to save. I seem kind of made for that, as if 't was what I'd got to do. I should feel sights better about it if I could make it evident what I was savin' for. If I had a child, now, Sarah Ann," and her voice was a little husky,—"if I had a child, I should think I was heapin' of it up because he was the one trained by the Lord to scatter it again for good. But here's Mr. Crowe and me, we can't do anything with money, and both of us like to keep things same's they've always been. Now Priscilla Dance was talking away like a mill-clapper, week before last. She'd think I would go right off and get one o' them new-fashioned gilt-and-white papers for the best room, and some new furniture, an' a marble-top table. And I looked at her, all struck up. 'Why,' says I, 'Priscilla, that nice old velvet paper ain't hurt a mite. I shouldn't feel 't was my best room without it. Dan'el says 't is the first thing he can remember rubbin' his little baby fingers on to it, and how splendid he thought them red roses was.' I maintain," continued Mrs. Crowe stoutly, "that folks wastes sights o' good money doin' just such foolish things. Tearin' out the insides o' meetin'-houses, and fixin' the pews different; 't was good enough as 't was with mendin'; then times come, an' they want to put it all back same's 't was before."

This touched upon an exciting subject to active members of that parish. Miss Binson and Mrs. Crowe belonged to opposite parties, and had at one time come as near hard feelings as they could, and yet escape them. Each hastened to speak of other things and to show her untouched friendliness.

"I do agree with you," said Sister Binson, "that few of us know what use to make of money, beyond every-day necessities. You've seen more o' the world than I have, and know what's expected. When it comes to taste and judgment about such things, I ought to defer to others;" and with this modest avowal the critical moment passed when there might have been an improper discussion.

In the silence that followed, the fact of their presence in a house of death grew more clear than before. There was a something disturbing in the noise of a mouse gnawing at the dry boards of a closet wall near by. Both the watchers looked up anxiously at the clock; it was almost the middle of the night, and the whole world seemed to have left them alone with their solemn duty. Only the brook was awake.

"Perhaps we might give a look up-stairs now," whispered Mrs. Crowe, as if she hoped to hear some reason against their going just then to the chamber of death; but Sister Binson rose, with a serious and yet satisfied countenance, and lifted the small lamp from the table. She was much more used to watching than Mrs. Crowe, and much less affected by it. They opened the door into a small entry with a steep stairway; they climbed the creaking stairs, and entered the cold upper room on tiptoe. Mrs. Crowe's heart began to beat very fast as the lamp was put on a high bureau, and made long, fixed shadows about the walls. She went hesitatingly toward the solemn shape under its white drapery, and felt a sense of remonstrance as Sarah Ann gently, but in a business-like way, turned back the thin sheet.

"Seems to me as she looks pleasanter and pleasanter," whispered Sarah Ann Binson impulsively, as they gazed at the white face with its wonderful smile. "To-morrow 't will all have faded out. I do believe they kind of wake up a day or two after they die, and it's then they go." She replaced the light covering, and they both turned quickly away; there was a chill in this upper room.

"'T is a great thing for anybody to have got through, ain't it?" said Mrs. Crowe softly, as she began to go down the stairs on tiptoe. The warm air form the kitchen beneath met them with a sense of welcome and shelter.

"I don' know why it is, but I feel as near again to Tempy down here as I do up there," replied Sister Binson. "I feel as if the air was full of her, kind of. I can sense things, now and then, that she seems to say. Now I never was one to take up with no nonsense of sperits and such, but I declare I felt as if she told me just now to put some more wood into the stove."

Mrs. Crowe preserved a gloomy silence. She had suspected before this that her companion was of a weaker and more credulous disposition than herself. "'T is a great thing to have got through," she repeated, ignoring definitely all that had last been said. "I suppose you know as well as I that Tempy was one that always feared death. Well, it's all put behind her now; she knows what 't is." Mrs. Crowe gave a little sigh, and Sister Binson's quick sympathies were stirred toward this other old friend, who also dreaded the great change.

"I'd never like to forgit almost those last words Tempy spoke plain to me," she said gently, like the comforter she truly was. "She looked up at me once or twice, that last afternoon after I come to set by her, and let Mis' Owen go home ; and I says, 'Can I do anything to ease you, Tempy?' and the tears come into my eyes so I couldn't see what kind of a nod she give me. 'No, Sarah Ann, you can't, dear,' says she; and then she got her breath again, and says she, looking at me real meanin', 'I'm only a-gettin' sleepier and sleepier; that's all there is,' says she, and smiled up at me kind of wishful, and shut her eyes. I knew well enough all she meant. She'd been lookin' out for a chance to tell me, and I don' know's she ever said much afterwards."

Mrs. Crowe was not knitting; she had been listening too eagerly. "Yes, 't will be a comfort to think of that sometimes," she said, in acknowledgment.

"I know that old Dr. Prince said once, in evenin' meetin', that he'd watched by many a dyin' bed, as we well knew, and enough o' his sick folks had been scared o' dyin' their whole lives through; but when they come to the last, he'd never seen one but was willin', and most were glad, to go. "'T is as natural as bein' born or livin' on,' he said. I don't know what had moved him to speak that night. You know he wa'n't in the habit of it, and 't was the monthly council of prayer for foreign missions anyways," said Sarah Ann; "but 't was a great stay to the mind to listen to his words of experience."

"There never was a better man," responded Mrs. Crowe, in a really cheerful tone. She had recovered from her feeling of nervous dread, the kitchen was so comfortable with lamplight and firelight; and just then the old clock began to tell the hour of twelve with leisurely whirring strokes.

Sister Binson laid aside her work, and rose quickly and went to the cupboard. "We'd better take a little to eat," she explained. "The night will go fast after this. I want to know if you went and made some o' your nice cupcake, while you was home to-day?" she asked, in a pleased tone; and Mrs. Crowe acknowledged such a gratifying piece of thoughtfulness for this humble friend who denied herself all luxuries. Sarah Ann brewed a generous cup of tea, and the watchers drew their chairs up to the table presently, and quelled their hunger with good country appetites. Sister Binson put a spoon into a small, old-fashioned glass of preserved quince, and passed it to her friend. She was most familiar with the house, and played the part of hostess. "Spread some o' this on your bread and butter," she said to Mrs. Crowe. "Tempy wanted me to use some three or four times, but I never felt to. I know she'd like to have us comfortable now, and would urge us to make a good supper, poor dear."

"What excellent preserves she did make!" mourned Mrs. Crowe. "None of us has got her light hand at doin' things tasty. She made the most o' everything, too. Now, she only had that one old quince-tree down in the far corner of the piece, but she'd go out in the spring and tend to it, and look at it so pleasant, and kind of expect the old thorny thing into bloomin'."

"She was just the same with folks," said Sarah Ann. "And she'd never git more'n a little apernful o' quinces, but she'd have every mite o' goodness out o' those, and set the glasses up onto her best-room closet shelf, so pleased. 'T wa'n't but a week ago to-morrow mornin' I fetched her a little taste o' jelly in a teaspoon; and she says 'Thank ye,' and took it, an' the minute she tasted it she looked up at me as worried as could be. 'Oh, I don't want to eat that,' says she. 'I always keep that in case o' sickness.' 'You're goin' to have the good o' one tumbler yourself,' says I. 'I'd just like to know who's sick now, if you ain't!' An' she couldn't help laughin', I spoke up so smart. Oh, dear me, how I shall miss talkin' over things with her! She always sensed things, and got just the p'int you meant."

"She didn't begin to age until two or three years ago, did she?" asked Mrs. Crowe. "I never saw anybody keep her looks as Tempy did. She looked young long after I begun to feel like an old woman. The doctor used to say 't was her young heart, and I don't know but what he was right. How she did do for other folks! There was one spell she wasn't at home at day to a fortnight. She got most of her livin' so, and that made her own potatoes and things last her through. None o' the young folks could get married without her, and all the old ones was disappointed if she wa'n't round when they was down with sickness and had to go. An' cleanin', or tailorin' for boys, or rug-hookin',—there was nothin' but what she could do as handy as most. 'I do love to work,'—ain't you heard her say that twenty times a week?"

Sarah Ann Binson nodded, and began to clear away the empty plates. "We may want a taste o' somethin' more towards mornin'," she said. "There's plenty in the closet here; and in case some comes from a distance to the funeral, we'll have a little table spread after we get back to the house."

"Yes, I was busy all the mornin'. I've cooked up a sight o' things to bring over," said Mrs. Crowe. "I felt 't was the last I could do for her."

They drew their chairs near the stove again, and took up their work. Sister Binson's rocking-chair creaked as she rocked; the brook sounded louder than ever. It was more lonely when nobody spoke, and presently Mrs. Crowe returned to her thoughts of growing old.

"Yes, Tempy aged all of a sudden. I remember I asked her if she felt as well as common, one day, and she laughed at me good. There, when Mr. Crowe begun to look old, I couldn't help feeling as if somethin' ailed him, and like as not 't was somethin' he was goin' to git right over, and I dosed him for it stiddy, half of one summer."

"How many things we shall be wanting to ask Tempy!" exclaimed Sarah Ann Binson, after a long pause. "I can't make up my mind to doin' without her. I wish folks could come back just once, and tell us how 't is where they've gone. Seems then we could do without 'em better."

The brook hurried on, the wind blew about the house now and then; the house itself was a silent place, and the supper, the warm fire, and an absence of any new topics for conversation made the watchers drowsy. Sister Binson closed her eyes first, to rest them for a minute; and Mrs. Crowe glanced at he compassionately, with a new sympathy for the hard-worked little woman. She made up her mind to let Sarah Ann have a good rest, while she kept watch alone; but in a few minutes her own knitting was dropped, and she, too, fell asleep. Overhead, the pale shape of Tempy Dent, the outworn body of that generous, loving-hearted, simple soul, slept on also in its white raiment. Perhaps Tempy herself stood near, and saw her own life and its surroundings with new understanding. Perhaps she herself was the only watcher.

Later, by some hours, Sarah Ann Binson woke with a start. There was a pale light of dawn outside the small windows. Inside the kitchen, the lamp burned dim. Mrs. Crowe awoke, too.

"I think Tempy'd be the first to say 't was just as well we both had some rest," she said, not without a guilty feeling.

Her companion went to the outer door, and opened it wide. The fresh air was none too cold, and the brook's voice was not nearly so loud as it had been in the midnight darkness. She could see the shapes of the hills, and the great shadows that lay across the lower country. The east was fast growing bright.

"'T will be a beautiful day for the funeral," she said, and turned again, with a sigh, to follow Mrs. Crowe up the stairs.

ALICE BROWN

Joint Owners in Spain

(1895)

*J*OINT Owners in Spain" was first collected in *Meadow-Grass: Tales of New England Life* (1895), Alice Brown's first volume of short stories and the book that launched her long career. She lived to be ninety years old (1857–1948), surviving changes in literary fashion to publish seventeen novels and nine short story collections in addition to poetry, plays, essays, biography, and travel sketches.

Brown dedicated *Meadow-Grass* to her friend "M.G.R.," Maria G. Reed.[1] Although I have not seen her mentioned in print, Reed is described in a Brown letter as "the dear friend who makes my family." From other letters we learn that the two lived together for some fifty years, from at least 1880 when Brown moved to Boston from Hampton Falls, her New Hampshire seacoast birthplace, until Reed's death some time between 1927 and 1938. In her later years Reed became blind and suffered from arthritis.

A more public friendship was Brown's relationship with her Boston neighbor, poet Louise Imogen Guiney. In the year *Meadow-Grass* appeared Brown and Guiney took a walking tour, which turned into a most pleasant "talking tour," they confessed, of England.[2] On their return they founded the Women's Rest Tour Association to help women make arrangements to vacation abroad with other women; the organization still exists. Brown and Guiney also collaborated on writing projects, producing a handbook for female tourists, an account of early New England heroines, and a laudatory study of Robert Louis Stevenson. After Guiney's death in 1920 Brown published a biography of her friend. She also burned their correspondence, making it impossible to reconstruct the relationship.

In fact, we know little about Alice Brown's life beyond the externals. Her parents were Elizabeth Lucas (Robinson) Brown and Levi Brown, and she had an older brother. She graduated in 1876 from Robinson Seminary in Exeter. She taught before finding editorial work in Boston. But the kind of information that might illuminate her work, such as the nature of her relationship with mother, father, and brother, the influence of teachers, and the motives that led to authorship, Brown felt we have no right to know. She led the most private of lives, hardly ever granting interviews and refusing to speak or read in public outside her beloved Boston Authors Club, and she tried to extend this privacy beyond death; in her will she forbids publication of her letters and asks recipients to destroy them as proof of friendship.[3]

Only a strong contradictory desire, the wish to be a popular author, could have induced Brown to accede to her publisher's demand for biographical details for promotional pamphlets. In 1916 she allowed herself to be interviewed with painfully awkward results, she fending the interviewer off with advice on gardening and comments such as "The author . . . doesn't really like to talk about himself. He's shy," and the frustrated interviewer exclaiming, "But what is she like and what does she think?" In 1927 Brown chose to interview herself instead and switched to the second person: "You scud off to Boston. . . . And since people seem to have a liking for New England stories, you fall into the habit of writing them. . . . then you write some novels, but somehow, when you come on them in print, they never seem quite right. There was always something you wanted to get into them and it never was there. What was it? You don't know." And so on.[4]

Perhaps the belief that good fences make good neighbors needs no explanation: privacy may be viewed as a basic human need, just as Brown, an admirer of Robert Frost, skillfully presents it in "Joint Owners in Spain." On the other hand, the inability to speak about oneself in the first person seems unusual enough to signal an area of great tension. Brown unluckily came of age after another writer she esteemed, Sarah Orne Jewett, during the period toward the end of the nineteenth century when intimate relationships between women were no longer considered normal. For women to be openly "different" and "not meant for motherhood," as Brown describes a friend in a letter, was to risk not simply disapproval but, as Nancy Sahli puts it, the "persecution of both society and their own potentially divided selves."[5] We may thus speculate about the something you wanted to get into print and couldn't and about the irony of a woman who wrote over forty books being at the same time cruelly silenced.

If Alice Brown's situation reminds us of that of Willa Cather, her contemporary, she resembles Cather (and also Edith Wharton) in her inability to conceive of the writer as female. *Vanishing Points* (1913), a collection of short stories about artists, portrays only male writers; *My Love and I* (1912), a novel about authorship, is told in the first person male. When a "serious writer" cannot be female, to say nothing of lesbian, no wonder "he" feels shy and reveals such an uneasy attitude toward "his" public. Brown alternately woos her readers and castigates them, lamenting her lack of popularity and complaining about the "democracy of taste and intellect" that is ruining the times.

One can find traces of this perhaps compensatory snobbery in "Joint Owners in Spain," where the old ladies prefer photography to art, having failed to accompany the narrator to Europe, and Mrs. Mitchell seems to stand in for the narrator in her condescension. Because it avoids the point-of-view problem, I prefer the dramatic version of "Joint Owners." The story easily lent itself to dramatization, and as a play it proved one of the most popular of Brown's works, far surpassing her prize-winning *Children of Earth* (1915), which she had hoped would establish her as a playwright. Once "Joint Owners" was produced at the Little Theatre in Chicago in 1912 it bought her bread, Brown said—if not all the bread, at least the butter and the jam. It seems to me still a fine play for amateur theater.

Was Brown, then, most talented as a dramatist? She was best known as a novelist, wanted to be remembered as a poet, and has been rediscovered lately as a short story writer in the local color tradition. It is her short story collections that are still in print, and critics in the 1970s introduced her as a local colorist.[6] However, very little has appeared on Brown since except for Deborah G. Lambert's assessment of the stories in *American Short-Story Writers, 1880–1910.*[7] Thorough biographical and critical studies may seem formidable undertakings because of the sheer volume of Brown's writings and the large number of her letters scattered in libraries (despite her dictum). Fittingly, in light of the gaps and silences I have mentioned, the most useful Brown bibliography is unpublished: Bonnie Gardner's extensive bibliography, which includes a list of letters, may be found in the Alice Brown collection at the University of New Hampshire Library.

BARBARA A. WHITE

The Old Ladies' Home, much to the sorrow of its inmates, "set back from the road." A long, box-bordered walk led from the great door down to the old turnpike, and thickly bowering lilac-bushes forced the eye to play an unsatisfied hide-and-seek with the view. The sequestered old ladies were quite unreconciled to their leaf-hung outlook; active life was presumably over for them, and all the more did they long to "see the passing" of the little world which had usurped their places. The house itself was very old, a stately, square structure, with pillars on either side of the door, and a fanlight above. It had remained unpainted now for many years, and had softened into a mellow lichen-gray, so harmonious and pleasing in the midst of summer's vital green, that the few artists who ever heard of Tiverton sought it out, to plant umbrella and easel in the garden, and sketch the stately relic; photographers, also, made it one of their accustomed haunts. Of the artists the old ladies disapproved, without a dissenting voice. It seemed a "shaller" proceeding to sit out there in the hot sun for no result save a wash of unreal colors on a white ground, or a few hasty lines indicating no solid reality; but the photographers were their constant delight, and they rejoiced in forming themselves into groups upon the green, to be "took" and carried away with the house.

One royal winter's day, there was a directors' meeting in the great south room, the matron's parlor, a spot bearing the happy charm of perfect loyalty to the past, with its great fireplace, iron dogs and crane, its settle and entrancing corner cupboards. The hard-working president of the board was speaking hastily and from a full heart, conscious that another instant's discussion might bring the tears to her eyes:—

"May I be allowed to say—it's irrelevant, I know, but I should like the satisfaction of saying it—that this is enough to make one vow never to have anything to do with an institution of any sort, from this time forth for evermore?"

For the moment had apparently come when a chronic annoyance must be recognized as unendurable. They had borne with the trial, inmates and directors, quite as cheerfully as most ordinary people accept the inevitable; but suddenly the tension had become too great, and the universal patience snapped. Two of the old ladies, Mrs. Blair and Miss Dyer, who were settled in the Home for life, and who, before going there, had shown no special waywardness of temper, had proved utterly incapable of living in peace with any available human being; and as the Home had insufficient accommodations, neither could be isolated to fight her "black butterflies" alone.

No inmate, though she were cousin to Hercules, could be given a room to herself; and the effect of this dual system on these two, possibly the most eccentric of the number, had proved disastrous in the extreme. Each had, in her own favorite fashion, "kicked over the traces," as the matron's son said in town-meeting (much to the joy of the village fathers), and to such purpose that, to continue the light-minded simile, very little harness was left to guide them withal. Mrs. Blair, being "high sperited," like all the Coxes from whom she sprung, had now so tyrannized over the last of her series of room-mates, so browbeaten and intimidated her, that the latter had actually taken to her bed with a slow fever of discouragement, announcing that "she'd ruther go to the poor-farm and done with it than resk her life there another night; and she'd like to know what had become of that hunderd dollars her nephew Thomas paid down in bills to get her into the Home, for she'd be thankful to them that laid it away so antic to hand it back afore another night went over her head, so 't she could board somewheres decent till 'twas gone, and then starve if she'd got to!"

If Miss Sarah Ann Dyer, known also as a disturber of the public peace, presented a less aggressive front to her kind, she was yet, in her own way, a cross and a hindrance to their spiritual growth. She, poor woman, lived in a scarcely varying state of hurt feeling; her tiny world seemed to her one close federation, existing for the sole purpose of infringing on her personal rights; and though she would not take the initiative in battle, she lifted up her voice in aggrieved lamentation over the tragic incidents decreed for her alone. She had perhaps never directly reproached her own unhappy room-mate for selecting a comfortable chair, for wearing squeaking shoes, or singing "Hearken, ye sprightly," somewhat early in the morning, but she chanted those ills through all her waking hours in a high, yet husky tone, broken by frequent sobs. And therefore, as a result of these domestic whirlwinds and too stagnant pools, came the directors' meeting, and the helpless protest of the exasperated president. The two cases were discussed for an hour longer, in the dreary fashion pertaining to a question which has long been supposed to have but one side; and then it remained for Mrs. Mitchell, the new director, to cut the knot with the energy of one to whom a difficulty is fresh.

"Has it ever occurred to you to put them together?" asked she. "They are impossible people; so, naturally, you have selected the very mildest and most Christian women to endure their nagging.

They can't live with the saints of the earth. Experience has proved that. Put them into one room, and let them fight it out together."

The motion was passed with something of that awe ever attending a Napoleonic decree, and passed, too, with the utmost good-breeding; for nobody mentioned the Kilkenny cats. The matron compressed her lips and lifted her brows, but said nothing; having exhausted her own resources, she was the more willing to take the superior attitude of good-natured scepticism.

The moving was speedily accomplished; and at ten o'clock, one morning, Mrs. Blair was ushered into the room where her forced colleague sat by the window, knitting. There the two were left alone. Miss Dyer looked up, and then heaved a tempestuous sigh over her work, in the manner of one not entirely surprised by its advent, but willing to suppress it, if such alleviation might be. She was a thin, colorless woman, and infinitely passive, save at those times when her nervous system conflicted with the scheme of the universe. Not so Mrs. Blair. She had black eyes, "like live coals," said her awed associates; and her skin was soft and white, albeit wrinkled. One could even believe she had reigned a beauty, as the tradition of the house declared. This morning, she held her head higher than ever, and disdained expression except that of an occasional nasal snort. She regarded the room with the air of an impartial though exacting critic; two little beds covered with rising-sun quilts, two little pine bureaus, two washstands. The sunshine lay upon the floor, and in that radiant pathway Miss Dyer sat.

"If I'd ha' thought I should ha' come to this," began Mrs. Blair, in the voice of one who speaks perforce after long sufferance, "I'd ha' died in my tracks afore I'd left my comfortable home down in Tiverton Holler. Story-'n'-a-half house, a good sullar, an' woods nigh-by full o' sarsaparilla an' goldthread! I've moved more times in this God-forsaken place than a Methodist preacher, fust one room an' then another; an' bad is the best. It was poor pickin's enough afore, but this is the crowner!"

Miss Dyer said nothing, but two large tears rolled down and dropped on her work. Mrs. Blair followed their course with gleaming eyes endowed with such uncomfortable activity that they seemed to pounce with every glance.

"What under the sun be you carryin' on like that for?" she asked, giving the handle of the water-pitcher an emphatic twitch to make it even with the world. "You 'ain't lost nobody, have ye, sence I moved in here?"

Miss Dyer put aside her knitting with ostentatious abnegation, and began rocking herself back and forth in her chair, which seemed not of itself to sway fast enough, and Mrs. Blair's voice rose again, ever higher and more metallic:—

"I dunno what you've got to complain of more 'n the rest of us. Look at that dress you've got on,—a good thick thibet, an' mine's a cheap, sleazy alpaca they palmed off on me because they knew my eyesight ain't what it was once. An' you're settin' right there in the sun, gittin' het through, an' it's cold as a barn over here by the door. My land! if it don't make me mad to see anybody without no more sperit than a wet rag! If you've lost anybody, why don't ye say so? An' if it's a mad fit, speak out an' say that! Give me anybody that's got a tongue in their head, I say!"

But Miss Dyer, with an unnecessary display of effort, was hitching her chair into the darkest corner of the room, the rockers hopelessly snarling her yarn at every move.

"I'm sure I wouldn't keep the sun off'n anybody," she said, tearfully. "It never come into my head to take it up, an' I don't claim no share of anything. I guess, if the truth was known, 'twould be seen I'd been used to a house lookin' south, an' the fore-room winders all of a glare o' light, day in an' day out, an' Madeira vines climbin' over 'em, an' a trellis by the front door; but that's all past an' gone, past an' gone! I never was one to take more 'n belonged to me; an' I don't care who says it, I never shall be. An' I'd hold to that, if 'twas the last word I had to speak!"

This negative sort of retort had an enfeebling effect upon Mrs. Blair.

"My land!" she exclaimed, helplessly. "Talk about my tongue! Vinegar's nothin' to cold molasses, if you've got to plough through it."

The other sighed, and leaned her head upon her hand in an attitude of extreme dejection. Mrs. Blair eyed her with the exasperation of one whose just challenge has been refused; she marched back and forth through the room, now smoothing a fold of the counterpane, with vicious care, and again pulling the braided rug to one side or the other, the while she sought new fuel for her rage. Without, the sun was lighting snowy knoll and hollow, and printing the fine-etched tracery of the trees against a crystal sky. The road was not usually much frequented in winter time, but just now it had been worn by the week's sledding into a shining track, and several sleighs went jingling up and down. Tiverton was seizing the opportunity of a perfect day and the best of "going," and was taking its way to market. The trivial happenings of this far-away world had thus far elicited no more than a passing glance from Mrs. Blair; she was too absorbed in domestic warfare even to peer down through the leafless lilac-boughs, in futile wonderment as to whose bells they might be, ringing merrily past. On one journey about the room, however, some chance arrested her gaze. She stopped, transfixed.

"Forever!" she cried. Her nervous, blue-veined hands clutched at her apron and held it; she was motionless for a moment. Yet the picture without would have been quite devoid of interest to the casual eye; it could have borne little significance save to one who knew the inner life history of the Tiverton Home, and thus might guess what slight events wrought all its joy and pain. A young man had set up his camera at the end of the walk, and thrown the cloth over his head, preparatory to taking the usual view of the house. Mrs. Blair recovered from her temporary inaction. She rushed to the window, and threw up the sash. Her husky voice broke strenuously upon the stillness:—

"Here! you keep right where you be! I'm goin' to be took! You wait till I come!"

She pulled down the window, and went in haste to the closet, in the excess of her eagerness stumbling recklessly forward into its depths.

"Where's my bandbox?" Her voice came piercingly from her temporary seclusion. "Where'd they put it? It ain't here in sight! My soul! where's my bunnit?"

These were apostrophes thrown off in extremity of feeling; they were not questions, and no listener, even with the most friendly disposition in the world, need have assumed the necessity of answering. So, wrapped in oblivion to all earthly considerations save that of her own inward gloom, the one person who might have responded merely swayed back and forth, in martyrized silence. But no such spiritual withdrawal could insure her safety. Mrs. Blair emerged from the closet, and darted across the room with the energy of one stung by a new despair. She seemed about to fall upon the neutral figure in the corner, but seized the chair-back instead, and shook it with such angry vigor that Miss Dyer cowered down in no simulated fright.

"Where's my green bandbox?" The words were emphasized by cumulative shakes. "Anybody that's took that away from me ought to be b'iled in ile! Hangin' 's too good for 'em, but le' me git my eye on 'em an' they shall swing for 't! Yes, they shall, higher 'n Gil'roy's kite!"

The victim put both trembling hands to her ears.

"I ain't deef!" she wailed.

"Deef? I don't care whether you're deef or dumb, or whether you're nummer 'n a beetle! It's my bandbox I'm arter. Isr'el in Egypt! you might grind some folks in a mortar an' you couldn't make 'em speak!"

It was of no use. Intimidation had been worse than hopeless; even bodily force would not avail. She cast one lurid glance at the supine figure, and gave up the quest in that direction as sheer waste of time. With new determination, she again essayed the closet, tossing shoes and rubbers behind her in an unsightly heap, quite heedless of the confusion of rights and lefts. At last, in a dark corner, behind a blue chest, she came upon her treasure. Too hurried now for reproaches, she drew it forth, and with trembling fingers untied the strings. Casting aside the cover, she produced a huge scoop bonnet of a long-past date, and setting it on her head, with the same fevered haste, tied over it the long figured veil destined always to make an inseparable part of her state array. She snatched her stella shawl from the drawer, threw it over her shoulders, and ran out of the room.

Miss Dyer was left quite bewildered by these erratic proceedings, but she had no mind to question them; so many stories were rife in the Home of the eccentricities embodied in the charitable phrase "Mis' Blair's way" that she would scarcely have been amazed had her terrible room-mate chosen to drive a coach and four up the chimney, or saddle the broom for a midnight revel. She drew a long breath of relief at the bliss of solitude, closed her eyes, and strove to regain the lost peace, which, as she vaguely remembered, had belonged to her once in a shadowy past.

Silence had come, but not to reign. Back flew Mrs. Blair, like a whirlwind. Her cheeks wore each a little hectic spot; her eyes were flaming. The figured veil, swept rudely to one side, was borne backwards on the wind of her coming, and her thin hair, even in those few seconds, had become wildly disarranged.

"He's gone!" she announced, passionately. "He kep' right on while I was findin' my bunnit. He come to take the house, an' he'd ha' took me an' been glad. An' when I got that plaguy front door open, he was jest drivin' away; an' I might ha' hollered till I was black in the face, an' then I couldn't ha' made him hear."

"I dunno what to say, nor what not to," remarked Miss Dyer, to her corner. "If I speak, I'm to blame; an' so I be if I keep still."

The other old lady had thrown herself into a chair, and was looking wrathfully before her.

"It's the same man that come from Sudleigh last August," she said, bitterly. "He took the house then, an' said he wanted another view when the leaves was off; an' that time I was laid up with my stiff ankle, an' didn't git into it, an' to-day my bunnit was hid, an' I lost it ag'in."

Her voice changed. To the listener, it took on an awful meaning.

"An' I should like to know whose fault it was. If them that owns the winder, an' set by it till they see him comin', had spoke up an' said, 'Mis' Blair, there's the photograph man. Don't you want to be took?' it wouldn't ha' been too late! If anybody had answered a civil question, an' said, 'Your bunnit-box sets there behind my blue chist,' it wouldn't ha' been too late then! An' I 'ain't had my likeness took sence I was twenty year old, an' went to Sudleigh Fair in my changeable *visite* an' leghorn hat, an' Jonathan wore the brocaded weskit he stood up in, the next week Thursday. It's enough to make a minister swear!"

Miss Dyer rocked back and forth.

"Dear me!" she wailed. "Dear me suz!"

The dinner-bell rang, creating a blessed diversion. Mrs. Blair, rendered absent-minded by her grief, went to the table still in her bonnet and veil; and this dramatic entrance gave rise to such morbid though unexpressed curiosity that every one forbore, for a time, to wonder why Miss Dyer did not appear. Later, however, when a tray was prepared and sent up to her (according to the programme of her bad days), the general commotion reached an almost unruly point, stimulated as it was by the matron's son, who found an opportunity to whisper one garrulous old lady that Miss Dyer had received bodily injury at the hands of her roommate, and that Mrs. Blair had put on her bonnet to be ready for the sheriff when he should arrive. This report, judiciously started, ran like prairie fire; and the house was all the afternoon in a pleasant state of excitement. Possibly the matron will never know why so many of the old ladies promenaded the corridors from dinnertime until long after early candlelight, while a few kept faithful yet agitated watch from the windows. For interest was divided; some preferred to see the sheriff's advent, and others found zest in the possibility of counting the groans of the prostrate victim.

When Mrs. Blair returned to the stage of action, she was much refreshed by her abundant meal and the strong tea which three times daily heartened her for battle. She laid aside her bonnet, and carefully folded the veil. Then she looked about her, and, persistently ignoring all the empty chairs, fixed an annihilating gaze on one where the dinner-tray still remained.

"I s'pose there's no need o' my settin' down," she remarked, bitingly. "It's all in the day's work. Some folks are waited on; some ain't. Some have their victuals brought to 'em an' pushed under their noses, an' some has to go to the table; when they're there, they can take it or leave it. The quality can keep their waiters settin' round day in an' day out, fillin' up every chair in the room. For my part, I should think they'd have an extension table moved in, an' a snowdrop cloth over it!"

Miss Dyer had become comparatively placid, but now she gave way to tears.

"Anybody can move that waiter that's a mind to," she said, tremulously. "I would myself, if I had the stren'th; but I 'ain't got it. I ain't a well woman, an' I 'ain't been this twenty year. If old Dr. Parks was alive this day, he'd say so. 'You 'ain't never had a chance,' he says to me. 'You've been pull-hauled one way or another sence you was born.' An' he never knew the wust on 't, for the wust hadn't come."

"Humph!" It was a royal and explosive note. It represented scorn for which Mrs. Blair could find no adequate utterance. She selected the straightest chair in the room, ostentatiously turned its back to her enemy, and seated herself. Then, taking out her knitting, she strove to keep silence; but that was too heavy a task, and at last she broke forth, with renewed bitterness,—

"To think of all the wood I've burnt up in my kitchen stove an' airtight, an' never thought nothin' of it! To think of all the wood there is now, growin' an' rottin' from Dan to Beersheba, an' I can't lay my fingers on it!"

"I dunno what you want o' wood. I'm sure this room's warm enough."

"You don't? Well, I'll tell ye. I want some two-inch boards, to nail up a partition in the middle o' this room, same as Josh Marden done to spite his wife. I don't want more 'n my own, but I want it mine."

Miss Dyer groaned, and drew an uncertain hand across her forehead.

"You wouldn't have no gre't of an outlay for boards," she said, drearily. "'Twouldn't have to be knee-high to keep me out. I'm no hand to go where I ain't wanted; an' if I ever was, I guess I'm cured on't now."

Mrs. Blair dropped her knitting in her lap. For an instant, she sat there motionless, in a growing rigidity; but light was dawning in her eyes. Suddenly she came to her feet, and tossed her knitting on the bed.

"Where's that piece o' chalk you had when you marked out your tumbler-quilt?" The words rang like a martial order.

Miss Dyer drew it forth from the ancient-looking bag, known as a cavo, which was ever at her side.

"Here 'tis," she said, in her forlornest quaver. "I hope you won't do nothin' out o' the way with it. I should hate to git into trouble here. I ain't that kind."

Mrs. Blair was too excited to hear or heed her. She was briefly, flashingly, taking in the possibilities of the room, her bright black eyes darting here and there with fiery insistence. Suddenly she went to the closet, and, diving to the bottom of a baggy pocket in her "t'other dress," drew forth a ball of twine. She chalked it, still in delighted haste, and forced one end upon her bewildered room-mate.

"You go out there to the middle square o' the front winder," she commanded, "an' hold your end o' the string down on the floor. I'll snap it."

Miss Dyer cast one despairing glance about her, and obeyed.

"Crazy!" she muttered. "Oh my land! she's crazy's a loon. I wisht Mis' Mitchell 'd pitch her tent here a spell!"

But Mrs. Blair was following out her purpose in a manner exceedingly methodical. Drawing out one bed, so that it stood directly opposite her kneeling helper, she passed the cord about the leg of the bedstead and made it fast; then, returning to the middle of the room, she snapped the line triumphantly. A faint chalkmark was left upon the floor.

"There!" she cried. "Leggo! Now, you gi' me the chalk, an' I'll go over it an' make it whiter."

She knelt and chalked with the utmost absorption, crawling along on her knees, quite heedless of the despised alpaca; and Miss Dyer, hovering in a corner, timorously watched her. Mrs. Blair staggered to her feet, entangled by her skirt, and pitching like a ship at sea.

"There!" she announced. "Now here's two rooms. The chalk-mark's the partition. You can have the mornin' sun, for I'd jest as soon live by a taller candle if I can have somethin' that's my own. I'll chalk a lane into the closet, an' we'll both keep a right o' way there. Now I'm to home, an' so be you. Don't you dast to speak a word to me unless you come an' knock here on my headboard,—that's the front door,—an' I won't to you. Well, if I ain't glad to be alone! I've hung my harp on a willer long enough!"

It was some time before the true meaning of the new arrangement penetrated Miss Dyer's slower intelligence; but presently she drew her chair nearer the window and thought a little, chuckling as she did so. She, too, was alone. The sensation was new and very pleasant. Mrs. Blair went back and forth through the closet-lane, putting her clothes away, with high good humor. Once or twice she sang a little—Derby's Ram and Lord Lovel—in a cracked voice. She was in love with solitude.

Just before tea, Mrs. Mitchell, in some trepidation, knocked at the door, to see the fruits of contention present and to come. She had expected to hear loud words; and the silence quite terrified her, emphasizing, as it did, her own guilty sense of personal responsibility. Miss Dyer gave one appealing look at Mrs. Blair, and then, with some indecision, went to open the door, for the latch was in her house.

"Well, here you are, comfortably settled!" began Mrs. Mitchell. She had the unmistakable tone of professional kindliness; yet it rang clear and true. "May I come in?"

"Set right down here," answered Miss Dyer, drawing forward a chair. "I'm real pleased to see ye."

"And how are you this afternoon?" This was addressed to the occupant of the other house, who, quite oblivious to any alien presence, stood busily rubbing the chalk-marks from her dress.

Mrs. Blair made no answer. She might have been stone deaf, and as dumb as the hearthstone bricks. Mrs. Mitchell cast an alarmed glance at her entertainer.

"Isn't she well?" she said, softly.

"It's a real pretty day, ain't it?" responded Miss Dyer. "If 'twas summer time, I should think there'd be a sea turn afore night. I like a sea turn myself. It smells jest like Old Boar's Head."

"I have brought you down some fruit." Mrs. Mitchell was still anxiously observing the silent figure, now absorbed in an apparently futile search in a brocaded work-bag. "Mrs. Blair, do you ever cut up bananas and oranges together?"

No answer. The visitor rose, and unwittingly stepped across the dividing line.

"Mrs. Blair—" she began, but she got no further.

Her hostess turned upon her, in surprised welcome.

"Well, if it ain't Mis' Mitchell! I can't say I didn't expect you, for I see you goin' into Miss Dyer's house not more 'n two minutes ago. Seems to me you make short calls. Now set right down here, where you can see out o' the winder. That square's cracked, but I guess the directors 'll put in another."

Mrs. Mitchell was amazed, but entirely interested. It was many a long day since any person, official or private, had met with cordiality from this quarter.

"I hope you and our friend are going to enjoy your room together," she essayed, with a hollow cheerfulness.

"I expect to be as gay as a cricket," returned Mrs. Blair, innocently. "An' I do trust I've got good neighbors. I like to keep to myself, but if I've got a neighbor, I want her to be somebody you can depend upon."

"I'm sure Miss Dyer means to be very neighborly." The director turned, with a smile, to include that lady in the conversation. But the local deafness had engulfed her. She was sitting peacefully by the window, with the air of one retired within herself, to think her own very remote thoughts. The visitor mentally improvised a little theory, and it seemed to fit the occasion. They had quarrelled, she thought, and each was disturbed at any notice bestowed on the other.

"I have been wondering whether you would both like to go sleighing with me some afternoon?" she ventured, with the humility so prone to assail humankind in a frank and shrewish presence. "The roads are in wonderful condition, and I don't believe you'd take cold. Do you know, I found Grandmother Eaton's foot-warmers, the other day! I'll bring them along."

"Law! I'd go anywheres to git out o' here," said Mrs. Blair, ruthlessly. "I dunno when I've set behind a horse, either. I guess the last time was the day I rid up here for good, an' then I didn't feel much like lookin' at outdoor. Well, I guess you *be* a new director, or you never'd ha' thought on 't!"

"How do you feel about it, Miss Dyer?" asked the visitor. "Will you go,—perhaps on Wednesday?"

The other householder moved uneasily. Her hands twitched at their knitting; a flush came over her cheeks, and she cast a childishly appealing glance at her neighbor across the chalkline. Her eyes were filling fast with tears. "Save me!" her look seemed to entreat. "Let me not lose this happy fortune!" Mrs. Blair interpreted the message, and rose to the occasion with the vigor of the intellectually great.

"Mis' Mitchell," she said, clearly, "I may be queer in my notions, but it makes me as nervous as a witch to have anybody hollerin' out o' my winders. I don't care whether it's company nor whether it's my own folks. If you want to speak to Miss Dyer, you come along here arter me,—don't you hit the partition now!—right out o' my door an' into her'n. 'Here, I'll knock! Miss Dyer, be you to home?"

The little old lady came forward, fluttering and radiant in the excess of her relief.

"Yes, I guess I be," she said, "an' all alone, too! I see you go by the winder, an' I was in hopes you'd come in!"

Then the situation dawned upon Mrs. Mitchell with an effect vastly surprising to the two old pensioners. She turned from one to the other, including them both in a look of warm loving-kindness. It was truly an illumination. Hitherto, they had thought chiefly of her winter cloak and nodding ostrich plume; now, at last, they saw her face, and read some part of its message.

"You poor souls!" she cried. "Do you care so much as that? O you poor souls!"

Miss Dyer fingered her apron and looked at the floor, but her companion turned brusquely away, even though she trod upon the partition in her haste.

"Law! it's nothin' to make such a handle of," she said. "Folks don't want to be under each other's noses all the time. I dunno's anybody could stan' it, unless 'twas an emmet. They seem to git along swarmin' round together."

Mrs. Mitchell left the room abruptly.

"Wednesday or Thursday, then!" she called over her shoulder.

The next forenoon, Mrs. Blair made her neighbor a long visit. Both old ladies had their knitting, and they sat peacefully swaying back and forth, recalling times past, and occasionally alluding to their happy Wednesday.

"What I really come in for," said Mrs. Blair, finally, "was to ask if you don't think both our settin'-rooms need new paper."

The other gave one bewildered glance about her.

"Why, 'tain't been on more 'n two weeks," she began; and then remembrance awoke in her, and she stopped. It was not the scene of their refuge and conflict that must be considered; it was the house of fancy built by each unto herself. Invention did not come easily to her as yet, and she spoke with some hesitation.

"I've had it in mind myself quite a spell, but somehow I 'ain't been able to fix on the right sort o' paper."

"What do you say to a kind of a straw color, all lit up with tulips?" inquired Mrs. Blair, triumphantly.

"Ain't that kind o' gay?"

"Gay? Well, you want it gay, don't ye? I dunno why folks seem to think they've got to live in a hearse because they expect to ride in one! What if we be gittin' on a little mite in years? We ain't underground yit, be we? I see a real good ninepenny paper once, all covered over with green brakes. I declare if 'twa'n't sweet pretty! Well, whether I paper or whether I don't, I've got some thoughts of a magenta sofy. I'm tired to death o' that old horsehair lounge that sets in my clock-room. Sometimes I wish the moths would tackle it, but I guess they've got more sense. I've al'ays said to myself I'd have a magenta sofy when I could git round to it, and I dunno 's I shall be any nearer to it than I be now."

"Well, you *are* tasty," said Miss Dyer, in some awe. "I dunno how you come to think o' that!"

"Priest Rowe had one when I wa'n't more 'n twenty. Some o' his relations give it to him (he married into the quality), an' I remember as if 'twas yesterday what a tew there was over it. An' I said to myself then, if ever I was prospered I'd have a magenta sofy. I 'ain't got to it till now, but now I'll have it if I die for 't."

"Well, I guess you're in the right on 't." Miss Dyer spoke absently, glancing from the window in growing trouble. "O Mis' Blair!" she continued, with a sudden burst of confidence, "you don't think there's a storm brewin', do you? If it snows Wednesday, I shall give up beat!"

Mrs. Blair, in her turn, peered at the smiling sky.

"I hope you ain't one o' them kind that thinks every fair day 's a weather breeder," she said. "Law, no! I don't b'lieve it will storm; an' if it does, why, there's other Wednesdays comin'!"

EDITH WHARTON

Friends

(1900)

*T*HROUGHOUT Edith Wharton's life (1862–1937) there existed a web of friendships with intellectual and provocative women, a web that spanned countries and decades. Some of her central friendships were constructed early in her life. Sara Norton, the daughter of a family friend, was a serious and quick-minded woman with whom Wharton corresponded for over twenty years. In these letters they exchanged literary opinions and political analyses, and Wharton relayed accounts of many of the important events of her life.[1] Later, in Florence in 1894, Wharton met a woman whose friendship would inspire her. Violet Paget, an extraordinarily intelligent English historian, had written *Studies of the Eighteenth Century in Italy* and other volumes Wharton greatly admired. Paget, who wrote under the name Vernon Lee, was one of the few people whose forceful intellectual conversation stunned even Wharton into silence. Despite Wharton's alleged distaste for lesbianism, her relationship with Paget was important to her development as a writer and lasted many years.

Wharton also liked women who were daring and slightly eccentric in their private lives. French poet Anna de Noailles was probably the first woman, besides Wharton, who was not content to provide only a lovely audience during the literary *salons* they both attended—she waved her hand wildly for silence when she paused for a drink during her intellectual monologues. Wharton called Noailles's remote relative-in-law Princess de Poix one of the two most "radioactive" women she knew. The other one was Philomène de Lévis-Mirepoix, a well-known journalist who wrote the prize-winning *Benediction* under the name Claude Sylve. Wharton so admired her work that she found a publisher for the first

American edition of *Benediction* and wrote the introduction herself. Literature was their meeting ground; Lévis-Mirepoix later recorded her memory of a time when Wharton communicated the importance of their friendship by sharing her most central commitment, her writing:

> And then, into the salon where the fire gleamed equally with the last roses, Edith brought the past. She brought it in the form of an album where there were carefully pasted (amid a number of rare photographs) clippings of critical articles about her first writings. I would sacrifice several visits, a trip, many walks with her than have this day lost to me! . . . With how much delicious affection she made me a participant in her earliest memories. And how certain I was that day (I have remained so ever since) of all the warmth hidden beneath the snow.[2]

Wharton chose a way out of the stultification of the imposed role of an upper-class woman by working hard at what she loved. Although she could be demanding, through her friendships she demonstrated her belief in the primacy of women's work, as the sustenance of her own life was her commitment to her art.

Born Edith Newbold Jones in 1862, the third child of Lucretia Rhinelander and George F. Jones, she was a descendant of two wealthy New York society families. Lucretia Jones tried to instill in her daughter the values of her society in which women's concerns were limited to marriage and wardrobes, even going so far as to forbid her daughter to read contemporary fiction. Despite her mother, young Edith's craving for intellectual stimulation was fed by her voracious reading of her father's library books and by her avid storytelling—her first novella, *Fast and Loose,* was written when she was fourteen. Although reluctant to encourage any literary endeavors, her parents did arrange to have a small book of Wharton's verse printed privately when she was sixteen. One of these poems was published in the *Atlantic Monthly;* soon after, two others appeared in the New York *World.* Yet it would be another decade before Wharton's next publication.

During this time, she was busy with the social obligations of a young woman of her class. After a previous engagement, Edith Jones consented to wed Edward ("Teddy") Wharton in April 1885. She found Teddy attractive and engaging, yet she soon found that they were sexually incompatible. Brought up "properly" by upper-class standards, she was kept ignorant of the sexual side of marriage: even on Edith's wedding night, Lucretia refused to enlighten her daughter about the smallest details. Perhaps due to that fact as much as anything Teddy might have done, their marriage was not consummated for three weeks and remained virtually sexless throughout their lives. The Whartons would have other troubles as well. Although he was active and vital before marrying and for some time in the early years of his marriage, Teddy suffered increasingly from ill health and experienced manic-depressive mood swings, especially during his wife's rising critical and financial success as a novelist. Relatively early in their marriage, Edith Wharton longed for release from her vows.

In 1908, noting in her diary that this was the first sexual passion she had ever felt, she began a relationship with Morton Fullerton. Fullerton, an extremely popular journalist, was the Paris correspondent for the London *Times,* reporting on everything from French political developments to new scientific theories. Fullerton was also involved with Katharine Fullerton, a woman whom he had grown up thinking was his sister. When they discovered they were cousins, Katharine proclaimed her love for him and they were engaged. Katharine had won the *Century* award for the best short story by a college graduate in 1900; when Fullerton told her of his affair with Wharton, Katharine retreated to a convent to work on her first novel. After breaking their engagement and marrying another man, Katharine Fullerton Gerould sent the manuscript of her novel to Edith Wharton, who encouraged her own publishers to print it. *Vain Oblations* was published in 1913, and Gerould went on to produce a sizable body of work over the next thirty years. Wharton had again shared her commitment to writing by making possible another woman's work.

Wharton's affair with Morton Fullerton lasted for three years. Teddy, in the meantime, was engaged in successive extramarital liaisons (even installing one of the women in Edith's house) as well as in embezzling some of his wife's money. They were finally divorced in 1913, after long estrangements and unsuccessful reconciliations.

The years of her marriage, however, were the ones in which Wharton struggled with her role as a writer, eventually devoting herself to fiction rather than verse. After publishing several short stories and being asked to produce a volume of them, Wharton suffered bouts of "nervous exhaustion," a combination of nausea, depression, and "an inability to think." To treat these symptoms, she took a "rest cure" in 1898—complete bed rest, three meals a day, and massage therapy. This provided her with what she longed for most: escape from their small New York and Newport homes and Teddy's unending presence there. The untroubled atmosphere of the rest cure (she had no visitors) allowed her to begin to resolve the conflict between the social expectations that she should be a wife and hostess and her ambition to become a writer. Her doctors at this time may have helped incidentally by encouraging her to work and by forbidding her to return to her cramped New York home with Teddy. This time to herself strengthened Wharton's writing commitment and career. After producing two collections of short stories—*Crucial Instances* (1901) and *The Descent of Man and Other Stories* (1904)—Wharton published a series of very popular and critically successful novels, beginning with *The House of Mirth* (1905). She earned a Pulitzer Prize (the first woman to do so) for *The Age of Innocence* (1920). Throughout her literary career she composed short stories and novellas and at one point concentrated on ghost stories.

Wharton, in 1923, became the first woman to receive an honorary Doctor of Letters degree from Yale University. In 1926, she and Mary E. Wilkins Freeman were elected to the National Institute of Arts and Letters in America. The following year, several Yale professors endeavored to nominate her for the Nobel Prize. Her later years, surrounded by friends, were characterized by a deepening serenity and a preoccupation with the substance of organized Christianity. She died of a stroke in 1937.

Wharton's vast literary output includes architecture books and literary criticism, novels, and eighty-six short stories. Her best stories, whether set in New England or New York, are insightful and carefully crafted; many focus on the social roles and restrictions imposed on women in a variety of situations.

As stories such as "Friends" demonstrate, one of the primary though unacknowledged influences on Wharton was late nineteenth-century women's literature. Wharton, who thought of herself as the protegée of no one, resented the opinion that some of her contemporaries—such as Henry James, a critically successful but never popular novelist—had greatly influenced her work. Her public allegiances were with writers of the nineteenth century, such as Jane Austen and George Eliot, although she carefully followed new American fiction by women: she called Anita Loos's *Gentlemen Prefer Blondes* "the great American novel" and later in life pronounced Colette "one of the greatest writers of our time." Additionally, the beginning of her career coincides with the publication of the mature works of such nineteenth-century American geniuses as Freeman and Sarah Orne Jewett. Although she deprecated these writers for portraying the "rosy" side of New England, their influence on her cannot be denied. Her analysis of society and her characterization of women's varied responses to its restrictions link her to this tradition. Perhaps she may have been compelled to distance herself from her literary foremothers to affirm her unique identity; however, her early stories especially demonstrate her debt to these women.

"Friends," first published in *Youth's Companion* in 1900[3] but not collected until its appearance in 1968 in volume 1 of *The Collected Short Stories of Edith Wharton,* explores the sacrifice one woman makes for her friend and the strength they both gain from the act. This story clearly shows Wharton's belief in the transforming power of female friendship. Penelope's act does not make her a martyr; it spurs her to change her life, to ally with other women against "the common troubles of her kind."

LEAH HACKLEMAN

Sailport is an ugly town. It makes, indeed, certain concessions to the eye in one or two streets on the hill, where there are elms, and houses set apart behind clipped hedges; but this favored quarter is a mere incident in the harsh progressiveness of a New England town seated on a capacious harbor and in touch with a widely radiating railway system.

The streets, too narrow for the present needs of the town, run between buildings of discordant character; the new brick warehouse, like a factory chimney with windows in it, looking down from its lean eminence on the low wooden "store" of a past generation, and the ambitious office building, with its astrologer's tower and rustications of sham granite, turning a contemptuous side wall on the recessed door and balustraded roof of the old dwelling house which had been adapted to commercial uses with the least possible outlay.

These streets, through which the electric cars rush with a rapidity dazing to the simple-minded and perilously fascinating to small boys on the way to school, are full of snow and mud in winter, of dust and garbage in summer. At each corner a narrow cross street leads the eye down to a glimpse of wooden wharves and a confusion of masts and smoke-stacks against a quiver of yellowish water. Nowhere is there the least peep of green, the smallest open space that spring may use as a signboard; even in the outlying districts, where cottages and tenements are being "run up" for the increasing population of laboring men and operatives, the patches of ground between the houses are not gardens, but waste spaces strewn with nameless refuse.

The inhabitants of Sailport would doubtless be surprised to hear their "city" (as they are careful to call it) thus characterized. The greater number are probably of the opinion that handsome is as handsome does; and according to the national interpretation of the adage, Sailport is doing very handsomely, increasing in private and civic wealth, and multiplying with astonishing rapidity its telephone poles and electric wires, its car tracks and factory chimneys.

To Penelope Bent, now emerging from the railway station, her traveling bag in hand, Sailport had never appeared ugly; or only with the homely, lovable ugliness of a face that has bent above one's first awakenings; a face that has always been there; that one would not exchange for any Venus of the museums.

She looked at it now, after her long journey, with an unexpected sense of relief, the consciousness of being once more in a place where Penelope Bent had an identity, where twenty friendly hearts would ache for her, if they but knew! She would have died rather than have them know. As she stepped from the station she shrank even from the scrutiny of the sunshine; yet she was not proof against the comfort of feeling that the sympathy she dreaded was within reach; and she almost smiled at the nod of the Irish apple woman who greeted her as she hurried down the steps.

Everything all these last days had been so unreal; she had journeyed far into such a strange world, passing through so endless a nightmare of unknown sights and sounds and names. Here all was peacefully, prosaically familiar; the streets deep in spring mud, the house fronts blotched with signboards, the hoardings with their flamboyant advertisements, the junction of car tracks and the peristyle of the Baptist Church opposite the station all formed a part of her earliest consciousness.

Although she returned to it all so heavily, although the mere fact of her return testified to a disaster too recent to tolerate the touch of thought, yet the spell of association was upon her before she had picked her way through the mud to the opposite sidewalk.

Miss Bent, in her neat traveling dress, her hat still protected from the contamination of the journey by the folds of a thick veil, did not look like a victim of Olympian ire. She had passed well beyond thirty, in appearance if not in years, and her small, spare figure and pale face suggested the flatness and premature discoloration of a pressed flower. There was, however, nothing else about her in accordance with so tender a simile, her air of almost military precision rather implying a past devoted to the punctual accomplishment of didactic duties.

Her whole mien, in fact, savored of the educational. Her small features were as neatly balanced as a sentence of Lindley Murray's and her black hair assumed, in parting on her forehead, the exact curves of a pair of copybook parentheses. The eyes alone played traitor to this well-tutored mask, all that was feminine and inconsequent in their possessor lurking there under a spring of moisture, like Truth at the bottom of her well.

It was a bright April day, and the clock in the Gothic tower, which an unbridled fancy had recently appended to the classic façade of the city hall, struck twelve as Miss Bent passed beneath it. For a moment she paused, glancing down the main street, congested, as usual at that hour, by the pressure of traffic; then she hastened along the narrow sidewalk, drawing down her veil, and pressing close to the sides of the houses to escape the contact of hurrying shoulders.

She had washed her face and smoothed her dress in the toilet room of the sleeping car, and there seemed to be no reason why she should not stop and see Mr. Boutwell for a moment on her way home.

She walked on hurriedly without raising her eyes, till at last, reaching a certain side street, she paused to glance at a building which faced her—a large brick building with brownstone angles and a massive porch. It stood by itself at the end of the street, with an air of moral superiority that at once proclaimed it to be one of the public schools of Sailport.

Miss Bent's heart began to beat. There were *her* windows—the three with geraniums on the sill, at the left-hand corner of the second story. Would she be sitting behind them again, in a day or two at her desk on the raised platform, facing the double file of benches? Why not, indeed? Why even raise the question? What possible doubt could there be of the place having been kept for her?

The whole school board had assured her of it when, a month earlier, laughing and crying, she had taken, as she thought, a last leave of them. "Till the next general meeting we shall engage a temporary substitute. One word from you, and we'll put you back—remember that."

How she had smiled then at such idle toying with impossibilities! But she had smiled through tears of gratification. It was so pleasant to feel that they had liked her, that they had valued her services; to know that no teacher had ever left the school amid such a chorus of lamentations, that none had ever been so urgently entreated by the school board to reconsider her determination and come back to them!

"Why not persuade Mr. Dayton to sell out in Louisville and go into business here?" one commissioner had even laughingly suggested; and she, taken by the humor of it, had promised to submit the plan to Mr. Dayton. It seemed all a part then—the tears, the regrets, the little professional jokes—of the general cumulative pleasantness of life; now the wish of the school board remained the one reed she had to cling to, and she told herself how thankful she ought to be that it was so strong a one.

How many women, after resigning such a place as hers, could comfort themselves with the hope of being able to return to it? How many, whom she knew, had spent years in the vain effort to get into one of the schools!

There was her friend, Vexilla Thurber, for instance—poor Vexilla! How hard she had tried for a place in Penelope's school, how long it had been the unattainable ambition of her life! And she had never even had a hope of success. All Miss Bent's efforts had been unavailing; the school board remained obdurate, retiring behind hazy generalities; but Mr. Boutwell, one of their number, confided to Miss Bent that her friend was not "smart enough."

In vain Miss Bent protested that Vexilla's apparent dullness was only timidity; in vain offered to answer for the sufficiency of her knowledge and for her untiring industry. The school board bowed in general acquiescence, but did not find Miss Thurber to their liking. In vain Miss Bent, letting her eyes speak, reminded them of her friend's difficult situation, with a helpless grandmother, a crippled brother and an idle sister to support; the board bowed again, implying that the public schools of Sailport were not asylums for the indigent.

And so, year after year, Miss Bent had to bear the same heavy news to her friend; and year after year Vexilla, smiling down her discomfiture, had to return to the underpaid toil of a few private lessons, combined with odd jobs in the way of bookkeeping and typewriting. At the recollection Miss Bent's eyes melted. Poor Vexilla— hers was the harder lot!

"Perhaps now, if they're *very* glad to get me back," Miss Bent murmured under her veil, "I may be able to do something for Vexilla." And she remembered with fresh thankfulness that her letter must have reached Mr. Boutwell three days before the meeting of the school board.

This fortifying thought hastened the step with which she sped along Main Street toward a shabby-looking building, with glass doors surmounted by an inscription declaring it to be the People's Library. Nothing in the interior of the library belied its outer shabbiness; the rooms, as she entered, emitted an odor of much-handled books that gave her a qualm after her draught of salt April air. At a desk near the door sat a young woman with a cold veal complexion and taffy-colored hair who, in the absence of more pressing duties, was engaged in polishing her nails.

"Is Mr. Boutwell in?" Miss Bent asked.

"Guess he's in his office."

Miss Bent walked down the room between the lines of dingy books to a door at the farther end.

A prompt "Come in" answered her knock, and she entered a room almost filled by a large writing table, at which a man sat in an office chair, collating catalogues.

He raised a pale face, elongated in one direction by the baldness of his high forehead, in the other by the vague neutral tints of his beard, and the expression of distress wrinkling his neuralgic-looking brows seemed involuntarily to contradict the smile of welcome that lent a sudden blueness to his spectacled gray eyes.

"Miss Bent!"

She stood before him, fingering her bag in a spasm of nervousness that gripped her throat.

"O Mr. Boutwell," broke from her at last, as she dropped into the seat he pushed forward. It was so unlike her usual mode of address, she was so little given to feminine falterings and incoherencies, that, under the contagion of her emotion, he could only stammer, "I'm afraid you've had a trying time." And at once he doubted if the words were in good taste.

His perturbation increased when she drew from her pocket a neatly folded handkerchief, and pushing back her veil, silently wiped her eyes.

She restored the handkerchief to her pocket and put her bag aside, keeping one wrist slipped through its handle, as, with the caution of the unaccustomed traveler, she had done during all the long hours of the journey. "You must excuse me," she said, "but I've been in the cars since yesterday afternoon, and I came right here from the station."

"You must be very tired!" he murmured.

"Oh no, not very, but I've been through a good deal."

She glanced vaguely about the little room, with its book-lined walls and the window looking out on a blind alley, full of rubbish.

"You didn't expect me back so soon, did you?" she added, with a sigh.

Boutwell had taken off his spectacles and was rubbing them with a bit of chamois skin. He coughed instead of replying.

"Isn't it a mercy I didn't take mother?" she went on in a tone of confidence that contrasted with her usual impersonal manner. "The long journey there and back would have been too awful for her. I've been so thankful ever since. It seemed to keep me from breaking down, and I needed something to do that. I've been through everything."

"I was afraid so," he answered, feeling now that she would not repudiate his sympathy. "I got your letter."

"Oh, my letter!" she exclaimed.

The blood rushed to her forehead. A few minutes ago, in passing the schoolhouse, she had felt very sure of the future; but now—Her hand slipped form the bag, rejoining the other which trembled on her knee. The librarian's brows were a projecting bunch of wrinkles.

"I got your letter, Miss Bent, but only yesterday."

"Only *yesterday!*"

"Yes, you unfortunately addressed it to me personally, instead of sending it to the school board, and—"

"I did that on purpose," she interposed, "to keep my—to keep it private. I didn't want to have everybody talking about my—my having broken off my engagement; mother doesn't even know yet; I couldn't bear to tell anybody but *you!*"

"I know, I know; I gathered that from what you wrote. But it was most unlucky that you wrote to me, for I've been away, up in Maine, for the last week with my wife's mother, who's been sick, and I only got back yesterday."

"Only yes-ter-day!" she repeated, dividing the words into syllables, as if they belonged to a foreign tongue which she did not perfectly understand. Then, suddenly lifting her head: "But my place—they must have filled my place?"

"It was filled three days ago at the general meeting. There was no help for it. No one could imagine—"

"No, no, of course—of course."

He had been afraid that she would cry again, but to his surprise she remained quite calm.

"Who has it?" she asked.

He hesitated a moment; the words seemed hard to say: "Your friend, Miss Thurber."

"Vexilla!"

The room swung round; her lips grew dry; she felt an inconsequent desire to laugh. "But Vexilla—Vexilla! You always said—why, not one of you would *look* at her—not even for the third primary— and now, my class! *My* class!"

She was bathed in a hot wave of anger. The whole air seemed thick with ingratitude and treachery, as if all these years she had walked in an atmosphere of lies. What did it mean? What could it mean? Perhaps, even while they were urging her to remain, imploring her to come back to them, they had been plotting her removal; possibly keeping Vexilla to fill this very place, while they glossed over with hypocritical excuses their refusal to give her a lesser one! And Vexilla herself—might not she, too, have had a hand in it? Who could tell, in a world that swarmed with such grinning incongruities?

"But Vexilla—Vexilla—" she repeated.

"I don't wonder at your surprise." Mr. Boutwell's familiar voice fell strangely on the tumult of her thoughts. "We've been unwilling to employ Miss Thurber for reasons with which you are perfectly familiar, and which you have often told me you thought inadequate. You remember how much you've talked with me about her; how often you've told me it was only shyness that made her appear so dull and hesitating; that she was really better educated than many of our present teachers." He paused, but Miss Bent made no answer.

"Well," he continued, "there were very few candidates for your place, and among them there was only one who appeared at all satisfactory to the board, and that was Miss Euphemia Staples. We had just decided to appoint her when she was called out West, to keep house for a brother who has lost his wife; and that left us without a single eligible applicant—for of course Miss Thurber was not among the applicants."

A low sound like a laugh escaped Miss Bent.

"At last somebody suggested Miss Thurber. It rather took us aback at first, but we hadn't much time to think the matter over, and there didn't seem to be anybody else. We recalled what you'd said about her—the board always thought a great deal of your opinion—and finally we sent for her. She was considerably overcome—she cried a good deal—and for a time it didn't seem as if we could get her to accept. She said she'd sooner have taken any other place in the school."

Miss Bent moved impatiently in her seat. Vexilla had evidently expressed all the proper sentiments; for once in her life she had not been tongue-tied; she seemed indeed to have surprised Mr. Boutwell by her eloquence. The supplanted teacher rose, feeling for her bag.

"I guess I'd better be going along," she murmured.

"Wait a minute, please; I haven't quite finished. I hope we shall see you back among us all the same, Miss Bent, for Miss Thurber accepted your place only on the condition that if by any chance you— you changed your mind and came back within the next few weeks, she should be permitted to resign. And I know she'll hold us to our agreement."

Miss Bent turned red, then pale. "Changed my mind? Changed my mind? How dare she?" Her anger dropped and she sank back into her chair. "Did she say that? Did she? Poor Vexilla! That she'd only accept on that condition? She made you promise? She made the whole board agree to it? Poor Vexilla—oh, poor Vexilla!"

"And what's more, she means it, too," Mr. Boutwell went on. "She's restless and worried at the idea of being in your place; says she can't get used to it; it don't seem natural to her. She's a devoted friend, Miss Bent."

"I know, I know."

"I met her only this morning on my way here, and she stopped to talk about you and tell me how she missed you. She said she'd give up her place in a minute to have you back here, and I believe she would, though from what I hear it means a good deal to her to be getting a regular salary. She's had a pretty hard time of it up to now, I guess."

"You met Vexilla this morning?" Miss Bent interrupted, without noticing his last words. "You didn't tell her—about me, did you, Mr. Boutwell?"

"I said nothing."

"Thank you—thank you. You always understand. I'm so confused myself; I don't yet know how I mean to act. Even mother doesn't suspect anything. She doesn't know I've come—she doesn't know but what I'm married!" She gave a constrained laugh and rose once more.

The laugh troubled Boutwell; it seemed to conceal some inaccessible disaster.

"Don't you think," he began, for the sake of saying something, "that it would have been wiser to let Mrs. Bent know? Won't she be considerably startled at seeing you?"

"I'm afraid she will; but I couldn't tell her in a letter; she'd have shown it to everybody. You know she just *has* to talk things over."

"I understand."

Miss Bent looked at him hesitatingly. "I guess I'll go now. I'm very grateful to you for not having spoken about my letter."

"Oh, that's all right," said the librarian, taking refuge again in the examination of his spectacles. "But, see here, Miss Bent, what are you going to do?"

"About what?"

"Why—the school."

"Oh, I don't know," she said slowly. "I'm so bewildered I can't think straight yet. I'll have to go home and quiet down a little. Only please don't let Vexilla know I'm here; don't tell anybody you've seen me; I'm so afraid she'll find out about it before I've seen her."

"Don't worry about that, Miss Bent."

"No; I know I can trust you."

Their hands met and she moved away, adding, as she reached the door, "I'll come in tomorrow and tell you what I've decided."

"Very well; but I'm sure Miss Thurber won't keep the place. I guess she's got a will of her own, and I don't believe you could make her stay if you tried."

Miss Bent turned back abruptly.

"O Mr. Boutwell, I don't know what you must think of me! I was perfectly hateful about Vexilla when you first told me—perfectly hateful! I don't see how I could behave so. As if she hadn't as much right to take my class as anybody else! But the fact is, I'm almost crazy. I don't seem to know what I'm doing—" Her eyes clung to Boutwell with a look of shipwrecked terror. "I must tell you—I must tell you! I can't endure it another minute by myself! What I wrote you wasn't true—about having broken off my engagement. There wasn't a word of truth in it. When I got to Louisville Mr. Dayton wasn't there. He'd gone off the day before, and nobody knew where he was. I had to get detectives—his partner helped me. It took us nearly a week to find him. He was away down in Texas—and he'd married another woman!"

Boutwell jumped up with a wrathful exclamation, but before it was out of his mouth the office door had closed on Miss Bent.

II

Late that afternoon Miss Bent, having unpacked her few possessions (she looked the other way as she slipped the gray cashmere with lace ruffles into a drawer by itself), sat in her little bedroom trying to think. The sense of familiarity which had soothed the first moments of her return to Sailport had given way to a profounder estrangement. As she glanced about the room, it seemed impossible that four walls which had held so much of her life should assume a look of such chill indifference. Every line of the furniture, every twist in the pattern of the wallpaper, seemed to repeat the same "I know thee not!" No, she was not the Penelope Bent who had lived there through so many happy, monotonous years; she was a stranger who had never been in the room before, and who knew as little of its history as it knew of hers.

The fanciful wanderings of her thoughts frightened her—she was not accustomed to such divagations; she felt herself on the brink of delirium. The interview with her mother had been terrible. She had told Mrs. Bent that her marriage was postponed, taking refuge in this euphuism under the merciless tenderness of the maternal gaze. It would have been so much easier to face indifference! Mrs. Bent's tremulous avoidance of surmises, her abruptly deflected questions, her unwonted acquiescences, seemed to intensify the vividness of the mute insight that lighted up every corner of her daughter's consciousness. The two women lived in that involuntary familiarity from which neither speech nor silence can give sanctuary.

Suddenly the solitude seemed to be full of her mother's eyes, and Miss Bent, starting up, moved toward the window. Twilight was falling, and a few steps in the open air might do her good. She put on her hat and veil, and unlocking her door, stepped into the cheerful sitting room beyond. Ivy and geranium throve on the sunny windows sill, and a lump of coal had just been kindled in the grate.

Mrs. Bent, a small, withered woman, rooted to her seat by some obscure ailment, looked up at her daughter with shrinking, inquisitive eyes. Miss Bent drew up the shawl about her mother's knees, and absently broke a yellow leaf from one of the geranium plants.

"Seems to me the geraniums have had too much water this last week," she said.

"I'm afraid they have, Penelope. Nobody's got your knack with them."

Miss Bent stirred the soil in the pot. "It needs loosening." She drew on her gloves, avoiding her mother's eye.

"You're going out a little way, Penelope?"

"Yes, I'll be back soon." She hesitated. "If anybody comes in, mother, don't—don't—"

Mrs. Bent's eyelids trembled; the violence of her protest confessed her weakness. "Penelope Bent, how can you think—"

"Oh, that's all right!" the daughter said, resignedly.

Although it was growing dark indoors, the spring daylight still lingered, and Miss Bent, instinctively seeking for solitude, turned up a quiet side street, disturbed only by the calls of a few children at play. The air brought little ease to her head, and she was conscious of a growing inability to think. Yet she knew that in a few hours she must act; she could not continue to keep her presence in Sailport a secret; had she cherished any such design, her mother's tongue would have frustrated it. She must prepare to meet Vexilla Thurber the next day; before they met she must decide on some course of action, and as yet no conclusion had suggested itself.

Try as she might to examine the problem before her, she could see but one point of it—that she had lost her place at the school, that the greater part of her savings had been absorbed by the journey to Louisville and the preparations for her wedding, and that now she was left stranded, with heavy expenses to face and without means of meeting them. Although Miss Bent had only her mother to support, she had found her salary barely sufficient for her needs. Her own tastes were simple, but Mrs. Bent's ill health taxed her daughter's purse with demands that had every quality of unexpectedness except that of inevitable recurrence.

Under such conditions, the future looked disheartening enough. She remembered Boutwell's words: "Miss Thurber won't keep the place"; but the suggestion they conveyed was intolerable. Of course, if something else could be found for Vexilla—but she smiled at herself for trusting her hopes to this frail hypothesis. Had not she and all Vexilla's friends been searching for years for that delusive something? Yes, but Boutwell had said that Vexilla would insist on resigning, and he was right in thinking that Vexilla had a will of her own. If Vexilla meant to resign, the whole of Sailport could not stop her. And if she resigned, what was to prevent—

Miss Bent pulled herself together. She had a sudden vision of Vexilla's household, with the infirm grandmother, the crippled brother, helpless as a baby, who lay in his chair playing with tin soldiers, the handsome, slatternly sister, who drifted back from every "job" that Vexilla obtained for her into a languid permanence of novel reading and street corner flirtation. Vexilla had three to support; Miss Bent but one. Yes, but if Vexilla insisted on resigning?

Down the empty street a woman's figure was approaching. Even in the failing light there was no mistaking the thick-set figure, the oscillating walk that suggested a ship with her steering gear out of order, or the round face framed in meek drab hair. Miss Bent glanced about in the instinctive attempt to escape; but it was too late.

"Penelope!"

"Vexilla!"

The two women faced each other, Miss Bent silent, Vexilla Thurber emitting her astonishment in a series of soft cries:

You, Penelope—*you!* Back in Sailport? Gracious mercy! But is it you, really? I feel as if it might be your ghost. Oh no, there's your cameo brooch! *Penelope*—why don't you say something?"

"You don't give me time, Vexilla; but I'm not a ghost—and I've come back."

"For mercy's sake! What in the world has happened? Penelope Bent, you've had some misfortune! You'd never have come back—has anything happened to *him?* I know something's happened—you look awful! What *is* it?"

Vexilla's agonized italics echoed through the silent street, and a woman on the opposite sidewalk slackened her pace to listen.

"I can't tell you here, Vexilla. Don't be so excited! I'll walk along with you a little way."

Her friend, clutching her arm, watched her with perturbed blue eyes.

"You needn't talk to *me*, Penelope—something has happened, or else you're sick; one or the other! You're as white as a sheet, and I can feel you trembling all over! Penelope—Penelope—you don't want me to go away and leave you? You aren't angry with me for—for meeting you?" Her apple face was wet with tears; they ran down unheeded, dabbling her fawn-colored dress.

"Nonsense, Vexilla! Why should I be angry with you for meeting me? I've only just got home, and I'm a little tired, that's all!"

"Oh, you poor soul, you're *dead* tired! I can see that. But, Penelope—" She drew closer, her voice sinking to a frightened whisper. "I don't quite understand—*are you married?*"

"No, I'm not married." Miss Bent glanced over her friend's shoulder and saw a group of people approaching. "But we can't stand here and talk, and I can't ask you to come and see me just now. Mother's in the parlor, and we couldn't talk before her."

"No, no; I know we couldn't," Miss Thurber emotionally acquiesced. "But why won't you come home with me for a few minutes? Do, Penelope! Lally will be getting supper for grandma and Phil, and we can have my room all to ourselves. Lally's getting real helpful, Penelope. She cares for grandma so nicely when I have to be out!"

Miss Bent hesitated. "Where were you going, Vexilla?"

"Me? I was only going to run down to Main Street for a minute to get some books. It's of no consequence—" She broke off suddenly and her color rose. The books of which she was in quest were probably the textbooks for her new class at the school. "Come with me, Penelope," she deprecatingly entreated.

"Very well," said Miss Bent, with sudden resolution; and they began to walk in the direction of Vexilla's home.

Vexilla, eased of her first agitation, respected her friend's reticence, and they moved on silently through the dusk, pricked here and there by the yellow points of the street lamps. At length they reached a house divided from the sidewalk by a strip of down-trodden earth enclosed with broken palings. Vexilla opened the door and led her friend through an entry smelling of boiled cabbage, and up a narrow staircase to the top of the house. On the upper landing she paused to say, with visible embarrassment, "You mustn't mind if Lally and Phil seem surprised to see you back. We've been talking so much about—"

"Yes, yes; I understand," Miss Bent hastily interposed.

Vexilla stepped into a low-ceilinged room which was almost in darkness.

"Why, Lally! Haven't you lighted the lamp? Haven't you got supper?"

Vexilla advanced into the room, leaving Miss Bent on the threshold.

"I can't see where I'm going! Where are the matches? Oh, here. It's a mercy I filled the lamp before I went out, anyway!"

She bent over a lamp which stood on the center table, and the room was presently revealed in all its shabby disorder. In an old bath chair near the window lay the paralyzed boy, his drawn face detached like a death's-head against the shawl thrust pillow-wise behind his head. Lally, the sister, dragging herself from the sofa on which she had been stretched, stepped listlessly into the lamplight, which illuminated the beauty of her heavy white face, helmeted with somber hair.

"Goodness!" she exclaimed. "That you, Miss Bent? Have you got married already? Vexilla never told us you were coming back!"

"Vexilla's got your place at school!" piped the paralyzed boy from the window.

Vexilla paid no heed. She had hurried toward her grandmother, a huge ruin of a woman with a face like a broken statue, who sat vaguely smiling in a rocking chair beside the stove.

"Gracious, Lally, you've left the stove door open, and there's a cinder right in grandma's lap!"

"Lally's been asleep!" the boy shrilly interposed. Vexilla smoothed the old woman's hair, straightened the knitted shawl about her shoulders, and closed the door of the stove. Lally had thrown herself back on the sofa, still gazing at Miss Bent under the projecting visor of her hair, while the boy began impatiently: "Vexilla, aren't you going to get supper?"

"No; Lally's going to." Vexilla turned to her friend. "Come this way, Penelope."

Miss Bent followed her down a passageway to a small room with two beds in it. Miss Thurber struck a match and lighted a lamp which stood on a desk piled with schoolbooks.

"Sit down and wait, please, Penelope. I'll be back in a minute."

She turned away, shutting the door after her, while Miss Bent sank into a chair. She longed to fly, to escape from the depressing influences of Vexilla's home to the orderly silence of her own little room. The cracked looking glass and threadbare carpet, the bed in which the helpless grandmother slept, all the evidences of Vexilla's hardships and privations, seemed to add their pressure to the weight upon her burdened nerves. Never before had life appeared so meaningless and cruel.

Vexilla returned, demonstrative and breathless, with a cup of steaming tea.

"Please drink it, Penelope, please do—you're regularly worn out. I can see you are. Just take a mouthful—I know it'll do you good!" Her blue eyes had the look of a dog begging to be noticed.

Miss Bent took the cup and leaned back, sipping the tea reluctantly, while Vexilla sat by in an ecstasy of mute contemplation.

"I do feel better," Miss Bent said at last, meeting her friend's gaze. "And now, Vexilla, we must talk."

She paused a moment, as if rallying her forces, and then began again: "I must tell you—"

Vexilla leaned forward. "Wait a minute, Penelope—there's something I must tell *you* first. I can't bear to have you speak a word before you know what's happened."

Miss Bent looked at her, half smiling. "I know," she said.

"You *know!* About the school?"

"Yes. I've seen Mr. Boutwell."

"Oh!" said Vexilla, in a long shudder of comprehension. For a moment or two both women were silent. Then Vexilla began to speak in quick, entreating tones.

"O Penelope, what *must* you have thought? It all happened so strangely! They sent for me, Penelope—of course I never would have dreamed of applying. Even if I'd been smart enough, I never would have applied for *your* place! And I always supposed they thought I was too stupid. You'd tried so often to get me into the schools that I didn't suppose there was any chance for me. When they sent for me I thought it must be a mistake. I couldn't believe it! And even when I found they really wanted me, I couldn't bear the idea, Penelope. I said if it had only been any other place but yours; but they said that was the only one that was vacant. And of course everybody said you'd never come back here—you were so positive you wouldn't, Penelope—" She paused, shrinking back from the unrevealed mystery of her friend's return. "And I've got so many to think of that it didn't seem as if I ought to refuse. But I said I'd only take it on one condition. I made them solemnly agree to that—that if you changed your mind and—and decided to come back to Sailport—"

"I know that, too," said Miss Bent, slowly. Bending forward, she kissed the wet cheek of her friend. Fresh tears rose to Vexilla's eyes; but the intensity of the resolve which animated her drove them back and subdued the quivering of her lips.

"I'm glad Mr. Boutwell told you, Penelope. I couldn't bear to have had you think, for one minute, even, that I'd have taken the place on any other terms."

"I knew you wouldn't, Vexilla!"

"O Penelope! How like you to say that!" In the rapture of being understood she ventured to lay one large hand on Miss Bent's. "There's nobody like you—nobody! Oh, it's so good to have you back!" Again she faltered, in fear of appearing to touch intentionally upon Penelope's enigmatic course.

Miss Bent did not speak. She sat motionless, her eyes fixed on a plush-framed photograph of herself that hung above Vexilla's desk. It was the only picture in the room.

"And there's another thing I want to tell you right off, Penelope! I know just what you are—always thinking of other people first and yourself last; and I don't want you to think it's any loss to me to—to give up that place. I don't want to keep it, Penelope! It's a relief to me to give it up. I never should have got used to it. I'm not half bright enough, anyway! I don't much believe they'd have kept me more than one term, even if—and it doesn't suit me, somehow! I'd rather go back to my old work. I—I think I'd have resigned, anyway. I'm sure I would, Penelope! The fact is, it ties me down too much—I'm more independent with my other work."

Miss Bent raised her eyes. "Your bookkeeping and typewriting, you mean? Where's your typewriter, by the way? It always used to stand on your desk."

In the faint candlelight she thought she saw Miss Thurber's color change.

"It's not here now."

"Where is it? What's become of it?"

"I—well, the fact is I sold it."

"You sold it? Why? Oh, because—I see." Miss Bent paused, struggling with a resentment that suddenly forced itself through her sympathy for her friend. She repressed the ungenerous impulse. What could be more natural than that Vexilla should sell her typewriter?

Miss Thurber went on precipitately "I guess I shan't have much time for typewriting, anyway. You see, it's going to be a great help to have had that appointment. I don't believe I'll have a bit of trouble getting private pupils now. Fact is, that's the real reason I was always so crazy to get into the schools. I never thought the work would really suit me—but it makes such a lot of difference if you can refer parents to the board! I guess I'll have more work than I can manage."

Miss Bent laughed, and rising from her seat, laid her hand on Vexilla's shoulder. "You're a goose, Vexilla! How do you know I'm going to stay in Sailport?"

"Penelope!"

Miss Thurber had also risen, and the two women stood facing each other.

"You don't know yet why I'm here," Miss Bent continued in the same bantering tone. "It seems to me you're taking a good deal for granted, aren't you?"

"O Penelope! I didn't mean—"

Miss Bent, withdrawing her hand, took a few hesitating steps across the room. Vexilla hung back, waiting for her to speak. "I'm going to tell you, Vexilla," she said at last.

"Yes," the other nodded.

There was another silence. Miss Bent seemed to find difficulty in choosing her words.

"My marriage isn't going to take place—just at present—that's all. When I got to Louisville I found—but I can't tell you all that now; it's too long. Perhaps tomorrow. I only got back this morning, and I had to explain it all to mother. Of course my coming back upset her a good deal."

"Don't say another word, Penelope! I can see how tired you are. Only tell me you're not in any trouble—"

Miss Bent met her gaze calmly.

"I'm not in any trouble, Vexilla. My marriage has been put off for reasons that—that are perfectly satisfactory to Mr. Dayton and myself. He's obliged to be away from Louisville a good deal just now— and I didn't want to stay out there alone—with mother here—"

"O Penelope—but couldn't he have let you know?" Vexilla cried, her sympathy outrunning her discretion.

"I'll explain all that another time. I only want to tell you that I've decided to leave Sailport with mother now, instead of waiting till— afterward. You know she was to have joined me in Louisville, and we've given up our rooms here, so we'd have to move on the first of May, anyhow." She now spoke without perceptible hesitation.

"But, Penelope, I don't understand!" Miss Thurber faltered. "Where are you going? You are not going back to Louisville right off?"

Miss Bent's face stiffened. "No; not there." She paused a moment. "I think we shall go to New York," she said at last. "Aunt Sarah Tillman, mother's younger sister, lives there, and I could get plenty to do in a big place like that. It's very easy, if you know some one who lives there. But it's not on my account; it's because of mother. She's a good deal upset by the change in my plans. She'd made up her mind to leave Sailport, and I'm afraid it would be hard for her to settle down again after making all her preparations to go. You know mother's very excitable."

"I know, but—"

"I've had a good many offers of work in New York," Miss Bent continued, ignoring the interruption. "My aunt's always writing to us to come and stay with her. She says she could get me half a dozen pupils right off. Her husband's related to a Presbyterian minister, with a large parish. And I don't know but what I should like the change, too. I feel rather restless myself."

Miss Thurber continued to gaze at her with a tender incredulity. "But New York—you've never been there—"

"Well, I don't know that it's too late to begin."

"No; but it's all so queer! Why, you've hardly ever been away from Sailport, Penelope! I can't think what you want to go to New York for."

Miss Bent rose again. Her lips were compressed and she forced the words through them with a certain precipitation. "New York is nearer Louisville, for one thing. You hadn't thought of that, I suppose?"

"No," Vexilla faltered.

"You know Mr. Dayton was never able to get as far east as this."

Miss Thurber colored. She felt that it was singularly obtuse of her not to have understood this. "To be sure," she murmured, "I never thought of it! You must excuse me, Penelope. I've asked you so many questions, and I know how tired you are! But I couldn't help it. It's all so sudden! I can't take it in yet—the idea of your going away again, just as I was so glad to have you back!"

Miss Bent was putting on her jacket and adjusting her brown veil. For a moment she did not speak, and some indefinable change in her face made Vexilla suddenly exclaim: "But *is* it true? Are you really going away?"

Miss Bent turned on her almost angrily. "I don't know what you mean! You talk as if I didn't know my own mind! I'm not in the habit of saying things I don't mean!"

"Oh, I know, but—" Vexilla's words ran into tears.

Miss Bent leaned forward and gently kissed her.

"Mother and I are going away in a few days, that's quite settled.

My reason for telling you so at once is that I was afraid you might do something foolish about the school."

"O Penelope, Penelope!"

"And I want you to keep the class, Vexilla. I particularly want you to keep it! I was so glad when Mr. Boutwell told me they'd given it to you! I couldn't bear to think of a stranger in my class. You must write me about the girls, Vexilla, and perhaps I can help you sometimes with your work."

"O Penelope! It seems as if I couldn't bear it—*your* class!"

"You're a goose, Vexilla, and now good-bye! It's dark, and mother will be getting worried."

"Let me walk home with you, Penelope. I feel as if I wasn't ever going to see you again."

"You silly child! You'll see me tomorrow, I hope. Come in the afternoon, while mother's taking her nap."

"You won't let me walk back with you now?"

"Not now. I want to be alone."

She opened the door and stepped hurriedly along the passageway ahead of Vexilla, passing, she hardly knew how, among the inmates of the living room, now gathered about an untidy supper table. On the landing Vexilla clung to her with another mute pressure, full of confused doubts and tremors; then she found herself on the staircase, and a moment later she was alone in the dim street.

For a while she stood irresolute, as if awaiting the subsidence of some strong wave of emotion; then, slowly, she began to move forward along the deserted sidewalk.

At the next corner, instead of turning homeward, she bent her steps toward Main Street, unconsciously quickening her pace as she advanced. She was in that curiously detached state when one's body seems like an inert mass, propelled from one point to another without conscious action of its own. In this condition she reached the corner where the brightly-lighted post-office windows projected their oblongs of yellow light across the shadows of Main Street. She pushed open one of the doors, and, going to a small window at the back of the office, asked for a sheet of paper and a stamped envelope.

Having received them, she withdrew to one of the shelves lining the wall, and dipped a ragged pen into the cup of grayish coagulated matter which a paternal government provides for the convenience of the peripatetic letter writer. She wrote a few lines, which she addressed to Mr. Boutwell, and having dropped the envelope into a letter box, she left the post office and turned toward home.

Her step had lost all hesitancy. She seemed to be moving with decision toward a definitely chosen goal. In the course of the past hour her whole relation to life had changed. The experience of the last weeks had flung her out of her orbit, whirling her through dread spaces of moral darkness and bewilderment. She seemed to have lost her connection with the general scheme of things, to have no further part in the fulfilment of the laws that made life comprehensible and duty a joyful impulse. Now the old sense of security had returned. There still loomed before her, in tragic amplitude, the wreck of her individual hope; but she had escaped from the falling ruins and stood safe, outside of herself, in touch once more with the common troubles of her kind, enfranchised forever from the bondage of a lonely grief.

ZONA GALE

Nobody Sick, Nobody Poor

(1907)

ONA Gale (1874–1938), the only child of Eliza Beers and Charles Franklin Gale, grew up in Portage, Wisconsin, a town of 5,000 whose rich history provided the material for her best work.

From earliest childhood Gale displayed an active imagination and a preference for solitary amusements. At the age of four she suffered a near fatal case of diphtheria, which left her in delicate health until adolescence. Unable to engage in rough-and-tumble play with other children, Gale developed a strong literary bent. Her favorite activities were listening to, reading, and eventually writing stories. She announced at age seven that she was going to be a writer and never deviated from that goal. Although her classmates liked Gale and she had a small circle of girlfriends with whom she did the things most little girls do, she lived most intensely in her inner world of fantasy. This created an impression of aloofness throughout her life.

Zona Gale's parents and their values were the major influences on her life. Both parents came from sturdy Anglo-Saxon pioneer stock and embodied such traditional virtues as hard work, honesty, frugality, and piety. Zona, the focal point of Eliza and Charlie Gale's lives, bore an imprint from both. The most powerful emotional bond of her life was with her mother. Tall, dignified, and handsome, Eliza Gale was a formidable woman. With her lively wit and talent at singing and playing the piano, she quickly became the center of attention at social gatherings. She was, on the one hand, commonsensical and down to earth and, on the other, imaginative and creative. A devout Presbyterian all of her adult life, she also possessed a strain of moral earnestness on which she frequently called to guide her in the raising of her daughter, something she regarded as a sacred trust. Above all, Eliza Gale had an iron will, a quality that she bequeathed to her only child.

Zona both adored and admired her father; she thought him the most noble man she had ever known. His slight build and small-boned frame made him look out of place in the cab of his locomotive engine, and indeed he was; but he worked forty-three years for the railroad, never earning more than $2,000 a year. His retiring nature concealed a pronounced individuality and a restless mind that led him to read deeply in the works of those who interested him most—Swedenborg, Spencer, Darwin, and Emerson. Zona, serious minded from childhood, inherited her father's inclination toward meditative reflection. Central to Charles Gale's world view was the principle of correspondences, wherein the material world is but the external manifestation of the great spiritual universe that lies behind it, which Emerson called the Oversoul.

The entire family believed that motherhood was a manifestation of one of the most important correspondences in the universe, the spiritual love and unity that binds all human beings together. Zona Gale's writing repeatedly makes clear that she believed women were morally superior to men because they were the microcosmic expressions of this macrocosmic force on which the human race depends. In this belief she was an essentialist. Throughout her life, Gale was committed to the betterment of humankind and strived unstintingly toward that end.

Although it was unusual for a young woman from her background to go to college, Gale's parents were determined to give her this advantage, regardless of any sacrifices it required. Zona earned both a bachelor's and a master's degree from the University of Wisconsin at Madison. Even more unusual was her decision to enter journalism, not a respectable profession for a well-bred, genteel young woman; but Zona Gale succeeded brilliantly as a reporter, both in Milwaukee and later in New York. While in New York, Gale became acquainted with magazine editors and acquired an aggressive agent. With these contacts established, Gale was able to return to Portage (and her parents) in 1904 and devote herself to writing the tales that soon brought her fame and financial independence.

Back home in Wisconsin Gale became caught up in the push for civic improvement, an outgrowth of Robert La Follette's work locally and the Progressive movement nationally. Next she advanced to suffragism and antimilitarism. Through these activities she made friends with some of the most distinguished women of the day: Jane Addams, Crystal Eastman, Charlotte Perkins Gilman, Alice Paul, and Lillian Wald, to cite only a few. Her growing literary celebrity put her in touch with all the greats and near-greats in the literary world of her day, which resulted in friendships with many women writers—Edith Wharton, Ellen Glasgow, Willa Cather, Margaret Widdemer, Elinor Wylie, Susan Glaspell, Rachel

Crothers, Fannie Hurst, Edna Ferber, Lula Vollmer, Dorothy Canfield Fisher, Margery Latimer, Anzia Yezierska, Marya Zaturenska, Meridel Le Sueur, and Jessie Fauset, among others. These women were diverse in age, race, religion, sexual preference, and level of success. Gale looked for goodness; other considerations were irrelevant. She also had many close male friends and associates, but the keystone of her life was her associations with other women. She reached out to them for solace, companionship, advice, affirmation, and, above all, help in furthering the causes they mutually espoused. (She belonged to Heterodoxy—that extraordinary group of radical professional women who met bimonthly in Greenwich Village—from its inception in 1912, probably at the behest of her special friend, Fola La Follette, Robert La Follette's eldest child.)

The winning of the Pulitzer Prize for drama in 1921 for the stage adaptation of *Miss Lulu Bett* provided Zona Gale with greater resources and influence to use in public service. This commitment continued until her death in December 1938.

"Nobody Sick, Nobody Poor," which first appeared in the *Delineator* in November 1907, comes from the Friendship Village series, a collection of tales about small town life that eventually filled five volumes. (Most of the Friendship Village stories were first published in such popular magazines as *Outlook, Everybody's,* and the *Delineator*). Like many of these tales, "Nobody Sick, Nobody Poor" reflects Gale's belief that women act as "mothers" to the community, spreading love and revealing the commonality she believed all human beings shared—if only they would recognize it.[1]

VIRGINIA COX

Two days before Thanksgiving the air was already filled with white turkey feathers, and I stood at a window and watched until the loneliness of my still house seemed like something pointing a mocking finger at me. When I could bear it no longer I went out in the snow, and through the soft drifts I fought my way up the Plank Road toward the village.

I had almost passed the little bundled figure before I recognized Calliope. She was walking in the middle of the road, as in Friendship we all walk in winter; and neither of us had umbrellas. I think that I distrust people who put up umbrellas on a country road in a fall of friendly flakes.

Instead of inquiring perfunctorily how I did, she greeted me with a fragment of what she had been thinking—which is always as if one were to open a door of his mind to you instead of signing you greeting from a closed window.

"I just been tellin' myself," she looked up to say without preface, "that if I could see one more good old-fashion' Thanksgivin', life'd sort o' smooth out. An' land knows, it needs some smoothin' out for me."

With this I remember that it was as if my own loneliness spoke for me. At my reply Calliope looked at me quickly—as if I, too, had opened a door.

"Sometimes Thanksgivin' *is* some like seein' the sun shine when you're feelin' rill rainy yourself," she said thoughtfully.

She held out her blue-mittened hand and let the flakes fall on it in stars and coronets.

"I wonder," she asked evenly, "if you'd help me get up a Thanksgivin' dinner for a few poor sick folks here in Friendship?"

In order to keep my self-respect, I recall that I was as ungracious as possible. I think I said that the day meant so little to me that I was willing to do anything to avoid spending it alone. A statement which seems to me now not to bristle with logic.

"That's nice of you," Calliope replied genially. Then she hesitated, looking down Daphne Street, which the Plank Road had become, toward certain white houses. There were the homes of Mis' Mayor Uppers, Mis' Holcomb-that-was-Mame-Bliss, and the Liberty sisters,—all substantial dignified houses, typical of the simple prosperity of the countryside.

"The only trouble," she added simply, "is that in Friendship I don't know a soul rill sick, nor a soul what you might call poor."

At this I laughed, unwillingly enough. Dear Calliope! Here indeed was a drawback to her project.

"Honestly," she said reflectively, "Friendship can't seem to do anything like any other town. When the new minister come here, he give out he was goin' to do settlement work. An' his second week in the place he come to me with a reg'lar hang-dog look. What kind of a town is this?' he says to me, disgusted. 'They ain't nobody sick in it an' they ain't nobody poor!' I guess he could 'a' got along without the poor—most of us can. But we mostly like to hev a few sick to carry the flowers off our house plants to, an' now an' then a tumbler o' jell. An' yet I've known weeks at a time when they wasn't a soul rill flat down sick in Friendship. It's so now. An' that's hard, when you're young an' enthusiastic, like the minister."

"But where are you going to find your guests then, Calliope?" I asked curiously.

"Well," she said brightly, "I was just plannin' as you come up with me. An' I says to myself: 'God give me to live in a little bit of a place where we've all got enough to get along on, an' Thanksgivin' finds us all in health. It looks like He'd afflicted us by lettin' us hev nobody to do for.' An' then it come to me that if we was to get up the dinner,—with all the misery an' hunger they is in the world,—God in His goodness would let some of it come our way to be fed. 'In the wilderness a cedar,' you know—as Liddy Ember an' I was always tellin' each other when we kep' shop together. An' so to-day I said to myself I'd go to work an' get up the dinner an' trust there'd be eaters for it."

"Why, Calliope," I said, "Calliope!"

"I ain't got much to do with, myself," she added apologetically; "the most I've got in my sullar, I guess, is a gallon jar o' watermelon pickles. I could give that. You don't think it sounds irreverent—connectin' God with a big dinner, so?" she asked anxiously.

And, at my reply:—

"Well, then," she said briskly, "let's step in an' see a few folks that might be able to tell us of somebody to do for. Let's ask Mis' Mayor Uppers an' Mis' Holcomb-that-was-Mame-Bliss, an' the Liberty girls."

Because I was lonely and idle, and because I dreaded inexpressibly going back to my still house, I went with her. Her ways were a kind of entertainment, and I remember that I believed my leisure to be infinite.

We turned first toward the big shuttered house of Mis' Mayor Uppers, to whom, although her husband had been a year ago removed from office, discredited, and had not since been seen in Friendship, we yet gave her old proud title, as if she had been Former Lady Mayoress. For the present mayor, Authority Hubblethwaite, was, as Calliope said, "unconnect."

I watched Mis' Uppers in some curiosity while Calliope explained that she was planning a dinner for the poor and sick,—"the lame and the sick that's comfortable enough off to eat,"—and could she suggest some poor and sick to ask? Mis' Uppers was like a vinegar cruet of mine, slim and tall, with a little grotesquely puckered face for a stopper, as if the whole known world were sour.

"I'm sure," she said humbly, "it's a nice i-dee. But I declare, I'm put to it to suggest. We ain't got nobody sick nor nobody poor in Friendship, you know."

"Don't you know of anybody kind o' hard up? Or somebody that, if they ain't down sick, feels sort o' spindlin'?" Calliope asked anxiously.

Mis' Uppers thought, rocking a little and running a pin in and out of a fold of her skirt.

"No," she said at length, "I don't know a soul. I think the church'd give a good deal if a real poor family'd come here to do for. Since the Cadozas went, we ain't known which way to look for poor, Mis' Ricker gettin' her fortune so puts her beyond the wolf. An' Peleg Bemus, you can't *get* him to take anything. No, I don't know of anybody real decently poor."

"An' nobody sick?" Calliope pressed her wistfully.

"Well, there's Mis' Crawford," admitted Mis' Uppers; "she had a spell o' lumbago two weeks ago, but I see her pass the house to-day. Mis' Brady was laid up with toothache, too, but the *Daily* last night said she'd had it out. An' Mis' Doctor Helman did have one o' her stomach attacks this week, an' Elzabella got out her dyin' dishes an' her dyin' linen from the still-room—you know how Mis' Doctor always brings out her nice things when she's sick, so't if she should die an' the neighbours come in, it'd all be shipshape. But she got better this time an' helped put 'em back. I declare it's hard to get up anything in the charity line here."

Calliope sat smiling a little, and I knew that it was because of her secret certainty that "some o' the hunger" would come her way, to be fed.

"I can't help thinkin'," she said quietly, "that we'll find somebody. An' I tell you what: if we do, can I count on you to help some?"

Mis' Uppers flushed with quick pleasure.

"Me, Calliope?" she said. And I remembered that they had told me how the Friendship Married Ladies' Cemetery Improvement Sodality had been unable to tempt Mis' Uppers to a single meeting since the mayor ran away. "Oh, but I couldn't though," she said wistfully.

"No need to go to the table if you don't want," Calliope told her. "Just bake up somethin' for us an' bring it over. Make a couple o' your cherry pies—did you get hold of any cherries to put up this year? Well, a couple o' your cherry pies an' a batch o' your nice drop sponge cakes," she directed. "Could you?"

Mis' Mayor Uppers looked up with a kind of light in her eyes.

"Why, yes," she said, "I could, I guess. I'll bake 'em Thanksgivin' mornin'. I—I was wonderin' how I'd put in the day."

When we stepped out in the snow again, Calliope's face was shining. Sometimes now, when my faith is weak in any good thing, I remember her look that November morning. But all that I thought then was how I was being entertained that lonely day.

The dear Liberty sisters were next, Lucy and Viny and Libbie Liberty. We went to the side door,—there were houses in Friendship whose front doors we tacitly understood that we were never expected to use,—and we found the sisters down cellar, with shawls over their head, feeding their hens through the cellar window, opening on the glassed-in coop under the porch.

In Friendship it is a point of etiquette for a morning caller never to interrupt the employment of a hostess. So we obeyed the summons of the Liberty sister to "come right down"; and we sat on a firkin and an inverted tub while Calliope told her plan and the hens fought for delectable morsels.

"My grief!" said Libbie Liberty tartly, "where you goin' to *get* your sick an' poor?"

Mis' Viny, balancing on the window ledge to reach for eggs, looked back at us.

"Friendship's so comfortable that way," she said, "I don't see how you can get up much of anything."

And little Miss Lucy, kneeling on the floor of the cellar to measure more feed, said without looking up:—

"You know, since mother died we ain't never done anything for holidays. No—we can't seem to want to think about Thanksgiving or Christmas or like that."

They all turned their grave lined faces toward us.

"We want to let the holidays just slip by without noticin'," Miss Viny told us. "Seems like it hurts less that way."

Libbie Liberty smiled wanly.

"Don't you know," she said, "when you hold your hand still in hot water, you don't feel how hot the water really is? But when you move around in it some, it begins to burn you. Well, when we let Thanksgiving an' Christmas alone, it ain't so bad. But when we start to move around in 'em—"

Her voice faltered and stopped.

"We miss mother terrible," Miss Lucy said simply.

Calliope put her blue mitten to her mouth, but her eyes she might not hide, and they were soft with sympathy.

"I know—I know," she said. "I remember the first Christmas after my mother died—I ached like the toothache all over me, an' I couldn't bear to open my presents. Nor the next year I couldn't either—I couldn't open my presents with any heart. But—" Calliope hesitated, "that second year," she said, "I found somethin' I could do. I saw I could fix up little things for other folks an' take some comfort in it. Like mother would of."

She was silent for a moment, looking thoughtfully at the three lonely figures in the dark cellar of their house.

"Your mother," she said abruptly, "stuffed the turkey for a year ago the last harvest home."

"Yes," they said.

"Look here," said Calliope; "if I can get some poor folks together,—or even *one* poor folk, or hungry,—will you three come to my house an' stuff the turkey? The way—I can't help thinkin' the way your mother would of, if she'd been here. An' then," Calliope went on briskly, "could you bring some fresh eggs an' make a pan o' custard over to my house? An' mebbe one o' you'd stir up a sunshine cake. You must know how to make your mother's sunshine cake?"

There was another silence in the cellar when Calliope had done, and for a minute I wondered if, after all, she had not failed, and if the bleeding of the three hearts might be so stanched. It was not self-reliant Libbie Liberty who spoke first; it was gentle Miss Lucy.

"I guess," she said, "I could, if we all do it. I know mother would of."

"Yes," Miss Viny nodded, "mother would of."

Libbie Liberty stood for a moment with compressed lips.

"It seems like not payin' respect to mother," she began; and then shook her head. "It ain't that," she said; "it's only missin' her when we begin to step around the kitchen, bakin' up for a holiday."

"I know—I know," Calliope said again. "That's why I said for you to come over in my kitchen. You come over there an' stir up the sunshine cake, too, an' bake it in my oven, so's we can hev it et hot. Will you do that?"

And after a little time they consented. If Calliope found any sick or poor, they would do that.

"We ain't gettin' many i-dees for guests," Calliope said, as we reached the street, "but we're gettin' helpers, anyway. An' some dinner, too."

Then we went to the house of Mis' Holcomb-that-was-Mame-Bliss—called so, of course, to distinguish her from the "Other" Holcombs.

"Don't you be shocked at her," Calliope warned me, as we closed Mis' Holcomb's gate behind us, "she's dreadful diff'r'nt an' bitter since Abigail was married last month. She's got hold o' some kind of a Persian book, in a decorated cover, from the City; an' now she says your soul is like when you look in a lookin'-glass—that there ain't really nothin' there. An' that the world's some wind an' the rest water, an' they ain't no God only your own breath—oh, poor Mis' Holcomb!" said Calliope. "I guess she ain't rill balanced. But we ought to go to see her. We always consult Mis' Holcomb about everything."

Poor Mis' Holcomb-that-was-Mame-Bliss! I can see her now in her comfortable dining room, where she sat cleaning her old silver, her thin, veined hands as fragile as her grandmother's spoons.

"Of course, you don't know," she said, when Calliope had unfolded her plans, "how useless it all seems to me. What's the use—I keep sayin' to myself now'-days; what's the use? You put so much pains on somethin', an' then it goes off an' leaves you. Mebbe it dies, an' everything's all wasted. There ain't anything to tie to. It's like lookin' in a glass all the while. It's seemin', it ain't bein'. We ain't certain o' nothin' but our breath, an' when that goes, what hev you got? What's the use, o' plannin' Thanksgivin' for anybody?"

"Well, if you're hungry, it's kind o' nice to get fed up," said Calliope, crisply. "Don't you know a soul that's hungry, Mame Bliss?"

She shook her head.

"No," she said, "I don't. Nor nobody sick in body."

"Nobody sick in body," Calliope repeated absently.

"Soul-sick an' soul-hungry you can't feed up," Mis' Holcomb added.

"I donno," said Calliope thoughtfully, "I donno but you can."

"No," Mis' Holcomb went on; "your soul's like yourself in the glass: they ain't anything there."

"I donno," Calliope said again; "some mornin's when I wake up with the sun shinin' in, I can feel my soul in me just as plain as plain."

Mis' Holcomb sighed.

"Life looks dreadful footless to me," she said.

"Well," said Calliope, "sometimes life *is* some like hearin' fire-crackers go off when you don't feel up to shootin' 'em yourself. When I'm like that, I always think if I'd go out an' buy a bunch or two, an' get somebody to give me a match, I could see more sense to things. Look here, Mame Bliss; if I get hold o' any folks to give the dinner for, will you help me some?"

"Yes," Mis' Holcomb assented half-heartedly, "I'll help you. I ain't nobody much in family, now Abigail's done what she has. They's only Eppleby, an' he won't be home Thanskg'vin this year. So I ain't nothin' else to do."

"That's the i-dee," said Calliope heartily; "if everything's foolish, it's just as foolish doin' nothin' as doin' somethin'. Will you bring over a kettleful o' boiled potatoes to my house Thanksgivin' noon? An' mash 'em an' whip 'em in my kitchen? I'll hev the milk to put in. You—you don't cook as much as some, do you, Mame?"

Did Calliope ask her that purposely? I am almost sure that she did. Mis' Holcomb's neck stiffened a little.

"I guess I can cook a thing or two beside mash' potatoes," she said, and thought for a minute. "How'd you like a pan o' 'scalloped oysters an' some baked macaroni with plenty o' cheese?" she demanded.

"Sounds like it'd go down awful easy," admitted Calliope, smiling. "It's just what we need to carry the dinner off full sail," she added earnestly.

"Well, I ain't nothin' else to do an' I'll make 'em," Mis' Holcomb promised. "Only it beats me who you can find to do for. If you don't get anybody, let me know before I order the oysters."

Calliope stood up, her little wrinkled face aglow; and I wondered at her confidence.

"You just go ahead an' order your oysters," she said. "That dinner's goin' to come off Thanksgivin' noon at twelve o'clock. An' you be there to help feed the hungry, Mame."

When we were on the street again, Calliope looked at me with her way of shy eagerness.

"Could you hev the dinner up to your house," she asked me, "if I do every bit o' the work?"

"Why, Calliope," I said, amazed at her persistence, "have it there, of course. But you haven't any guests yet."

She nodded at me through the falling flakes.

"You say you ain't got much to be thankful for," she said, "so I thought mebbe you'd put in the time that way. Don't you worry about folks to eat the dinner. I'll tell Mis' Holcomb an' the others to come to your house—an' I'll get the food an' the folks. Don't you worry! An' I'll bring my watermelon pickles an' a bowl o' cream for Mis' Holcomb's potatoes, an' I'll furnish the turkey—a big one. The rest of us'll get the dinner in your kitchen Thanksgivin' mornin'. My!" she said, "seems though life's smoothin' out fer me a'ready. Goodby—it's 'most noon."

She hurried up Daphne Street in the snow, and I turned toward my lonely house. But I remember that I was planning how I would make my table pretty, and how I would add a delicacy or two from the City for this strange holiday feast. And I found myself hurrying to look over certain long-disused linen and silver, and to see whether my Cloth-o'-Gold rose might be counted on to bloom by Thursday noon.

II

"We'll set the table for seven folks," said Calliope, at my house on Thanksgiving morning.

"Seven!" I echoed. "But where in the world did you ever find seven, Calliope?"

"I found 'em," she answered. "I knew I could find hungry folks to do for if I tried, an' I found 'em. You'll see. I sha'n't say another word. They'll be here by twelve sharp. Did the turkey come?"

Yes, the turkey had come, and almost as she spoke the dear Liberty sisters arrived to dress and stuff it, and to make ready the pan of custard, and to "stir up" the sunshine cake. I could guess how the pleasant bustle in my kitchen would hurt them by its holiday air, and I carried them off to see my Cloth-o'-Gold rose which had opened in the night, to the very crimson heart of it. And I told them of the seven guests whom, after all, Calliope had actually contrived to marshal to her dinner. And in the midst of our almost gay speculation on this, they went at their share of the task.

The three moved about their office gravely at first, Libbie Liberty keeping her back to us as she worked, Miss Viny scrupulously intent on the delicate clatter of the egg-beater, Miss Lucy with eyes downcast on the sage she rolled. I noted how Calliope made little excuses to pass near each of them, with now a touch of the hand and now a pat on a shoulder, and all the while she talked briskly of ways and means and recipes, and should there be onions in the dressing or

should there not be? We took a vote on this and were about to chop
the onions in when Mis' Holcomb's little maid arrived at my kitchen
door with a bowl of oysters which Mis' Holcomb had had left from
the 'scallop, an' wouldn't we like 'em in the stuffin'? Roast turkey
stuffed with oysters! I saw Libbie Liberty's eyes brighten so delight-
edly that I brought out a jar of seedless raisins and another of preserved cherries to add to the custard, and then a bag of sweet almonds to be blanched and split for the cake o' sunshine. Surely, one
of us said, the seven guests could be preparing for their Thanksgiving dinner with no more zest than we were putting into that dinner
for their sakes. "Seven guests!" we said over and again. "Calliope,
how did you do it! When everybody says there's nobody in Friendship that's either sick or poor?"

"Nobody sick, nobody poor!" Calliope exclaimed, piling a dish
with watermelon pickles. "Land, you might think that was the town
motto. Well, the town don't know everything. Don't you ask me so
many questions."

Before eleven o'clock Mis' Mayor Uppers tapped at my back door,
with two deep-dish cherry pies in a basket, and a row of her delicate,
feathery sponge cakes and a jar of pineapple and pie-plant preserves
"to chink in." She drew a deep breath and stood looking about the
kitchen.

"Throw off your things an' help, Mis' Uppers," Calliope admonished her, one hand on the cellar door. "I'm just goin' down for some
sweet potatoes Mis' Holcomb sent over this morning, an' you might
get 'em ready, if you will. We ain't goin' to let you off now, spite of
what you've done for us."

So Mis' Mayor Uppers hung up her shawl and washed the sweet
potatoes. And my kitchen was fragrant with spices and flavourings
and an odorous oven, and there was no end of savoury business to
be at. I found myself glad of the interest of these others in the day
and glad of the stirring in my lonely house. Even if their bustle could
not lessen my own loneliness, it was pleasant, I said to myself, to see
them quicken with interest; and the whole affair entertained my infinite leisure. After all, I was not required to be thankful. I merely
loaned my house, cosey in its glittering drifts of turkey feathers, and
the day was no more and no less to me than before, though I own
that I did feel more than an amused interest in Calliope's guests.
Whom, in Friendship, had she found "to do for," I detected myself
speculating with real interest as in the dining room, with one and

another to help me, I made ready my table. My prettiest dishes and silver, the Cloth-o'-Gold rose, and my yellow-shaded candles made little auxiliary welcomes. Whoever Calliope's guests were, we would do them honour and give them the best we had. And in the midst of all came from the City the box with my gift of hothouse fruit and a rosebud for every plate. "Calliope!" I cried, as I went back to the kitchen, "Calliope, it's nearly twelve now. Tell us who the guests are, or we won't finish dinner!"

Calliope laughed and shook her head and opened the door for Mis' Holcomb-that-was-Mame-Bliss, who entered, followed by her little maid, both laden with good things.

"I prepared for seven," Mis' Holcomb said. "That was the word you sent me—but where you got your seven sick an' poor in Friendship beats me. I'll stay an' help for a while—but to me it all seems like so much monkey work."

We worked with a will that last half-hour, and the spirit of the kitchen came upon them all. I watched them, amused and pleased at Mis' Mayor Uppers's flushed anxiety over the sweet potatoes, at Libbie Liberty furiously basting the turkey, and at Miss Lucy exclaiming with delight as she unwrapped the rosebuds from their moss. But I think that Mis' Holcomb pleased me most, for with the utensils of housewifery in her hands she seemed utterly to have forgotten that there is no use in anything at all. This was not wonderful in the presence of such a feathery cream of mashed potatoes and such aromatic coffee as she made. *There* was something to tie to. Those were real, at any rate, and beyond all seeming.

Just before twelve Calliope caught off her apron and pulled down her sleeves.

"Now," she said, "I'm going to welcome the guests. I can—can't I?" she begged me. "Everything's all ready but putting on. I won't need to come out here again; when I ring the bell on the sideboard, dish it up an' bring it in, all together—turkey ahead an' vegetables followin'. Mis' Holcomb, you help 'em, won't you? An' then you can leave if you want. Talk about an old-fashion' Thanksgivin'. My!"

"Who *has* she got?" Libbie Liberty burst out, basting the turkey. "I declare, I'm nervous as a witch, I'm so curious!"

And then the clock struck twelve, and a minute after we heard Calliope tinkle a silvery summons on the call-bell.

I remember that it was Mis' Holcomb herself—to whom nothing mattered—who rather lost her head as we served our feast, and who

was about putting in dishes both her oysters and her macaroni instead of carrying in the fair, brown, smoking bake pans. But at last
we were ready—Mis' Holcomb at our head with the turkey, the
others following with both hands filled, and I with the coffee-pot. As
they gave the signal to start, something—it may have been the mystery before us, or the good things about us, or the mere look of the
Thanksgiving snow on the window-sills—seemed to catch at the
hearts of them all, and they laughed a little, almost joyously, those
five for whom joy had seemed done, and I found myself laughing too.

So we six filed into the dining room to serve whomever Calliope
had found "to do for." I wonder that I had not guessed before. There
stood Calliope at the foot of the table, with its lighted candles and its
Cloth-o'-Gold rose, and the other six chairs were quite vacant.

"Sit down!" Calliope cried to us, with tears and laughter in her
voice. "Sit down, all six of you. Don't you see? Didn't you know? Ain't
we soul-sick an' soul-hungry, all of us? An' I tell you, this is goin' to
do our souls good—an' our stomachs too!"

Nobody dropped anything, even in the flood of our amazement.
We managed to get our savoury burden on the table, and some way
we found ourselves in the chairs—I at the head of my table where
Calliope led me. And we all talked at once, exclaiming and question-
ing, with sudden thanskgiving in our hearts that in the world such
things may be.

"I was hungry an' sick," Calliope was telling, "for an old-fashion'
Thanksgivin'—or anything that'd smooth life out some. But I says to
myself, 'It looks like God had afflicted us by not givin' us anybody to
do for.' An' then I started out to find some poor an' some sick—an'
each one o' you knows what I found. An' I ask' myself before I got
home that day, 'Why not them an' me?' There's lots o' kinds o' things
to do on Thanksgivin' Day. Are you ever goin' to forgive me?"

I think that we all answered at once. But what we all meant was
what Mis' Holcomb-that-was-Mame-Bliss said, as she sat flushed and
smiling behind the coffee-cups:—

"I declare, I feel something like I ain't felt since I don't know when!"

And Calliope nodded at her.

"I guess that's your soul, Mame Bliss," she said. "You can always
feel it if you go to work an' act as if you got one. I'll take my coffee
clear."

And as we laughed, and as I looked down my table at my guests, I felt with a wonder that was like belief. How my heart leaped up within me and how it glowed! And I knew a mist of tears in my eyes, and something like happiness possessed me.

And I understood, with infinite thanksgiving, that, if I would have it so, my little house need never be wholly lonely any more.

SUI SIN FAR

The Heart's Desire

(1912)

 ***T**HE Heart's Desire"* appears among
the "Tales of Chinese Children" in the second half of Sui Sin Far's collection of stories *Mrs. Spring Fragrance* (1912).[1] All the stories in this collection had previously appeared in such major magazines as *Independent,
Hampton's, Century, New York Evening Post, Good Housekeeping, Over-
land, Out West, New England, Ladies' Home Journal, Gentlewoman, Short
Stories,* and *Sunset.* Sui Sin Far (meaning narcissus or, literally, water fragrant flower) was the pseudonym of Edith Maud Eaton (1865–1914),
the first person of Chinese ancestry in American letters to make the
Chinese-American perspective central to her writing. She lived and
worked during the period of the most virulent sinophobia in America:
when Chinese were lynched, driven en masse out of town, robbed, and
even murdered without legal recourse; and when the Chinese Exclusion
Act was first passed (1882) and twice renewed (1892 and 1902). (It was
repealed only in 1943.) Edith Eaton's assumption of a Chinese pseudonym—an assertion of Chinese pride at a time when other Chinese-
Americans and Chinese-Eurasians (including her sister Winnifred Eaton)
were passing for white, Japanese, or Mexican—was an extraordinary act
of defiance and courage. In numerous articles and stories she fought
against the prevailing prejudicial views of the Chinese as heathen, un-
assimilable, filthy, and treacherous; she showed them to be human, dignified, noble, loving, and long-suffering. She strove for understanding
and acceptance among different races and classes.

"The Heart's Desire" is a story of a special kind of love. It is typical of
other Sui Sin Far stories in taking as the norm the Chinese perspective
and Chinese cultural trappings (Golden Lily feet, a euphemism for

bound feet; lotus flowers; marble bridges; silks and peacock fans). But it is atypical in form as it is not a realistic short story but, rather, an exquisite, exotic parable with a fairy-tale quality and a crystal-clear moral. Li Chung O'Yam is a type rather than a person; at the beginning, she embodies the highest ideal in physical form and material well-being that Chinese society could envision for its girls and yet, or because of this, she is unhappy. Her deepest heart's desire cannot be satisfied by the circumstances of her birth, by material finery, by a father, a mother, or a brother, but only by a friendship of her choosing with another girl. Their difference in class and wealth is insignificant; what matters is that they are soul mates. The story asserts not only the centrality of friendships between women across class lines but also the sacredness of individual choice.

In her own life Edith Eaton certainly valued and exercised her right to make her own choices, but as to her friendships with women, we have very little specific information. The only sources I have uncovered are limited: her own seven-and-a-half-page essay "Leaves from the Mental Portfolio of an Eurasian";[2] her sister Winnifred's autobiography, *Me;*[3] Winnifred's biography of another sister, *Marion, the Story of an Artist's Model;*[4] correspondence and conversations with Winnifred's grandson;[5] and an article in a Seattle publication.[6]

Edith was the eldest daughter of fourteen children born to a Chinese woman, Grace Trefusus (1847–1922), and her English painter husband, Edward Eaton (1839–1915). According to family legend, Grace Trefusus, also known in the family as Lotus Blossom, had been stolen from her home by a band of acrobats, then rescued and adopted by an English missionary couple in China. As Grace is described in "Leaves," she was "English bred with English ways and manner of dress" and had been "brought up in a Presbyterian college." In Shanghai, at sixteen, Grace was married, and shortly thereafter the young couple went to England. She was still in her early twenties when she and Edward immigrated to America, but she was already the mother of six. Edith was born in England, ten months after her brother Edward Charles. She came to America at age six, first living in Hudson City, New York, and later Montreal.

"Leaves" is full of the suffering Edith endured due to her mother's ethnicity. In one episode, she and her older brother return home, scratched and torn after a battle they had fought against children who had taunted them with "Chinky, chinky Chinaman, yellow-face, pig-tail, rat-eater." Her feisty mother's reaction to their stated victory is a smile of satisfaction while their peace-loving father pretends to be more interested in the newspaper. Happier memories of Eaton family life were recorded in *Marion,* giving us a picture of an extremely poor but lively, close-knit family, for whom painting and poetry were everyday staples:

Our family had always loved poetry. Mama used to read Tennyson's "Idylls of the King," and we knew all of the characters and even played them as children. Moreover, papa and Ada [Edith] and Charles [Edward] and even Nora [Winnifred] could all write poetry. Ada [Edith] made up poems about every little incident in our lives. . . . She . . . wrote a poem about our Panama hen who died. She said the wicked cock hen, a hen we had that could crow like a cock, had killed her. How we laughed over that poem.

Edith was further described in *Marion* as "the most unselfish of girls," who "used to bring everything she earned to mama. She fretted all the time about the family and especially mama, to whom . . . she was almost fanatically loyal." Edith expresses her sensitivity and empathy for her mother in this passage: "My mother's screams of agony when a baby is born almost drive me wild, and long after her pangs have subsided I feel them in my own body. Sometimes it is a week before I can get to sleep after such an experience." Edith took her position as eldest daughter seriously and used to wait up at nights worrying when siblings, even her older brother, went out. After leaving home to work at various jobs from typist to journalist, from Jamaica, West Indies, to San Francisco and Seattle, Edith continuously and dutifully sent home money for her parents and the younger children.

In Seattle, where she lived for a decade, Edith Eaton seems to have had several close friendships with women. She is enthusiastic in her descriptions of them—"women who braced and enlightened me, women to whom the things of the mind and the heart appealed; women who were individuals, not merely the daughters of their parents, the wives of their husbands; women who taught me that nationality was no bar to friendship with those whose friendship was worthwhile"—but is not specific about them as individuals.

Among her own sisters, Grace, in 1912, became the first Chinese-American woman admitted to the Chicago Bar and distinguished herself by fighting for tenants' and women's rights. Winnifred, calling herself Onoto Watanna and claiming Nagasaki as her birthplace, became a highly successful writer of "Japanese" romances, publishing hundreds of short stories and nearly two dozen novels, many of which went into multiple printings and foreign translations. One, *A Japanese Nightingale*, became a Broadway play and competed in 1903 with David Belasco's production of *Madame Butterfly*.

Although eclipsed by Winnifred's productivity and popularity, Edith wrote with sisterly loyalty of Chinese-Eurasians who passed as Japanese-Eurasians: "The unfortunate Chinese Eurasians. Are not those who compel them to thus cringe more to be blamed than they?" Using the parlance of the world, Edith called herself a "very serious and sober-minded spinster," but she was proud of her self-sufficiency. She died in Montreal in April 1914, at age forty-nine. In honor of her efforts on their behalf, the Chinese community placed a special stone on her tomb with an inscription that, freely translated, means "The righteous one forgets not China."[7]

AMY LING

She was dainty, slender, and of waxen pallor. Her eyes were long and drooping, her eyebrows finely arched. She had the tiniest Golden Lily feet and the glossiest black hair. Her name was Li Chung O'Yam, and she lived in a sad, beautiful old palace surrounded by a sad, beautiful old garden, situated on a charming island in the middle of a lake. This lake was spanned by marble bridges, entwined with green creepers, reaching to the mainland. No boats were ever seen on its waters but the pink lotus lily floated thereon and swans of marvellous whiteness.

Li Chung O'Yam wore priceless silks and radiant jewels. The rarest flowers bloomed for her alone. Her food and drink were of the finest flavors and served in the purest gold and silver plates and goblets. The sweetest music lulled her to sleep.

Yet Li Chung O'Yam was not happy. In the midst of the grandeur of her enchanted palace, she sighed for she knew not what.

"She is weary of being alone," said one of the attendants. And he who ruled all within the palace save Li Chung O'Yam, said: "Bring her a father!"

A portly old mandarin was brought to O'Yam. She made humble obeisance, and her august father inquired ceremoniously as to the state of her health, but she sighed and was still weary.

"We have made a mistake; it is a mother she needs," said they.

A comely matron, robed in rich silks and waving a beautiful peacock feather fan, was presented to O'Yam as her mother. The lady delivered herself of much good advice and wise instruction as to deportment and speech, but O'Yam turned herself on her silken cushions and wished to say goodbye to her mother.

Then they led O'Yam into a courtyard which was profusely illuminated with brilliant lanterns and flaring torches. There were a number of little boys of about her own age dancing on stilts. One little fellow, dressed all in scarlet and flourishing a small sword, was pointed out to her as her brother. O'Yam was amused for a few moments, but in a little while she was tired of the noise and confusion.

In despair, they who lived but to please her consulted amongst themselves. O'Yam, overhearing them, said: "Trouble not your minds. I will find my own heart's ease."

Then she called for her carrier dove, and had an attendant bind under its wing a note which she had written. The dove went forth and flew with the note to where a little girl named Ku Yum, with a face as round as a harvest moon, and a mouth like a red vine leaf, was hugging a cat to keep her warm and sucking her finger to prevent her from being hungry. To this little girl the dove delivered O'Yam's message, then returned to its mistress.

"Bring me my dolls and my cats, and attire me in my brightest and best," cried O'Yam.

When Ku Yum came slowly over one of the marble bridges towards the palace wherein dwelt Li Chung O'Yam, she wore a blue cotton blouse, carried a peg doll in one hand and her cat in another. O'Yam ran to greet her and brought her into the castle hall. Ku Yum looked at O'Yam, at her radiant apparel, at her cats and her dolls.

"Ah!" she exclaimed. "How beautifully you are robed! In the same colors as I. And behold, your dolls and your cats, are they not much like mine?"

"Indeed they are," replied O'Yam, lifting carefully the peg doll and patting the rough fur of Ku Yum's cat.

Then she called her people together and said to them:

"Behold, I have found my heart's desire—a little sister."

And forever after O'Yam and Ku Yum lived happily together in a glad, beautiful old palace, surrounded by a glad, beautiful old garden, on a charming little island in the middle of a lake.

ANZIA YEZIERSKA

A Bed for the Night

(1923)

$\mathcal{A}$LTHOUGH two and a half million Jews came to America between 1882 and 1924, Anzia Yezierska was the only woman of this generation of Jewish immigrants who wrote a body of fiction in the acquired language of English. Briefly famous in the 1920s, Yezierska felt that she had a messianic calling to speak to America for all of New York's Lower East Side. Yet the creative process was difficult for her. As she herself remarked, "I burn up in this all-consuming desire my family, my friends, my loves, my clothes, my food, my very life."

As an immigrant Jewish woman from a working-class background, Yezierska was quadruply marginal to the literary and cultural traditions of mainstream American society. How did she achieve what other women of her generation of Jewish immigrants could not? By choosing a single life-style—an unusual act in her cultural context—she had a "room of her own," as Virginia Woolf put it, in which to write. She received support from her older sisters and women teachers and writers. Identification with her mother provided material; identification with her father gave her a sense of mission. A brief romantic relationship with philosopher and educator John Dewey was a source of inspiration.

Her writing is noteworthy for its sustained focus on the problems of immigrant women, adept use of Yiddish-English dialect, and emotionally charged style. This style, criticized by reviewers who looked for restraint and subtlety in women's writing, was actually derived from the Yiddish oral tradition, with its female village storytellers, and suited the verbal vehemence of the women about whom she wrote. Critics also said that her fiction was extremely autobiographical (perhaps because her protagonists or narrators were almost always immigrant women), but examination reveals it to be true to the emotions rather than the facts of her life. Yezierska herself was more educated and well read than her ghetto characters, to mention one significant difference. In her fiction, she drew from the experiences of other immigrants as well as her own.

Anzia Yezierska was born about 1881 in the Russian-Polish village of Plinsk. One of ten children of Pearl and Baruch Yeziersky, she arrived in America with her family at about the age of fifteen. Yezierska worked in sweatshops, laundries, and as a maid while studying English in night school. A settlement worker helped her to get a scholarship to Columbia College's domestic science teacher training program; to enter, Yezierska fabricated a high school diploma.

In 1905, Yezierska started teaching domestic science, although she disliked the subject intensely. While attending Rand School classes in social theory, she met radical feminist Henrietta Rodman, who encouraged Yezierska in her writing. At this point, she started using her European name of Anzia Yezierska rather than Hattie Mayer, the name she was given at Ellis Island.

In 1910, Yezierska married lawyer Jacob Gordon; the marriage was annulled shortly because Yezierska wanted a spiritual, not a physical, union. A year later, she married (by religious ceremony only) their mutual friend, teacher Arnold Levitas. She gave birth to a daughter, Louise, in 1912. After several difficult years of marriage, Yezierska and Levitas finally separated; Louise, now four, was cared for by Levitas and his mother. Yezierska focused on her writing and visited Louise once a week.

Yezierska's first published story, "The Free Vacation House" (1915), describes an overworked immigrant mother's frustration with organized charity's attempts to help her. Yezierska based the story on her older sister Annie's experience with charities, but charged the story with pain and humiliation that her sister, who returned to the free vacation house, apparently did not feel.

In 1917, Yezierska barged into John Dewey's Columbia University office to enlist his aid in obtaining a permanent teaching certificate, which she had been denied. As proof of her abilities, she showed him her writing. From 1917 to 1918, she audited his seminars. Their brief and probably unconsummated romance ended after the summer of 1918. For Dewey, Yezierska was a window onto the Jewish ghetto and the inspiration for over twenty love poems. For Yezierska, Dewey represented mainstream America and the paternal approval she did not receive from own highly religious father. Dewey encouraged her and introduced her to editors; his influence outlasted their relationship.

For Yezierska, writing involved the Jewish male's scholarly ideal rather than the Jewish female's "enabling" one. Yezierska came to see her writing as a religious calling, requiring isolation and resembling her father's religious calling in importance. She reports writing in the mornings and evenings, the same times that he prayed.

In her most anthologized story, "The Fat of the Land," the main character, Hanneh Breineh, was based on her mother. It was chosen the best of *Best Short Stories of 1919.* In 1920, Houghton Mifflin published *Hungry Hearts,* a collection of short stories. After Hearst newspapers publicized this book, Goldwyn movie studios hired Yezierska to write screenplays. The short stories of *Hungry Hearts* and her first novel, *Salome of the Tenements,* became two movies, the prints and negatives of which have since irretrievably disintegrated. Yezierska felt that her creativity dried up in Hollywood. She returned to New York, where she was mostly reclusive, but sometimes had lunch with the Algonquin Hotel group of writers.

Despite fears about writing, Yezierska wrote more short stories (collected in *Children of Loneliness,* 1923) and three more novels. *Bread Givers* (1925), about her family, was the most polished; it was followed by *Arrogant Beggar* (1927), about public and private charity, and *All I Could Never Be* (1932), about her relationship with Dewey. This last one was written during Yezierska's University of Wisconsin Zona Gale Fellowship for writers in residence. Louise attended the university at the same time and helped her mother edit the book.

Yezierska's fictionalized autobiography, *Red Ribbon on a White Horse* (1950), describes her Hollywood and Works Progress Administration (WPA) Writers' Project experiences. It corrected inaccuracies in her Hollywood publicity and recalled Yezierska to the public. Throughout the fifties, she wrote *New York Times* book reviews and sometimes lectured. She developed her fictional voice of the old woman, speaker for the aged poor, at this time. Until 1966, Yezierska lived by herself in New York, but then moved near her daughter Louise, who hired transcribers for the writing Yezierska continued even when nearly blind. Anzia Yezierska died in a nursing home near Claremont, California, on November 21, 1970, at nearly ninety years of age.

Whether Yezierska was writing about young immigrant Jewish women, or the elderly, alienated urban poor, she expressed the feelings of characters marginal to the American mainstream. "A Bed for the Night," originally published in *Children of Loneliness,* emphasizes recurrent themes in Yezierska's writing: only the poor, those who have nothing to lose, actually help the poor; only that which is given from the heart is not demeaning to the receiver. Yezierska often writes about young women struggling to survive in a harsh urban environment. Ironically, although both women in this story are economic outcasts, the social conventions that have defined their status also divide them from each other.

Largely because of recent interest in women and ethnic writers, other works of Yezierska's have been reprinted in book form.[1] Two biographies[2] are also available.

SALLY ANN DRUCKER

A drizzling rain had begun to fall. I was wet and chilled to the bone. I had just left the free ward of a hospital where I had been taken when ill with the flu. It was good to be home again! Even tho what I called home were but the dim, narrow halls of a rooming-house. With a sigh of relief I dropped my suit-case in the vestibule.

As the door swung open, the landlady met me with: "Your room is taken. Your things are in the cellar."

"My room?" I stammered, white with fear. "Oh no—please Mrs. Pelz!"

"I got a chance to rent your room at such a good price, I couldn't afford to hold it."

"But you promised to keep it for me while I was away. And I paid you for it—"

"The landlord raised me my rent and I got to get it out from the roomers," she defended. "I got four hungry mouths to feed—"

"But maybe I would have paid you a little more," I pleaded, "if you had only told me. I have to go back to work to-day. How can I get another room at a moment's notice?"

"We all got to look out for ourselves. I am getting more than twice as much as you paid me from this new lodger," she finished triumphantly. "And no housekeeping privileges."

"You must give me time!" My voice rose into a shriek. "You can't put a girl out into the street at a moment's notice. There are laws in America—"

"There are no laws for roomers."

"*No law for roomers?*" All my weakness and helplessness rushed out of me in a fury of rebellion. "*No law for roomers?*"

"I could have put your things out in the street when your week was up. But being you were sick, I was kind enough to keep them in the cellar. But your room is taken." She said with finality. "I got to let my rooms to them as pay the most. I got to feed my own children first. I can't carry the whole world on my back."

I tried to speak. But no voice came to my lips. I felt struck with a club on the head. I could only stare at her. And I must have been staring for some time without seeing her for I had not noticed she had gone till I heard a voice from the upper stairs, "Are you still there?"

"Oh—yes—yes—I—I—am—going—going." I tried to rouse my stunned senses which seemed struck to the earth.

"There's no money in letting rooms to girls," my landlady continued, as she came down to open the door for me. "They're always cooking, or washing, or ironing and using out my gas. This new roomer I never hear nor see except in the morning when he goes to work and at night when he comes to sleep."

I staggered out in a bewildered daze. I leaned against the cold iron lamp-post. It seemed so kind, so warm. Even the chill, drizzling rain beating on my face was almost human. Slowly, my numbed brain began to recollect where I was. Where should I turn? To whom? I faced an endless maze of endless streets. All about me strangers— seas of jostling strangers. I was alone—shelterless!

All that I had suffered in rooming-houses, rushed over me. I had never really lived or breathed like a free, human being. My closed door assured me no privacy. I lived in constant dread of any moment being pounced upon by my landlady for daring to be alive. I dared not hang out my clothes on a line in the fresh air. I was forced to wash and dry them stealthily at night, over chairs and on my trunk. I was under the same restraint when I did my simple cooking altho I paid dearly for the gas I used.

This ceaseless strain of don't move here and don't step there, was far from my idea of home. But still it was shelter from the streets. I had become almost used to it. I had almost learned not to be crushed by it. Now, I was shut out—kicked out like a homeless dog.

All thoughts of reporting at my office left my mind. I walked and walked, driven by despair. Tears pressed in my throat, but my eyes were dry as sand.

I tried to struggle out of my depression. I looked through the furnished-room sections of the city. There were no cheap rooms to be had. The prices asked for the few left, were ten, twelve, and fifteen dollars a week.

I earn twenty-five dollars a week as a stenographer. I am compelled to dress neatly to hold down my job. And with clothes and food so high, how could I possibly pay more than one third of my salary for rent?

In my darkness I saw a light—a vision of the Settlement. As an immigrant I had joined one of the social clubs there and I remembered there was a residence somewhere in that building for the workers. Surely they would take me in till I had found a place where I could live.

"I'm in such trouble!" I stammered, as I entered the office of the head resident. "My landlady put me out because I couldn't pay the raise in rent."

"The housing problem is appalling," Miss Ward agreed, with her usual professional friendliness. "I wish I could let you stay with us, my child, but our place is only for social workers."

"Where should I go?" I struggled to keep back my tears. "I'm so terribly alone."

"Now—now, dear child," Miss Ward patted my shoulder encouragingly. "You mustn't give way like that. Of course I'll give you the addresses of mothers of our neighborhood."

One swift glance at the calm, well-fed face and I felt instantly that Miss Ward had never known the terror of homelessness.

"You know, dear, I want to help you all I can," smiled Miss Ward, trying to be kind, "and I'm always glad when my girls come to me."

"What was the use of my coming to you?" I was in no mood for her make-believe Settlement smile. "If you don't take me in, aren't you pushing me in the street—joining hands with my landlady?"

"Why—my dear!" The mask of smiling kindness dropped from Miss Ward's face. Her voice cooled. "Surely you will find a room in this long list of addresses I am giving you."

I went to a dozen places. It was the same everywhere. No rooms were to be had at the price I could afford.

Crushed again and again, the habit of hope still asserted itself. I suddenly remembered there was one person from whom I was almost sure of getting help—an American woman who had befriended me while still an immigrant in the factory. Her money had made it possible for me to take up the stenographic course. Full of renewed hope I sped along the streets. My buoyant faith ever expectant could think of one outcome only.

Mrs. Olney had just finished dictating to her secretary, when the maid ushered me into the luxurious library.

"How good it is to see you! What can I do for you?" The touch of Mrs. Olney's fine hand, the sound of her lovely voice was like the warming breath of sunshine to a frozen thing. A choking came in my throat. Tears blinded me.

"If it wasn't a case of life and death, I wouldn't have bothered you so early in the morning."

"What's the trouble, my child?" Mrs. Olney was all concern.

"I can't stand it any longer! Get me a place where I can live!" And I told her of my experiences with my landlady and my hopeless room-hunting.

"I have many young friends who are in just your plight," Mrs. Olney consoled, "And I'm sending them all to the Better Housing Bureau."

I felt as tho a powerful lamp went out suddenly within my soul. A sharp chill seized me. The chasm that divides those who have and those who have not yawned between us. The face I had loved and worshiped receded and grew dim under my searching gaze.

Here was a childless woman with a house full of rooms to herself. Here was a philanthropist who gave thousands of dollars to help the poor. And here I tried to tell her that I was driven out into the street—shelterless. And her answer to my aching need was, "The Better Housing Bureau."

Again I turned to the unfeeling glare of the streets. A terrible loneliness bled in my heart. Such tearing, grinding pain was dragging me to the earth! I could barely hold myself up on my feet. "Ach! Only for a room to rest!" And I staggered like a dizzy drunkard to the Better Housing Bureau.

At the waiting-room I paused in breathless admiration. The soft grays and blues of the walls and hangings, the deep-seated divans, the flowers scattered in effective profusion, soothed and rested me like silent music. Even the smoothly fitting gown of the housing specialist seemed almost part of the color scheme.

As I approached the mahogany desk, I felt shabby—uncomfortable in this flawless atmosphere, but I managed somehow to tell of my need. I had no sooner explained the kind of room I could afford than the lady requested the twenty-five cents registration fee.

"I want to see the room first," I demanded.

"All our applicants pay in advance."

"I have only a two dollar bill and I don't get my pay till Monday."

"Oh, that's all right. I'll change it," she offered obligingly. And she took my one remaining bill.

"Where were you born? What is your religion?"

"I came for a room and not to be inquisitioned," I retorted.

"We are compelled to keep statistics of all our applicants."

Resentfully, I gave her the desired information and with the addresses she had given me, I recommenced my search. At the end of another futile hour of room-hunting there was added to the twenty-five cents registration fee, an expense of fifteen cents for carfare. And I was still homeless.

I had been expecting to hear from my sister who had married a prosperous merchant and whom I hadn't seen for years. In my agitation, I had forgotten to ask for my mail and I went back to see about it. A telegram had come, stating that my sister was staying at the Astor and I was to meet her there for lunch.

I hastened to her. For, altho she was now rich and comfortable, I felt that after all she was my sister and she would help me out.

"How shabby you look!" She cast a disapproving glance at me from head to foot. "Couldn't you dress decently to meet me, when you knew I was staying at this fashionable hotel?"

I told her of my plight.

"Why not go to a hotel till you find a suitable room?" she blandly advised.

My laughter sounded unreal so loud it was, as I remembered her, "Before the French Revolution, when starving people came to the queen's palace clamoring for bread, the queen innocently exclaimed, 'Why don't they eat cake?'"

"How disagreeable you are! You think of no one but yourself. I've come here for a little change, to get away from my own troubles and here you come with your hatefulness.

I hadn't known the relief of laughter, but now that I was started I couldn't stop, no more than I could stop staring at her. I tried to associate this new being of silks and jewels with the woman who had worked side by side with me in the factory.

"How you act! I think you're crazy," she admonished and glanced at her wrist-watch. "I'm late for my appointment with the manicurist. I have to have my nails done after this dusty railway trip."

And I had been surprised at the insensate settlement worker, at my uncomprehending American friend who knew not the meaning of want. Yet here was my own sister, my own flesh and blood, reared in the same ghetto, nurtured in the same poverty, ground in the same sweat-shop treadmill, and because she had a few years of prosperity, because she ate well and dressed well and was secure, she was deaf to my cry.

Where I could hope for understanding, where I could turn for shelter, where I was to lay my head that very night, I knew not. But this much suddenly came to me, I was due to report for work that day. I was shut out on every side, but there in my office at least, awaited me the warmth and sunshine of an assured welcome. My employer would understand and let me take off the remainder of the day to continue my search.

I found him out and instead, awaiting me, was a pile of mail which he had left word I should attend to. The next hour was torture. My power of concentration had deserted me. I tapped the keys of my typewriter with my fingers, but my brain was torn with worry, my nerves ready to snap. The day was nearly spent. Night was coming on and I had no place to lay my head.

I was finishing the last of the letters when he came. After a friendly greeting, he turned to the letters. I dared not interrupt until the mail was signed.

"Girl! What's wrong? That's not like you!" He stared at me. "There are a dozen mistakes in each letter."

A blur. Everything seemed to twist and turn around me. Red and black spots blinded me. A clenched hand pounded his desk and I heard a voice, that seemed to come from me, screaming like a lunatic. "I have no home—no home—not even a bed for the night!"

Then all I remember is the man's kindly tone as he handed me a glass of water. "Are you feeling better?" he asked.

"My landlady put me out." I said between labored breaths. "Oh-h I'm so lonely! Not a place to lay my head!"

I saw him fumble for his pocketbook and look at me strangely. His burning gaze seemed to strip me naked—pierce me through and through from head to foot. Something hurt so deep I choked with shame. I seized my hat and coat and ran out.

It was getting dark when I reached the entrance of Central Park. Exhausted, I dropped to the nearest bench. I didn't even know I was crying.

"Are you lonely, little one?" A hand slipped around my waist and a dapper, young chap moved closer. "Are you lonely?" he repeated.

I let him talk. I knew he had nothing real to offer, but I was so tired, so ready to drop the burden of my weary body that I had no resistance in me. "There's no place for me," I thought to myself. "Everyone shuts me out. What difference what becomes of me? Who cares?"

My head dropped to his shoulder. And the cry broke from me, "I have no place to sleep in tonight."

"Sleep?" I could feel him draw in his breath and a bloodshot gleam leaped into his eyes. "You should worry. I'll take care of that."

He flashed a roll of bills tauntingly. "How about it kiddo? Can you change me a twenty-dollar bill?"

As his other hand reached for me, I wrenched loose from him as from the cloying touch of pitch. "I wish I were that kind! I wish I were your kind! But I'm not!"

His hands dropped from the touch of me as tho his flesh was scorched and I found I was alone.

I walked again. At the nearest telephone pay station I called up the women's hotels. None had a room left for less than two dollars. My remaining cash was forty cents short. The Better Housing Bureau had robbed me of my last hope of shelter.

I passed Fifth Avenue and Park Avenue mansions. Many were closed, standing empty. I began counting the windows, the rooms. Hundreds and hundreds of empty rooms, hundreds and hundreds of luxuriously furnished homes, and I homeless—shut-out. I felt I was abandoned by God and man and no one cared if I perished or went mad. I had a fresh sense of why the spirit of revolution was abroad in the land.

Blindly I retraced my steps to the park bench. I saw and felt nothing but a devouring sense of fear. It suddenly came over me that I was not living in a world of human beings, but in a jungle of savages who gorged themselves with food, gorged themselves with rooms, while I implored only a bed for the night. And I implored in vain.

I felt the chaos and destruction of the good and the beautiful within me and around me. The sight of people who lived in homes and ate three meals a day filled me with the fury of hate. The wrongs and injustices of the hungry and the homeless of all past ages burst from my soul like the smouldering lava of a blazing volcano. Earthquakes of rebellion raced through my body and brain. I fell prone against the bench and wept not tears, but blood.

"Move along! No loitering here!" The policeman's club tapped me on the shoulder. Then a woman stopped and bent over me.

I couldn't move. I couldn't lift my head.

"Tell your friend to cut out the sob-stuff," the officer continued, flourishing his club authoritatively. "On your way both of youse. Y'know better than to loaf around here, Mag."

The woman put her hand on mine in a friendly, little gesture of protection. "Leave her alone! Can't you see she's all in? I'll take care of her."

Her touch filled me with the warmth of shelter. I didn't know who or what she was but I trusted her.

"Poor kid!—What ails her? It's a rough world all alone."

There was no pity in her tone, but comprehension, fellowship. From childhood I'd had my friendships and many were dear to me. But this woman without a word, without a greeting, had sounded the depths of understanding that I never knew existed. Even as I looked up at her she lifted me from the bench and almost carried me through the arbor of trees to the park entrance. My own mother couldn't have been more gentle. For a moment it seemed to me as if the spirit of my dead mother had risen from her grave in the guise of this unknown friend.

Only once the silence between us was broken. "Down on your luck, kid?" Her grip tightened on my arm. "I've been there myself. I know all about it."

She knew so well, what need had she of answer? The refrain came back to me: "Only themselves understand themselves and the likes of themselves, as souls only understand souls."

In a darkened side street we paused in front of a brownstone house with shutters drawn.

"Here we are! Now for some grub! I'll bet a nickel you ain't ate all day." She vaulted the rickety stairs two at a time and led the way into her little room. With a gay assertiveness she planted me into her one comfortable chair attempting no apology for her poverty—a poverty that winked from every corner and could not be concealed. Flinging off her street clothes she donned a crimson kimona and rummaged through the soap box in which her cooking things were kept. She wrung her hands with despair as if she suffered because she couldn't change herself into food.

Ah! The magic of love! It was only tea and toast and an outer crust of cheese she offered—but she offered it with the bounty of a princess. Only the kind look in her face and the smell of the steaming tray as she handed it to me—and I was filled before I touched the food to my lips. Somehow this woman who had so little had fed me as people with stuffed larders never could.

Under the spell of a hospitality so real that it hurt as divine, beautiful things hurt, I felt ashamed of my hysterical worries. I looked up at her and marveled. She was so full of God-like grace—and so unconscious of it!

Not until she had tucked the covers warmly around me did I realize that I was occupying the only couch she had.

"But where will you sleep?" I questioned.

A funny little laugh broke from her. "I should worry where I sleep."

"It's so snug and comfy," I yawned, my eyes heavy with fatigue. "It's good to take from you—"

"Take? Aw, dry up kid! You ain't taking nothing," she protested, embarassed. "Tear off some sleep and forget it."

"I'll get close to the wall, and make room for you," I murmured as I dropped off to sleep.

When I woke up I found, to my surprise, the woman was sleeping in a chair with a shawl wrapped around her like a huge statue. The half of the bed which I had left for her had remained untouched.

"You were sleeping so sound, I didn't want to wake you," she said as she hurried to prepare the breakfast.

I rose refreshed, restored—sane. It was more than gratitude that rushed out of my heart to her. I felt I belonged to some one, I had found home at last.

As I was ready to leave for work, I turned to her. "I am coming back tonight," I said.

She fell back of a sudden as if I had struck her. From the quick pain that shone in her face, I knew I had hurt something deep within her. Her eyes met mine in a fixed gaze but she did not see me, but stared through me into the vacancy of space. She seemed to have forgotten my presence and when she spoke her voice was like that of one in a trance. "You don't know what you're asking. I—ain't—no—good."

"You no good? God from the world! Where would I have been without you? Even my own sister shut me out—Of them all, you alone opened the door and spread for me all you had."

"I ain't so stuck on myself as the *good* people, altho I was as good as any of them at the start. But the first time I got into trouble, instead of helping me, they gave me the marble stare and the frozen heart and drove me to the bad."

I looked closely at her, at the dyed hair, the roughed lips, the defiant look of the woman driven by the Pharisees from the steps of the temple. Then I saw beneath. It was as tho her body dropped away from her and there stood revealed, her soul—the sorrows that gave her understanding—the shame and the heart-break that she turned into love.

"What is good or bad?" I challenged. "All I know is that I was hungry and you fed me. Shelterless and you sheltered me. Broken in spirit and you made me whole—"

"That stuff's all right, but you're better off out of here—"

I started toward her in mute protest.

"Don't touch me," she cried. "Can't you see—the smut all over me? Ain't it in my face?"

Her voice broke. And like one possessed of sudden fury, she seized me by the shoulder and shoved me out.

As the door slammed, I heard sobbing—loosened torrents of woe. I sank to my knees. A light not of this earth poured through the door that had shut on me. A holiness enveloped me.

This woman had changed the world for me. I could love the people I had hated yesterday. There was that something new in me, a light that the dingiest rooming house could not dim, nor all the tyranny of the landlady shut out.

Vague, half-remembered words flashed before me in letters of fire. "Despised and rejected of men"—a woman of sorrows and acquainted with grief.

AGNES REPPLIER

Sin

(1938)

*A*GNES Repplier's "Sin," a complex story of friendship, independence, and the gender gap, moves from a natural childhood happiness through psychological anguish to a spiritual joy likened to that of "the blessed saints in Paradise." Some of its intensity emerges from its autobiographical nature, some from its setting—a context all but erased from the current American scene. Catholic boarding schools for girls operated by communities of nuns of European origin in nineteenth- and early twentieth-century America created an atmosphere that gave rise to great friendships and great sins. The nuns themselves, products of a patriarchal religious tradition that allows literal-minded people to use divine authority for their own ends, practiced what they had been taught, sometimes turning religious discipline into psychological tyranny.

Fortunately for Repplier and for the protagonist of her story, the Sisters (then called Madames) of the Sacred Heart, who operated Eden Hall at Torresdale, Pennsylvania, the setting for "Sin," were well-educated women. Although school regulations—such as the superior's reading all incoming and outgoing correspondence—were patterned on conventual discipline, the Madames included women of wisdom and humor who knew when to punish, when to blink at youthful capers, and, as in the case of Madame Bouron, when to honor a commitment more mature than its maker's years.

Like her protagonist, Repplier delighted in her first school experience, which she recounts in the amusing *In Our Convent Days* (1905). Born in Philadelphia, April 1, 1855, of German Catholic lineage, Repplier grew up in a highly disciplined home. Her father, John George Repplier, engaged in a coal mining and processing business, paid little attention to his family. The care and education of the children fell to his second wife, Agnes's mother, Agnes Mathias Repplier, who did not relish the responsibility. Young Agnes, unable to compete successfully with either her intelligent and beautiful elder sister, Mary, or her clever and handsome younger brother, Louis, for her mother's attention, developed a rebellious streak that persisted throughout her youth.

When she learned to read—an early ordeal, as was learning to tell time—she was enrolled in Eden Hall. Compared to her disciplined home, the school seemed to Repplier a "libertine's Heaven." "Little girls brimming over with a superfluity of energy would absorb my simplified emotions. To some of them my heart would go out in quick recognition of companionship. A few of them were destined . . . to be my friends for life. . . . If ever a ten-year-old was fitted for a communal life," she wrote in *Eight Decades* (1937), "I was that happy child."[1] The dearest of those friends was Elizabeth Robins, later Pennell, art critic and historian. Another was Lilly Milton of "Sin."

Soon after the incident described in "Sin" Repplier was dismissed from the school, probably for repeated infractions of the rules. Subsequently she attended a school conducted by Agnes Irwin, later the first dean of Radcliffe College. Although Repplier idolized Irwin, she could not resist testing their friendship. Openly refusing an assignment, she once again found herself dismissed.

Undaunted, Repplier set out to educate herself. In addition to reading steadily, she also spent time writing. When her father lost the family fortune, Repplier began to send out the stories she had written, eventually placing every one. At the age of twenty she met Father Isaac Hecker, friend of Henry David Thoreau and the Alcott family, founder of the Paulist order, and editor of the *Catholic World*. Recognizing Repplier's limited knowledge of life and her extensive knowledge of literature, he advised her to turn to the essay. Repplier's incisive mind and sharp wit soon made her a frequent contributor to the *Catholic World*, the *Atlantic Monthly* (edited at that time by Thomas Bailey Aldrich, who became her friend and literary mentor), *Lippincott's*, the *Nation*, and other journals. In just over half a century she wrote ninety essays for the *Atlantic Monthly* alone, collecting many of them and others in more than twenty volumes. "Sin" appeared in the June 1938 issue.

Writing, lecturing, and international travel became Repplier's way of life. Concurrently, she developed numerous friendships and associations of varied intensity. Repplier considered her mother a remarkable woman and influence. "My Mother," she said, "was the first woman I knew who used her own mind."[2] Repplier's sister Mary, who became a respected teacher, was in later years a trusted friend, as was Cornelia Frothingham.

Distinguished writers whom Repplier knew included Mary E. Wilkins Freeman, Julia Ward Howe, Henry James, Sarah Orne Jewett, Edith Wharton, and Walt Whitman. Close male friends were Harrison Morris, J. William White (whom she credited with saving her life by operating on her for cancer), Horace Howard Furness, Dr. S. Weir Mitchell, and the British writer Andrew Lang, with whom she carried on a correspondence that bordered on intimacy until the two writers met.

Despite her friendships with women, Repplier claimed no feminist leanings, although she wished women to have the vote and equality with men in the workplace. She had no time for reformers. She opposed people like Jane Addams, whom she debated publicly on the stage child issue. The only cause she espoused and for which she wrote and spoke passionately was American opposition to the Germans in World War I. Repplier died in 1950.

From one perspective, "Sin" is a tribute to the essence of friendship— the willingness to sacrifice one's self for one's friend—and an acknowledgment that friendship can exist on many levels and bridge disparate ages and ranks. While the young protagonist takes her own fierce love for Lilly as a given, she finds Madame Bouron's capacity for friendship stunning. By taking on herself the appearance of evil, Madame Bouron knowingly adds to the student myth developed through the years. Simultaneously, she explodes the myth in the mind of the young protagonist, who in order to be true to Lilly may never share the newly acquired knowledge with others.

From another perspective, the story is a declaration of independence. The protagonist, like Huck Finn, takes a stand when she tells the first lie, and the courage she develops from that action enables her to stand by it, even if it means telling the deed in confession, facing Madame Bouron, and reaffirming the lie to Lilly despite possible expulsion from the school. This sense of independence is what all people must acquire at some point in life—the willingness to take responsibility for what they feel they must do, even if, as in the story "Sin," it means eternal damnation. As such decisions must often be kept secret, they carry the note of cosmic loneliness that in time all adults recognize.

Repplier intensifies the irony by setting the climax in the context of the First Friday Novena. In pre-Vatican II days, many Catholics put great stress on receiving communion on nine consecutive First Fridays, the practice Jesus reportedly informed St. Margaret Mary at Paray-le-monial would "guarantee" salvation. When Madame Rayburn reminds the protagonist that Thursday is the day for confession, she advances the action and conflict significantly. The protagonist's failure to go to confession and communion would raise questions in the minds of pupils and teachers alike. Failure to tell the "sin" in confession would result in sacrilege.

The systemic pressures seem compounded to drive the protagonist to distraction. Her determination to surmount the barriers earns the reader's admiration.

Repplier, too, deserves applause, for she does not let Madame Bouron off easily. Although herself a victim of the patriarchal religious system of which she is an agent, Madame Bouron is "as good as gold," only "according to the standards of childhood."[3]

LUCY M. FREIBERT

I was twelve years old, and very happy in my convent school. I did not particularly mind studying my lessons, and I sometimes persuaded the less experienced nuns to accept a retentive memory as a substitute for intelligent understanding, with which it has nothing to do. I "got along" with other children, and I enjoyed my friends; and of such simple things is the life of a child composed.

Then came a disturbing letter from my mother, a letter which threatened the heart of my content. It was sensible and reasonable, and it said very plainly and very kindly that I had better not make an especial friend of Lilly Milton; "not an exclusive friend," wrote my mother, "not one whom you would expect to see intimately after you leave school."

I knew what all that meant. I was as innocent as a kitten; but divorces were not common in those conservative years, and Mrs. Milton had as many to her credit as if she were living—a highly esteemed and popular lady—to-day. I regretted my mother's tendency to confuse issues with unimportant details (a mistake which grown-up people often made), and I felt sure that if she knew Lilly—who was also as innocent as a kitten, and was blessed with the sweetest temper that God ever gave a little girl—she would be delighted that I had such an excellent friend. So I went on happily enough until ten days later, when Madame Rayburn, a nun for whom I cherished a very warm affection, was talking to me upon a familiar theme—the diverse ways in which I might improve my classwork and my general behavior. The subject did not interest me deeply—repetition had staled its vivacity—until my companion said the one thing that had plainly been uppermost in her mind: "And Agnes, how did you come to tell Lilly Milton that your mother did not want you to go with her? I never thought you could have been so deliberately unkind."

This brought me to my feet with a bound. "Tell Lilly!" I cried. "You could not have believed such a thing. It was Madame Bouron who told her."

A silence followed this revelation. The convent discipline was as strict for the nuns as for the pupils, and it was not their custom to criticize their superiors. Madame Bouron was mistress general, ranking next to the august head, and of infinitely more importance to us. She was a cold, severe, sardonic woman, and the general dislike felt for her had shaped itself into a cult. I had accepted this cult in simple good faith, having no personal grudge until she did this dreadful thing; and I may add that it was the eminently unwise custom of reading all the letters written to or by the pupils which stood responsible for the trouble. The order of nuns was a French one, and the habit of surveillance, which did not seem amiss in France, was ill-adapted to America. I had never before wasted a thought upon it. My weekly home letter and the less frequent but more communicative epistles from my mother might have been read in the market place for all I cared, until this miserable episode proved that a bad usage may be trusted to produce, sooner or later, bad results.

It was with visible reluctance that Madame Rayburn said after a long pause: "That alters the case. If Madame Bouron told Lilly, she must have had some good reason for doing so."

"There was no good reason," I protested. "There couldn't have been. But it doesn't matter. I told Lilly it wasn't so, and she believed me."

Madame Rayburn stared at me aghast. "You told Lilly it was not so?" she repeated.

I nodded. "I could not find out for two days what was the matter," I explained; "but I got it out of her at last, and I told her that my mother had never written a line to me about her. And she believed me."

"But my dear child," said the nun, "you have told a grievous lie. What is more, you have borne false witness against your neighbor. When you said to Lilly that your mother had not written that letter, you made her believe that Madame Bouron had lied to her."

"She didn't mind believing that," I observed cheerfully, "and there was nothing else that I could say to make her feel all right."

"But a lie is a lie," protested the nun. "You will have to tell Lilly the truth."

I said nothing, but my silence was not the silence of acquiescence. Madame Rayburn must have recognized this fact, for she took another line of attack. When she spoke next, it was a in a low voice and very earnestly. "Listen to me," she said. "Friday is the first of May. You are going to confession on Thursday. You will tell Father O'Harra the whole story just as you have told it to me, and whatever he bids you do, you must do it. Remember that if you go to confession and do not tell this you will commit the very great sin of sacrilege; and if you do not obey your confessor you will commit the sin of open disobedience to the Church."

I was more than a little frightened. It seemed to me that for the first time in my life I was confronted by grown-up iniquities to which I had been a stranger. The thought sobered me for two days. On the third I went to confession, and when I had finished with my customary offenses—which, as they seldom varied, were probably as familiar to the priest as they were to me—I told my serious tale. The silence with which it was received bore witness to its seriousness. No question was asked me; I had been too explicit to render questions needful. But after two minutes (which seemed like two hours) of thinking my confessor said: "A lie is a lie. It must be retracted. To-morrow you will do one of two things. You will tell your friend the truth, or you will tell Madame Bouron the whole story just as you told it to me. Do you understand?"

"Yes," I said in a faint little voice, no louder than a sigh.

"And you will do as I bid you?"

"Yes," I breathed again.

"Then I will give you absolution, and you may go to Communion. But remember, no later than to-morrow. Believe me, it will get no easier by delay."

Of that I felt tolerably sure, and it was with the courage of desperation that I knocked the next morning at the door of Madame Bouron's office. She gave me a glance of wonderment (I had never before paid her a voluntary call), and without pause or preamble I told my tale, told it with such bald uncompromising verity that it sounded worse than ever. She listened at first in amazement, then in anger. "So Lilly thinks I lied to her," she said at last.

"Yes," I answered.

"And suppose I send for her now and undeceive her."

"You can't do that," I said. "I should tell her again my mother did not write the letter, and she would believe me."

"If you told another such lie, you would be sent from the school."

"If I were sent home, Lilly would believe me. She would believe me all the more."

The anger died out of Madame Bouron's eyes, and a look of bewilderment came into them. I am disposed to think that, despite her wide experience as nun and teacher, she had never before encountered an *idée fixe,* and found out that the pyramids are flexible compared to it. "You know," she said uncertainly, "that sooner or later you will have to do as your mother desires."

I made no answer. The "sooner or later" did not interest me at all. I was living now.

There was another long pause. When Madame Bouron spoke again it was in a grave and low voice. "I wish I had said nothing about your mother's letter," she said. "I thought I could settle matters quickly that way, but I was mistaken, and I must take the consequences of my error. You may go now. I will not speak to Lilly, or to anyone else about this affair."

I did not go. I sat stunned, and asking myself if she knew all that her silence would imply. Children seldom give adults much credit for intelligence. "But," I began feebly—

"But me no buts," she interrupted, rising to her feet, "I know what you are going to say: but I have not been the head of a school for years without bearing more than one injustice."

Now when I heard these words sadly spoken something broke up inside of me. It did not break gently, like the dissolving of a cloud; it broke like the bursting of a dam. Sobs shook my lean little body as though they would have torn it apart. Tears blinded me. With difficulty I gasped out three words. "You are good," I said.

Madame Bouron propelled me gently to the door, which I could not see because of my tears. "I wish I could say as much for you," she answered, "but I cannot. You have been very bad. You have been false to your mother, to whom you owe respect and obedience; you have been false to me; and you have been false to God. But you have been true to your friend."

She put me out of the door, and I stood in the corridor facing the clock. I was still shaken by sobs, but my heart was light as a bird.

And, believe it or not, the supreme reason for my happiness was—not that my difficulties were over, though I was glad of that; and not that Lilly was safe from hurt, though I was glad of that; but that Madame Bouron, whom I had thought bad, had proved herself to be, according to the standards of childhood, as good as gold. My joy was like the joy of the blessed saints in Paradise.

DOROTHY PARKER

The Standard of Living

(1941)

*I*F Parker, born in 1893, were alive today, she might be a stand-up comedian. In the Roaring Twenties, however, she was a sit-down writer plagued by writer's block and the fragile social insecurity epitomized by her wry verse with its pungent punch lines ("For art is a form of catharsis / And love is a permanent flop") and her stories of flappers and matrons seeking, but seldom securing, the comforts of unimpeachable social status and true love.

Parker was the daughter of a Scot, Eliza Marston Rothschild, and J. Henry Rothschild, a prosperous Manhattan clothier. Her mother died shortly after Dorothy's two-months-premature birth. She disliked both her Jewish father and her Christian stepmother, who sent her for some years to the nearby Blessed Sacrament Convent School (and who regularly asked, "Did you love Jesus today?") before "finishing" her education at the fashionable Miss Dana's in Morristown, New Jersey, in 1911. Parker later characterized her young self as "a plain, disagreeable little child" and said she wanted to write her autobiography if only to call it *Mongrel,* which epitomized her detested self-image as "a mongrel that wanted to be a thoroughbred."

Within a decade, however, as an insouciant journalist at *Vogue* (1913–16) and *Vanity Fair* (1916–20), she found the ideal social milieu, the verbally glib, self-promoting Round Table at the Algonquin Hotel. There, during daily lunches and afternoon drinking bouts, these *bons vivants*—including Robert Benchley, George S. Kaufman, Alexander Woolcott, and Harold Ross, who founded the *New Yorker* in 1925—practiced the repartee (some would say smart-aleck style) that characterized their writing. Indeed during the 1920s and early 1930s Parker wrote her best work, the verse, stories, and reviews, wisecracking and wary, that made her the toast of New York—the antithesis of the Little Old Lady from Dubuque, that mythic arbiter of midwestern middle-class morality and taste.

Her volumes of verse (not serious "poetry," she claimed) include *Enough Rope* (1926), *Sunset Gun* (1928), and *Death and Taxes* (1931). They are mostly lamentations for loves lost, never found, or gone awry ("Scratch a lover, and find a foe"). Her short stories, collected in *Laments for the Living* (1930), *After Such Pleasures* (1933), and *Here Lies* (1939) are of three conspicuous types. These include dramatic monologues; devastating, ironic self-characterizations of unsure women hopelessly dependent on insensitive or heartless men ("A Telephone Call"); and social satires patronizing to the urban upper crust ("Horsie"). The best are incisive portraits of more subtle, fully developed characters, usually women, as found in Parker's masterpiece, "Big Blonde," winner of the O. Henry Memorial Prize for the best short story of 1929.

Parker herself seemed as inconstant as the men whose fickleness her poetry condemns, and as insecure and personally unhappy as many of her women characters. In 1917, she married a handsome Wall Street broker, well-connected, heavy-drinking Edwin Pond Parker II, who soon left for two years' military service. When he returned they separated and were divorced in 1928. She had an abortion in 1923 and attempted suicide; followed by a series of brief affairs—in 1925 with playwright Charles MacArthur, in 1926 with tobacco heir Seward Collins, and in 1927 with businessman John Garrett. In 1928 she began a liaison with bisexual actor Alan Campbell, who became the major supporter—and inhibitor (because of their joint dependence on alcohol)—of her later literary career. They married (1933), divorced (1947), remarried (1950), separated (1953), and reunited in 1956 until Campbell's death in 1963. In the 1930s and 1940s Parker collaborated on film scripts with Ross Evans, including *A Star is Born* (1937) and *Lady Windemere's Fan* (1949). Her dramatic collaborations—*Close Harmony,* 1929, with Elmer Rice; *The Coast of Illyria,* 1945, with Ross Evans; and *The Ladies of the Corridor,* 1954, with Arnaud D'Usseau—present the tortured lives of Charles and Mary Lamb, and of elderly women dying in a hotel; they were not commercially successful. Later Parker was blacklisted for her liberal political views, and increasingly abusive of alcohol; her writing became sporadic and unreliable. She died, alone and isolated, in a New York hotel in 1967. *The Portable Dorothy Parker* (1944, rev. 1976) is her only work currently in print.

"The Standard of Living," which first appeared in the *New Yorker* in 1941, is an unusual story for Parker in that it depicts a true friendship between two young working women (always "girls" to Parker) who so value their association with each other that the interchangeable young men who join them from time to time are incidental to their lives. Annabel and Midge work next to one another, lunch together every noon, and spend most evenings and weekends together, playing out their fantasy lives according to the unwritten rules that they alone generate and they alone can understand.

LYNN Z. BLOOM

Annabel and Midge came out of the tea room with the arrogant slow gait of the leisured, for their Saturday afternoon stretched ahead of them. They had lunched, as was their wont, on sugar, starches, oils, and butter-fats. Usually they ate sandwiches of spongy new white bread greased with butter and mayonnaise; they ate thick wedges of cake lying wet beneath ice cream and whipped cream and melted chocolate gritty with nuts. As alternates, they ate patties, sweating beads of inferior oil, containing bits of bland meat bogged in pale, stiffening sauce; they ate pastries, limber under rigid icing, filled with an indeterminate yellow sweet stuff, not still solid, not yet liquid, like salve that has been left in the sun. They chose no other sort of food, nor did they consider it. And their skin was like the petals of wood anemones, and their bellies were as flat and their flanks as lean as those of young Indian braves.

Annabel and Midge had been best friends almost from the day that Midge had found a job as stenographer with the firm that employed Annabel. By now, Annabel, two years longer in the stenographic department, had worked up to the wages of eighteen dollars and fifty cents a week; Midge was still at sixteen dollars. Each girl lived at home with her family and paid half her salary to its support.

The girls sat side by side at their desks, they lunched together every noon, together they set out for home at the end of the day's work. Many of their evenings and most of their Sundays were passed in each other's company. Often they were joined by two young men, but there was no steadiness to any such quartet; the two young men would give place, unlamented, to two other young men, and lament would have been inappropriate, really, since the newcomers were scarcely distinguishable from their predecessors. Invariably the girls spent the fine idle hours of their hot-weather Saturday afternoons together. Constant use had not worn ragged the fabric of their friendship.

They looked alike, though the resemblance did not lie in their features. It was in the shape of their bodies, their movements, their style, and their adornments. Annabel and Midge did, and completely, all that young office workers are besought not to do. They painted their lips and their nails, they darkened their lashes and lightened their hair, and scent seemed to shimmer from them. They wore thin, bright dresses, tight over their breasts and high on their legs, and tilted slippers, fancifully strapped. They looked conspicuous and cheap and charming.

Now, as they walked across to Fifth Avenue with their skirts swirled by the hot wind, they received audible admiration. Young men grouped lethargically about newsstands awarded them murmurs, exclamations, even—the ultimate tribute—whistles. Annabel and Midge passed without the condescension of hurrying their pace: they held their heads higher and set their feet with exquisite precision, as if they stepped over the necks of peasants.

Always the girls went to walk on Fifth Avenue on their free afternoons, for it was the ideal ground for their favorite game. The game could be played anywhere, and, indeed, was, but the great shop windows stimulated the two players to their best form.

Annabel had invented the game; or rather she had evolved it from an old one. Basically, it was no more than the ancient sport of whatwould-you-do-if-you-had-a-million dollars? But Annabel had drawn a new set of rules for it, had narrowed it, pointed it, made it stricter. Like all games, it was the more absorbing for being more difficult.

Annabel's version went like this: You must suppose that somebody dies and leaves you a million dollars, cool. But there is a condition to the bequest. It is stated in the will that you must spend every nickel of the money on yourself.

There lay the hazard of the game. If, when playing it, you forgot, and listed among your expenditures the rental of a new apartment for your family, for example, you lost your turn to the other player. It was astonishing how many—and some of them among the experts, too—would forfeit all their innings by such slips.

It was essential, of course, that it be played in passionate seriousness. Each purchase must be carefully considered and, if necessary, supported by argument. There was no zest to playing wildly. Once Annabel had introduced the game to Sylvia, another girl who worked in the office. She explained the rules to Sylvia and then offered her the gambit "What would be the first thing you'd do?" Sylvia had not shown the decency of even a second of hesitation. "Well," she said, "the first thing I'd do. I'd go out and hire somebody to shoot Mrs. Gary Cooper, and then . . ." So it is to be seen that she was no fun.

But Annabel and Midge were surely born to be comrades, for Midge played the game like a master from the moment she learned it. It was she who added the touches that made the whole thing cozier. According to Midge's innovations, the eccentric who died and left you the money was not anybody you loved, or, for the matter of that, anybody you even knew. It was somebody who had seen you somewhere and had thought, "That girl ought to have lots of nice things. I'm going to leave her a million dollars when I die." And the death was to be neither untimely nor painful. Your benefactor, full of years and comfortably ready to depart, was to slip softly away during sleep and go right to heaven. These embroideries permitted Annabel and Midge to play their game in the luxury of peaceful consciences.

Midge played with a seriousness that was not only proper but extreme. The single strain on the girls' friendship had followed an announcement once made by Annabel that the first thing she would buy with her million dollars would be a silver-fox coat. It was as if she had struck Midge across the mouth. When Midge recovered her breath, she cried that she couldn't imagine how Annabel could do such a thing—silver-fox coats were common! Annabel defended her taste with the retort that they were not common, either. Midge then said that they were so. She added that everybody had a silver-fox coat. She went on, with perhaps a slight loss of head, to declare that she herself wouldn't be caught dead in silver fox.

For the next few days, though the girls saw each other as constantly, their conversation was careful and infrequent, and they did not once play their game. Then one morning, as soon as Annabel entered the office, she came to Midge and said that she had changed her mind. She would not buy a silver-fox coat with any part of her million dollars. Immediately on receiving the legacy, she would select a coat of mink.

Midge smiled and her eyes shone. "I think," she said, "you're doing absolutely the right thing."

Now, as they walked along Fifth Avenue, they played the game anew. It was one of those days with which September is repeatedly cursed; hot and glaring, with slivers of dust in the wind. People drooped and shambled, but the girls carried themselves tall and walked a straight line, as befitted young heiresses on their afternoon promenade. There was no longer need for them to start the game at its formal opening, Annabel went direct to the heart of it.

"All right," she said. "So you've got this million dollars. So what would be the first thing you'd do?"

"Well the first thing I'd do," Midge said. "I'd get a mink coat." But she said it mechanically, as if she were giving the memorized answer to an expected question.

"Yes," Annabel said, "I think you ought to. The terribly dark kind of mink." But she, too, spoke as if by rote. It was too hot; fur, no matter how dark and sleek and supple, was horrid to the thoughts.

They stepped along in silence for a while. Then Midge's eye was caught by a shop window. Cool, lovely gleamings were there set off by chaste and elegant darkness.

"No," Midge said. "I take it back. I wouldn't get a mink coat the first thing. Know what I'd do? I'd get a string of pearls. Real pearls."

Annabel's eyes turned to follow Midge's.

"Yes," she said, slowly. "I think that's kind of a good idea. And it would make sense, too. Because you can wear pearls with anything."

Together they went over to the shop window and stood pressed against it. It contained but one object—a double row of great, even pearls clasped by a deep emerald around a little pink velvet throat.

"What do you suppose they cost?" Annabel said.

"Gee, I don't know," Midge said. "Plenty, I guess."

"Like a thousand dollars?" Annabel said.

"Oh, I guess like more," Midge said. "On account of the emerald."

"Well, like ten thousand dollars?" Annabel said.

"Gee, I wouldn't even know," Midge said.

The devil nudged Annabel in the ribs. "Dare you to go in and price them," she said.

"Like fun!" Midge said.

"Dare you," Annabel said.

"Why, a store like this wouldn't even be open this afternoon," Midge said.

"Yes, it is so, too," Annabel said. "People just came out. And there's a doorman on. Dare you."

"Well," Midge said. "But you've got to come too."

They tendered thanks, icily, to the doorman for ushering them into the shop. It was cool and quiet, a broad, gracious room with paneled walls and soft carpet. But the girls wore expressions of bitter disdain, as if they stood in a sty.

A slim, immaculate clerk came to them and bowed. His neat face showed no astonishment at their appearance.

"Good afternoon," he said. He implied that he would never forget it if they would grant him the favor of accepting his soft-spoken greeting.

"Good afternoon," Annabel and Midge said together, and in like freezing accents.

"Is there something—?" the clerk said.

"Oh, we're just looking," Annabel said. It was as if she flung the words down from a dais.

The clerk bowed.

"My friend and myself merely happened to be passing," Midge said, and stopped, seeming to listen to the phrase. "My friend here and myself," she went on, "merely happened to be wondering how much are those pearls you've got in your window."

"Ah, yes." the clerk said. "The double rope. That is two hundred and fifty thousand dollars, Madam."

"I see," Midge said.

The clerk bowed." An exceptionally beautiful necklace," he said. "Would you care to look at it?"

"No, thank you," Annabel said.

"My friend and myself merely happened to be passing," Midge said.

They turned to go; to go, from their manner, where the tumbrel awaited them. The clerk sprang ahead and opened the door. He bowed as they swept by him.

The girls went on along the Avenue and disdain was still on their faces.

"Honestly!" Annabel said. "Can you imagine a think like that?"

"Two hundred and fifty thousand dollars!" Midge said. "That's a quarter of a million dollars right there!"

"He's got his nerve!" Annabel said.

They walked on. Slowly the disdain went, slowly and completely as if drained from them, and with it went the regal carriage and tread. Their shoulders dropped and they dragged their feet: they bumped against each other, without notice or apology, and caromed away again. They were silent and their eyes were cloudy.

Suddenly Midge straightened her back, flung her head high, and spoke, clear and strong.

"Listen, Annabel," she said. "Look. Suppose there was this terribly rich person, see? You don't know this person, but this person has seen you somewhere and wants to do something for you. Well, it's a terribly old person, see? And so this person dies, just like going to sleep, and leaves you ten million dollars. Now, what would be the first thing you'd do?"

MARJORIE WORTHINGTON

Hunger

(1941)

*M*ARJORIE Worthington was born in 1898 or possibly 1900 in New York City, the daughter of Rose (Samuels) Muir and Oscar Muir. She seems to have had a fairly secure family life as a child and referred to her parents and sister as "conventional." As a young woman just out of high school, she was drawn to social work. During World War I she volunteered as a nurse's aid in a children's ward. After an infant died in her arms, she abandoned her nursing career and joined the American Red Cross, writing up psychiatric histories.

Eventually she studied journalism at New York University. Seeking a job in publishing, she found a minor position with the *International Book Review,* an adjunct of the *Literary Digest.* She was married very briefly to a reporter on the New York *Morning Sun* and in 1923 married Lyman Worthington, who worked in the advertising department of the New York *Daily News.* He was successful enough to allow her to quit her job and begin a novel. The Worthingtons had been married three benign years when they were invited to play bridge with another couple, the Seabrooks.

Willie and Marjorie felt an immediate attraction. After a short courtship, they each left their spouses and sailed for France and the bohemian life. There they met well-known literary figures—Gertrude Stein and Alice B. Toklas, Aldous and Maria Huxley, for instance—and were mostly prosperous and happy.

Worthington wrote of Seabrook, almost gratefully, "Willie, behind whose shining light I could always bask in comfortable obscurity." But Seabrook's shining light sometimes threatened to extinguish Worthington's. She wrote of a particularly hectic time in her life, "I had so little time to myself, with trying to run a big house and feed a lot of guests and keep Willie from drowning in despair and alcohol, that when I could get away to that quiet room above the garage my fingers raced like mad to get as much written as possible in the time that was mine." The fact that she was not able to make a full commitment to her work is not surprising in a society that accepts the idea that "people who need people are the luckiest people in the world" and that treats the consorts of well-known men as also-rans. Nevertheless, while she was with Seabrook, Worthington produced several novels, which were well received: *Spider Web* (1930), *Mrs. Taylor* (1932), *Scarlet Josephine* (1933), and *Come, My Coach* (1935). A fifth novel, *Manhattan Solo* (1937), was written after the couple returned from France to the United States.

In 1935, after Seabrook stopped drinking alcohol for a period, Worthington and Seabrook were married. They had a few good years together in a small town in upstate New York, but their life together was overshadowed by a serious sexual incompatibility, Seabrook's dependence on alcohol, and Worthington's dependence on him. Seabrook began drinking heavily again and became involved with another woman in a sadomasochistic affair. Worthington left; their divorce was granted in 1941.

Worthington found life without Seabrook very bleak. Although she saw several short stories published during this period, it was years before she began to write books again. When she did, she turned to nonfiction—a biography of Louisa May Alcott, *Miss Alcott of Concord* (1958); *Immortal Lovers: Heloise and Abelard* (1960); and the story of her marriage, *The Strange World of Willie Seabrook* (1966). She died in 1976.

Worthington's story "Hunger" appeared in *Harper's Bazaar* in 1942, but was actually written earlier. She describes its inception:

> Who knows where the idea for a story comes from, or how it comes? An impression, a spoken phrase, the nod of a head or another gesture— at any rate, I was in a receptive frame of mind. Willie was away on an assignment, and I was not only lonely but secretly worried. . . . I couldn't explain just why I was worried, . . . But I felt that although we were safe together, out there in the world beyond our nine acres lurked all kinds of enemies. . . .
>
> The history of "Hunger" is a Cinderella story and should be encouraging to young writers. Willie liked it when I showed it to him, and I sent it to an agent I had at the time. She returned it, saying she was sorry but she just didn't believe in it, so I put it away in a desk drawer and forgot it. A long time after that, . . . friends came to see us . . . I didn't want to admit [I hadn't been writing] and I showed it to them. They were enthusiastic and insisted I send it off again. . . . It was sold to *Harper's Bazaar*,

the first magazine to see it. To my infinite surprise and joy, that story was selected by both the O'Brien and the O.Henry prize collections of short stories for the same year, and afterwards it appeared in numerous anthologies.[1]

The power of "Hunger" lies not only in its depiction of physical hunger but in its undercurrent of the insatiable hunger for intimacy. In order to realize even a few, imperfect moments of intimacy, some of us are willing to give away whatever we have. This is not nobility or sacrifice, but necessity.

There is also a hint of cannibalism or vampirism in "Hunger," for human beings often feed on each other emotionally, just as Worthington and Seabrook did until there was no nourishment left for either of them. Worthington was able to pull away from her relationship with Seabrook; but she admits that when she did, she lost her desire and ability to write poetry, and abandoned her career as a novelist too. Sensing the danger of an all-consuming affair, she left it, leaving much of herself behind as well.

BETTY BURNETT

Madame Lenzel hurried along the first-floor corridor of the Grassmount School for Girls. She was a tall woman, who walked with a stoop, carrying her large head forward, as though the weight of her untidy gray hair were too much for her. She was nearsighted, but since she had broken the glasses which she had brought with her from Austria, in that hasty flight two years ago, she had been unable to afford a visit to an American oculist.

She was unusually excited today, because she was having a visitor. She had been with the school, as teacher of German and French, for six months. She had been so relieved to get the position, after the long search for work, that she had been almost happy. There had been no time to feel strange or lonely.

But today she was aware of the starved loneliness she had known for her old friends. The Countess Natalie Pozinska was waiting in the library, to be her invited guest for a night at the school. Miss Thompson, the headmistress, to whom she had shown Natalie's letter, had sanctioned the invitation. Natalie was Polish, of an old and aristocratic family. Madame Lenzel had known her in Vienna, when she, Madame, held a salon every Thursday. Of all the people who gathered there, Natalie had been the gayest and most entertaining. After the fall of Poland, Madame had thought often of her old friend, and wondered what had become of her. And then, this week, had arrived a letter saying that Natalie had been in New York a year and had just discovered that her old friend Madame Lenzel was teaching in a girl's school. She wrote she would love to pay a little visit so that they could talk about old times and, as exiles in a new country, console each other.

At the door of the library, behind which she could hear the crackling of logs in the fireplace, Madame Lenzel paused. Perhaps she should have gone to her room after her last class and changed from the old gray skirt and mended sweater to something brighter and more dressy. The Countess Pozinska had been famous for her attention to style, for her grooming. She would not want her old friend to feel sorry for her, or sad. Natalie had been so gay. How wonderful it would be to hear her infectious laugh again. What did clothes matter? . . . They would get over that first embarrassment of inspection and soon be telling funny stories. . . . Yes, they would somehow find things to laugh about, in spite of the tragedies. Natalie was like that, with her fine sense of humor.

Madame's lips twisted into a smile as she pushed open the door of the library, and called out, "Natalie! How good to see you" before her nearsighted eyes could make out more than a dark blur on the divan before the fire.

A small form rose, with an answering cry, shrill and ecstatic: "Ilsa! *Que c'est bon!*"

There was an interchange of French exclamations, and then the two were holding hands—the Austrian woman's large and bony, the Countess Pozinska's small and like little claws, with sharp pointed nails.

They devoured each other for a moment or two, and Madame Lenzel, in her honesty, felt a sharp stab of pain. Could this little woman with the dark circles under her eyes and the sallow complexion be the beautiful Natalie she had known in Vienna? It was impossible. She could see every detail now that they were close together: the discolored skin, the hair that was purple from cheap dyes, instead of being black and glossy; the velvet turban that was dusty and needed brushing; the old silk dress that was bunched here and there, to give it a style it had not. What had happened to the Countess Pozinska? The one old Doctor Stern, Madame's closest friend, had once called the brightest star in the firmament over Vienna? The eyes, now studying Madame, were like sharp gimlets, not stars.

"Poor thing," Madame thought with dismay. "What a time she must have had!" She gave the Countess's hand a squeeze, and said, gruffly, to cover her emotions: "Sit down, please. You must be tired after your train trip from New York. Soon we will have tea, when Miss Thompson finishes her class. A nice tea, Natalie. There . . . sit down and warm yourself. It's a beautiful fire, isn't it? They have endless supplies of wood here. . . . I'll put on another log."

Clumsily she bent over the fire and shoved a log on top of the others, glad to hide her face until she had recovered from her first shock.

The library was a comfortable and beautiful room. Madame Lenzel, when she first arranged for the Countess's visit, had been proud that she could receive her friend in a place almost as luxurious and well run as those to which they had both once been accustomed. This house had belonged formerly to a wealthy American family, with traditions. The school, under Miss Thompson, had kept the original atmosphere as far as possible.

They sat, now, next to each other, on the divan before the fire. They began, slowly at first and a little shyly, to talk of themselves, but they kept it brief. They could not, all at once, tell the real story of their exile. They went, with relief, to a discussion of their friends: this one was in Princeton, teaching; that one was in Lisbon, awaiting passage; another was in the South of France. Doctor Stern, Madame's dearest friend in Vienna, was, she said, in Zurich. Madame hoped, someday, to arrange for his passage. Thank God, he was with friends, not alone. She did not tell Natalie she was saving part of her salary, each month, to bring the brilliant old man to America.

They talked, but there was a gulf between them. And there was no laughter. None at all.

Suddenly, a log fell, and in the blaze that followed this displacement, Madame saw the Countess's hands. They were dirty—they were little dark claws with dirt ingrained. She was about to suggest, belatedly, that perhaps after her journey, the Countess would like to wash. But at that moment Natalie's eyes followed hers, and the Countess said, unexpectedly:

"You are wondering what has become of my jewels, Ilsa. Naturally. But I decided not to wear them to the country. I left them in my hotel room, and as you came in, I was worrying about them. Do you think they will be safe?"

Madame Lenzel was too surprised to do anything except make a clucking sound with her tongue.

The Countess went on, leaning forward and placing one of the soiled little claws on Madame's knee: "Never mind," she said, "I was always careless. But now my jewels mean more to me than before. And do you know why? Because, dear Ilsa, I have made a will. I didn't mean to tell you so soon . . . but I have really made a will leaving all my jewels to you, my dear. Now, don't look surprised. I asked myself, whom have I left in the world? No one. I thought of you . . . my old friend, Madame Lenzel. I wrote out the will, before a lawyer . . . and I put the document along with other papers in my box at the bank."

Madame Lenzel gasped. The room was hot and she felt embarrassed. Her mouth just opened and closed because there was nothing to say.

The Countess said quickly, "Don't thank me, Ilsa. I want no thanks. But you shall have them all some day . . . the diamond rings, the pearls . . . the little garnet cross you used to admire . . . all of them. *Voilà.*"

Madame Lenzel felt the newly sharp eyes of Natalie upon her and she blushed. What was there to say to such nonsense? Suddenly she felt a chill. "She wants something from me," she thought. "She talks this foolishness because she is going to ask for something. And I have nothing to give her, poor thing. If I help anybody, it must be the good little Doctor Stern. I will have to disappoint her."

She looked at the Countess. She determined to tell her the truth. To say, "Dear Natalie, I know you have lost your jewels. How could you have kept them? I know this is all a story made up because you are suffering from shame. Please relax. Be natural with me. We are both at a place where there can be no shame." But at that very moment, the door opened, and Miss Thompson entered the library.

She was an attractive woman in her early forties. She wore heather-blue tweeds and a sweater to match. Her light brown hair was becomingly cut and well cared for. When she came into a room she brought with her a wholesome atmosphere of fresh air plus a scent of Yardley soap. She spoke with a Boston accent and was obviously aware of her superiority over most people. To Madame's surprise, she seemed actually impressed when she was introduced to the Countess Pozinska.

Natalie had risen, to acknowledge the introduction charmingly, with just the right amount of condescension. Madame Lenzel had no need to have felt a momentary embarrassment. Her clothes might be shabby, she could be covered with train dust—and worse—but she was still the Countess Pozinska.

Madame Lenzel relinquished her seat on the divan and moved to the other side of the tea table, which the houseman had just arranged. Natalie and Miss Thompson began a lengthy conversation in French which they both seemed to be enjoying.

It was a specially nice tea today, Madame Lenzel noted with satisfaction. There were scones, and Danish pastry, large chocolate peppermints, and an iced layer cake. She drank some tea first, because she needed it, and then she helped herself generously and began to eat.

She was on her third buttered scone, when she noticed that Natalie was laughing, and it seemed, even though faintly, at least somewhat like her former gay laughter. Her dark little face was animated. She was being charming, trying to please, just as she used to be on the days of Madame Lenzel's salon.

Madame Lenzel poured herself another cup of tea, and then, suddenly, her spine stiffened. She heard Natalie say, in a purring voice:

"But there is nobody who knows as good a German as Madame. I used to go to her just for the pleasure of hearing the classic, pure German spoken as it should be. Of course, in my turn, I taught Madame a little French. Remember, Ilsa, the trouble you had with the French r's? It is funny how seldom a member of the Germanic races can manage a Parisian accent. With us Poles, it seems to come easy."

Madame choked on a crumb, put her tiny tea napkin to her face, and turned crimson. Could Natalie have forgotten that she, Madame Lenzel, was hired here to *teach* the French language? Could it be possible she had come to insinuate herself into the school at the expense of her friend? Ach, no. It was unthinkable. Natalie was talking so fast and trying so hard to be charming that she did not realize what she was saying.

"Eat, Natalie," Madame Lenzel said, suddenly, thrusting a plate of scones toward the Countess. "Don't talk quite so much. You are missing a fine tea."

Miss Thompson poured a fresh cup of tea for the Countess Pozinska, but the headmistress was gazing thoughtfully at Madame Lenzel. She said, "What a treat it will be for the girls tonight to hear French so beautifully spoken." And Madame Lenzel felt a chill in her heart.

"How nice it is here," the Countess said, in English. "I feel almost at home, already. I am used to big houses in the country, am I not, Ilsa? But our house near Warsaw was old. It dated from the fifth century. . . ."

In the brief period between tea and dinner, there was not time for Madame Lenzel and the Countess to have their long talk about old days in Vienna. Madame Lenzel was busy running a bath for her guest, who was sharing her room with her. She was worried, too, and found it difficult to be natural.

If the Countess was aware of this restraint, she did not show it. She came back from the bathroom, wrapped in a soiled pink kimono. Her purple hair was damp, her features pinched with cold, but she was singing a gay little tune.

As she dressed, she kept up a bright chatter, as though to divert Madame Lenzel's attention from the girdle that was frayed, the fussy French underwear that was faded and torn, the long silk stockings with white clocks up the ankles and runs up the backs.

When it came time for her to put on a mussed black Chantilly lace evening dress, Madame had to help her pin the shoulder straps to her brassière. There were other places that needed pinning, and in disgust, Madame picked up a needle and threaded it.

"What for?" asked the Countess. "Why bother to sew this old rag? I shall throw it away when I leave. I was not sure whether one dressed for dinner here, and at the last moment I threw this thing in my bag. For the country I always wore my oldest things. It looks all right, though, doesn't it? It is still . . . chic?" She was pathetically anxious to please.

To Madame Lenzel, the Countess looked like an aging nightclub performer. The lace dress was too low in front and in back; it was not in good taste for the occasion. For a moment the Devil whispered in Madame Lenzel's ear.

Then, with a grunt, Madame searched in a drawer and brought out a beautiful black fringed shawl. She threw it over the Countess's bare shoulders. "Here," she said roughly, "you will be cold. Do not take it off, not once tonight."

For a second the Countess Pozinska stared at her. Then with a little laugh she said, "*Merci,*" and drew the shawl across her breast.

Dinner was served at eight o'clock, in a beautiful room on long polished tables lighted by candles. Miss Thompson said grace, after which they sat down, the Countess at the right of the headmistress and Madame Lenzel on her left, instead of down near the end of the table as usual. Miss Thompson's assistant sat at the foot of the table, and in between, spaced by a few selected teachers, were the school-girls. They wore neat silk afternoon dresses, while the teachers wore dinner dresses of insipid taffetas and silks. Among them, the Count-ess Pozinska looked like a little black crow.

Madame Lenzel ate her soup noisily and with enjoyment. When she wiped her mouth and looked up she saw the Countess's soup being removed, untouched. Natalie was telling an amusing story in French, and the girls were listening. Miss Thompson beamed.

It was the same with the fish course. Natalie pecked at the sole, and stopped eating to tell the young girl next to her about her expe-riences traveling from Lisbon to America on the Clipper. Madame was startled, because she had seen the third-class label of the steam-ship *Excelsior* on the Countess's suitcase. But the girls were interested.

When the meat arrived, Madame was almost beside herself for fear that Natalie would send the beef away untouched. She very nearly leaned across the table to say, "Stop talking for a while, Natalie. Eat!" It pained her that anyone as pinched-looking as the Countess should be so indifferent to food. But Natalie, all smiles, was answering ques-tions about Poland, describing its splendors before the invasion. It was educational, and told in exquisite French, and Miss Thompson was encouraging her.

Once the Countess paused, to search in a voluminous tapestry bag which she held in her lap. At last she drew out a soiled hand-kerchief, wiped her nose delicately and swiftly, and put the un-sightly object away before anybody but Madame Lenzel had noticed.

After that, Madame heard the click of the big bag several times, and wished, too late, she had lent Natalie one of her own clean handkerchiefs. "She has become a slop," Madame said to herself in-dignantly. "But she can still charm everyone, as she did all of us when she was an *élégante.*"

She seemed to have completely captivated the headmistress, who invited Madame and the Countess to take coffee with her after din-ner in her private sitting room.

"And what are your plans . . . for . . . the duration?" Miss Thompson asked as she poured the Countess's coffee.

Natalie shrugged her shoulders. "Who knows?" she answered simply. "Beggars cannot be choosers. I would do anything, but it is so hard to find what to do . . . in a new country. Not everybody has Madame Lenzel's good fortune. But, of course, not everybody deserves it." She laughed and patted Madame Lenzel's hand.

"I wish," Miss Thompson said earnestly, "I could afford two language teachers. I have thought it would be nice to have a French table at meals, where students of French would not be permitted to speak English at all."

Madame Lenzel sat up stiffly. The little spoon dropped from her saucer and she stooped to pick it up. Why had she not been told about Miss Thompson's wish for a French table? Why, not until now?

"My girls," Madame said, when she leaned back in her chair again, "my girls in advanced French are doing very well, Miss Thompson. Nancy Bourne will be ready to pass her entrance examinations for Smith, as you wished. They are all doing satisfactory work . . . very."

"Oh, I know that, Madame Lenzel," Miss Thompson said, "I know you are an excellent teacher and the girls are devoted to you. I hope you don't think any criticism of you was intended?"

"No," Madame said, somewhat mollified. "No. I quite understand. You are most kind."

The Countess rushed into the uncomfortable silence to say, "Alas, French may become a dead language, you know . . . like Latin and Greek, and nobody will need to know how it is spoken. Poor France." She opened her bag again, to take out her handkerchief . . . and wipe her eyes.

"That will never be," Madame Lenzel cried out. "As long as I teach German, I teach French, too." She glared around the room, and saw by the clock that it was ten o'clock.

"So," she said, rising, "it is time to retire. We must thank Miss Thompson for her kindness, Natalie, and then I will take you to my room."

The Countess took Miss Thompson's hand and said fervently, "I shall not forget your kindness to me, and what a pleasure it has been to be here, in this beautiful place. No matter what happens to me, I shall remember your hospitality."

As they mounted the stairs to Madame Lenzel's room, the Countess whispered, "Did you notice, Ilsa, that she had on her desk the

Almanac de Gotha as well as her Social Register? They are snobs, these little American teachers, aren't they?" She smiled with satisfaction, and Madame Lenzel longed to slap her.

While the Countess made herself ready for the night, Madame Lenzel pulled aside the curtain at one of her windows and stood looking out on the dark garden, and the woods beyond. Many evenings she had stood this way, before going to sleep. It was so quiet, so peaceful.

Tomorrow, Natalie would be gone, and no harm would have come of the visit. After her classes tomorrow, Madame promised herself a long walk in the woods. She would find autumn leaves to bring back to the house, even if there were no other flowers. She was ashamed of herself, but she felt she could not wait for the morrow to come, so that she could have her room back, and her privacy.

She turned around at a peculiar sound from one of the twin beds. Natalie was sitting propped against the pillows. She had thrown Madame's black shawl over her nightgown. In front of her was the enormous brocade bag, from which she was calmly taking out a soft roll, already buttered, a greasy cold scone, a piece of beef, and some chocolate peppermints. She began eating greedily, her sharp teeth gleaming—first the meat and bread, then the pastry. The candies, from the dish Miss Thompson had offered her and from which she had seemed to accept one little piece, she now swallowed whole, without chewing.

As though hypnotized, Madame Lenzel approached the bed. She couldn't say a word.

When the last crumb had disappeared, the Countess looked up and stared at Madame Lenzel.

"But," Madame faltered, "but, why did you not eat these when they were offered to you? What are you . . . a . . . a squirrel?"

"Do you think," the Countess said fiercely, "that I wanted anyone to know how hungry I was?"

Madame Lenzel sank down on the foot of the bed.

"Of course I am hungry," the Countess was almost shouting now. "I have been starving, do you hear? Starving for months and months. . . ." Then suddenly she buried her face in the bed clothes and began to sob.

Madame Lenzel did not stop her. She walked to the window again and looked out. To be hungry—she knew what that was. At first you thought it could not happen to you, then you realized it was happening. You got sick from it and frightened, and unless you were very good, you got demoralized. Honor, decency, everything became secondary to the void in your stomach. Ach, God, poor Natalie. Her own eyes were moist when she turned back to the room.

"Compose yourself, Natalie," she said sternly. "I will be back in a few moments."

In her old gray flannel bathrobe and the leather bedroom slippers that were like battered old barges, Madame Lenzel walked slowly downstairs to the headmistress's bedroom. She knocked timidly at the door.

Miss Thompson had not yet gone to bed. She was sitting before the fire, reading. She greeted Madame Lenzel kindly, and told her to sit down.

Madame Lenzel sat on the edge of a chair, clasping and unclasping her hands a few times before she spoke. She was thinking of her old friend, Professor Stern, and she sighed. At last she took the plunge.

"Miss Thompson, I come to suggest that my friend, the Countess Pozinska, and I divided the language work. I could teach French and German literature and grammar . . . and she could teach the conversation. She was once famous for her conversation. The young ladies would learn much from her . . . manners, and poise . . . all that. . . ."

Miss Thompson seemed interested. She closed her book, but she said, with a sigh, "That would be nice, Madame Lenzel. But my budget will not permit another teaching salary. I'm sorry."

Madame Lenzel nearly lost her balance in her eagerness. "Salary!" she exclaimed. "What does that matter? A few dollars more or less . . . we will divide my salary, and so it shall be just the same to you. But we are both, in a manner of speaking, homeless. We can share my room comfortably . . . and as for the food . . . my friend Natalie eats like a bird, as you may have noticed." She tried to smile, as though she had said something funny.

There was a silence and then the headmistress picked up her book again. "I think it can be arranged," she said slowly. "Yes, I'm sure it can."

Madame Lenzel thanked her heartily and strode to the door. As she opened it, Miss Thompson said, "I think you are being very generous."

Madame Lenzel blushed scarlet and said, "Ridiculous." She shut the door and made hastily for the stairs. As she reached the top landing she stopped to catch her breath.

"Poor Doctor Stern," she thought. "He will have to wait now a long time before I can send him passage money. But at least, in Zurich he has friends. He will never be hungry."

As she started to open her own door, she noticed that the Countess was a noisy sleeper. She gave a deep sigh, shrugged her shoulders, and entered the room on tiptoe.

FRANCES GRAY PATTON

A Nice Name

(1949)

*J*N 1951 a newspaper reviewer chastised Frances Gray Patton for her aversion to publicity. "She has to get over this," he said. But she never did. During the most active years of her writing career—from the mid-1940s through the 1960s—Patton (b. 1906) published as much as she wanted, wherever she wanted—from the *New Yorker* to *Ladies' Home Journal*. But she didn't always want to. She preferred instead to be "absorbed in domestic trivia—cooking, gardening" and raising her children. After a grandchild's birth in 1955, her book publisher, Jonothan Dodd, wrote to her, "Stop cooing at that baby—and get on with that book." Today, at age eighty-five, she is still a refreshing presence, true to the portrait of her in printed interviews: friendly, loving, and thoughtful. Patton is a woman able to laugh at herself and the world. She says, for instance, that she writes in the basement, where "wet towels and other things sort of flap in my face." Her stories are mostly lighthearted, funny pieces she calls "gentle satire" in which, she claims, "I am trying to preserve a somewhat objective point of view, a view which shows me that everybody (nobody in my stories at least, is very mean), that everybody, including myself, is slightly ridiculous."

But Patton also says of her stories that "they often seem frivolous, humorous, but underneath each one is a pretty sober thought." Indeed, Patton's are enduring stories, especially those that preserve the traces of an all-but-suppressed antiracist consciousness among white women. "A Nice Name" is one of Patton's most powerful achievements; it should be linked to stories such as "A Piece of Bread" (1944), a troubling account of a young white girl's fear of a chain gang repairing the street in front of her house and her plagued conscience after refusing to bring one of the inmates food.

Patton normally draws her characters from the upper-middle classes of southern whites. Her most moving stories are those that prod the contradictions of the characters' liberalism. Sometimes those contradictions emerge in relationships with black maids; sometimes they surface in the McCarthy years as the characters' easy assumption of security is shattered when they are falsely accused, coerced into conformity, or denied such basic freedoms as the right to question and disagree. Patton's stories are often ones in which white characters confront dangerous political pressures or find allies among black people. In her stories white and black women are able to meet, however briefly, to share something of significance. The forces that pull them apart again, and away from their own basic values, are named.

The scanty record of Patton's early life suggests an intelligent and lively girl who decided early on a literary career. Her mother, Mary S. MacRae Gray, published occasional stories in *St. Nicholas Magazine* and *Youth's Companion;* her father, Robert Lilly Gray, and two brothers were journalists. "Fanny," as she was known in the family, said of her father's influence, that he "gave me the respect most men reserve for their sons. He took my writing seriously." Later Patton would say,

> I like economy in writing, probably because I had a newspaperman for a father. I believe that the more briefly a thing can be said without being done in a jerky manner, the better it is. For that reason every sentence I write is to me an important sentence. I go over my manuscripts and cut out sentences. I also believe in the one right word. . . . I want to write like any good reporter—to describe the scene of my stories honestly; to tell the truth about my characters; to avoid sloppiness, malice, and platitude; to write readably.

Patton's writing has always found an eager audience. While in her teens, she won a playwriting fellowship at the University of North Carolina after attending Trinity College (now Duke University) for a year and working briefly with the Stuart Walker stock company in Cincinnati, Ohio. The drama program at Chapel Hill in those years—the early 1920s—was an exciting one. Frederick Koch and others were developing what they called "folk theater" or "people's theater," in which plays were constructed from local legends, stories, and traditions. The Carolina playmakers, apparently an interracial company, inspired the production of native theater nationwide. Frances Gray produced two plays with the group. In 1924, *The Beaded Buckle* was produced and published in *Carolina Folk-Plays*. The next year, when the Playmakers Theatre was dedicated on November 23, the production of her (unpublished) play *Out of the Past* was the opening event. Frances Gray never graduated from the university because she refused to take first-year math.

In 1927, she married Lewis Patton, fresh out of graduate school and new to the faculty of English at Chapel Hill. She quickly settled into a happy existence as a faculty wife, free to "go her own way" and write as much as she wished. After several years, she gave birth to a son and, later, twin daughters. She wrote little while her children were young, but returned to it at her husband's insistence in the 1940s.

Patton's writing career from that point on was a charmed one. Her first published short story, "A Piece of Bread" (1944), won the O. Henry prize in 1945 and attracted publishers' attention. Patton's stories began to appear in a variety of popular magazines: *Harper's, McCall's, Ladies Home Journal, Charm, Colliers, New Yorker.* Her work was sometimes anthologized, and she won several more prizes. In 1951 Patton published her first collection of short stories, *The Finer Things of Life,* which was well received, as was her second collection in 1955, *A Piece of Luck, and Other Stories.* Her third collection, consisting primarily of reprints, is *Twenty-Eight Stories* (1969).

Patton is best known for her only published novel, *Good Morning, Miss Dove,* which evolved from one of her earliest short stories. The novel is about a geography teacher in a small town, a woman Patton says is "a rebel, so conventional as to be unconventional." Despite her severity, or perhaps because of it, the "terrible" Miss Dove exercised an enormous influence on at least two generations of the townsfolk. She enchanted her audience, who compared the book to *Our Town.* She captivated Patton herself who admitted that "I started writing Miss Dove with a little malice in my mind. After all, I thought children should be quite free. But then I began to sympathize with the teacher. . ." and Miss Dove escaped, transcending Patton's original intentions. The first Miss Dove story appeared in *Ladies' Home Journal* in 1947. Readers loved it, clamored for more, and finally for the novel, which was released by Dodd in October 1954, serialized by the *Journal* as a "novelette" in November, and selected by the Book of the Month Club in 1955—the same year the novel was made into a Hollywood film starring Jennifer Jones. In the years following, *Miss Dove* was translated into several foreign languages and adapted for the stage. Although in 1973 Patton told a reporter that she was at work on "something large," it was never, apparently, completed.

In 1949 "A Nice Name" appeared in the *New Yorker* and was awarded a prize from the Society for Intercultural Education. Soon after that it was reprinted in the *Negro Digest.* One critic described Patton's *New Yorker* stories as "distinguished by their overwhelming accuracy, their painful attention to detail. Never is there a mischosen word, an inept phrase, a misplaced emphasis. They have the slick perfection of freshly laid concrete."

"A Nice Name" is typical of Patton's stories in its subject: conventional people. Patton explains, "I felt they were neglected in literature and I think there are more of them and they are the people who in the long run, when they change, affect the world."

Although readers today will be alert to the issue of race and racial difference in "A Nice Name," Patton herself would emphasize that "it is about a relation between two *people,* not two races," "that every person . . . is an individual, no matter how he may appear outwardly, he cannot be put into a category. There is always this possibility in each life, quiet as it may be, for personal idiosyncratic expansion and reaction. Each person's life is important to him. Everyone thinks he is different, and everyone is."

In "A Nice Name," Josephine struggles with her own difference, her urge to think and to create as a writer. But surrounding her, suffocating her, is a society that values not difference but conformity. Josephine is offered a choice—which, significantly, she experiences through the conflicting claims of her female friends. Often Patton's stories end at moments of confusion and decision, the characters stifled and constrained, but yearning for justice. "A Nice Name" is one of these, stories that set readers, too, onto a field of conflict as we examine the prejudices and their consequent limitations that we share with the characters.

GLYNIS CARR

The postman was late this morning, and Josephine Archer loitered, waiting for him. She ran upstairs to dab scent on her handkerchief; she moved a vase of everlastings from a table to the piano; she did a number of useless things because she didn't want to leave the house before he came. Finally, though, she decided that she'd have to go on.

She was going, as she went every Friday morning, to Amy Webb's house, out on the edge of town. Jane Banks and Kate Honeycutt would be there, too. All the girls, as they still called themselves at forty-odd, were trying to make some extra money, on account of the inflation. Their husbands' incomes were larger than they'd ever been, but you couldn't tell what might happen with labor in the saddle and Mr. Truman returned to office. (Even here in North Carolina, which had gone heavily Democratic, most of the "representative people" were sorry the country wasn't having a change.) Now that her own children were in boarding school, Josephine had time to tutor other children—the ones who had not gone away and who were having trouble with their studies; Jane and Kate baked angel cakes; and Amy, who had no children, had taken up what she called the beauty business. She was the local agent for a cosmetic firm that sold its wares by appointment or other genteel methods. Once a week, the old friends met together to have a facial and a gossip, and maybe to buy a lipstick or a bar of fancy soap from Amy. Josephine, the high-brow of the group, attempted to preserve an attitude of condescension toward these sessions (Sam, her husband, considered them silly as hell), but she really enjoyed them. She was attached to the girls, and, after all, getting your skin toned up made more sense than playing morning bridge.

When Josephine stepped out on the porch, she heard Liza singing to herself as she swept the front steps. The long strokes of her broom kept time with her low, slow-moving song and swooped up little airy clouds of dust that twinkled in the mild winter sunshine. Liza was a dark, elderly colored woman who wore square steel-rimmed spectacles and an air of moral superiority.

"Isn't this a fine day?" Josephine said.

"Yes, Ma'am," said Liza. "I never see the winter come in so easy." She stood aside to let Josephine pass. "Wait a minute, Miss Josie. Your princess shows behind."

"Oh, damn!" said Josephine. "I haven't time to fix it."

"Yes'm, you is," Liza said. "The streetcar just now went down. Step here."

Like a docile child, Josephine did as she was told. Liza selected a small gilt pin from the chain of linked safety pins that dangled on her bosom. She lifted Josephine's coat, thrust a chilly hand under the waistband of her skirt, yanked at the offending slip, and pinned a tuck securely in it. "Now you look nice," she said.

"How would I manage without you, Liza?" Josephine murmured gratefully.

"I reckon you'd flounder," Liza said. "You needs me to look after you. I ain't had advantages, like some. I can't read, and I can't write, and I can't use that dial phone good, but I knows how to work." Her face glowed. This was a topic she liked to enlarge upon. "Cook, clean up, tend to white folks—ain't no decent work I can't do." She paused, deliberating. "'Cept teach school," she added honestly. "I never tried that." Her tone implied that she had given a pedagogical career due consideration and had rejected it as unworthy of her talents.

Smiling, Josephine went down the path. She was very fond of Liza. Twenty years ago, when she engaged her, at six dollars a week, she'd been certain that she'd found a treasure, and time had proved her right. Liza was getting twenty-five now, with Sundays off, but she hadn't changed. She was just as humble and self-respecting as ever. It was plain silly to say that all darkies were spoiled by prosperity, Josephine thought, feeling pleasantly liberal—a lot of white people were, for that matter. It was a question of character, not color. She would discuss that with the girls this morning; they needed shaking out of their fixed ideas, and, besides, it would be fun to hear what they'd say. It would be provoking, too, for their opinions ran naturally to the pious and stuffy, but she would be rewarded by some gem of complacency that she could quote to Sam, or could use in a letter.

The postman came along just as she shut the iron gate behind her. He had a letter for her—the one from Mrs. Marshall that she'd been hoping for. She read it standing on the corner, waiting for the streetcar to come. It was a charming letter, witty and entertaining, and poignant at the end, in a stark, almost poetic way that moved Josephine deeply. Her vision seemed to widen, to brighten, and all the accustomed details of her life seemed more important than they really were.

Every time Josephine got one of Mrs. Marshall's letters, the same thing would happen to her. She would feel curiously alive, as if the sun had suddenly broken through a ceiling of colorless cloud. She would notice the angle of a shadow, the feel of the air, the green interstices of the old bricks in the sidewalk; she would observe the people who passed, perceiving in them some below-the-surface quality that made them significant; and she would start sorting and sifting her impressions for use in the letter she was soon, herself, to write in reply.

She folded the letter and put it in her pocketbook. She was aware of the sunlight, lying like a warm hand between her shoulder blades, and she look around at the town of New Hope—a dull little town, actually, that hadn't changed or wanted to change in all the years she'd known it—and as she tried to find the words that would carry its essential flavor, it became not dull at all but perfectly sweet and serene, a town reflecting a sort of Wordsworthian continuity. She could still hear Liza crooning on the porch, and some winter birds, seduced, no doubt, by the unseasonable weather into a mood of vernal optimism (now, *that* sounded stilted), were twittering. Peering down the hill where New Hope's one trolley line ran—from the courthouse square, at the bottom, to the city limits, a mile beyond her corner—Josephine saw the rooftops still wet and shining with dew, and the green dome of the courthouse—that indescribable, nostalgic green of weathered copper—rising, like a structure lighter than air, above the handkerchief-fog that had settled in the low part of town. She couldn't see the streetcar, but she knew how it looked, sitting idle at the foot of the square while the motorman drank a Coca-Cola in Boone's Drugstore. Soon the car, painted jonquil yellow and driven by a bad-tempered motorman, would emerge from the mist and come bouncing up the hill as it had bounced since she could remember. When it was halfway up, the wires would begin to hum. First, they would carry a droning murmur, then a louder sound, insistent and gay, until you expected them to burst out singing. She would get on and ride out to join the girls at Amy's. But in the meantime it was pleasant to stand here in the sun, playing with her thoughts and thinking about the letter in her purse.

The trolley wires had begun to hum. The yellow car jerked jauntily up the hill and stopped to take Josephine on.

On the way out to Amy's, she reread her letter. Up to now, the exchange had been hardly more than a delightful game of wits. Josephine and her correspondent, whom she had never seen, had vied with each other, each striving to cap the other's latest letter with a better one of her own. But today's letter was different. It was like the beginning of something—an overture to the sort of friendship you read about in books, in which there is no call for explanations or reserves, because of a perfect junction of sympathies.

The correspondence had begun in an accidental way. When Josephine had started coaching school children, she had rediscovered a forgotten pleasure. She had found that she still liked Latin. Years before, when her Great-Uncle Ashbel, a profane, yellow-visaged old gentleman wasting away of a liver ailment, had propped himself up in bed and introduced her to that language, she had been an apt pupil, but Uncle Ash had died, and Josephine, realizing that a passion for gerunds was considered queer by her contemporaries, had curbed it accordingly. Now, in the comparative safety of middle age, she had felt bold enough to risk an unconventional enthusiasm. She had sought to arouse that enthusiasm in the children she taught. After drilling them in their conjunctions, she had read them snatches of Horace and Vergil, explaining what she read and making them repeat the Latin after her, to "get its feeling on the tongue." Her experiment had appeared to work, for even Jane Banks' bat-brained twins had stopped fooling with their hair while they recited. Flushed with success, Josephine had written a letter to the local newspaper, and had immediately felt sheepish about having done so. The letter, advocating a reformed technique in the teaching of beginners' Latin, had been ignored by the local teachers, but there'd been this one woman, Mrs. Marshall, from an obscure place in Virginia, who had written to her. An acquaintance had clipped Mrs. Archer's letter for her, Mrs. Marshall wrote, adding that she herself was a teacher and had used that method for years. Although the children in her country scool didn't come from privileged homes, they had, she said, the gift of rhythm and a liking for accented syllables. Most of them would have to go to work young, and some educators might think it foolish to teach them any Latin at all, but she looked at it another way. Life was going to be hard for these children; any richness she could put into their minds was little enough. Someday the ring of noble words might come back to them, easing their worry and making them happy for a moment.

That first letter, though it had pleased Josephine, had made her feel shy. Theoretically, she admired the unguarded sincerity of a person who could bring out phrases like "the ring of noble words," but she suspected that this sort of writing was a bit high-flown. However, she'd shown the letter to the girls and they'd thought it wonderful. Somehow, that had reassured her.

"She must be a bril-l-iant woman!" Kate Honeycutt had said, rolling the "l"s on her tongue. Her rosy complexion, on which the crow Thought had never stamped his foot, had glowed rosier with awe. To Kate, the willing perusal of a single printed page indicated an intellectual temperature that flirted with brain fever. "And look at her nice name!"

It *was* a nice name, Josephine had thought, saying it over to herself. The woman had signed herself Hannah Lee Marshall—(Mrs.) Hannah Lee Marshall. It sounded like a name that had been handed down with love through generations—a legacy as honored as an

Early Georgian spoon. It suggested an accustomed, plain-as-an-old-shoe gentility so entirely untainted with pretentiousness that it needn't even be afraid of fancy phrases, when they came from the heart. Josephine had written then to thank Mrs. Marshall for her interest, and after a correct interval Mrs. Marshall had written again. The second letter had firmly established her as a lady; it had been as serious as the first but more restrained, more—well, more like a letter Josephine might have written. Like the one she *had* written. Josephine had replied a second time, and from then on the correspondence had flourished.

Josephine had always been fond of writing letters, but until now she'd been given scant opportunity to practice the art. Of course, there'd been that one literary beau when she was nineteen, but he hadn't lasted long. She still recalled him with a kind of stubborn gratitude, though at the time she'd come to think him as funny as her friends had. She'd met him at a Chapel Hill commencement. He hadn't attended the dances, because he wasn't a fraternity man, but in his cap and gown at the Senior Reception he'd looked like everybody else. He'd written her a number of letters that summer, all very elevated and full of metaphor and sentiment, and she had written to him. Every Sunday, while her family slept off its dinner, she had retired to the library, and there, with the help of Bartlett and Roget, she had composed her weekly epistle. The boy had called her "the modern Madame de Staël" (she had looked up de Staël in the Britannica) and had quoted Pater, to the effect that she gave him "a quickened, multiplied consciousness."

Unfortunately, he had come to see her. He had looked very raw and "country." He had had a red neck and a large Adam's apple, and he'd been painfully conscious of his manners. At dinner, when he spilled a drop of gravy on the cloth, he had exclaimed, "Oh, pardon me! That was unpardonable!" He had become a family joke, of course, but, even so, Josephine would have continued the correspondence if her mother hadn't said, "Now, Josie, you can't hurt that poor boy's feelings! Just go on writing to him, but be careful not to encourage him. Make your letters shorter, skip a week now and then, and gradually let them stop altogether." That had taken the edge off the whole thing.

Josephine's other correspondence had been mostly family letters. Cousins wrote to tell about Mamie's engagement—"such a nice boy, a third generation Sigma Nu"—or about Aunt Sadie's varicose veins.

Josephine's children wrote from school asking for week-end permission or for "those old saddle oxfords I think I left in the storm closet." One could hardly offer in return a prose poem about the mist in the courthouse square. That was the sort of thing one could send only to a Mrs. Marshall.

The two women wrote to each other with increasing frequency, and they didn't for long confine themselves to the problems of teaching Latin. They discussed food and religion and art. They made epigrams on the weather. They philosophized and polished their sentences. Occasionally, Josephine turned again to Bartlett and Roget. Once, she invited Mrs. Marshall to visit her, and when her invitation met with an evasive refusal, she'd been almost offended. It had seemed too much of a piece with Mrs. Marshall's general reticence, for, candid to a degree about her inner life, the lady told next to nothing of her circumstances or background. Reserve was a sign of breeding, to be sure, but Josephine felt that Mrs. Marshall had an excess of that virtue. And the odd way she continued to sign herself, with "Mrs." in parentheses! As if to remind me that I'm only a professional acquaintance, Josephine thought, somewhat petulantly. As if she fears I'll presume!

Yet the anonymous nature of the correspondence—for writing "Dear Mrs. Marshall" was as private as writing "Dear Diary"—was a charm against self-consciousness. Josephine dropped her own restraint and wrote personal things. She poked fun at Sam and at the girls, and she embroidered on old recollections that she'd rarely shared with anyone.

Sunday had been the anniversary of Uncle Ash's death, and Josephine had written Mrs. Marshall about the winter she had studied Latin with him. As she described an afternoon spent in his room, she had almost been there again. She smelled the fatpine fire, and the narcissus blooming in a bowl of pebbles, and the acrid medicine in a glass—all those odors that couldn't quite disguise the odor of mortality. She saw the books piled all over the dressers and tables and half the bed, too, and the old man sitting up high, so that he could breathe, and the moments when his eyes seemed to struggle against the dull, toxic glaze that settled on them. (That was why he'd given her the lessons, she supposed—to keep his faculties alive.) She heard his outraged voice saying, "Christ, no! It's dative, not ablative! Dative, dative! I should think your goddam instinct would have told you!"

She had related all that to Mrs. Marshall, and at last Mrs. Marshall had verged upon the personal. At the end of the long letter that had come today, after a criticism of Graham Greene's latest novel, a recipe for hickory-nut cake, and a fine description of cloud formations in the Virginia foothills, she had said, "When I think of your uncle among his books, I think of my father. He was ill for a long time, too, but he had no books to sustain him. He would have understood the joys of the Sabine farm, but he never heard of it."

That was going pretty far, Josephine thought—and for a Virginian, especially—to confess that one's own father hadn't been an educated man! It amounted to a laying of the cards on the table, to a declaration of the utmost confidence. When I write her next, Josephine determined, I shall call her Hannah.

The car stopped at the end of the line. The cross motorman leaped off and angrily reversed his trolley pole. At a more leisurely speed, Josephine followed him. Then she hurried up the half block to Amy's house.

Mossy, Amy's cherished maid, greeted her at the door. "Lawzy, Miss Jo," she said, "you-all comes steppin' high, an' Miss Katie an' Miss Janie cain't sashay roun' de cawnah on dey own two footses. I done tell 'em they-all gwine be big as me, an' Miss Jo gwine hol' on t' huh shape."

"Mr. Archer needed the car today," Josephine said, and was instantly furious with herself for stooping to an explanation. She couldn't stand Mossy. She disapproved of familiar servants and suspected this one of playing professional darky. Mossy was a fat, oily-black woman, whose sly and greedy eyes belied her ingratiating simper. And she used "you-all" in the singular. She must have got her dialect from the radio.

"Lemme res' yo' bonnet," Mossy said, snatching Josephine's hat and regarding it with contempt. "Go on up to Miss Amy's room. De other ladies is up dar, puttin' on dey nekkid jays." She waited complacently for appreciative laughter from Josephine. "Dat's whut I calls dem flimsy wrappers dat don't hide nutn," she said, in the peeved manner of an after-dinner speaker who is forced to diagram his little joke. "Nekkid jays. Nekkid as a jay bird."

Josephine smiled as affably as she could and went upstairs. Amy's room was dainty and restful. The walls were painted pale violet and the Venetian blinds were drawn, because Amy believed the ritual of beauty required an atmosphere of sanctuary. Sun came through in thin slices and made a Jacob's ladder on the carpet. Generally, the room was full of chatter, but today the girls sat quietly on the chaise longue, underneath the row of Godey prints. Their hair was drawn back from their foreheads, and their faces, glistening with cold cream, had a look of solemn innocence. So they had looked at school, Josephine thought with a rush of affection, when they had been deep in some weighty matter like the nature of eternal punishment or just how wrong it was to kiss a boy before he'd given you his fraternity pin.

"Jo-Jo, darling!" Amy said, rising. "We've saved the prettiest negligée for you. Have you heard Mossy's version of 'negligée'? It's a scream."

"She told me," Josephine said. "Hey there, everybody."

From a lingerie closet that looked stocked for a long, luxurious illness, Amy took a fragile concoction of lace and chiffon. She was a tall woman whose least movement had grace. Now, as she offered the garment to Josephine, her gesture conveyed the notion of a kind of Olympian compassion.

"Isn't it pretty!" Josephine cried. "It looks like a frappé." She took off her suit and blouse.

"Your slip's hiked up," Kate said. She came and removed Liza's safety pin, and helped Josephine into the wrapper.

"You're first, Jo," Amy said, arranging a row of bottles and jars on a table beside the bed. She spread a clean towel on the pillow. "Lie down, now, and relax. Let all the little muscles go slack."

Josephine stretched out on the bed. Amy gazed down at her with an unaccountable air of indecision. Kate and Jane were silent. Josephine had the sudden conviction that they were all about to tell her something, and that whatever it was would be unpleasant. Jane looked uneasily at Amy. Amy shrugged.

"By the way, Jo," Jane said, "have you heard from Mrs. M. lately?"

"I heard today," Josephine said. "An awfully nice letter."

"That's a coincidence," Jane said, "because we heard, too—indirectly. Mary Lou Hunter has just been up that way, and she's solved your mystery."

Josephine sat up. Amy sat down beside her and took her hand.

"You see, we were just dead with curiosity," Jane said. "So when we heard Mary Lou was going up there to her niece's wedding, we asked her to do some detective work. We thought we'd surprise you. Mary Lou came home last night." She licked her lips nervously. "You tell her, Amy. You talked to Mary Lou."

Amy stroked Josephine's hand. "Your Mrs. Marshall is a remarkable person," she began slowly. "She's far better educated than any of us ever dreamed of being. Even than you, Jo."

"That's apparent in her letters," Josephine said.

"I mean she's really cultivated," Amy went on. "It's not only that she teaches school; she plays the piano beautifully—classical music."

"She reads French for fun," Kate said, wide-eyed.

"There's just this one thing," said Amy.

"One teentsy-weentsy thing!" Kate chirped.

"Hush up, Kate. This isn't funny," Jane said.

"I think it is," Kate said. "One way you look at it, it's funny."

"Well," Josephine said, trying to sound flippant, "is she living in sin?"

"Oh, no," Amy said. "She's highly respected in her community. Very charitable, and a power for good, and . . ." Her voice trailed away. She looked hopefully at Jane. Jane shook her head. "Well," Amy said flatly, "she's colored."

"What?" Josephine gasped. Then she saw the girls watching her, wanting to see how she would act. "I need to light a Murad," she said.

"Here's a Camel, if that will help," Jane said. "Is it all right, Amy?"

"Yes," said Amy, who usually would not let the girls smoke during treatments, because she thought tobacco smoke injurious to the creams and lotions she worked with. "This time. I think she needs it."

Josephine drew smoke deep into her lungs. It made her dizzy, the way the first cigarette of the day often did. She blew it out on a whistle of wonder.

"Aren't you flabbergasted?" said Kate.

"Give me time to take it in," Josephine said. But she realized, with a definite sense of shock, that she wasn't particularly surprised, really, and that what she'd learned didn't make much difference. Of course, it explained some things—Mrs. Marshall's personal reticence, for instance, and the absence of a wary sophistication that might have prevented her from using those high-sounding, hackneyed expressions, like "noble words" and "richness in their minds,"

so innocently, as if they were still fresh and potent. And that paren-
thetical prefix to her signature—what did it mean? Was it simple
ignorance of usage? Or was it pride, a jealous insistence upon her
right to the appellative? Josephine tried to picture her by thinking of
Liza, whom she loved, and of Mossy, whom she detested, and of a
number of other Negroes, to whom she was amiably indifferent. But
she couldn't do it. It was strange, now she came to think of it, that
she had never visualized Hannah Lee Marshall in the flesh. All that
the name had ever evoked for her had been a sense of nimble spirits,
of candor of mind, and of a lovely variety of experience in a world
that had a warm glow. And that was all it evoked now.

"Yes, Jo, she's colored," Amy said. "Her story's like a fairy tale, except that it doesn't end happily. Do you want to hear it?"

"Naturally," Josephine said.

"Well, she was raised on this little farm in Virginia. They say her
parents were the finest type of Negroes—humble and self-respecting. The kind that's gone with the wind. They had a whole mess of
children, and most of them didn't amount to much, but this Mrs.
Marshall—" She laughed apologetically. "I reckon I ought to call her
Hannah now—this one girl was awfully smart and pretty. You know
darky girls *can* be pretty. They say she had that right clear brown
skin—"

"I know," Josephine said.

"Some Northern people came down there for the summer and
hired Hannah to look after their children. They were advanced
thinkers, so they got crazy over her and took her home with them
and treated her like a member of the family. They sent her to college
and even let her travel in Europe."

"Misguided kindness," said Jane.

"Well, yes," Amy agreed, "but they didn't know any better. People
who weren't brought up with darkies don't understand them like we
do. Anyhow, Hannah married a doctor in the North—a colored doctor—but he left her, or something. She had no children, and her
father was old and sick, so she came home to nurse him. And after
he died, she had this idea that she ought to stay there and help her
people. So she did."

One way you look at it," Kate said gravely, "it's sad."

Josephine felt called upon to say something. "I'm astonished,"
she said.

"Of course you are, honey," Amy said. "It isn't your fault."

"It's that woman's fault," Jane said hotly. "Writing to Jo like that. Letting on she was an equal. I think we should expose her!"

"No," Amy said. "That wouldn't be Christian. She's had a strange life and a lonely one. She probably never considered the position she was placing Jo in."

"Maybe she thought Jo-Jo was a nigger, too," Kate said.

Jane put her face in her hands and moaned with laughter. Amy made a try for composure, but the effort was beyond her. Kate laughed because the others did, and because she thought she must have said something clever. Josephine began to laugh, too. She leaned against Amy's shoulder and laughed until she cried.

"Stop it," Amy said. "You'll get hysterical. Do you want some ammonia?"

"No. I'm all right," Josephine said.

"But listen," said Jane. "There's another thing to consider. Jo asked her to come to see her. Suppose she does?"

"I've considered that," Amy said. "There needn't be any embarrassment. Mrs. Marshall will go into Jo's bedroom and they'll have a nice, long chat about Latin. Then she can go home with Liza. Or she can come out here and stay with Mossy. Mossy has a double bed, with an inner-spring mattress."

Josephine stared at her. I couldn't have heard that, she thought. For an instant, she herself seemed to become Mrs. Marshall—being received with kind courtesy, being dismissed and told she could sleep in the bed beside fat Mossy. Oh, for heaven's sake! Amy must be joking. But Amy rarely joked, and she was not joking now. Her noble brow was unravaged by humor or doubt. Her lips were curved—not in a smile but in their perpetual expression of confident goodness. "Lie back, now," she said, "and let's get on with the treatment."

Josephine lay back. Kate and Jane started to paint their toenails, talking quietly between themselves as they compared the relative merits of Tropic Pink and Forbidden Apple. I don't have to stay here if I don't want to, Josephine thought suddenly. What am I doing here anyway, in this silly room, with these silly women? I'm a free agent. I can put on my clothes and go home, and write a letter to my friend Hannah Marshall. But Amy had laid a wet compress on her eyes. Amy had begun, with strong, competent fingers, to work cream into her face. "Your tissues are starved," Amy said.

Josephine surrendered for the moment to the rhythm of the massage and tried to recover the feeling of calm exhilaration that she had known an hour earlier. But the mood had flown. All she remembered now was a smug, dowdy town and a tedious, bossy darky sweeping in a slovenly way. (Why did she have to raise all that dust?) The windows were open, and presently she heard the beginning of a resonance in the air. It came from the trolley wires, down at the corner. Soon the dinky car would be heard rattling and banging along the tracks, but now there was only this monotonous humming noise—like a whine, like a long complaint, like the fretful, recurrent loneliness of the human mind.

Why, that's pretty good, Josephine thought with a stab of pleasure. I must remember to use that in a letter.

"Now, Joe," Amy said gently, without disturbing the regular rotary motion of her fingertips, "don't hurt that poor woman's feelings! You'll have to go on writing—for a time, at least. Maybe you could mention the race business casually, as if you'd known about her all along. And you can skip a letter now and then. And gradually— without doing anything cruel, you know. . . ."

Josephine stiffened.

"Let all the little muscles go slack," Amy said.

ALICE CHILDRESS

In the Laundry Room

(1956)

*F*LORENCE, the play Alice Childress published and produced in 1949, depicts a black woman and a white woman discussing racial issues in a segregated bus station. Unable to transcend hierarchies based on color, the women lose the opportunity for genuine interchange. Although these two women meet in mutually familiar territory, history prevents them from entering into an untainted exchange. In "In the Laundry Room" Childress again depicted a black woman and a white woman meeting in familiar territory, this time trying to find a basis for interacting as individuals instead of playing the roles that history, custom, and mythology have assigned them. The difference in this story is that the black woman is Mildred, the daring, iconoclastic domestic worker in *Like One of the Family . . . conversations from a domestic's life* (1986),[1] from which this story is taken, whose trademark is challenging the norm and championing the unpredictable.

The element of daring in Mildred's character—daring to call a white woman a liar, to insist that a fellow domestic confront her own fears and prejudices, to subvert the status quo—is characteristic also of Alice Childress (born October 12, 1920). Having migrated from South Carolina to New York when such transitions might have been popular if not profitable, Childress learned early that a supportive network was what one needed to be daring.

Her first and most influential friend was her grandmother, Eliza White. Not only did she take Childress to New York, but she instilled in her those values that proved essential in her later life: confidence in herself in spite of opposition, ambition to reach new heights, trust in her own ability. Childress recalls that her grandmother helped shape her creative imagination. Eliza White had a "deep interest in writing" and would encourage her granddaughter to "write things down," asserting of various pieces that "we should keep this" and stuffing these writings into the "oversized pocketbook" she kept for such occasions.[2] Childress and White would also clip newspaper articles and speculate on what had *not* been covered. And the two of them would sit at the window on 118th Street between Lenox and 7th Avenues and speculate about people passing by.

Mrs. White encouraged young Alice to explore not only her imagination, but the empirical world around her. She took Childress to art galleries, museums, the Italian and Jewish shopping areas, and to explore other sights in the city. Thinking at the time only that she was "going out with Mama," Childress later realized how invaluable those experiences had been in the shaping of her creative imagination and her identity as an artist.

Her grandmother exposed her to other experiences that were equally influential. A member of Salem Church of Harlem, of which the poet Countee Cullen's father was minister, Mrs. White took Childress to hear readings of poetry from works by Cullen, Langston Hughes, and Paul Laurence Dunbar, and to operas and other musical programs put on by the church. White and Childress attended cultural discussions in private homes of members of the Amapa Society as well as programs sponsored by various YMCAs throughout the city.

Childress recounts that Sunday afternoons with her grandmother's circle of friends were especially significant. All from Charleston, South Carolina, they inspired Childress to stay in touch with her roots; this influence is clearly evident in Childress's play *Wedding Band* (1966), her novel *A Short Walk* (1979), and the musical drama *Gullah* (1984). Childress credits this group's "intense attachment to where they came from" as the source of her accurate depictions of the people, the culture, and the history of South Carolina and the Sea Island territory about which she writes. They, in turn, recognized that she was special; they frequently said to Mrs. White, "That child's been here before," meaning that Childress had the wisdom of an elder though she was still a young child.

One of Childress's early teachers recognized her talent when Childress was only ten years old (she was already writing stories by this time). The young white teacher knew that few blacks had been successful in the theater, but she nonetheless expressed confidence in Childress's abilities and encouraged her theatrical ambitions. "When you have a gift," she said, "you use it" in spite of any obstacles posed by race.

During the 1930s and 1940s, when Childress worked at a variety of jobs—machinist, photo retoucher, salesperson, insurance agent, domestic—to support her young daughter and herself, she needed a supportive network for child care as well as for encouragement to continue as an actress and writer. Mrs. Ruth Brown took care of Childress's daughter during part of that time, and Mrs. Helen Mead, a black woman who owned the Little Brown Schoolhouse, also provided a safe and productive environment for her daughter.

Childress peopled her fictional and dramatic worlds with domestics (*Like One of the Family,* 1956), seamstresses and bakers (*Wedding Band,* 1966), and other working-class individuals. She also portrayed failed and retrieved love affairs among this group (*Mojo: A Black Love Story,* 1970). In other works she depicted revolutionaries who were not on the front lines of the uprising of the 1960s (*Wine in the Wilderness,* 1969). Equally as iconoclastic as her character Mildred, Childress refused to allow a director to change an ending for one of her plays; to allow *Trouble in Mind* (1955), her most successful play, to be optioned for Broadway; or to write about topics that critics considered appropriate for black artists, such as those sprinkled with anti-white messages. She could write about interracial love (*Wedding Band*) without sensationalizing it, and she could be hopeful enough to portray a thirteen-year-old drug addict who might indeed, through some miracle of faith and with the help of friends, find the strength to alter his self-destructive habits (*A Hero Ain't Nothin' but a Sandwich,* 1973). Her most recent work, *Those Other People* (1989), deals with sexual and racial difference.

During her work with *Freedom* magazine, Childress's friendships with Paul Robeson, W.E.B. Du Bois, and Lorraine Hansberry provided formal intellectual support for her development as an artist. In her year working with this group, she and Hansberry would occasionally produce "mini-shows" for Robeson, combinations of prose and song that won his approval. Hansberry wrote the first review of one of Childress's plays. Robeson was the model for pursuing what one believed in, and both Childress and Hansberry learned well from him. Once he admonished them not to appear on a public program with him, saying, "You may be punished for it, you know." They made the appearance. Du Bois also taught Childress the need for serious "working artists."

Childress's husband Nathan Woodard has provided the friendship that she values most; she says that there is "no friendship to compare with it in my life." He has encouraged her in her writing, interrupted his own work to complete music for hers, and traveled extensively with her. They worked together in producing *Young Martin Luther King* (1969) as well as the more recent production of *Gullah* (1984); Woodard took six weeks away from his professional activities to assist Childress in producing a full-length version of *Gullah* at the University of Massachusetts at Amherst (it played for 120 performances in the shortened version that they produced earlier in South Carolina).

Childress also has theatrical and academic friends who are sympathetic to her artistic identity and who respect what she has tried to achieve. Ruby Dee played the lead role in four productions of *Wedding Band* and wrote an article on the political climate that prevented its staging. Theater scholar Rosemary Curb early looked at Childress's drama and wrote in response to what she had done—not to what she should have done, as others were wont to respond.[3] Childress and Mildred inspired my first critical study, *From Mammies to Militants: Domestics in Black American Literature* (1982).[4]

TRUDIER HARRIS

Marge . . . Sometimes it seems like the devil and all his imps are tryin' to wear your soul case out. . . . Sit down, Marge, and act like you got nothin' to do. . . . No, don't make no coffee, just sit. . . .

Today was laundry day and I took Mrs. M . . .'s clothes down to the basement to put them in the automatic machine. In a little while another houseworker comes down—a white woman. She dumps her clothes on the bench and since my bundle is already in the washer I go over to sit down on the bench and happen to brush against her dirty clothes. . . . Well sir! She gives me a kinda sickly grin and snatched her clothes away quick. . . .

Now, you know, Marge, that it was nothin' but the devil in her makin' her snatch that bundle away 'cause she thought I might give her folks gallopin' pellagra or somethin'. Well, honey, you know what the devil in me wanted to do! . . . You are right! . . . My hand was just itchin' to pop her in the mouth, but I remembered how my niece Jean has been tellin' me that *poppin'* people is not the way to solve problems. . . . So I calmed myself and said, "Sister, why did you snatch those things and look so flustered?" She turned red and says, "I was just makin' room for you." Still keepin' calm, I says, "You are a liar." . . . And then she hung her head.

"Sister," I said, "you are a houseworker and I am a houseworker— now will you favor me by answering some questions?" She nodded her head. . . . The first thing I asked her was how much she made for a week's work and, believe it or not, Marge, she earns less than I do and *that ain't easy*. . . . Then I asked her, "Does the woman you work for ask you in a *friendly* way to do extra things that ain't in the bargain and then later on get *demandin'* about it?" . . . She nods, yes. . . . "Tell me, young woman," I went on, "does she cram eight hours of work into five and call it *part time?*" . . . She nods yes again. . . .

Then, Marge, I added, "I am not your enemy, so don't get mad with me just because you ain't free!" . . . Then she speaks up fast, "I am free!" . . . . "All right," I said. "How about me goin' over to your house tonight for supper?" . . . "Oh," she says, "I room with people and I don't think they . . ." I cut her off. . . . "If you're free," I said, "you can pick your own friends without fear."

Wait a minute, Marge, let me tell it now. . . . "How come," I asked her, "the folks I work for are willin' to have me put my hands all over their chopped meat patties and yet ask me to hang my coat in the kitchen closet instead of in the hall with theirs?" . . . By this time, Marge, she looked pure bewildered. . . . "Oh," she said, "it's all so mixed up I don't understand!"

"Well, it'll all get clearer as we go along," I said. . . . "Now when you got to plunge your hands in all them dirty clothes in order to put them in the machine . . . how come you can't see that it's a whole lot safer and makes more sense to put your hand in mine and be friends?" Well, Marge, she took my hand and said, "I want to be friends!"

I was so glad I hadn't popped her, Marge. The good Lord only knows how hard it is to do things the right way and make peace. . . . All right now, let's have the coffee, Marge.

DELORIS HARRISON

A Friend for a Season

(1969)

*D*ELORIS Netzband and I are friends for a season. "We had friendships the way plays have runs on Broadway," says her protagonist Cheryl in "A Friend for a Season." So too are we friends, Netzband and I—our friendship has been running eight seasons now, during summertimes when Netzband returns stateside from Cairo, Egypt.

Netzband, who writes under the name Deloris Harrison, is a woman who has lived in many different and vastly separate worlds—black Harlem; an intensely secular large urban university; an all-male, almost all-white elite university; a New England small city; an all-white high school; the Netherlands; Egypt. She has made friends in many of those worlds, friendships that have survived her departure from each world. The ability to survive in all of those different environments is something special; the ability to enter into and maintain friendships with people rooted in those various worlds is most unusual, and undoubtedly has something to teach us.

This summer Deloris Netzband came up to the Vermont farmhouse I live in (for years the same town, same house, same husband) and we talked about writing and teaching and about our college-age children. (Her daughter Germaine is a junior at Yale.) Netzband wore green shadow over her eyes in the shape of triangles like Nefertiti's. She looked marvelous. Through the open windows, the noise of a tractor mowing out in the field created a pause in our conversation. In that moment I imagined her gazing out of the heart of some faraway city in the dry desert heat, through shafts of dusty sunlight, across a river I know only the name of—the Atbara perhaps—at gray-green palms, the curve of a white felucca sail. I marveled at how much she has seen, how much she has been able to reconcile. Then, I envied her her life.

But she was not always so free. "I write often about children," Deloris Netzband says. "In childhood you are so vulnerable. The things that happen to you are so arbitrary—where you live, where you go to school, whether your parents are divorced. It's like the idea the Greeks had about fate . . . the godlike nature of authorities." In spite of their circumstances, the children in her stories, like Cheryl in "A Friend for a Season," dare to feel a tenuous pride for what they do have. Many of Netzband's stories are set in Harlem, where she grew up. In another of Netzband's stories, "My Mother and Me," the first-person narrator, an adolescent boy, is told at school to draw a floor plan of the apartment where he lives alone with his mother. When it is finished and he hands it in to his drafting teacher, the teacher looks at the shoebox floor plan and refuses to believe it. In another story, "Going Home," the narrator recalls her Harlem childhood and the trips she and her mother took "fourth Sundays" to her grandmother's home in Virginia in the country, "where backward hicks come from." When the grandparents have all died and there is no real family left for her, the mother in the story decides never to return for fourth Sunday. With a stoicism typical of the children in the stories, the narrator says, "While I did not in the following years miss those excursions, I'm sure she did; but then we had our lives to live, our times to suffer through and our home to make for ourselves."

And so there is a movement in each story, as in "A Friend for a Season," toward condensation, as hopes and dreams and finally even nostalgia are swept out by authority and circumstance and a denser reality settles in. At the moment of deepest suffering, the writing takes on solidity; the child looks around, records the cold breeze, the smell of garbage from across the river, the unscrubbed hallway—the street, "where everyone is equal." One senses that this is the moment of understanding, of acceptance, even of affirmation.

Although Netzband grew up in New York, she was born in the family home in Virginia. Bought and paid for in 1926 by her grandfather, this farm was the first in Bedford Country to be owned by blacks. Her own childhood had its share of dreams: she wanted to be an opera singer for her father who sang and encouraged her to sing. She wanted to be a doctor. She wanted to be a writer. Like Cheryl in "A Friend for a Season," Netzband's life took a turn at the divorce of her parents, when she was in second grade. She grew close to her mother, a hospital administrator, a woman whose warmth and confidence may have set free Netzband's sense of humor, that jiggly laugh you shared with your best friend when you were both twelve.

She was admitted to Radcliffe at the age of sixteen, but Radcliffe officials thought she was too young and suggested she wait a year. Instead,

Netzband enrolled in St. Joseph's College and, in 1958, received her B.A. Although she wanted to find something in the field of writing, Netzband tried every major newspaper, magazine, radio and television station and "met a brick wall." "The barriers were not ready to come down," Netzband said. "It was a time of recession, of tremendous discrimination against blacks, against women." Instead, she got an M.A. from New York University and did a year of social work. Then she took a teaching exam, became certified, and taught at De Witt Clinton High School for seven years. In 1966–67, she taught in the Netherlands for a year as a Fulbright exchange teacher. She returned and, on May 15, 1968, finished the last page of her manuscript *We Shall Live in Peace,* a children's book on Martin Luther King. The next day, May 16, her daughter Germaine was born.

In the years following she taught at City College of New York; at Dartmouth College from 1970 to 1972, when it was still an all-male institution; and at Windham College in Vermont as visiting creative writing professor. She taught later for Lebanon College in Lebanon, New Hampshire, which is where I met her. I was a student in her contemporary American fiction course. Currently, Netzband is head of the English Department of Cairo American College in Cairo, Egypt.

Netzband has described the writing of the following story:[1] "I wrote 'A Friend for a Season' in the Netherlands, in a small town south near the border of Belgium. It was in a house I rented from a schoolmaster who had become blind at the age of seventy. The study was lined with books; he touched each one and told me its title. It was a pleasant room. The desk looked out over a park. I sat there and wrote this story. It was the first experience for me of how you can transcend place and time."

MARGARET W. MERRILL

As children we had friends the way plays have runs on Broadway. In the fall, fresh from camp—or, more likely, a two-month hiatus in the South with grandparents—we looked around the schoolyard and saw new faces. By the crumbling concrete wall where the boys played handball you might see a frightened little girl just arrived from the South, innocent to the ways of New York. Or you might for the first time find value in an old face. Last year (as you called the months before summer vacation) this person had seemed too childish or not childish enough, and so you were oblivious of each other.

Now you suddenly found beauty and worth in each other. You became friends for a season.

This was the girl who saw you through some climactic, devastating season in your life and became synonymous with it, although in most cases she had nothing to do with it.

If it was autumn, you roller-skated together; you watched the sun seem to move farther and farther away from the earth while you swung together in the park—both of you eager to fly high, as you once had, but growing ashamed that you still loved the swings, the monkey bars and the seesaws. You went to the library together. You walked home from school together.

By spring there was often a new friend, and you played hopscotch and jumped double-dutch. You walked farther away from the neighborhood. You would sit quietly like country children, as most likely you should have been, having been born in some green Southern land. You would look up at the sun through thin city trees and feel happy to be alive. Talk flowed easily with a bag of potato chips or a large dill pickle between you.

One day in the middle of March I met Phyllis Green in the doorway of MacFarland's Candy Store. Although Phyllis and I had gone to the same school for over a year, we had never approached each other.

"Hi, Cheryl. Haigies on your potato chips," she said, speaking as naturally as if we had been friends for a long time.

Phyllis had skinny legs and big feet, and so did I. There was usually a hole in the back of one of her socks, and the socks always rode down in her large, down-at-heel shoes. Phyllis walked in the middle of winter through the dull gray streets of Harlem with her coat flapping open and hanging lopsided. Her short hair was in braids. Usually either a braid was coming loose or a half-tied ribbon hung precariously from it. Phyllis was carefree, happy; and I—I was already like an unhappy mouse. She was my best friend for a while.

It was a bright day, the first one we had had since the long, dark winter. It was nearly one o'clock, and time to return to school after lunch.

MacFarland's Candy Store faced the schoolyard, and I could see the lines of students (boys at the two eastern doors and girls at the two western doors) beginning to move inside the building. Only a few belligerent boys still played handball, or stood just outside the gate, as if undecided whether or not to return to the battlefield of classrooms. Their brown and black faces were covered with sweat because they had been either playing handball or running senselessly and insanely—running to exorcise a frustrated devil within themselves. On their faces was a sense of impending defeat. As always, they had discarded their jackets with defiant bravado, daring the temperature to drop again. At this they always lost too.

The girls' entrances were always locked first. In an effort to coax the gate hangers inside, the boys' doors were left open till last. None of the boys moved toward the sanctuary inside. Only Phyllis and I approached it, hand in hand.

Phyllis had an easy walk. She moved gracefully despite the way her coat hung and the size of her feet.

"I sure liked that movie, didn't you, Cheryl?" she asked. "It was good—I mean, the way he could jump all over the place and swing and everything. I mean, I never did see nothing like that, especially swinging around with a girl in his arms and sword-fighting at the same time. Don't you think it was great?" Her voice was alive with excitement.

"Yes. I certainly wish I could do it," I added. "I read *The Count of Monte Cristo* and he did all that stuff too, but it's different to see it."

"You read a lot, don't you?" She shivered as she spoke. The wind had blown her lightweight coat open and pierced the thin cotton of her dress. I was aware for the first time that she was not as warmly dressed as I. Under my heavy coat I wore a long-sleeved sweater and a winter skirt; I also had on my woolen cap, knee socks and sturdy Oxfords. Despite them I still felt the chill of winter.

"I love to read. It's lots of fun," I said after several moments.

When we reached her house, we stood on the stoop, both reluctant to leave each other. There was a lot of walking in these relationships but not too much traffic inside each other's homes. That was too private and personal. There might be brothers and sisters with different names, a strange man in stylish clothes or someone drunk upon the floor. That was too sordid. Savagely you guarded your home and with deep respect you observed the code. The stoop was all right, and even the dingy hallway was not above a visit from a friend. But best of all was the street.

"Let me walk you to your house," she said finally.

"Okay."

I didn't want to leave her that way either. We walked toward Sev-

enth Avenue, stopping along the way to look into dimly lighted hall-
ways, all the while noticing other children doing the same.

We had reached my stoop. I lived in Seventh Avenue in a house
that once was well kept by its inhabitants. There had been a cleaner,
more prosperous look about it than the buildings crammed together
in the block. The tree-lined boulevard on a glorious spring day held
a grandeur and elegance that once had stirred pride in people like
my father and mother. They had felt apart from the Negroes who
lived farther into the block. But change had come; neglect was eating
away at the once-stately buildings with aristocratic names. Already
the professionals had taken flight to Sugar Hill, to Queens and
Brooklyn, leaving people like my parents behind with nothing but
their pride to sustain them.

"Well, Cheryl, I guess I better be going," Phyllis said to me as we
stood at the steps of my building. Both my parents worked, and as a
result I was alone at home a great deal. Unlike the other children, I
did not think I needed to guard the sanctity of my home. In fact, I
thought my home and my parents were something special and singularly wonderful, and I would have liked to share them with everyone. True, there were things I didn't wish my friends to know; for
example, in the last few months there had been long, terrible arguments between my parents. But especially on Saturdays, when my
father was at work, I would have liked to have a visitor. Before I
could ask Phyllis, although I knew she saw the question on my face,
she had hurried away, as though frightened by the thought that she
might have to do the same.

I stood in the cold on the stoop, looking across the wide avenue. I
thought of my father and mother. I could see his handsome, cara-
mel-colored face, his crinkly kind of black hair, which he wore a
little longer than most colored men. And next to him I saw my
mother's light, cream-colored skin, her large, hazel eyes and soft,
wispy brown hair. She had a tendency to be plump and was con-
tinually dieting. They were dressed to go out dancing and to listen to
some jazz at "Wells'" or "Small's." There was none of the strain of the
past on their faces, and I felt an arrogant pride at having such attractive, intelligent parents.

And they were intelligent. My mother worked as a typist at the
Municipal Building and answered the phone for a commissioner. My
father did not deliver mail but sorted it. Occasionally when a man
was sick, he took over a window at the main post office, where he

worked. He was always full of stories of those days—how white people registered such surprise and tried to hide their hostility when they saw him. But more than their jobs, it was the fact that my mother and father talked and read a lot. That made me know we were a lot better than most Negro families. I felt above the code of the other children, and would have welcomed Phyllis gladly into my home. . . .

"Damn it, Lettie! Why do you have to say the same thing over and over again? Don't you think I want the best for Cheryl, just like you do? I'm breaking my back trying to save money so we can get the hell out of here, and you're crying the blues all the time. Don't you ever let up on a man? I'm tired of hearing about it. I've been wearing the same damn suit since I got out of the Army. That's right—ten years! I know the neighborhood is falling apart, that they're practically selling dope in the hallway and that my daughter has to wade through drunks to get to the playground. You act like I'm not scuffling like a g.d. nigger to save her for something better. I had three lousy beers. These Italian guys working off the trucks said, 'Hey, come on, man—have a couple with us!' What am I supposed to say?"

He now speaks in a whiny, Uncle Tom's voice: "'No, I can't go, Mr. Bossman, 'cause Miss Charlie thinks three lousy beers stand between her and a house in Queens. She thinks my daughter can't go to college or something because I have three stinking beers.' And when the checks come, what then? Sneak off to the men's room like a scared rat? Hell no!" He stopped for a moment, as if gathering his strength, and then continued more violently than before:

"I gotta once and a while say, 'Listen, man, let me pay for this round,' without you pulling your nightgown tight around your body and locking me out for it."

"Jesse, all I said was we didn't save anything this check, and that's no good." My mother's voice was low and painful. "We've got to keep saving or we'll never get anywhere."

I heard it all through the thin wall that separated our bedrooms. I heard the quarrel, my mother turn over her large body, my father's heavy breathing. I stuck my arms out of the covers, testing the temperature of the room. It was cold.

There was never any heat on Saturday night, because the super devoted this time to drinking. His wife made a fire during the day, but at night the real cold of winter settled into the old building. If my mother decided to wait up for my father, she would light the oven and sit in the kitchen, or watch TV while lying wrapped in blankets on the couch.

On happy nights my father would bring some barbecued spare-ribs and several cans of beer and they would laugh and listen to the phonograph. He liked to listen to what he called "low-down blues," and he loved to hear "Going to Chicago." When Joe Williams sang, "There ain't nothin' a monkey woman can do for me," he would laugh his loud, sincerely happy laugh and reach out to touch my mother. I never saw him do it, but I always knew he did, because I then would hear my mother say, "Oh, Jesse, you're such a fool." It was playful, loving talk that I felt a part of, that made me feel warm all over, in spite of the cold apartment.

He would answer her by saying, "Come on and dance, babe." They would move around the tiny living room, bumping into furniture, laughing softly to themselves. Then my father would say, "Lettie, leave the dishes and let's go to bed." My mother would open the door to my room, and in the narrow crack of light I could see her plump silhouette.

"It's a wonder you didn't wake Cheryl with all the noise you was making," she whispered.

"Did I wake up my baby?" he asked softly. I never answered, even though I was awake. They would close the door and go into their bedroom and I would go to sleep happy.

But that was long ago—or at least, that's how I felt. There were endless Saturdays of arguments and angry words that blotted out those happy times. It seemed as though my father came home later and later, and all the time I became more aware that it was actually very cold in the house and not at all happy.

"Do you think I want any of that stuff you dish out? Listen, un-wrap it! Hang it out on the line, for all I care. You save it all up and give it to God or the g.d. priest in church."

"Jesse, will you stop yelling? Cheryl is right in the next room, and she doesn't need to hear your filthy mouth. Nobody decent wants to have anything to do with you, smelling like a beer barrel all the time."

"So what? So I had seven or eight beers. What the hell, I knew there wasn't a damn thing to come home to."

"I told you, Cheryl is too big and she can hear everything that goes on in here."

"She's nothing but a baby, and anyway, what's wrong with her hearing us? I'm your husband, ain't I? I'm her father! How do you think I got to be her father if I didn't—"

"For God's sake, Jesse, lower your voice! Let's go to sleep. It must be three thirty."

"Lettie . . . ain't nothing' a monkey woman can do for me . . ." he half-sung.

I heard them for a half hour more, making the same sounds that they always did, but later my mother went to the bathroom. I stood in my bare feet, shivering, outside the closed door.

"Mommy, I got to pee-pee," I said.

I heard her crying and then the toilet flush and the water running. I was seized with panic.

"Are you all right, Mommy?"

"Certainly, sweetheart. Wait just a minute and Mommy will be out," she called to me.

I rushed into the bathroom, not waiting, convinced that she was ill. When I saw her special hot-water bottle with a long tube attached to it, I was convinced, and a torrent of tears rushed from my eyes. She stood over me, still holding the bag awkwardly in her hands. I pressed my face against her and burrowed my head into her stomach. We stood there like that until we heard my father's voice.

"Can't I come in?" He opened the door and stood scratching his head. "Well, this is quite a family; everybody's up and around at four o'clock in the morning like it's afternoon. How about it—can Daddy have some privacy?"

He was in a cheerful mood, and once we left the bathroom, I could hear him whistling. My mother went to the kitchen, and I knew that in a few minutes we would have something good to eat because we were all awake.

Both of us were wearing robes and my mother had on bedroom slippers, but my father wore only his underwear, the whiteness of which stood out handsomely against his brown, well-built body. He reminded me of Errol Flynn, whom I had just seen in a film. I thought my father as beautiful as he, if not more so.

"Daddy, can you sword-fight?" I asked.

My father had been in the Second World War, and although I had been a baby at the time, I was convinced that he had been a hero.

"Sure, Pumpkin! Daddy can do everything!" His eyes were smiling, and it seemed hard to believe that he had spoken so violently to my mother only a short while before, "Boy, could I go for some Sherman's Barbecue," he said. He put his large, strong hands over my eyes. I could smell the odor of his body, which was so different from that of my mother's or my own. Even when he took his hands away, I could feel the pressure and warmth they had created across my face.

"Like magic," he said as he closed the refrigerator.

"Jesse, put some clothes on," my mother said in an unkind and brittle voice. In a softer tone she added, "You'll catch your death of cold."

My mother had turned on the oven to make the kitchen comfortable. She heated the meal, taking it from paper plates and putting it on our own dishes. When it was fixed, my father returned to the room, wearing an old Army sweater and a worn pair of pants. There was something wicked about being up and eating at four o'clock. The thought that everyone was asleep and that this was our very own time made it more precious. Even my mother had got into the spirit of it. She was smiling, and her hazel eyes were not clouded as they had been earlier.

"Daddy, I got a new friend. Her name is Phyllis Green."

We had finished eating, and my parents sat back drinking beer, my father from the can, my mother from a glass.

"Oh, yeah? What ever happened to the light-skinned little girl who lives down the street—what's her name?"

"Rosalind," I said coldly, annoyed that he could not keep up with my friends any better than that. "Oh, she's a drip and I hate her."

"Cheryl, that's not right. You shouldn't hate anybody," my mother said. My father's only comment was a muffled laugh.

"Well, she's not very smart," I continued, feeling cozy and having the sudden desire to talk and talk. I wanted to talk for hours, to extend this moment beyond the confines of its time. "She has skinny legs and big feet," I continued.

"Just like my Pumpkin," my father joked.

"Oh, Cheryl's just at that age. She'll develop nicely when she's a teen-ager, and that's not so far away from now."

I was happy that my mother had so quickly come to my defense. But my father just ran his hand across my hair, which was sticking up from having lain in bed.

"She's just a baby. Always will be Daddy's baby."

It sounded like the beginning of the old argument, and struck a cold terror in me so fierce that I grasped my father's hand tightly and began to talk feverishly.

"Phyllis is my best friend. We're going to the library to listen to stories and I'm going to stay at her house and help her look after her little brother, and we go to the movies together and eat MacFarland's potato chips and everything. . . ."

My parents weren't listening to me. They stared at each other across the table.

"All right, Lettie, so we won't ever get the hell out of this place. So we can't afford to have another baby and you're gonna work the rest of your life. I make seventy-five dollars a week—that's it. Do you think they'll ever give me a permanent place at the front window? Do you seriously think that I'll ever be a supervisor over all those white guys? Not in another fifty years! Sure, the Supreme Court can say they've got to integrate schools, but that don't change things for me. It's not that easy. . . . Oh, Lettie, it's dragging me down. It's dragging me down. It'll take a lifetime to save five thousand dollars. And I get tired of not having a car, not being able to go out for a drink once in a while. Tired of saving! But you don't seem to understand. You sit there with your righteous attitude and make me pay for every inch."

Suddenly, with an almost embarrassed expression on their faces, they looked at me. Neither spoke for quite a while, and when my mother did, her voice was strained and unnatural.

"Cheryl, go to bed. It's so late. Go to bed, honey."

My father echoed her. "That's right, Pumpkin. You better hit the sack."

Before I went to bed, I walked to one end of the table into my father's arms and received his hug, then to the other end. As I did, I noticed that the paint was peeling off the table. It was old. My mother kissed me. My feet were cold against the floor, and I rushed to bed, eager to find the warmth and security I missed.

Phyllis took a handful of potato chips. Her hands, like her feet, were oversized. She looked across the Harlem River toward the Bronx. It was bright, and spring actually had come to the city. There was no escaping it, and somehow beauty could be found everywhere. Phyllis and I had decided to go down to the river. We had walked to the pier, along a street lined with factories, and tin buildings for storage. Already there were boys who had come to take a quick plunge in the water or to sit on the docks and fish with a piece of string. They never, to my knowledge, caught anything, but the time passed, the sun was gentle and kind and there was always laughter.

I had suggested that we take this walk after school so that I could muster up the courage to talk to her, more than to enjoy the glorious day. Things lay heavy inside me. Although Phyllis and I went to the movies together on Saturdays, walked through the streets together, swung in the swings and even had gone as far down town as 65th Street to the zoo together, a polite awkwardness hung between us. It didn't matter that I had coerced her into going to the library with me or that we had gossiped about our former friends. What was important was that we never had really talked about our families. Neither of us had met the other's parents or set foot in the other's house.

Easter vacation had come and gone, and for those ten days we hadn't seen each other. When the holidays were over we greeted each other with genuine delight, yet I had no more idea how she had passed those days than she had of how I had spent mine.

As we stood side by side on the pier, our hands greasy from potato chips, we appeared close. It did not seem possible that there could be secrets between us, but we had learned from necessity to live by the rules of friendship. Now, however, I felt compelled to violate them.

"Does your father live with you?" I asked after a long time. My voice sounded strange and far off and not credible. This startled me, as my question did Phyllis.

She answered, however, quite casually. "No. I never seen him."

"Do you miss not having a father?" I asked. She appeared at the moment much taller and older than I. She hesitated and then spoke. "No, I don't miss something I never had. My brother's father comes around sometimes, but he don't like me 'cause I'm dark."

I couldn't think of anything to say. I had not expected her to have problems too. I had thought that because she never spoke or cried or seemed affected by anything, there were no hurts for her, only for me.

"Phyllis . . ." I began. I moved the bag of potato chips between us. Clumsily I offered her the last handful. I felt sure that I would cry, and tried to prevent it by looking up into the sky. "My father went away. He doesn't live with us any more," I finally managed to say.

"Oh," she commented unemotionally. "Did he fight with your mama a lot?"

"No," I answered quickly. I was appalled that my father should be accused of hurting my mother.

"Then why did he go away?" she asked.

"I don't know," I replied. I thought I had told too much already. There were things I didn't understand myself. Obviously she couldn't understand what had happened in my home. There had been no drunken fights or policemen or running up and down the stairs in the middle of the night. I had come home from the movies one Saturday and my mother, with no tears in her eyes but a frightful shaking in her large body, had said simply that my father would not be coming home, that he had decided to live somewhere else but that he still loved me and always would. When he was settled he would come and see me. And on Easter Sunday he had come. They had talked in low voices in the living room and he had taken me on his lap for a little while. Then he was gone. I had an address and phone number in Brooklyn. It could have been any stranger's.

"Phyllis, let's start back," I said. It was getting dark and there was a cold breeze and the smell of garbage from the river. When we reached my stoop, Phyllis stood on the sidewalk as I proceeded up the stairs. I turned to say good-by and saw that she was ready to follow me. For the first time I had no desire for her to come into my house. The super rarely scrubbed the hallway and the light had been out for nearly a week. I could not articulate it, but now I was no better than she, and that was the greatest pain. She could never enter my house or meet my family. All I could do was offer to walk her back to her house, for the street was the only place where we were equal.

PAULA GUNN ALLEN

They Make Their Climb

(1979)

*O*NE summer day in the late 1970s, Paula Gunn Allen and I drove out to visit her maternal grandmother at Cubero, near Laguna Pueblo. Mrs. Gottlieb still lived then in her rock house beneath big cottonwoods, next to the old Cubero Trading Company, the store Paula's dad used to run. I remember the sun dappling through deep-silled windows over a spill of geraniums and wandering Jew, and the new bookmobile copy of John Nichols's *The Magic Journey* that Mrs. Gottlieb was reading ("I don't know what you girls think, *you're* the English professors, but it seems like I just can't get into this one . . ."). Our two little boys, who had been rabbit-punching each other in the back seat most of the drive, became calm and affable in her kitchen.

Later that afternoon, we took Caleb and Sully out to the mesa top east of the village and watched our brave sons leap the deep crevices that Ephanie dares Elena to cross in "They Make Their Climb." "*Be careful!*" we yelled, giggling and jumping some ourselves, wishing for them and for us the courage to jump, the delight of jumping, and the care to keep from falling. "They Make Their Climb" is about how fear and guilt can shame children into believing that any jump is crazy—that any spontaneous act of joy is a fall, when, in truth, courage and care, risk and security, jumping and falling may be twinned halves of a single act. Around Laguna Pueblo (called Guadalupe in the story) they tell a lot of stories about twins, about women who go adventuring, about double-natured actions and beings, but more on that in a moment.

Paula (b. 1939) grew up in Cubero, New Mexico, one of several villages settled by people from the Keresan-speaking, matrifocal Laguna Pueblo as they needed more physical or political space than the mother pueblo afforded. Over the last three centuries, these outlying Laguna villages have incorporated the families of a wide variety of people—Spanish and Mexican soldiers, farmers, and ranchers; Scottish and German traders; Irish cavalry members who came West to hunt down "renegade" Navajo and Apache; Lebanese merchants who arrived with peddler's packs from points very far east indeed. Among the Lebanese came Paula's paternal great-grandfather, who used to boast that he had crossed the seven seas to come to New Mexico Territory. There were always members of other American Indian tribes; later on people came with the railroads or to work in the gypsum and uranium mines.

Anthropologists such as Elsie Clews Parsons, who dismissed Laguna in the 1920s as not a "real" pueblo, have been deluded by their own notions of what is Indian, unable to see that what may be most Indian is to be dynamic and inclusive rather than restricted by Anglo stereotypes. All of Paula's work invites us to remember stories, and to forget—or, rather, to *recognize*—stereotypes. Meanwhile, Laguna goes on. The Laguna communities have been famous locally for centuries for lively internecine squabbles, wonderful gossip and stories, and for women of unusual beauty and power. In my generation, the Laguna have given us an astonishing number of writers—Harold Littlebird; Paula herself; her sister, Carollee Sanchez; her cousin, Leslie Silko.

Paula herself embodies both the diversity and deep-rootedness of the Laguna people. Her essay "The Autobiography of a Confluence" in *I Tell You Now* (1987)[1] recounts her early years with equal emphasis on family, neighbors, and the terrain that nurtured her. Her mother, Ethel Gottlieb Francis, of Laguna-Sioux-Scottish descent, is a small-boned, elegant, fiercely intelligent woman. In her house you are fed, fussed over, questioned, instantly engaged in telling and listening to stories. Her father, E. Lee Francis, is a Lebanese cowboy turned rancher, trader, and politician. He served as Lieutenant Governor of New Mexico for a while, but in his youth he had such a reputation for being hot-blooded that the Gottliebs forbade him to court their daughter. I have heard Paula's parents tell antiphonally the romance and high comedy of their elopement (she sneaked out of her sorority house to meet him where he waited in an open jalopy; the roads were muddy; the justice of the peace at Bernalillo did not believe their story for a minute). Five kids, five decades, and many stories later, they are still married.

A storytelling family, as I say, whose stories catalogue and celebrate the complex weaving of their heritage. *That* is very Laguna. So is their five children's wisdom in choosing what to accept or reject of the cultural mainstream, gauging whether or not its assumptions square with the truths of their own experience.

That particular wisdom is hard won; a child can die in the getting of it. In *The Woman Who Owned the Shadows* (1983),[2] the novel of which the following story forms a part, and in an interview with Joseph Bruchac in his *Survival This Way* (1987),[3] Paula has spoken of her years beyond Cubero—of rigid parochial schools, of colleges and graduate schools nearly equally parochial in their own way, of her fears for her own sanity. When she says the 1968 publication of Scott Momaday's *House Made of Dawn*[4] saved her life, she means that literally. The perceptions of Momaday's mixed-blood hero first confirmed the validity of her own, assured her she was not crazy to miss a landscape as intensely as she would miss her mother, friends, lovers. The novel assured her it was not she alone who understood the world as so multiple, so alive with spirit and peopled by spirits. Moreover, the book in itself was testimony that people could gain control over their own senses of deprivation and difference in sufficient degree to write powerfully about them. And that she has done.

Read on its own, "They Make Their Climb" bears grim witness to the effect on girl children of the world's conspiracy to crush their adventurousness, spontaneity, sexuality, and particular love for one another, frightening them into a passive, dispirited femininity. Homophobia is the most obvious reason for the adults' decision to separate Ephanie and Elena. Ironically, it is the one reason that does not at first occur to Ephanie in her stunned innocence. But other reasons that do occur to her, reasons of class, color, and culture, are operative here as well, despite Elena's belief that their "sin" is "only the way we've been lately." Like Cherrie Moraga and Alice Walker, Paula knows that it is an old trick of the white patriarchy to whittle complex matters down to single issues.

Paula has often pointed out that even well-meaning white feminists may misread American Indian writing as they approach it from outside the cultures.[5] It is important in reading this story to be aware that Ephanie's—and Paula's—Keresan heritage fosters rather than discourages strong women and woman-centeredness. It adds immeasurably to know about the Keresan origin stories about twin sister spirits, one light and one dark, who become estranged; about Yellow Woman, an ancestor spirit who, in story after story, strays beyond the safe spiritual and physical boundaries of the pueblo, usually to the ultimate enrichment of her people; about The Woman Who Fell from The Sky, who fell and *survived*. Larger narratives encompass Paula's story. In her writings they are alluded to, told, and remembered. The spirit women in those stories are among Ephanie's friends; they sustain her and ensure her survival.

The well-made tale, the single narrative standing apart, is not an American Indian convention. In tribal culture, single stories work as parts of cycles. They grow out of a matrix, a mother lode of tradition. I do not question the excellence of the Western European short story genre or women's primacy in that genre; I do not value novels above stories. But "They Make Their Climb" is part of a context, a weaving that extends not only into Paula's story but beyond it into the greater weaving of Keresan story cycles. Ephanie's story is about understanding her own personal stories through the older ones. As tribal storytellers such as Paula are always reminding us, the thing about real stories is that they are never in the past. They are always continuing, still happening.

PATRICIA CLARK SMITH

It had been the apple tree. The long spring days there. With the girl. They had watched the village going. They had watched the clouds. When they thirsted they climbed down from the branches and walked to the nearby spring. Took a long sweet drink.

Elena had taught Ephanie about the weeds. Which to eat. When they had gathered prickly pears in the summer, brushing carefully the tiny spines from the fruit before they ate. They had wandered the mesas and climbed the nearer peaks. Together they had dreamed. Sharing. They never talked about growing up. What that would mean.

They had ridden horses. Pretended to be ranchers. Chased the village cattle around the town. Suffered scoldings for it. Learned to be trick riders. Roy Rogers and Hopalong Cassidy. Maybe they could be stunt men in Hollywood if they got good enough at it. If they could learn to jump from the rooftop onto the horse's back. They had chased the clouds.

Or lying, dreaming, had watched them, tracing faces and glorious beast shapes in the piling, billowing thunderheads. On July mornings they had gone out from their separate homes, laughing, feet bare and joyful in the road's early dust. The early wind cool and fresh, the bright sunlight making promises it would never keep. They had lain together in the alfalfa field of Elena's father, quiet, at peace.

They were children and there was much they did not know.

In their seasons they grew. Walking the road between their houses, lying languorous and innocent in the blooming boughs of the apple tree. Amid the fruiting limbs. And had known themselves and their surroundings in terms of each other's eyes. Though their lives were very different, their identity was such that the differences were never strange. They had secret names for each other, half joking, half descriptive, Snow White and Rose Red, they named themselves, in recognition of the fairness of Elena, the duskiness of Ephanie. In recognition also of the closeness they shared, those friends.

The events that measured their shared lives were counted in the places that they roamed, and Ephanie always remembered her childhood that way. The river, the waterfall, the graveyard, the valley, the mesas, the peaks. Each crevice they leaped over. Each danger they challenged, each stone, each blade of grass. A particularity that would shape her life.

They had especially loved the shadows. Where they grew, lavender, violet, purple, or where those shadows would recede. On the mountain slopes and closer by, beneath the shading trees. And the blue enfolding distance surrounding that meant the farthest peaks. Shared with them in their eyes, in their stories, but where, together, they had never been.

In all those years, in spite of distance, in spite of difference, in spite of change, they understood the exact measure of their relationship, the twining, the twinning. There were photographs of them from that time. Because Elena's gold-tinged hair looked dark in the photograph's light, no one could say which was Elena, which Ephanie. With each other they were each one doubled. They were thus complete.

Jump.

Fall.

Remember you are flying. Say you are a bird.

She had said that, Ephanie. Had urged Elena to leap the great crevices between the huge sandstone formations that shaped the mesas they roamed. Some of the leaps were wide and the ground far below. She had always done the leading. Elena, devoted, did what Ephanie decided. Or it seemed that way.

Ephanie didn't want to remember it that way. Wanted the fact to be that Elena had gone on her own windings, ones not of Ephanie's making. And in some cases, that was true. There were some things that, no matter how Ephanie urged them, Elena would not do. Some ways in which she remained safe within her own keeping. Sometimes, when she had adamantly refused, Ephanie would give up and go back to her own home. And it also went, sometimes, the other way.

They did not argue. They did not fight. Elena would do what was of her own wanting. And while it seemed that the dark girl was leading, the fair one did the guiding. And in her quiet, unargumentative, unobtrusive way, she kept them both safe within the limits of their youthful abilities, gave the lessons and boundaries that encompassed their lives.

Kept them safe. Or almost so. Except for that one time that she hadn't. Kept them safe. Had missed some signal. Had turned aside in some way, away or toward, a split second too soon, too late. Had not known in time not to speak. Had not known what her words, in time, in consequence, would create.

Perhaps it had been the shadows that betrayed her. The certain angle of light that somehow disoriented her. Perhaps so accustomed to being safe, she did not know the danger, any danger that might tear the web of their being. Shredding. Shattering. Splintering.

Or maybe it was the sun. The bright, the pitiless, the unwavering sun.

But whatever had disturbed her knowing, her keeping in time with the turns and twists of their sharing, their lives, in that splitting second everyone had abandoned Ephanie. Everything had gone away.

It was on a certain day. They went hiking. Exploring. They went walking. It was an adventure. One they had planned for a long time. Ever since they were small. They planned to walk to Picacho. The peak. That rose, igneous formation, straight up from the surrounding plain. The arid floor of the semi-desert of their homeland.

They wanted to climb the peak. To go to the top. To see. Elena said you could see the next village. The one that was invisible from where they lived. She told Ephanie the story, one she had recounted before. Much of what Ephanie knew about the people and land around them she learned from Elena. She didn't hear much that others told her. Not for many years.

Not that others had not spoken. Had not told her stories, had not given ideas, opinions, methods. They had. Some part of Ephanie recorded what they told her. What they said. But she did not acknowledge it until later. Not for many years. She did not understand how that had happened. But it did.

They had planned in the last days before their journey very well. Deciding what to take. What would not be too heavy to carry. What would not get in their way. What to wear, for comfort and protection, in the heat, against the stone. Which shirts, which length pants, which shoes. They knew they would get thirsty. It was July.

They wore tennis shoes and jeans. Usually they went barefoot from spring well into fall. Every chance they got. But this journey was special. It signified accomplishing. That they were grown. That they knew something, could put it into use.

They took oranges. For the juice. They knew how to use them, slit the rind with a toughened thumbnail, in a circle. Peel the small circle of rind away from the flesh. Press finger into the fruit, firmly, gently. So as not to lose too much juice. The juice was precious. It would sustain them. Then put the opening thus made to their mouths. Sucking. When all the juice was thus taken, they would split open the fruit and eat the pulp. And the white furry lining of the rind. Elena said it was sweet. That it was healthy.

Ephanie never ate an orange that way later. It didn't seem right. She didn't know why she wouldn't. Like her dislike of spiders. Which made no sense either. She remembered how it had gone, that journey, and why they had learned to eat oranges that particular way. She didn't understand her unwillingness to follow that child-hood ritual. Not for a long time. And she found the lining bitter. Peeled it carefully away from the fruit all of her adult life. Threw it away.

But she loved the smell of oranges. The orange oil that clung to her hands when she was done. Its fragrance. Its echoing almost re-membered pain. She would sniff it, dreaming, empty in thought, empty in mind, on her way to the faucet to wash it off her hands. And in the flood of water and soap she would banish what she did not know. Averting. Avoiding. Voiding. Pain.

They met in the early morning. While the cool wind blew down from the mountain. The way they were going was into the wind. The earth sparkled. The leaves. The sun was just getting started. Like a light from elsewhere it touched their eyes, their hands. They shiv-ered slightly, shaking. They began to walk. Taking the road that curved upward. Upward and out. They were leaving. They knew that. They knew they would never return.

They didn't talk about that intuition, but walked, silent, amiable, close. They listened to the soft padding of their footfall on the dusty road, watched their shadows move, silent, alongside of them. Elena told Ephanie how high the peak was. Much taller than it looked. They speculated about climbing it. Ephanie was afraid of heights that had no branches to hold on to, but she never let on. She had never let on.

The great isolate rock rose maybe a hundred feet from the ground. Its top was slender, precarious. It stood alone, gray and silent, reaching into the sky. It was a proud rock. A formation. It brooded there on the plain between the villages. It guarded the road to the mountain. Sentinel.

The story it bore was an old one. Familiar. Everywhere. They remembered the old tale as they watched the rock grow larger, approaching it. About the woman who had a lover. Who had died in a war. She was pregnant. Lonely, desperate, she went to Picacho, climbed to the top, jumped to her death. That was one version, the one Elena's Chicano people told.

There was another version, one that Ephanie's Guadalupe people told. The woman was in love with a youth she was forbidden to marry. He was a stranger, and she had fallen in love with him somehow. Maybe he was a Navajo. Maybe he was a Ute. But her love was hopeless from the start. Then the people found out that she was seeing the youth secretly. They were very angry. They scolded her. Said the things that would happen to the people because of her actions. Shamed her. Hurt and angry, she had gone to Picacho. Climbed to the top. Jumped to her death.

Ephanie imagined that climb. The woman finding places to put her hands. Her feet. Tentative, climbing. Tentative but sure. Shaking. She climbed to the place where the rock was narrowest. Where the drop was straight and steep. Dizzy she had stood there, thinking perhaps, of her anguish, of her rage, of her grief. Wondering, maybe, if whether what she contemplated was wise. No one knew what she had been thinking. They must have wondered about it. They must have told themselves stories about what had gone through her mind as she stood, wavering, just on the edge of the narrow rock bridge that connected the two slightly taller peaks of the formation.

From there she could have seen the wide sweep of the land, barren, hungry, powerful as it raised itself slow and serene toward the lower slopes of the mountains to the north beyond Picacho and was there lost to the wilderness of tabletop hills, soaring slopes, green grasses, flowers, shadows, springs, cliffs, and above them the treeless towering peak. Where it became wilderness. Where it came home.

She could have seen that, looking northward. Where the mountain called Ts'pin'a, Woman Veiled in Clouds, waited, brooding, majestic, almost monstrously powerful. Or she could look southward, eastward, toward the lands the people tended, that held and nurtured them. But probably she had not looked outward. Had not seen the sky, the piling, moving thunderheads. The gold in them. The purpling blue. The dazzling, eye-splitting white. The bellies of them pregnant, ripe with rain about to be born. The living promise of their towering strength. For if she had seen them, would she have jumped.

She Is Swept Away

By the time they got to the foot of the peak it was late morning. The sun was high and the earth around them looked flat. Sunbitten. The shadows had retreated to cooler places for the long day. Ephanie, slender, sturdy, brown, and Elena, slender, sturdy, hair tinged with gold, lightly olive skin deepened almost brown by the summer sun, sat down to rest amid the grey boulders that lay in piles at the base of the peak. They ate their oranges. Looked at the climb that faced them, uneasy. The gray rock soared above their heads, almost smooth. Ephanie looked at Elena for reassurance, thinking how beautiful her friend was, sweating, laughing. Wanted to reach out and touch her face. To hold her hand, brown and sturdy like her own. Reached and touched the smooth brown skin, brushed tenderly back the gold-streaked hair.

"When we get home," she said, "let's go to the apple tree and cool off."

"I can't," Elena said. "I have to go with my mother to town. We're going to stay a few days at my sister's." She looked away from Ephanie. Looked at the ground. Ephanie felt uneasiness crawling around in her stomach. She shifted her weight away from Elena. She didn't know why she felt what way. "Let's go on up," she said.

They climbed. Elena went first. Finding places to put hands and feet. They pretended they were mountains, climbing Mount Everest. They didn't have ropes, but they knew about testing rock and brush before trusting weight to them. They climbed over the boulders and up the first stage of the climb. That part was fairly easy. It was steep, but there was a broad abuttment that circled most of the peak, as though supporting its slender, massive skyward thrust. The abutment was hard packed dirt, light sandstone and the gray rock, probably volcanic, that formed Picacho.

They came to a resting place, high above the valley floor. It was very hot. They sat and looked around them. The rest of the peak rose above them along a narrow path that rose toward it from where they sat. A sheer drop on either side. Dizzy. Can we cross that. They looked into each other's eyes. Daring. Testing. Their old familiar way. "I don't think I can get across that. It makes me dizzy," Ephanie said. Elena said, since Ephanie had admitted her fear, "just crawl across it. That's what I'm going to do. I'm not going to try and walk across. We can crawl. It's not far." And she began crawling across the smooth sand that lay over the rock bridge that stretched between them and the smooth curving roundness of the farther peak. "Look down," Elena said. "It's really far."

Ephanie, on hands and knees, crept behind Elena. Feeling foolish, scared. Foolish in her fearfulness. Shaking. She did look down. It was a long way to the ground. She imagined falling. Smashing herself on the rocks below. How Elena would manage. Going home to tell them she had fallen. How the woman long ago had fallen. From here.

They got across the narrow bridge and stood up, clinging to the gray rock of the highest point that rose some three feet above their feet. They climbed up on it, scotting their bodies up and then turning to lie stomach-down on the flat peak. They looked down, over the back side of the peak. Saw the mountain a few miles beyond. "Let's stand up," one of them said. They stood, trembling slightly, and looked around. They saw the villages, one north of them, the other, just beyond it to the west.

They rested for awhile, wishing they hadn't left the rest of the oranges down below. They realized they still had to climb back down. The part they were always forgetting. As they examined the descent, Elena said, "Ephanie, there's something I have to tell you." She didn't look at her friend. She looked at her hands. Sweating and lightly streaked where the sweat had washed some of the dust of their climb away. "I can't come over to your place anymore."

The sun was blazing down on them, unconcerned. It was so hot. Ephanie looked at Elena's hands intently. She didn't speak for a long time. She couldn't swallow. She couldn't breathe. For some reason her chest hurt. Aching. She didn't know why. Anything.

She tried to think, to understand. They had been together all their lives. What did Elena mean. She wondered if it was because she had more. Of everything. Dresses, boarding school, a bigger house. A store-owner for a father. A trader.

Elena's father had a small cantina that he owned. But he didn't make a lot of money at it. He drove a school bus, to make ends meet.

Elena's house had three rooms. Besides the kitchen. They were all used for sleeping. One of them they used as a living room too. One of them was very small, hardly large enough for the tiny iron bedstead it held. Five or six people lived there, depending on whether her brothers were both there or not. They didn't have running water, and their toilet was outdoors. Ephanie thought maybe that was what was the matter. That they were growing up. That now that they were nearing adulthood, such things mattered. Were seen in some way that caused anger, caused shame.

When Ephanie didn't say anything for so long, Elena said, "It's because my mother thinks we spend too much time with each other." She looked at Ephanie, eyes shut against her. Not closed, open, but nothing of herself coming through them. Nothing in them taking her in. Ephanie sat, thinking she was dreaming. This didn't make any sense. What could be wrong. What could be happening. How could she not see Elena. Be with her. Who would she be with then, if not Elena.

She put out her hand. Took hold of Elena's arm. Held it, tightly. Swaying. She looked over the side of the peak. Thought about flying. Dropping off. She thought of going to sleep.

She moved so that she could put her hand on Elena's arm. Held her like that, staring. Trying to speak. Not being able to. There were no words. Only too many thoughts, feelings, churning in her like the whirlwind, chindi, dust devils on the valley floor below. "What are you talking about," she finally said. Her voice sounded strange in her ears.

Elena tried to back away, get loose from Ephanie's hand. Pulled away, but not completely. She looked at Ephanie. Her face was wet. Beads of sweat had formed along her upper lip. She wiped them away with the back of her hand. Her eyes looked flat, gave off no light. Her light brown eyes that were flecked with gold. Her brown face had a few freckles scattered over it. They stood out now, sharp.

"You know," she said, her voice low. "The way we've been lately. Hugging and giggling. You know." She looked down at her hands, twisting against themselves in her lap. "I asked the sister about that, after school. She said it was the devil. That I mustn't do anything like that. That it was a sin. And she told my mother. She says I can't come over any more."

Ephanie sat. Stunned. Mind empty. Stomach a cold cold stone. The hot sun blazed on her head. She felt sick. She felt herself shrinking within. Understood, wordlessly, exactly what Elena was saying. How she could understand what Ephanie had not understood. That they were becoming lovers. That they were in love. That their loving had to stop. To end. That she was falling. Had fallen. Would not recover from the fall, smashing, the rocks. That they were in her, not on the ground.

She finally remembered to take her hand off of Elena's arm. To put it in her pocket. She stood up again. Almost lost her balance. How will we ever get down, she wondered. She couldn't see very well. She realized her eyes were blurred with tears. "Why did you do that," she said. "How could you tell anyone? How did you know, what made you ask? Why didn't you ask me." And realized the futility of her words. The enormity of the abyss she was falling into. The endless, endless depth of the void.

"I was scared. I thought it was wrong. It is." Elena looked at Ephanie, eyes defiant, flat and hard, closed.

"Then why did we come today. Why get me all the way up here and then tell me?" Ephanie felt her face begin to crumble, to give way. Like the arroyo bank gave way in the summer rains. She didn't want Elena to see her like that, giving in to anguish, to weakness, to tears.

"I'm sorry." That was all Elena would say.

They got down from the peak the way they had come, using lifelong habits of caution and practice to guide them. In silence they walked the long way back to the village. Elena went inside when they came to her house. Ephanie went the rest of the way, not so far however long it seemed, alone. She went to the apple tree and climbed up into it. Hid her face in the leaves. She sat there, hiding, for a very long time.

GRACE PALEY

Friends

(1979)

$\mathcal{G}$RACE Paley is best known for
her story collections: *The Little Disturbances of Man* (1959), *Enormous
Changes at the Last Minute* (1974), and *Later the Same Day* (1985). She
also teaches, lectures, and writes essays and poetry; she published her
first book of poems, *Leaning Forward,* in 1986. Living in Vermont with
her second husband, the writer and activist Bob Nichols, and also in
New York City in the same Greenwich Village apartment where her children finished growing up, Grace Paley is now "a famous writer." All of
her work enjoys the popularity of readers as well as the admiration of
scholars and critics. She has received several major awards and grants,
including the prestigious Senior Fellowship of the Literature Program of
the National Endowment for the Arts, and was chosen the first state author of New York. Both *The Dictionary of Literary Biography,* volume 28
("Twentieth Century American Jewish Writers"), and *American Women
Writers,* volume 3, include essays about her.

Born in the Bronx in 1922, a third and late child to Manya Ridnyik
and Isaac Goodside, Grace grew up with a kitchenful of Jewish women.
Her grandmother, mother, aunts, and older sister spoke, shouted, and
lullabyed in Russian, Yiddish, and English. She grew into a neighborhood of women whose ethnic origins resisted the heat of the melting pot.
The voices of those women, each one sharply differentiated—and the
variegated voices of the neighborhood people from her own child-raising
years—are the voices we hear when we read her fiction.

Because Grace Paley's father came to the United States and then, like
Alexandra's father in "Enormous Changes at the Last Minute," went
"to medical school, and shot like a surface-to-air missile right into the

middle class," she grew up in material comfort. But her parents' earlier progressive sensibilities, their Russian socialist origins, became the foundation of Grace's consciousness of class privilege and her understanding of the political roots of personal life.

Her mother died of cancer in the early years of World War II, ending a lengthy illness that had painfully coincided with much of Grace's adolescence and complicated their relationship. The death came soon after Grace married her first husband, Jess Paley; their children, Nora and Danny, who grew up in the sixties, know the character of their maternal grandmother as we readers do—through her appearances as characters and personae in Grace's stories and poems. Their grandfather, however, was an important figure in their early lives, as he always had been in their mother's. Paley explains in a note to readers of *Enormous Changes at the Last Minute* that her father is "the father" in all her stories; he appears in several—notably as a poet, a socialist thinker, a sick and dying old man, and a critic of the life and writing of a daughter remarkably like Grace Paley.

With the exception of one or two stories that she never published, Paley wrote only poetry until she was over thirty years old. In her early years, like most artists, she copied both traditional and contemporary masters, reading Keats and Auden—with whom she studied at the New School for Social Research in New York. An apprentice, she assumed an English accent in syntax, diction, and subject; but she began to seek her own voice after Auden asked her, "Do the people you *know* talk like that? Do *you* talk like that?"

Possessed of the poetic sensibility, Grace Paley has been from her earliest years a "story hearer." When she was a child she would sit under the kitchen table while the grown-ups talked politics and family gossip, which were indistinguishable. An outstanding student in grammar school (the model for young Shirley Abramowitz in "The Loudest Voice" in *The Little Disturbances of Man*) when she got to junior high and high school, Grace was more interested in listening to the stories and voices all around her than in listening to her teachers. Though she entered Hunter College in the late 1930s, from which she was expected to follow her brother and sister into responsible adulthood, she soon dropped out. She would intend to go to class, would even want to go to class, but on the way into the building, up the stairs, she'd hear something that would catch her and take her away, right back down the stairs and out of the building.

By the late 1960s, much of what she heard was being said by children and young people—and especially by other mothers. The civil rights movement and the anti-war movement—the growing activism of neighborhood people in the parks and the PTA—sent Grace Paley to school the way Hunter College never did. Initially reluctant to speak in public, she became an organizer and spokeswoman; she traveled to Chile, the USSR, Vietnam, China, El Salvador, and Nicaragua. Picketing and passing out leaflets at draft boards, protesting on the White House lawn, demonstrating against the construction of nuclear power plants—arrested, tried, and jailed: Grace's political actions are fundamental to and inseparable from her art.

By the mid-1970s she had begun to write about the lives of women and children in discernibly feminist terms. Her earliest fiction is un-self-consciously woman-centered; the stories in *The Little Disturbances of Man,* though they focus on relationships between women and men, are filled with women living together in families and neighborhoods. But by the end of *Enormous Changes at the Last Minute* (including "Debts," in which a friend is acknowledged as the writer's inspiration; "Faith in the Afternoon," in which Gittel Darwin's relationship with Celia Hegel-Shtein is an issue seeking definition; "Northeast Playground," in which the eleven unwed mothers on relief are a model support group; "Faith in a Tree," in which the mothers who are *not* "friends" are those who "never grab another mother's kid when he falls and cries"; and especially "Living," in which Faith and Ellen are "dying" together) friendship between women—especially mothers—has become overtly political, inextricable from movement toward social change. In the final story, "The Long Distance Runner," white Faith and black Mrs. Luddy not only embody the struggle against racism but also, in their sudden intimacy, define heterosexual women's response to male supremacy as they exchange and analyze the substance of each other's lives.

By the mid-1980s, when *Later the Same Day* appeared, Paley's feminist politics had strengthened and become more apparent in her fiction. Three long stories in it develop women's friendship as a primary theme ("Ruthy and Edie," "The Expensive Moment," and "Friends"); two more present that theme prominently ("Love" and "Listening," the first and last stories of the collection); another two feature groups of women friends ("Somewhere Else" and "Zagrowsky Tells"). As she had with the final story in *Enormous Changes at the Last Minute,* Paley concluded her third collection by describing the intensity of women's struggle to bond politically and personally through the confrontation between straight Faith and lesbian Cassie.

In a short piece called "Midrash on Happiness,"[1] Faith (who is her most apparently autobiographical character) admits that, even in the face of global pain, "sometimes walking with a friend I forget the world." In her fiction, Grace Paley never forgets, but writes into her stories the friendship that causes that forgetting. In these stories, women friends move through their minds, their neighborhoods and the world, seeking justice—which is truth, and comfort—which is love.

JUDITH ARCANA

To put us at our ease, to quiet our hearts as she lay dying, our dear friend Selena said, Life, after all, has not been an unrelieved horror—you know, I *did* have many wonderful years with her.

She pointed to a child who leaned out of a portrait on the wall—long brown hair, white pinafore, head and shoulders forward.

Eagerness, said Susan. Ann closed her eyes.

On the same wall three little girls were photographed in a school-yard. They were in furious discussion; they were holding hands. Right in the middle of the coffee table, framed, in autumn colors, a handsome young woman of eighteen sat on an enormous horse—aloof, disinterested, a rider. One night this young woman, Selena's child, was found in a rooming house in a distant city, dead. The police called. They said, Do you have a daughter named Abby?

And with *him,* too, our friend Selena said. We had good times, Max and I. You know that.

There were no photographs of *him.* He was married to another woman and had a new, stalwart girl of about six, to whom no harm would ever come, her mother believed.

Our dear Selena had gotten out of bed. Heavily but with a comic dance, she soft-shoed to the bathroom, singing, "Those were the days, my friend . . ."

Later that evening, Ann, Susan, and I were enduring our five-hour train ride to home. After one hour of silence and one hour of coffee and the sandwiches Selena had given us (she actually stood, leaned her big soft excavated body against the kitchen table to make those sandwiches), Ann said, Well, we'll never see *her* again.

Who says? Anyway, listen, said Susan. Think of it. Abby isn't the only kid who died. What about that great guy, remember Bill Dalrymple—he was a non-cooperator or a deserter? And Bob Simon. They were killed in automobile accidents. Matthew, Jeannie, Mike. Remember Al Lurie—he was murdered on Sixth Street—and that little kid Brenda, who O.D.'d on your roof, Ann? The tendency, I suppose, is to forget. You people don't remember them.

What do you mean, "you people"? Ann asked. You're talking to *us.*

I began to apologize for not knowing them all. Most of them were older than my kids, I said.

Of course, the child Abby was exactly in my time of knowing and in all my places of paying attention—the park, the school, our street. But oh! it's true! Selena's Abby was not the only one of that beloved generation of our children murdered by cars, lost to war, to drugs, to madness.

Selena's main problem, Ann said—you know, she didn't tell the truth.

What?

A few hot human truthful words are powerful enough, Ann thinks, to steam all God's chemical mistakes and society's slimy lies out of her life. We all believe in that power, my friends and I, but sometimes . . . the heat.

Anyway, I always thought Selena had told us a lot. For instance, we knew she was an orphan. There were six, seven other children. She was the youngest. She was forty-two years old before someone informed her that her mother had *not* died in childbirthing her. It was some terrible sickness. And she had lived close to her mother's body—at her breast, in fact—until she was eight months old. Whew! said Selena. What a relief! I'd always felt I was the one who'd killed her.

Your family stinks, we told her. They really held you up for grief.

Oh, people, she said. Forget it. They did a lot of nice things for me too. Me and Abby. Forget it. Who has the time?

That's what I mean, said Ann. Selena should have gone after them with an ax.

More information: Selena's two sisters brought her to a Home. They were ashamed that at sixteen and nineteen they could not take care of her. They kept hugging her. They were sure she'd cry. They took her to a room—not a room, a dormitory with about eight beds. This is your bed, Lena. This is your table for your things. This little drawer is for your toothbrush. All for me? she asked. No one else can use it? Only me. That's all? Artie can't come? Franky can't come? Right?

Believe me, Selena said, those were happy days at Home.

Facts, said Ann, just facts. Not necessarily the *truth*.

I don't think it's right to complain about the character of the dying or start hustling all their motives into the spotlight like that. Isn't it amazing enough, the bravery of that private inclusive intentional community?

It wouldn't help not to be brave, said Selena. You'll see.

She wanted to get back to bed. Susan moved to help her.

Thanks, our Selena said, leaning on another person for the first time in her entire life. The trouble is, when I stand, it hurts me here all down my back. Nothing they can do about it. All the chemotherapy. No more chemistry left in me to therapeut. Ha! Did you know before I came to New York and met you I used to work in that hospital? I was supervisor in gynecology. Nursing. They were my friends, the doctors. They weren't so snotty then. David Clark, big surgeon. He couldn't look at me last week. He kept saying, Lena . . . Lena . . . Like that. We were in North Africa the same year—'44, I think. I told him, Davy, I've been around a long enough time. I haven't missed too much. He knows it. But I didn't want to make him look at me. Ugh, my damn feet are a pain in the neck.

Recent research, said Susan, tells us that it's the neck that's a pain in the feet.

Always something new, said Selena, our dear friend.

On the way back to the bed, she stopped at her desk. There were about twenty snapshots scattered across it—the baby, the child, the young woman. Here, she said to me, take this one. It's a shot of Abby and your Richard in front of the school—third grade? What a day! The show those kids put on! What a bunch of kids! What's Richard doing now?

Oh, who knows? Horsing around someplace. Spain. These days, it's Spain. Who knows where he is? They're all the same.

Why did I say that? I knew exactly where he was. He writes. In fact, he found a broken phone and was able to call every day for a week—mostly to give orders to his brother but also to say, Are you O.K., Ma? How's your new boyfriend, did he smile yet?

The kids, they're all the same, I said.

It was only politeness, I think, not to pour my boy's light, noisy face into that dark afternoon. Richard used to say in his early mean teens, You'd sell us down the river to keep Selena happy and innocent. It's true. Whenever Selena would say, I don't know, Abby has some peculiar friends, I'd answer for stupid comfort, You should see Richard's.

Still, he's in Spain, Selena said. At least you know that. It's probably interesting. He'll learn a lot. Richard is a wonderful boy, Faith. He acts like a wise guy but he's not. You know the night Abby died, when the police called me and told me? That was my first night's sleep in two years. I *knew* where she was.

Selena said this very matter-of-factly—just offering a few informative sentences.

But Ann, listening, said Oh!—she called out to us all, Oh!—and began to sob. Her straightforwardness had become an arrow and gone right into her own heart.

Then a deep tear-drying breath: I want a picture too, she said.

Yes. Yes, wait, I have one here someplace. Abby and Judy and that Spanish kid Victor. Where is it? Ah. Here!

Three nine-year-old children sat high on that long-armed sycamore in the park, dangling their legs on someone's patient head—smooth dark hair, parted in the middle. Was that head Kitty's?

Our dear friend laughed. Another great day, she said. Wasn't it? I remember you two sizing up the men. I *had* one at the time—I thought. Some joke. Here, take it. I have two copies. but you ought to get it enlarged. When this you see, remember me. Ha-ha. Well, girls—excuse me, I mean ladies—it's time for me to rest.

She took Susan's arm and continued that awful walk to her bed.

We didn't move. We had a long journey ahead of us and had expected a little more comforting before we set off.

No, she said. You'll only miss the express. I'm not in much pain. I've got lots of painkiller. See?

The tabletop was full of little bottles.

I just want to lie down and think of Abby.

It was true, the local could cost us an extra two hours at least. I looked at Ann. It had been hard for her to come at all. Still, we couldn't move. We stood there before Selena in a row. Three old friends. Selena pressed her lips together, ordered her eyes into cold distance.

I know that face. Once, years ago, when the children were children, it had been placed modestly in front of J. Hoffner, the principal of the elementary school.

He'd said, No! Without training you cannot tutor these kids. There are real problems. You have to know *how to teach*.

Our P.T.A. had decided to offer some one-to-one tutorial help for the Spanish kids, who were stuck in crowded classrooms with exhausted teachers among little middle-class achievers. He had said, in a written communication to show seriousness and then in personal confrontation to *prove* seriousness, that he could not allow it. And the board of ed itself had said no. (All this no-ness was to lead to some terrible events in the schools and neighborhoods of our poor yes-requiring city.) But most of the women in our P.T.A. were independent—by necessity and disposition. We were, in fact, the soft-speaking tough souls of anarchy.

I had Fridays off that year. At about 11 A.M. I'd bypass the principal's office and run up to the fourth floor. I'd take Robert Figueroa to the end of the hall, and we'd work away at storytelling for about twenty minutes. Then we would write the beautiful letters of the alphabet invented by smart foreigners long ago to fool time and distance.

That day, Selena and her stubborn face remained in the office for at least two hours. Finally, Mr. Hoffner, besieged, said that because she was a nurse, she would be allowed to help out by taking the littlest children to the modern difficult toilet. Some of them, he said, had just come from the barbarous hills beyond Maricao. Selena said O.K., she'd do that. In the toilet she taught the little girls which way to wipe, as she had taught her own little girl a couple of years earlier. At three o'clock she brought them home for cookies and milk. The children of that year ate cookies in her kitchen until the end of the sixth grade.

Now, what did we learn in that year of my Friday afternoons off? The following: Though the world cannot be changed by talking to one child at a time, it may at least be known.

Anyway, Selena placed into our eyes for long remembrance that useful stubborn face. She said, No. Listen to me, you people. Please. I don't have lots of time. What I want . . . I want to lie down and think about Abby. Nothing special. Just think about her, you know.

In the train Susan fell asleep immediately. She woke up from time to time, because the speed of the new wheels and the resistance of the old track gave us some terrible jolts. Once, she opened her eyes wide and said, You know, Ann's right. You don't get sick like that for nothing. I mean, she didn't even mention him.

Why should she? She hasn't even seen him, I said. Susan, you still have him-itis, the dread disease of females.

Yeah? And you don't? Anyway, he *was* around quite a bit. He was there every day, nearly, when the kid died.

Abby. I didn't like to hear "the kid." I wanted to say "Abby" the way I've said "Selena"—so those names can take thickness and strength and fall back into the world with their weight.

Abby, you know, was a wonderful child. She was in Richard's classes every class till high school. Good-hearted little girl from the beginning, noticeably kind—for a kid, I mean. Smart.

That's true, said Ann, very kind. She'd give away Selena's last shirt. Oh yes, they were all wonderful little girls and wonderful little boys.

Chrissy *is* wonderful, Susan said.

She *is,* I said.

Middle kids aren't supposed to be, but she is. She put herself through college—I didn't have a cent—and now she has this fellowship. And, you know, she never did take any crap from boys. She's something.

Ann went swaying up the aisle to the bathroom. First she said, Oh, all of them—just wohunderful.

I loved Selena, Susan said, but she never talked to me enough. Maybe she talked to you women more, about things. Men.

Then Susan fell asleep.

Ann sat down opposite me. She looked straight into my eyes with a narrow squint. It often connotes accusation.

Be careful—you're wrecking your laugh lines, I said.

Screw you, she said. You're kidding around. Do you realize I don't know where Mickey is? You know, you've been lucky. You always have been. Since you were a little kid. Papa and Mama's darling.

As is usual in conversations, I said a couple of things out loud and kept a few structured remarks for interior mulling and righteousness. I thought: She's never even met my folks. I thought: What a rotten thing to say. Luck—isn't it something like an insult?

I said, Annie, I'm only forty-eight. There's lots of time for me to be totally wrecked—if I live, I mean.

Then I tried to knock wood, but we were sitting in plush and leaning on plastic. Wood! I shouted. Please, some wood? Anybody here have a matchstick?

Oh, shut up, she said. Anyway, death doesn't count.

I tried to think of a couple of sorrows as irreversible as death. But truthfully nothing in my life can compare to hers: a son, a boy of fifteen, who disappears before your very eyes into a darkness or a light behind his own, from which neither hugging nor hitting can bring him. If you shout, Come back, come back, he won't come. Mickey, Mickey, Mickey, we once screamed, as though he were twenty miles away instead of right in front of us in a kitchen chair; but he refused to return. And when he did, twelve hours later, he left immediately for California.

Well, some bad things have happened in my life, I said.

What? You were born a woman? Is that it?

She was, of course, mocking me this time, referring to an old discussion about feminism and Judaism. Actually, on the prism of isms, both of those do have to be looked at together once in a while.

Well, I said, my mother died a couple of years ago and I still feel it. I think *Ma* sometimes and I lose my breath. I miss her. You understand that. Your mother's seventy-six. You have to admit it's nice still having her.

She's very sick, Ann said. Half the time she's out of it.

I decided not to describe my mother's death. I could have done so and made Ann even more miserable. But I thought I'd save that for her next attack on me. These constrictions of her spirit were coming closer and closer together. Probably a great enmity was about to be born.

Susan's eyes opened. The death or dying of someone near or dear often makes people irritable, she stated. (She's been taking a course in relationships *and* interrelationships.) The real name of my seminar is Skills: Personal Friendship and Community. It's a very good course despite your snide remarks.

While we talked, a number of cities passed us, going in the opposite direction. I had tried to look at New London through the dusk of the windows. Now I was missing New Haven. The conductor explained, smiling: Lady, if the windows were clean, half of you'd be dead. The tracks are lined with sharpshooters.

Do you believe that? I hate people to talk that way.

He may be exaggerating, Susan said, but don't wash the window.

A man leaned across the aisle. Ladies, he said, I do believe it. According to what I hear of this part of the country, it don't seem unplausible.

Susan turned to see if he was worth engaging in political dialogue.

You've forgotten Selena already, Ann said. All of us have. Then you'll make this nice memorial service for her and everyone will stand up and say a few words and then we'll forget her again—for good. What'll you say at the memorial, Faith?

It's not right to talk like that. She's not dead yet, Annie.

Yes, she is, said Ann.

We discovered the next day that give or take an hour or two, Ann had been correct. It was a combination—David Clark, surgeon, said—of being sick unto real death and having a tabletop full of little bottles.

Now, why are you taking all those hormones? Susan had asked Selena a couple of years earlier. They were visiting New Orleans. It was Mardi Gras.

Oh, they're mostly vitamins, Selena said. Besides, I want to be young and beautiful. She made a joking pirouette.

Susan said, That's absolutely ridiculous.

But Susan's seven or eight years younger than Selena. What did she know? Because: People *do* want to be young and beautiful. When they meet in the street, male or female, if they're getting older they look at each other's face a little ashamed. It's clear they want to say, Excuse me, I didn't mean to draw attention to mortality and gravity all at once. I didn't want to remind you, my dear friend, of our coming eviction, first from liveliness, then from life. To which, most of the time, the friend's eyes will courteously reply, My dear, it's nothing at all. I hardly noticed.

Luckily, I learned recently how to get out of that deep well of melancholy. Anyone can do it. You grab at roots of the littlest future, sometimes just stubs of conversation. Though some believe you miss a great deal of depth by not sinking down down down.

Susan, I asked, you still seeing Ed Flores?

Went back to his wife.

Lucky she didn't kill you, said Ann. I'd never fool around with a Spanish guy. They all have tough ladies back in the barrio.

No, said Susan, she's unusual. I met her at a meeting. We had an amazing talk. Luisa is a very fine woman. She's one of the office-worker organizers I told you about. She only needs him two more years, she says. Because the kids—they're girls—need to be watched a little in their neighborhood. The neighborhood is definitely not good. He's a good father but not such a great husband.

I'd call that a word to the wise.

Well, you know me—I don't want a husband. I like a male person around. I hate to do without. Anyway, listen to this. She, Luisa, whispers in my ear the other day, she whispers, Suzie, in two years you still want him, I promise you, you got him. Really. I may still want him then. He's only about forty-five now. Still got a lot of spunk. I'll have my degree in two years. Chrissy will be out of the house.

Two years! In two years we'll all be dead, said Ann.

I know she didn't mean all of us. She meant Mickey. That boy of hers would surely be killed in one of the drugstores or whorehouses of Chicago, New Orleans, San Francisco. I'm in a big beautiful city, he said when he called last month. Makes New York look like a garbage tank.

Mickey! Where?

Ha-ha, he said, and hung up.

Soon he'd be picked up for vagrancy, dealing, small thievery, or simply screaming dirty words at night under a citizen's window. Then Ann would fly to the town or not fly to the town to disentangle him, depending on a confluence of financial reality and psychiatric advice.

How *is* Mickey? Selena had said. In fact, that was her first sentence when we came, solemn and embarrassed, into her sunny front room that was full of the light and shadow of windy courtyard trees. We said, each in her own way, How are you feeling, Selena? She said, O.K., first things first. Let's talk about important things. How's Richard? How's Tonto? How's John? How's Chrissy? How's Judy? How's Mickey?

I don't want to talk about Mickey, said Ann.

Oh, let's talk about him, talk about him, Selena said, taking Ann's hand. Let's all think before it's too late. How did it start? Oh, for godsake talk about him.

Susan and I were smart enough to keep our mouths shut.

Nobody knows, nobody knows anything. Why? Where? Everybody has an idea, theories, and writes articles. Nobody knows.

Ann said this sternly. She didn't whine. She wouldn't lean too far into Selena's softness, but listening to Selena speak Mickey's name, she could sit in her chair more easily. I watched. It was interesting. Ann breathed deeply in and out the way we've learned in our Thursday-night yoga class. She was able to rest her body a little bit.

We were riding the rails of the trough called Park-Avenue-in-the-

Bronx. Susan had turned from us to talk to the man across the aisle.
She was explaining that the war in Vietnam was not yet over and
would not be, as far as she was concerned, until we repaired the
dikes we'd bombed and paid for some of the hopeless ecological
damage. He didn't see it that way. Fifty thousand American lives, our
own boys—we'd paid, he said. He asked us if we agreed with Susan.
Every word, we said.

You don't look like hippies. He laughed. Then his face changed.
As the resident face-reader, I decided he was thinking: Adventure.
He may have hit a mother lode of late counterculture in three opin-
ionated left-wing ladies. That was the nice part of his face. The other
part was the sly out-of-town-husband-in-New-York look.

I'd like to see you again, he said to Susan.

Oh? Well, come to dinner day after tomorrow. Only two of my
kids will be home. You ought to have at least one decent meal in
New York.

Kids? His face thought it over. Thanks. Sure, he said. I'll come.

Ann muttered, She's impossible. She did it again.

Oh, Susan's O.K., I said. She's just right in there. Isn't that good?
This is a long ride, said Ann.

Then we were in the darkness that precedes Grand Central.

We're irritable, Susan explained to her new pal. We're angry with
our friend Selena for dying. The reason is, we want her to be present
when we're dying. We all require a mother or mother-surrogate to
fix our pillows on that final occasion, and we were counting on her
to be that person.

I know just what you mean, he said. You'd like to have someone
around. A little fuss, maybe.

Something like that. Right, Faith?

It always takes me a minute to slide under the style of her public-
address system. I agreed. Yes.

The train stopped hard, in a grinding agony of opposing tech-
nologies.

Right. Wrong. Who cares? Ann said. She didn't have to die. She
really wrecked everything.

Oh, Annie, I said.

Shut up, will you? Both of you, said Ann, nearly breaking our
knees as she jammed past us and out of the train.

Then Susan, like a New York hostess, began to tell that man all our private troubles—the mistake of the World Trade Center, Westway, the decay of the South Bronx, the rage in Williamsburg. She rose with him on the escalator, gabbing into evening friendship and, hopefully, a happy night.

At home Anthony, my youngest son, said, Hello, you just missed Richard. He's in Paris now. He had to call collect.

Collect? From Paris?

He saw my sad face and made one of the herb teas used by his peer group to calm their overwrought natures. He does want to improve my pretty good health and spirits. His friends have a book that says a person should, if properly nutritioned, live forever. He wants me to give it a try. He also believes that the human race, its brains and good looks, will end in his time.

At about 11:30 he went out to live the pleasures of his eighteen-year-old nighttime life.

At 3 A.M. he found me washing the floors and making little apartment repairs.

More tea, Mom? he asked. He sat down to keep me company. O.K., Faith. I know you feel terrible. But how come Selena never realized about Abby?

Anthony, what the hell do I realize about you?

Come on, you had to be blind. I was just a little kid, and I saw. Honest to God, Ma.

Listen, Tonto. Basically Abby was O.K. She was. You don't know yet what their times can do to a person.

Here she goes with her goody-goodies—everything is so groovy wonderful far-out terrific. Next thing, you'll say people are darling and the world is *so* nice and round that Union Carbide will never blow it up.

I have never said anything as hopeful as that. And why to all our knowledge of that sad day did Tonto at 3 A.M. have to add the fact of the world?

The next night Max called from North Carolina. How's Selena? I'm flying up, he said. I have one early-morning appointment. Then I'm canceling everything.

At 7 A.M. Annie called. I had barely brushed my morning teeth. It was hard, she said. The whole damn thing. I don't mean Selena. All of us. In the train. None of you seemed real to me.

Real? Reality, huh? Listen, how about coming over for breakfast?—I don't have to get going until after nine. I have this neat sourdough rye?

No, she said. Oh Christ, no. No!

I remember Ann's eyes and the hat she wore the day we first looked at each other. Our babies had just stepped howling out of the sandbox on their new walking legs. We picked them up. Over their sandy heads we smiled. I think a bond was sealed then, at least as useful as the vow we'd all sworn with husbands to whom we're no longer married. Hindsight, usually looked down upon, is probably as valuable as foresight, since it does include a few facts.

Meanwhile, Anthony's world—poor, dense, defenseless thing— rolls round and round. Living and dying are fastened to its surface and stuffed into its softer parts.

He was right to call my attention to its suffering and danger. He was right to harass my responsible nature. But I was right to invent for my friends and our children a report on these private deaths and the condition of our lifelong attachments.

GLORIA NAYLOR

Etta Mae Johnson

(1982)

*I*N the late 1800s, thousands of blacks trekked to southern hamlets such as Robinsonville, Mississippi, located in Tunica County in the northwestern corner of the state, to work unrelentingly in the cotton fields as sharecroppers. Today in Robinsonville only vestiges of this era remain, including a few boarded up buildings and a few aging laborers.[1] What is significant about this place is that it was the humble beginning for hundreds of blacks including Gloria Naylor's parents, Alberta McAlpin and Roosevelt Naylor, who migrated from the South to northern urban centers with aspirations of obtaining the American dream.

Gloria Naylor, a telephone operator turned writer, was born January 25, 1950, in New York City. Prior to becoming an author, Naylor worked as a Jehovah's Witness evangelist for ten years. At age twenty-five, she entered Brooklyn's Medgar Evers College with aspirations of becoming a nurse. She transferred to Brooklyn College and received her B.A. in 1981. In the same month that she received her degree, she completed the manuscript for her first novel, *The Women of Brewster Place* (1982),[2] of which the story "Etta Mae Johnson" forms a part. In 1983, she completed her M.A. in Afro-American studies at Yale University. Since then she has maintained a number of appointments at various institutions, including Cummington Community of the Arts (Cummington, Massachusetts), George Washington University, and New York University. In the fall of 1985, she served as a United States Information Agency Cultural Exchange Lecturer in India.

Although Naylor grew up in Queens, the rural town of Robinsonville had an indelible impact on her life. She has vivid memories of her mother telling stories of how she worked in the cotton fields during her spare afternoons to earn the money needed to purchase books from various book clubs. Growing up in Mississippi during the Jim Crow era, Alberta McAlpin Naylor, along with millions of other blacks, was barred from the public libraries. At that time, for blacks to obtain books of any kind was a hard-earned luxury.

When *The Women of Brewster Place* won the National Book Award for first novel, Gloria Naylor in her acceptance speech proclaimed that her passionate love of books came from her mother's side of the family. It was Naylor's mother who introduced her as well as her two sisters to the library in New York City. Naylor recalls her taking them by the hand and saying, "You see all those books? Once you can write your name, all these books'll be yours."[3] It was her mother who encouraged this quiet and reserved child to use the written medium as a vehicle of self-expression and gave her her first diary. Over the years this diary, Naylor claims, "was followed by reams and reams of paper that eventually culminated in *The Women of Brewster Place*."[4] Naylor wrote an adaptation of the book for public television's 1985–86 season of "American Playhouse." *Brewster Place* was made into an ABC mini-series featuring a host of celebrated actors including Cicely Tyson and Paul Winfield.

With three books completed (*Brewster Place,* 1982; *Linden Hills,* 1985; and *Mama Day,* 1987) and a fourth one (*Bailey's Cafe*) well on the way, Naylor's achievements as a writer are quite remarkable, especially given that up until age twenty-seven she had no knowledge that black women had a literary tradition. In a creative writing class during her sophomore year at Brooklyn College, she was required to read one novel written by a black woman. It was Toni Morrison's *The Bluest Eye,*[5] a novel that explores the denigration of black female beauty along with the spiritual demoralization of a society obsessed with notions of the idealized blonde, blue-eyed standard of beauty—"the Mary Jane Look." This obsession has the community so paralyzed that a little black girl's desperate cry for acceptance goes unheeded. Naylor claims that reading this novel validated her desire to pick up the pen and write as a black woman. Her education in northern integrated schools had taught her that novels were something that white males wrote, the exception being a couple of black male writers and a few privileged white women writers. "Who was I to argue that Ellison, Austen, Dickens, the Brontës, Baldwin, and Faulkner weren't masters? They were and are."[6] *Brewster Place* was her first attempt to legitimize the American black woman's story in its varied and multidimensional forms.

Brewster Place, which could be located in any urban American northern city, is one of several housing units on worthless land in an overpopulated district, walled off from the predominantly white major business area. The wall isolates the black inhabitants geographically from the central activities of the city, standing as a symbol of their historical disenfranchisement in this country. Indeed this wall is the physical counterpart of the pervasive Jim Crow mentality that Alberta McAlpin Naylor and millions of other blacks contended with in the South. This wall, conceived out of racist and classist notions, comes to represent the psychological and spiritual degeneration of a neighborhood infested with poverty, crime, and despair.

The Women of Brewster Place is structured around the narratives of seven different women who, for various reasons, wind up in Brewster Place. Although they vary in age, background, sexual preference, and political consciousness, as black women they share a common oppression. In the midst of their obstacles, they maintain an enduring spirit that is strengthened by a sense of female communion. Etta Mae Johnson, one of the central figures in the novel, defies segregationist attitudes of Rock Vale, Tennessee, her hometown: "she looked them [whites] straight in the face while putting in her father's order at the dry goods store, when she reserved her sirs and mams for those she thought deserving, and when she smiled only if pleased, regardless of whose presence she was in" (59–60). A collector of Billie Holiday albums, this iconoclast defies the sexual mores of the black community with her "ain't-nobody's-business-if-I-do" attitude. Roaming from city to city, from the South to the North, she becomes disillusioned, finding no place willing to accept her on her own terms. After countless thwarted love affairs, she is ultimately sustained by the enduring friendship of Mattie Michael, particularly in her middle-aged years when her waning seductive charms land her one more time in bed with a man she assumes is her potential knight in shining armor. "I oughta find me a good man and settle down to live quiet in my old age," Etta Mae Johnson says. The one-night stand becomes her dream deferred.

Each of Naylor's four novels is part of a quartet. She appears to be weaving a tightly constructed mythology of white and black America that comes full circle when characters and places alluded to in one novel take center stage in another. Naylor's work, fiction and nonfiction, consistently explores the dynamics of such controversial topics as poverty, racism, sexism, classism, and homophobia, with the black community as the primary setting for her material. She has expressed her views in a variety of publications including *Essence, Ms., Publishers Weekly, People,* and *Life.* In 1986, she was a columnist for *The New York Times.*

In her work Naylor celebrates the enduring spirit that she has observed in her mother and other black women who somehow manage to triumph in spite of very limited personal circumstances.[7] Women such as Etta Mae Johnson who defy the system to maintain their own standards remain a central motif in her work. Naylor believes that women's affirmation of self is inherently connected to their sense of female communion, a resource historically used to promote psychological and spiritual maturity.

CAROL TAYLOR

The unpainted walls of the long rectangular room were soaked with the smell of greasy chicken and warm, headless beer. The brown and pink faces floated above the trails of used cigarette smoke like bodiless carnival balloons. The plump yellow woman with white gardenias pinned to the side of her head stood with her back pressed against the peeling sides of the baby grand and tried to pierce the bloated hum in the room with her thin scratchy voice. Undisturbed that she remained for the most part ignored, she motioned for the piano player to begin.

It wasn't the music or the words or the woman that took that room by its throat until it gasped for air—it was the pain. There was a young southern girl, Etta Johnson, pushed up in a corner table, and she never forgot. The music, the woman, the words.

> *I love my man*
> *I'm a lie if I say I don't*
> *I love my man*
> *I'm a lie if I say I don't*
> *But I'll quit my man*
> *I'm a lie if I say I won't*
>
> *My man wouldn't give me no breakfast*
> *Wouldn't give me no dinner*
> *Squawked about my supper*
> *Then he put me out of doors*
> *Had the nerve to lay*
> *A matchbox to my clothes*
> *I didn't have so many*
> *But I had a long, long, way to go*

Children bloomed on Brewster Place during July and August with their colorful shorts and tops plastered against gold, ebony, and nutbrown legs and arms; they decorated the street, rivaling the geraniums and ivy found on the manicured boulevard downtown. The

summer heat seemed to draw the people from their cramped apartments onto the stoops, as it drew the tiny drops of perspiration from
their foreheads and backs.

The apple-green Cadillac with the white vinyl roof and Florida
plates turned into Brewster like a greased cobra. Since Etta had
stopped at a Mobil station three blocks away to wash off the evidence of a hot, dusty 1200-mile odyssey home, the chrome caught
the rays of the high afternoon sun and flung them back into its face.
She had chosen her time well.

The children, free from the conditioned restraints of their older
counterparts, ran along the sidewalks flanking this curious, slow-
moving addition to their world. Every eye on the block, either
openly or covertly, was on the door of the car when it opened. They
were rewarded by the appearance of a pair of white leather sandals
attached to narrow ankles and slightly bowed, shapely legs. The
willow-green sundress, only ten minutes old on the short chestnut
woman, clung to a body that had finished a close second in its race
with time. Large two-toned sunglasses hid the weariness that had
defied the freshly applied mascara and burnt-ivory shadow. After
taking twice the time needed to stretch herself, she reached into the
back seat of the car and pulled out her plastic clothes bag and Billie
Holiday albums.

The children's curiosity reached the end of its short life span, and
they drifted back to their various games. The adults sucked their teeth
in disappointment, and the more envious felt self-righteousness
twist the corners of their mouths. It was only Etta. Looked like she'd
done all right by herself—this time around.

Slowly she carried herself across the street—head high and eyes
fixed unwaveringly on her destination. The half-dozen albums were
clutched in front of her chest like cardboard armor:

> *There ain't nothing I ever do*
> *Or nothing I ever say*
> *That folks don't criticize me*
> *But I'm going to do*
> *Just what I want to, anyway*
> *And don't care just what people say*
> *If I should take a notion*
> *To jump into the ocean*
> *Ain't nobody's business if I do . . .*

Any who bothered to greet her never used her first name. No one called Etta Mae "Etta," except in their minds; and when they spoke to each other about her, it was Etta Johnson; but when they addressed her directly, it was always Miss Johnson. This baffled her because she knew what they thought about her, and she'd always call them by their first names and invited them to do the same with her. But after a few awkward attempts, they'd fall back into the pattern they were somehow comfortable with. Etta didn't know if this was to keep the distance on her side or theirs, but it was there. And she had learned to tread through these alien undercurrents so well that to a casual observer she had mastered the ancient secret of walking on water.

Mattie sat in her frayed brocade armchair, pushed up to the front window, and watched her friend's brave approach through the dusty screen. Still toting around them oversized records, she thought. That woman is a puzzlement.

Mattie rose to open the door so Etta wouldn't have to struggle to knock with her arms full. "Lord, child, thank you," she gushed, out of breath. "The younger I get, the higher those steps seem to stretch."

She dumped her load on the sofa and swept off her sun-glasses. She breathed deeply of the freedom she found in Mattie's presence. Here she had no choice but to be herself. The carefully erected decoys she was constantly shuffling and changing to fit the situation were of no use here. Etta and Mattie went way back, a singular term that claimed co-knowledge of all the important events in their lives and almost all of the unimportant ones. And by rights of this possession, it tolerated no secrets.

"Sit on down and take a breather. Must have been a hard trip. When you first said you were coming, I didn't expect you to be driving."

"To tell the truth, I didn't expect it myself, Mattie. But Simeon got very ornery when I said I was heading home, and he refused to give me the money he'd promised for my plane fare. So I said, just give me half and I'll take the train. Well, he wasn't gonna even do that. And Mattie, you know I'll be damned if I was coming into this city on a raggedy old Greyhound. So one night he was by my place all drunk up and snoring, and as kindly as you please, I took the car keys and registration and so here I am."

"My God, woman! You stole the man's car?"

"Stole—nothing. He owes me that and then some."

"Yeah, but the police don't wanna hear that. It's a wonder the highway patrol ain't stopped you before now."

"They ain't stopped me because Simeon didn't report it."

"How you know that?"

"His wife's daddy is the sheriff of that county." Laughter hung dangerously on the edge of the two women's eyes and lips.

"Yeah, but he could say you picked his pockets."

Etta went to her clothes bag and pulled out a pair of pink and red monogrammed shorts. "I'd have to be a damned good pickpocket to get away with all this." The laughter lost its weak hold on their mouths and went bouncing crazily against the walls of the living room.

> *Them that's got, shall get*
> *Them that's not, shall lose*
> *So the Bible says*
> *And it still is news*

Each time the laughter would try to lie still, the two women would look at each other and send it hurling between them, once again.

> *Mama may have*
> *Papa may have*
> *But God bless the child*
> *That's got his own*
> *That's got his own*

"Lord, Tut, you're a caution." Mattie wiped the tears off her cheeks with the back of a huge dark hand.

Etta was unable to count the years that had passed since she had heard someone call her that. Look a' that baby gal strutting around here like a bantam. You think she'd be the wife of King Tut. The name had stayed because she never lost the walk. The washed-out grime and red mud of backwoods Rock Vale, Tennessee, might wrap itself around her bare feet and coat the back of her strong fleshy legs, but Etta always had her shoulders flung behind her collarbone and her chin thrust toward the horizon that came to mean everything Rock Vale did not.

Etta spent her teenage years in constant trouble. Rock Vale had no place for a black woman who was not only unwilling to play by the rules, but whose spirit challenged the very right of the game to exist. The whites in Rock Vale were painfully reminded of this rebellion when she looked them straight in the face while putting in her father's order at the dry goods store, when she reserved her sirs and mams for those she thought deserving, and when she smiled only if pleased, regardless of whose presence she was in. That Johnson gal wasn't being an uppity nigger, as talk had it; she was just being herself.

> Southern trees bear strange fruit
> Blood on the leaves and blood at the root
> Black bodies swinging
> In the southern breeze
> Strange fruit hanging
> From the poplar trees

But Rutherford County wasn't ready for Etta's blooming independence, and so she left one rainy summer night about three hours ahead of dawn and Johnny Brick's furious pursuing relatives. Mattie wrote and told her they had waited in ambush for two days on the county line, and then had returned and burned down her father's barn. The sheriff told Mr. Johnson that he had gotten off mighty light—considering. Mr. Johnson thought so, too. After reading Mattie's letter, Etta was sorry she hadn't killed the horny white bastard when she had the chance.

Rock Vale had followed her to Memphis, Detroit, Chicago, and even to New York. Etta soon found out that America wasn't ready for her yet—not in 1937. And so along with the countless other disillusioned, restless children of Ham with so much to give and nowhere to give it, she took her talents to the street. And she learned to get over, to hook herself to any promising rising black star, and when he burnt out, she found another.

Her youth had ebbed away quickly under the steady pressure of the changing times, but she was existing as she always had. Even if someone had bothered to stop and tell her that the universe had expanded for her, just an inch, she wouldn't have known how to shine alone.

Etta and Mattie had taken totally different roads that with all of their deceptive winding had both ended up on Brewster Place. Their laughter now drew them into a conspiratorial circle against all the Simeons outside of that dead-end street, and it didn't stop until they were both weak from the tears that flowed down their faces.

"So," Mattie said, blowing her nose on a large cotton handkerchief, "trusting you stay out of jail, what you plan on doing now?"

"Child, I couldn't tell you." Etta dropped back down on the couch. "I should be able to get a coupla thousand for the car to tide me over till another business opportunity comes along."

Mattie raised one eyebrow just a whisper of an inch. "Ain't it time you got yourself a regular job? These last few years them *business opportunities* been fewer and farther between."

Etta sucked her small white teeth. "A job doing what? Come on, Mattie, what kind of experience I got? Six months here, three there. I oughta find me a good man and settle down to live quiet in my old age." She combed her fingers confidently through the thick sandy hair that only needed slight tinting at the roots and mentally gave herself another fifteen years before she had to worry about this ulti-mate fate.

Mattie, watching the creeping tiredness in her eyes, gave her five. "You done met a few promising ones along the way, Etta."

"No, honey, it just seemed so. Let's face it, Mattie. All the good men are either dead or waiting to be born."

"Why don't you come to meeting with me tonight. There's a few settle-minded men in our church, some widowers and such. And a little prayer wouldn't hurt your soul one bit."

"I'll thank you to leave my soul well alone, Mattie Michael. And if your church is so full of upright Christian men, why you ain't snagged one yet?"

"Etta, I done banked them fires a long time ago, but seeing that you still keeping up steam . . ." Her eyes were full of playful kindness.

"Just barely, Mattie, just barely."

And laughter rolled inside of 2E, once again.

"Etta, Etta Mae!" Mattie banged on the bathroom door. "Come on out now. You making me late for the meeting."

"Just another second, Mattie. The church ain't gonna walk away."

"Lord," Mattie grumbled, "she ain't bigger than a minute, so it shouldn't take more than that to get ready."

Etta came out of the bathroom in an exaggerated rush. "My, my, you the most impatient Christian I know."

"Probably, the only Christian you know." Mattie refused to be hu-mored as she bent to gather up her sweater and purse. She turned and was stunned with a barrage of colors. A huge white straw hat reigned over layers of gold and pearl beads draped over too much bosom and too little dress. "You plan on dazzling the Lord, Etta?"

"Well, honey," Etta said, looking down the back of her stocking leg to double-check for runs, "last I heard, He wasn't available. You got more recent news?"

"Um, um, um." Mattie pressed her lips together and shook her head slowly to swallow down the laughter she felt crawling up her throat. Realizing she wasn't going to succeed, she quickly turned her face from Etta and headed toward the door. "Just bring your blasphemin' self on downstairs. I done already missed morning services waiting on you today."

Canaan Baptist Church, a brooding, ashen giant, sat in the middle of a block of rundown private homes. Its multi-colored, dome-shaped eyes glowered into the darkness. Fierce clapping and thunderous organ chords came barreling out of its mouth. Evening services had begun.

Canaan's congregation, the poor who lived in a thirty-block area around Brewster Place, still worshiped God loudly. They could not afford the refined, muted benediction of the more prosperous blacks who went to Sinai Baptist on the northern end of the city, and because each of their requests for comfort was so pressing, they took no chances that He did not hear them.

> When Israel was in Egypt's land
> Let my people go
> Oppressed so hard, they could not stand
> Let my people go

The words were as ancient as the origin of their misery, but the tempo had picked up threefold in its evolution from the cotton fields. They were now sung with the frantic determination of a people who realized that the world was swiftly changing but for some mystic, complex reason their burden had not.

> God said to go down
> Go down
> Brother Moses
> Brother Moses
> To the shore of the great Nile River

The choir clapped and stomped each syllable into a devastating reality, and just as it did, the congregation reached up, grabbed the phrase, and tried to clap and stomp it back into oblivion.

Go to Egypt
Go to Egypt
Tell Pharaoh
Tell Pharaoh
Let my people go

Etta entered the back of the church like a reluctant prodigal, prepared at best to be amused. The alien pounding and the heat and the dark glistening bodies dragged her back, back past the cold ashes of her innocence to a time when pain could be castrated on the sharp edges of iron-studded faith. The blood rushed to her temples and began to throb in unison with the musical pleas around her.

Yes, my God is a mighty God
Lord, deliver
And he set old Israel free
Swallowed that Egyptian army
Lord, deliver
With the waves of the great Red Sea

Etta glanced at Mattie, who was swaying and humming and she saw that the lines in her face had almost totally vanished. She had left Etta in just that moment for a place where she was free. Sadly, Etta looked at her, at them all, and was very envious. Unaccustomed to the irritating texture of doubt, she felt tears as its abrasiveness grated over the fragile skin of her life. Could there have been another way?

The song ended with a huge expulsion of air, and the congregation sat down as one body.

"Come on, let's get us a seat," Mattie tugged her by the arm.

The grizzled church deacon with his suit hanging loosely off his stooped shoulders went up to the pulpit to read the church business.

"That's one of the widowers I was telling you about," Mattie whispered, and poked Etta.

"Ummm." The pressure on her arm brought Etta back onto the uncomfortable wooden pew. But she didn't want to stay there, so she climbed back out the window, through the glass eyes of the seven-foot Good Shepherd, and started again the futile weaving of invisible ifs and slippery mights into an equally unattainable past.

The scenes of her life reeled out before her with the same aging script, but now hindsight sat as the omniscient director and had the young star of her epic recite different brilliant lines and make the sort of stunning decisions that propelled her into the cushioned front pews on the right of the minister's podim. There she sat with the deacons' wives, officers of the Ladies' Auxiliary, and head usherettes. And like them, she would wear on her back a hundred pairs of respectful eyes earned the hard way, and not the way she had earned the red sundress, which she now self-consciously tugged up in the front. Was it too late?

The official business completed, the treasurer pulled at his frayed lapels, cleared his throat, and announced the guest speaker for the night.

The man was magnificent.

He glided to the podium with the effortlessness of a well-oiled machine and stood still for an interminable long moment. He eyed the congregation confidently. He only needed their attention for that split second because once he got it, he was going to wrap his voice around their souls and squeeze until they screamed to be relieved. They knew it was coming and waited expectantly, breathing in unison as one body. First he played with them and threw out fine silken threads that stroked their heart muscles ever so gently. They trembled ecstatically at the touch and invited more. The threads multiplied and entwined themselves solidly around the one pulsating organ they had become and tightened slightly, testing them for a reaction.

The "Amen, brothers" and "Yes, Jesus" were his permission to take that short hop from the heart to the soul and lay all pretense of gentleness aside. Now he would have to push and pound with clenched fists in order to be felt, and he dared not stop the fierce rhythm of his voice until their replies had reached that fevered pitch of satisfaction. Yes, Lord—grind out the unheated tenements! Merciful Jesus—shove aside the low-paying boss man. Perfect Father— fill me, fill me till there's no room, no room for nothing else, not even that great big world out there that exacts such a strange penalty for my being born black.

It was hard work. There was so much in them that had to be replaced. The minister's chest was heaving in long spasms, and the sweat was pouring down his gray temples and rolling under his chin. His rich voice was now hoarse, and his legs and raised arms trembled on the edge of collapse. And as always they were satisfied a half-breath before he reached the end of his endurance. They sat back, limp and spent, but momentarily at peace. There was no price too high for this service. At that instant they would have followed him to do battle with the emperor of the world, and all he was going to ask of them was money for the "Lord's work." And they would willingly give over half of their little to keep this man in comfort.

Etta had not been listening to the message; she was watching the man. His body moved with the air of one who had not known recent deprivation. The tone of his skin and the fullness around his jawline told her that he was well-off, even before she got close enough to see the manicured hands and diamond pinkie ring.

The techniques he had used to brand himself on the minds of the congregation were not new to her. She'd encountered talent like that in poolrooms, nightclubs, grimy second-floor insurance offices, numbers dens, and on a dozen street corners. But here was a different sort of power. The jungle-sharpened instincts of a man like that could move her up to the front of the church, ahead of the deacons' wives and Ladies' Auxiliary, off of Brewster Place for good. She would find not only luxury but a place that complemented the type of woman she had fought all these years to become.

"Mattie, is that your regular minister?" she whispered.

"Who, Reverend Woods? No, he just visits on occasion, but he sure can preach, can't he?"

"What you know about him, he married?"

Mattie cut her eyes at Etta. "I should have figured it wasn't the sermon that moved you. At least wait till after the prayer before you jump all into the man's business."

During the closing song and prayer Etta was planning how she was going to maneuver Mattie to the front of the church and into introducing her to Reverend Woods. It wasn't going to be as difficult as she thought. Moreland T. Woods had noticed Etta from the moment she'd entered the chruch. She stood out like a bright red bird among the drab morality that dried up the breasts and formed rolls around the stomachs of the other church sisters. This woman was still dripping with the juices of a full-fleshed life—the kind of life he was soon to get up and damn into hell for the rest of the congregation—but how it fitted her well. He had to swallow to remove the excess fluid from his mouth before he got up to preach.

Now the problem was to make his way to the back of the church before she left without seeming to be in a particular hurry. A half-dozen back slaps, handshakes, and thank-you sisters only found him about ten feet up the aisle, and he was growing impatient. However, he didn't dare to turn his neck and look in the direction where he'd last seen her. He felt a hand on his upper arm and turned to see a grim-faced Mattie flanked by the woman in the scarlet dress.

"Reverend Woods, I really enjoyed your sermon," Mattie said.

"Why, thank you, sister—sister?"

"Sister Michael, Mattie Michael." While he was addressing his words to her, the smile he sent over her shoulder to Etta was undeniable.

"Especially the part," Mattie raised her voice a little, "About throwing away temptation to preserve the soul. That was a mighty fine point."

"The Lord moves me and I speak, Sister Michael. I'm just a humble instrument for his voice."

The direction and intent of his smile was not lost to Etta. She inched her way in front of Mattie. "I enjoyed it, too, Reverend Woods. It's been a long time since I heard preaching like that." She increased the pressure of her fingers on Mattie's arm.

"Oh, excuse my manners. Reverend Woods, this is an old friend of mine, Etta Mae Johnson. Etta Mae, Reverend Woods." She intoned the words as if she were reciting a eulogy.

"Please to meet you, Sister Johnson." He beamed down on the small woman and purposely held her hand a fraction longer than usual. "You must be a new member—I don't recall seeing you the times I've been here before."

"Well, no, Reverend, I'm not a member of the congregation, but I was raised up in the church. You know how it is, as you get older sometimes you stray away. But after your sermon, I'm truly thinking of coming back."

Mattie tensed, hoping that the lightning that God was surely going to strike Etta with wouldn't hit her by mistake.

"Well, you know what the Bible says, sister. The angels rejoice more over one sinner who turns around than over ninety-nine righteous ones."

"Yes, indeed, and I'm sure a shepherd like you has helped to turn many back to the fold." She looked up and gave him the full benefit of her round dark eyes, grateful she hadn't put on that third coat of mascara.

"I try, Sister Johnson, I try."

"It's a shame Mrs. Woods wasn't here tonight to hear you. I'm sure she must be mighty proud of your work."

"My wife has gone to her glory, Sister Johnson. I think of myself now as a man alone—rest her soul."

"Yes, rest her soul," Etta sighed.

"Please, Lord, yes," Mattie muttered, giving out the only sincere request among the three. The intensity of her appeal startled them, and they turned to look at her. "Only knows how hard this life is, she's better in the arms of Jesus."

"Yes"—Etta narrowed her eyes at Mattie and then turned back to the minister—"I can testify to that. Being a woman alone, it seems all the more hard. Sometimes you don't know where to turn."

Moreland Woods knew Etta was the type of woman who not only knew which way to turn, but, more often than not, had built her own roads when nothing else was accessible. But he was enjoying this game immensely—almost as much as the growing heat creeping into his groin.

"Well, if I can be of any assistance, Sister Johnson, don't hesitate to ask. I couldn't sleep knowing one of the Lord's sheep is troubled. As a matter of fact, if you have anything you would like to discuss with me this evening, I'd be glad to escort you home."

"I don't have my own place. You see, I'm just up from out of state and staying with my friend Mattie here."

"Well, perhaps we could all go out for coffee."

"Thank you, but I'll have to decline, Reverend," Mattie volunteered before Etta did it for her. "The services have me all tired out, but if Etta wants to, she's welcome."

"That'll be just fine," Etta said.

"Good, good." And now it was his turn to give her the benefit of a mouth full of strong, gold-capped teeth. "Just let me say good-bye to a few folks here, and I'll meet you outside."

"Girl, you oughta patent that speed and sell it to the airplane companies," Mattie said outside. "'After that sermon, Reverend, I'm thinking of coming back'—indeed!"

"Aw, hush your fussing."

"I declare if you had batted them lashes just a little faster, we'd of had a dust storm in there."

"You said you wanted me to meet some nice men. Well, I met one."

"Etta, I meant a man who'd be serious about settling down with you." Mattie was exasperated. "Why, you're going on like a schoolgirl. Can't you see what he's got in mind?"

Etta turned an indignant face toward Mattie. "The only thing I see is that you're telling me I'm not good enough for a man like that. Oh, no, not Etta Johnson. No upstanding decent man could ever see anything in her but a quick good time. Well, I'll tell you something, Mattie Michael. I've always traveled first class, maybe not in the way you'd approve with all your fine Christian principles, but it's done all right by me. And I'm gonna keep going top drawer till I leave this earth. Don't you think I got a mirror? Each year there's a new line to cover. I lay down with this body an get up with it every morning, and each morning it cries for just a little more rest than it did the day before. Well, I'm finally gonna get that rest, and it's going to be with a man like Reverend Woods. And you and the rest of those slack-mouthed gossips on Brewster be damned!" Tears frosted the edges of her last words. "They'll be humming a different tune when I show up there the wife of a big preacher. I've always known what they say about me behind my back, but I never thought you were right in there with them."

Mattie was stunned by Etta's tirade. How could Etta have so totally misunderstood her words? What had happened back there to stuff up her senses to the point that she had missed the obvious? Surely she could not believe that the vibrations coming from that unholy game of charades in the church aisle would lead to something as permanent as marriage? Why, it had been nothing but the opening gestures to a mating dance. Mattie had gone through the same motions at least once in her life, and Etta must have known a dozen variations to it that were a mystery to her. And yet, somehow, back there it had been played to a music that had totally distorted the steps for her friend. Mattie suddenly felt the helplessness of a person who is forced to explain that for which there are no words.

She quietly turned her back and started down the steps. There was no need to defend herself against Etta's accusations. They shared at least a hundred memories that could belie those cruel words. Let them speak for her.

Sometimes being a friend means mastering the art of timing. There is a time for silence. A time to let go and allow people to hurl themselves into their own destiny. And a time to prepare to pick up the pieces when it's all over. Mattie realized that this moment called for all three.

"I'll see ya when you get home, Etta," she threw gently over her shoulder.

Etta watched the bulky figure become slowly enveloped by the shadows. Her angry words had formed a thick mucus in her throat, and she couldn't swallow them down. She started to run into the darkness where she'd seen Mattie disappear, but at that instant Moreland Woods came out of the lighted church, beaming.

He took her arm and helped her into the front seat of his car. Her back sank into the deep upholstered leather, and the smell of the freshly vacuumed carpet was mellow in her nostrils. All of the natural night sounds of the city were blocked by the thick tinted windows and the hum of the air conditioner, but they trailed persistently behind the polished back of the vehicle as it turned and headed down the long gray boulevard.

> *Smooth road*
> *Clear day*
> *But why am I the only one*
> *Traveling this way*
> *How strange the road to love*
> *Can be so easy*
> *Can there be a detour ahead?*

Moreland Woods was captivated by the beautiful woman at his side. Her firm brown flesh and bright eyes carried the essence of nectar from some untamed exotic flower, and the fragrance was causing a pleasant disturbance at the pit of his stomach. He marveled at how excellently she played the game. A less alert observer might have been taken in, but his survival depended upon knowing people, knowing exactly how much to give and how little to take. It was this razor-thin instinct that had catapulted him to the head of his profession and that would keep him there.

And although she cut her cards with a reckless confidence, pushed her chips into the middle of the table as though the supply was unlimited, and could sit out the game until dawn, he knew. Oh, yes. Let her win a few, and then he would win just a few more, and she would be bankrupt long before the sun was up. And then there would be only one thing left to place on the table—and she would, because the stakes they were playing for were very high. But she was going to lose that last deal. She would lose because when she first sat down in that car she had everything riding on the fact that he didn't know the game existed.

And so it went. All evening Etta had been in another world, weaving his tailored suit and the smell of his expensive cologne into a custom-made future for herself. It took his last floundering thrusts into her body to bring her back to reality. She arrived in enough time to feel him beating against her like a dying walrus, until he shuddered and was still.

She kept her eyes closed because she knew when she opened them there would be the old familiar sights around her. To her right would be the plastic-coated nightstand that matched the cheaply carved headboard of the bed she lay in. She felt the bleached coarseness of the sheet under her sweaty back and predicted the roughness of the worn carpet path that led from the bed to the white-tiled bathroom with bright fluorescent lights, sterilized towels, and tissue-wrapped water glasses. There would be two or three small thin rectangles of soap wrapped in bright waxy covers that bore the name of the hotel.

She didn't try to visualize what the name would be. It didn't matter. They were all the same, all meshed together into one lump that rested like an iron ball on her chest. And the expression on the face of this breathing mass to her left would be the same as all the others. She could turn now and go through the rituals that would tie up the evening for them both, but she wanted just one more second of this soothing darkness before she had to face the echoes of the locking doors she knew would be in his eyes.

Etta got out of the car unassisted and didn't bother to turn and watch the taillights as it pulled off down the deserted avenue adjacent to Brewster Place. She had asked him to leave her at the corner because there was no point in his having to make a U-turn in the dead-end street, and it was less than a hundred yards to her door. Moreland was relieved that she had made it easy for him, because it had been a long day and he was anxious to get home and go to sleep. But then, the whole business had gone pretty smoothly after they left the hotel. He hadn't even been called upon to use any of the excuses he had prepared for why it would be a while before he'd see her again. A slight frown crossed his forehead as he realized that she had seemed as eager to get away from him as he had been to leave. Well, he shrugged his shoulders and placated his dented ego, that's the nice part about the worldly women. They understand the temporary weakness of the flesh and don't make it out to be something bigger than it is. They can have a good time without pawing and hanging all onto a man. Maybe I should drop around sometime. He glanced into his rearview mirror and saw that Etta was still standing on the corner, looking straight ahead into Brewster. There was something about the slumped profile of her body, silhouetted against the dim street light, that caused him to press down on the accelerator.

Etta stood looking at the wall that closed off Brewster from the avenues farther north and found it hard to believe that it had been just this afternoon when she had seen it. It had looked so different then, with the August sun highlighting the browns and reds of the bricks and the young children bouncing their rubber balls against its side. Now it crouched there in the thin predawn light, like a pulsating mouth awaiting her arrival. She shook her head sharply to rid herself of the illusion, but an uncanny fear gripped her, and her legs felt like lead. If I walk into this street, she thought, I'll never come back. I'll never get out. Oh, dear God, I am so tired—so very tired.

Etta removed her hat and massaged her tight forehead. Then, giving a resigned sigh, she started slowly down the street. Had her neighbors been out on their front stoops, she could have passed through their milling clusters as anonymously as the night wind. They had seen her come down that street once in a broken Chevy that had about five hundred dollars' worth of contraband liquor in its trunk, and there was even the time she'd come home with a broken nose she'd gotten in some hair-raising escapade in St. Louis, but never had she walked among them with a broken spirit. This middle-aged woman in the wrinkled dress and wilted straw hat would have been a stranger to them.

When Etta got to the stoop, she noticed there was a light under the shade at Mattie's window, and she strained to hear what actually sounded like music coming from behind the screen. Mattie was playing her records! Etta stood very still, trying to decipher the broken air waves into intelligible sound, but she couldn't make out the words. She stopped straining when it suddenly came to her that it wasn't important what song it was—someone was waiting up for her. Someone who would deny fiercely that there had been any concern—just a little indigestion from them fried onions that kept me from sleeping. Thought I'd pass the time by figuring out what you see in all this loose-life music.

Etta laughed softly to herself as she climbed the steps toward the light and the love and the comfort that awaited her.

J. CALIFORNIA COOPER

A Jewel for a Friend

(1984)

*E*VEN before she could read, J. California Cooper was telling stories. As a child growing up in Berkeley, California, she performed melodramas for her father and mother (who was so devoted to reading that she cooked with a book in her hand). Cooper's first collection of stories, *A Piece of Mine* (1984), was the first book published by Alice Walker and Robert Allen's Wild Trees Press, and it is where "A Jewel for a Friend" initially appeared. Walker had seen several of Cooper's plays performed and suggested that they be made into short stories. "Girl, I got so many other stories, I'll do something new," the playwright replied. And she did.

Cooper's nineteen one-act plays have been performed on stage, public television, college campuses, and community radio. *Strangers* won the Black Playwright of the Year award in 1978 from the Black Repertory Theatre in Berkeley. *Lovers* is anthologized in a collection called *Center Stage*.

Sales of her other two books of short stories, *Homemade Love* (1986) and *Some Soul to Keep* (1987), remain steady, which is highly unusual for short story collections from trade publishers. Cooper further supports herself by giving spirited readings at libraries and colleges. She says she is shy but that her characters commandeer her voice and movements when she dons her "big, wide, yellow dress with green flowers" to do a reading.

Cooper's characters show up in her mind and start talking to her when she is alone and undistracted. Each one is the voice of someone who knows the events or people involved with absolute authenticity. For example, she told me that the story "Sisters in the Rain" from *Some Soul to Keep* was being told by a schoolteacher until the events passed out of her purview; then that woman's daughter "stepped up" to continue the tale. Cooper has to "fight to stop listening and try to write down" what her characters are saying. She often asks them to repeat themselves and later fills in descriptions of what she saw as they were talking. She says of the process, "It's like a show in my mind."

Her gutsy characters have to "fight their way from the bottom" to achieve whatever peace and prosperity they can wrest from life. "My people win because they work hard and they suffer and they have integrity," she says. "I give them such hard troubles—sometimes I sit and cry because I know I have to get them to make it even a little harder on themselves." None of them are taken from life: "I don't know any of these people," she says. "A Jewel for a Friend," which was written in one day, began after Cooper had been lingering in a graveyard. "When I woke up, that child [Pearl] was chipping stone and starting in to tell the story."

Cemeteries have a great effect on Cooper: "Death means you are gone. You may have done some stuff and nobody ever knew it. So let me put you here in a story." She crowds many people into the acknowledgments to her collections: "No one has to do anything for you, and when they do, girl, you just have to remember." No terse, oblique dedications for her. They come from "a big heart with a whole lotta people in it" and include her family, publishers and editors, people who inspired her, the female ancestors she never knew, the children of the future, and all the readers who have ever loved her books.

These readers are all kinds of people. She receives mail from the barely literate conveying how empowering they found her books as well as psychologists asking her where she studied. Most of her characters appear to speak in a black idiom, yet Cooper says she wants her narratives to reflect the struggles of people everywhere and her voices to be primarily those of "the uneducated," undifferentiated by race. Several stories, however, deal directly with white-black marriages and the healing of the wounds of prejudice they bring about. "You really got my grandmother," people of diverse ethnic backgrounds have told her. Judging by responses like this and by sales of her books, the chord of racial and interpersonal harmony struck by J. California Cooper resonates for many readers.

JANET PALMER MULLANEY

I have my son bring me down here to this homegrown graveyard two or three times a week so I can clean it and sweep it and sit here among my friends in my rocking chair under this Sycamore tree, where I will be buried one day, soon now, I hope. I'm ninety years old and I am tired . . . and I miss all my friends too. I come back to visit them because ain't nobody left in town but a few old doddering fools I didn't bother with when I was younger so why go bothern now just cause we all hangin on? Its peaceful here. The wind is soft, the sun is gentle even in the deep summer. Maybe its the cold that comes from under the ground that keeps it cool. I don't know. I only know that I like to rest here in my final restin place and know how its gonna be a thousand years after I am put here under that stone I have bought and paid for long ago . . . long ago.

After I eat my lunch and rest a bit, I gets down to my real work here in this graveyard! I pack a hammer and chisel in my bags and when I's alone, I take them and go over to Tommy Jones' beautiful tombstone his fancy daughter bought for him and chip, grind and break away little pieces of it! Been doin it for eleven years now and its most half gone. I ain't gonna die til its all gone! Then I be at peace! I ain't got to tell a wise one that I hate Tommy Jones, you must know that yourself now! . . . If I am killin his tombstone! I hate him. See, his wife, my friend, Pearl, used to lay next to him, but I had her moved, kinda secret like, least without tellin anyone. I hired two mens to dig her coffin up and move her over here next to where I'm going to be and they didn't know nobody and ain't told nobody. It don't matter none noway cause who gon pay somebody to dig her up again? And put her back? Who cares bout her? . . . and where she lay for eternity? Nobody! But me . . . I do.

See, we growed up together. I am Ruby and she is Pearl and we was jewels. We use to always say that. We use to act out how these jewels would act. I was always strong, deep red and solid deep. She was brown but she was all lightness and frail and innocent, smooth and weak and later on I realized, made out of pain.

I grew up in a big sprawling family and my sons take after them, while Pearl growed up in a little puny one. Her mama kissed her daddy's ass til he kicked her's on way from here! That's her grave way over there . . . Way, way over there in the corner. That's his with that cement marker, from when he died two years later from six bullets in his face by another woman what didn't take that kickin stuff! Well, they say what goes around . . . But "they" says all kinda things . . . can't be sure bout nothin "they" says. Just watch your Bible . . . that's the best thing I ever seen and I'm ninety! Now!

Anyway, Pearl and me grew up round here, went to school and all. A two room school with a hall down the middle. Pearl nice and everybody should of liked her, but they didn't. Them girls was always pickin on her, til I get in it. See, I was not so nice and everybody did like me! Just loved me sometime! I pertected her. I wouldn't let nobody hurt her! Some of em got mad at me, but what could they do? I rather fight than eat! Use to eat a'plenty too! I was a big strong, long-armed and long-legged girl. Big head, short hair. I loved my eyes tho! Oh, they was pretty. They still strong! And I had pretty hands, even with all that field work, they still was pretty! My great grandchildren takes care of em for me now . . . rubs em and all. So I can get out here two or three times a week and hammer Tommy Jones' gravestone. Its almost half gone now . . . so am I.

When we got to marryin time . . . everybody got to that, some in love and some just tryin to get away from a home what was full of house work and field work and baby sister and brother work. I don't know how we was all too dumb to know, even when we got married and in a place of our own, it was all headin down to the same road we thought we was gettin away from! Well, I went after Gee Cee! He was the biggest boy out there and suited me just fine! I use to run that man with rocks and sticks and beat him up even. He wouldn't hurt me, you know, just play. But I finally got him to thinkin he loved me and one night, over there by the creek behind the church, way behind the church, I gave him somethin he musta not forgot . . . and we was soon gettin married. I didn't forget it . . . I named it George, Jr. That was my first son.

In the meantime the boys all seem to like Pearl and she grinned at all of em! She seem to be kinda extra stuck on that skinny rail, Tommy Jones, with the bare spot on the side of his head! He liked everybody! A girl couldn't pass by him without his hand on em, quick and fast and gone. I didn't like him! Too shifty for me . . . a liar! I can't stand a liar! His family had a little money and he always looked nice but he still wasn't nothin but a nice lookin liar what was shifty! Still and all, when I had done pushed Pearl around a few times tryin to make her not like him, he began to press on her and every way she turned, he was there! He just wouldn't let up when he saw I didn't like him for her! He gave her little trinkets and little cakes, flowers, home picked. Finally she let him in her deepest life and soon she was pregnant and then he got mad cause he had to marry her! I fought against that and when he found out it made him grin all the way through the little ceremony. I was her best lady or whatever you call it, cause I was her best friend.

Then everything was over and we was all married and havin children and life got a roll on and we had to roll with it and that took all our energies to survive and soon we was back in the same picture we had run away from cept the faces had changed. Stead of mama's faces, they was ours. And daddy's was the men we had married. Lots of times the stove and sink was the same and the plow was the same. In time, the mules changed.

Well, in time, everything happened. I had three sons and two daughters, big ones! Liked to kill me even gettin here! Pearl had one son and one daughter. Son was just like his daddy and daughter was frail and sickly. I think love makes you healthy and I think that child was sickly cause wasn't much love in that house of Pearl's, not much laughter. Tommy Jones, after the second child, never made love to Pearl again regular, maybe a year or two or three apart. She stayed faithful, but hell, faithful to what? He had done inherited some money and was burnin these roads up! He'd be a hundred miles away for a week or two, whole lotta times. Pearl worked, takin them children with her when I could'n keep em. But I had to rest sometimes, hell! I had five of my own and I had done told her bout that Tommy Jones anyway! But I still looked out for her and fed em when she couldn't. Yet and still, when he came home he just fall in the bed and sleep and sleep til time to get up and bathe and dress in the clothes he bought hisself and leave them again! If she cry and complain he just laugh and leave. I guess that's what you call leavin them laughin or somethin!

One day he slapped her and when he saw she wasn't gonna do nothin but just cry and take it, that came to be a regular thing! For years, I mean years, I never went over her house to take food when she didn't have some beatin up marks on her! I mean it! That's when she started comin over to the cemetery to clean it up and find her place. She also began savin a nickle here and a dime there to pay for her gravestone. That's what she dreamed about! Can you imagine that?!! A young, sposed to be healthy woman day-dreamin bout dyin!!? Well, she did! And carried that money faithfully to the white man sells them things and paid on a neat little ruby colored stone, what he was puttin her name on, just leavin the dates out! Now!

My sons was gettin married, havin babies, strong like they mama and papa, when her son got killed, trying to be like his daddy! He had done screwed the wrong man's daughter! They put what was left of him in that grave over there, behind that bush of roses Pearl planted years ago to remember him by. Well, what can I say? I'm a mother, she was a mother, you love them no matter what! The daughter had strengthened up and was goin on to school somewhere with the help of her father's people. And you know, she didn't give her mother no concern, no respect? Treated her like the house dog in a manger. I just don't blieve you can have any luck like that! It takes time, sometime, to get the payback, but time is always rollin on and one day, it will roll over you! Anyway even when the daughter had made it up to a young lady and was schoolin with the sons and daughters of black business people, she almost forgot her daddy too! She was gonna marry a man with SOMETHIN and she didn't want them at the weddin! Now! And tole em! Her daddy went anyway, so she dressed him cause he was broke now, and after the weddin, got his drunk ass out of town quick as lightnin cross the sky and he came home and taunted Pearl that her own daughter didn't love her! Now!

Well, time went on, I had troubles with such a big family, grandchildren comin and all. Love, love, love everywhere, cause I didn't low nothin else! Pretty faces, pretty smiles, round, fat stomachs, and pigtails flying everywhere and pretty nappy-headed boys growin up to be president someday, even if they never were . . . they was my presidents and congressmen! I could chew em up and swollow em sometimes, even today, grown as they are! We could take care of our problems, they was just livin problems . . . everyday kinds.

Pearl just seem to get quiet way back in her mind and heart. She went on, but she was workin harder to pay for that tombstone. The name was complete, only the last date was open and finally it was paid for. With blood, sweat and tears for true . . . seem like that's too much to pay for dyin!

One night I had bathed and smelled myself up for that old hard head of mine, Gee Cee, when a neighbor of Pearl's came runnin over screamin that Tommy Jones was really beatin up on Pearl. I threw my clothes on fast as I could and ran all the way and I was comin into some age then, runnin was not what I planned to do much of! When I got there, he had done seen me comin and he was gone, long gone, on them long, narrow, quick to run to mischief feet of his! I had got there in time to keep him from accidently killin her, but she was pretty well beat! He had wanted her rent and food money, she said, but she would not give it to him, so he beat her. She cried and held on to me, she was so frail, so little, but she was still pretty to me, little grey hairs and all. She thanked me as I washed her and changed the bed and combed her hair and fed her some warm soup and milk. She cried a little as she was tellin me all she ever wanted was a little love like I had. I cried too and told her that's all anybody wants.

When I was through fixin her and she was restin nice and easy, I sat by the bed and pulled the covers up and she said, "Hold my hand, I'm so cold." Well I grabbed her hand and held, then I rubbed her arms tryin to keep her warm and alive. Then, I don't know, life just kept rollin and I began to rub her whole little beautiful sore body . . . all over . . . and when I got to them bruised places I kissed them and licked them too and placed my body beside her body in her bed and the love for her just flowed and flowed. One minute I loved her like a child, the next like a mother, then she was the mother, then I was the child, then as a woman friend, then as a man. Ohhhhh, I loved her. I didn't know exactly what to do but my body did it for me and I did everything I could to make her feel loved and make her feel like Gee Cee makes me feel, so I did everything I could that he had ever done to me to make me feel good, but I forgot Gee Cee . . . and I cried. Not sad crying, happy cryin, and my tears and my love were all over her and she was holding me. She was holding me . . . so close, so close. Then we slept and when I wakened up, I went home . . . and I felt good, not bad. I know you don't need nothin "forever," just so you get close to love sometime.

Well Pearl got better. When we saw each other, we weren't embarrassed or shamed. She hit me on my shoulder and I thumped her on her head as we had done all our lives anyway. We never did it again, we didn't have to!

Pearl wasn't made, I guess, for the kind of life she had somehow chosen, so a few years later she died and Tommy Jones picked her plot, right over there where she used to be, and put her there and the tombstone man put that old-brand-new ruby colored gravestone on her grave. The preacher said a few words cause there wasn't much to pay him with and we all went home to our own lifes, of course.

Soon, I commence to comin over here and sweepin and cleanin up and plantin plants around, and this ole Sycamore tree Pearl had planted at her house was moved over here before Tommy Jones got put out for not payin rent. I planted it right here over where Gee Cee, me and Pearl gonna be. I likes shade. Anyway I was out here so much that's how I was able to notice the day Pearl's tombstone disappeared. Well, I like to died! I knew what that tombstone had gone through to get there! Right away I had my sons get out and find out what had happened and they found out that Tommy Jones was livin mighty hard and was mighty broke and had stole that tombstone and took it way off and sold it for a few dollars! You can chisel the name off, you know? But I can't understand what anyone would want a used tombstone for! I mean, for God's sake, get your own!! At least die first-class even if you couldn't live that way! Well, we couldn't find how to get it back so that's when I started payin on another one for her, and yes, for me and Gee Cee too. They's paid for now.

In the meantime, liquor and hard livin and a knife put Tommy Jones to rest, and imagine this, that daughter of theirs came down here and bought ONE gravestone for her DADDY!!! To hold up her name I guess, but that's all she did, then she left! Ain't been back!

Well, life goes on, don't it! Whew!

Now I come here over the years and chip away and chisel and hammer away cause he don't deserve no stone since he stole Pearl's. He never give her nothin but them two babies what was just like him and then he stole the last most important thing she wanted! So me, I'm gonna see that he don't have one either! When it's through, I'm gonna be through, then the gravestone man can bring them two stones over here, they bought and paid for! And he can place them here beside each other, for the rest of thousands of years. I'm in the middle, between Gee Cee and Pearl, like I'm sposed to be. They don't say much, but Ruby and the dates and Pearl's on hers, and the dates. Then my husband's name and the children on mine and her children's on hers. And that's all. I mean, how much can a gravestone say anyway?

Afterword

After Ruby died at 91 years of age, Gee Cee was still living at 90 years of age and he had a marker laid across the two graves saying, "Friends, all the way to the End." It's still there.

MARIA BRUNO

The Feeder

(1985)

*M*ARIA Bruno, born August 14, 1948, in Detroit, Michigan, loved living in her Italian neighborhood with her parents and older brother. She remembers vividly her grandmother's kitchen, "filled with silver pots, large wooden spoons, giant cans of imported olive oil with a foreign script I could not decipher, or homemade noodles drying on spindly racks." She remembers the women and children of the family, sitting at the table after the Sunday meal, "dipping thick crusts into the leftover sauce or snacking on grapes," and talking, telling the stories that chart her life, their lives, the lives so many of us can recall and re-create.

When Maria was nine, her family moved to the affluent Detroit suburb of Birmingham, where the public school system was open and creative. She wrote constantly, and when she was in high school, wrote plays, which her classmates produced. But what she was writing was not the woman-centered narrative she might have learned from her grandmother and mother. The difficulties of being a "woman writer" were obvious even in adolescence. As Bruno recalls,

> Since fourth grade, I wrote quietly in my room every night. I wrote Westerns, with swarthy bearded male heroes. My women were practically invisible: a Miss Kitty or two lurking somewhere in the background, beauty marks and all, speaking in soft, adoring monosyllables to the "real" heroes who got to ride horses, guzzle hard whiskey, and say strong things like: "This town isn't big enough for the two of us (pause), Jesse!" As I got older and outgrew the only female writers I knew, Beverly Cleary and Nancy Keene (who created Ramona Quimby and Nancy

Drew), I shifted my allegiance to the female heroes readily available to me—actresses and singers. So I found my female heroes. I won a Natalie Wood look-alike contest in the eleventh grade; practiced saying "What a dump!" in Bette Davis's gritty, cigarette-swinging falsetto; and lip-synched to The Chiffons, mouthing angry lyrics about lost boyfriends and territorial rights into a makeshift microphone—a plastic dolphin I had won at Marineland. But all the while, I, the secret writer, was channeling my real need to write, to find literary predecessors, to find female heroes in literature—and in the world, period—into fantasy.

Her writing stopped when she entered Michigan State University as a dual theater and English major (reading only two women writers in more than fifty credits of English courses). Late in her junior year, she married the man who was to father her daughters—Emily, now 20, and Rebecca, now 15. With the help of her former roommates, Maria finished her degree on schedule, in 1970.

Her marriage lasted fourteen years. In 1981, Bruno completed the M.A. in Creative Writing at Michigan State, after she resumed her writing following a dozen years of silence. (She describes the sequence of events: "During a diaper run to the local grocery store, I picked up a copy of Alix K. Shulman's *Memoirs of an Ex-Prom Queen*. The next week I went back for Lisa Alther, and the week after that, Marge Piercy. I was hooked. I had discovered stories written by women, filled with women characters I actually liked. I wrote my first short story when I was thirty-one, and I haven't stopped writing since.") In 1984, Maria won the *Ms.* magazine fiction contest with her story "A Matter of Disguise," a tale of a woman who gives up her male lover rather than her women friends. In 1986, she completed her Ph.D., combining a thesis on a woman-centered composition program with a collection of her own fiction. She now teaches in the American Thought and Language Department at Michigan State University.

"The Feeder"[1] is less humorous than many of Bruno's stories. There is no way it could include the wonderfully mocking—sometimes ribald—cynicism that marks much of her work. It is a highly serious story because the abusive relationships and the eating disorders that mar women's lives are themselves so serious. In the story, Bruno shows the compassion of one woman for another, the willingness to reach past conventional behavior to help a sister, even at the cost of one's own marriage. In writing this story, Bruno drew on a real-life situation in which the abused wife did eventually leave her husband—but without telling her friends until long past the divorce. The changes Bruno made in the fictional account, and the devastating portraits of the power-hungry husbands, make the story an explicit account of women's friendship in the face of macho sexual and economic force that is clearly malignant. As

Alma and Sylvia grope their way toward a language that will express the inexpressible—even the unthinkable—the reader is drawn into the seemingly comic yet simultaneously angry narrative. Characterized by their fat and too-lean bodies, as if their selves and souls were imaged only by their fatty tissues, Bruno's women find both identity and power in their friendships. "The Feeder" is a fiction that is, unfortunately, obviously germane to the abuses of affection so prevalent in the 1980s. Bruno's genius is in presenting a narrative for which so little precedent exists. She credits her strong belief in the value of women's bonding as the catalyst for this story.

Bruno is presently finishing a new collection of short stories and beginning work on a novel.

LINDA WAGNER-MARTIN

That summer day Alma Winters came to lunch, I noticed she had lost weight. She had lost the fullness of her breasts, the pinkish flesh of her cheeks, and could have been a small boy sitting there, instead of a grown woman playing with the food on her plate. Her once fiercely platinum hair was a faded brown, cropped close to her head with rigid sprouts standing upright at her crown and temples. Her gray eyes seemed much larger than I ever remembered, glass marbles fixed in a dull yellowed skin. Alma did not look at me as she arranged the meal into forced geometric designs on her plate. There was a sense of primordial ritual as she played with the food, separating it into squares and triangles with the tines of her fork, then pushing the food together into a larger rectangle. It was only after several minutes of this ceremonial rite that she took a bite. She showed no measure of enjoyment in her food, which could have been tasteless stones, the way she labored to swallow. Periodically she would lay down her fork, reach for her water goblet, and take measured mechanical sips, her lips never leaving the rim of the glass.

I felt like a cow next to her. My breasts were round and full from nursing my daughter Jenny, and David had joked just that morning that my arms and legs were getting to look like baby sea whales. I felt misshapen, a flesh balloon, sweat trickling down my inner thighs, making my print shift stick to my skin. I smelled of cooking grease and soured milk. I was uncomfortable in the late summer heat. Alma was cool and composed.

Jenny, who was seated in her highchair, squirmed momentarily and threw a large pasty noodle on the floor. She whined and I knew she wanted my breast. I lifted her out of the highchair, wiped the tomato sauce away from her face with a napkin, and opened the top button of my dress. Jenny maneuvered herself into a comfortable position, letting her smooth cheek disappear into the soft white breast, her lips blowing little fish kisses until she reached the nipple. Alma did not look up. She rearranged the food on her plate.

"It's too bad David can't be home for lunch," I said, shifting Jenny deeper into my arm for more leverage. "He would have loved to have seen you."

"Oh really?" she asked, taking a small even bite of the noodle.

"But then, I'm kind of glad we had this time to talk alone."

Alma neatly wiped her mouth with the cloth napkin, appearing to be finished, even though a great deal of food was left on her plate. I noticed fine strands of brown hair growing above her lip, alien shadows to this formerly very feminine creature.

"So," I paused, "When did you begin losing all this weight?"

"Oh, it's all come about gradually," she answered.

The breast milk from my untended breast seeped through the fabric of my dress, I was embarrassed, and shifted Jenny, who at nine months seemed too big and cumbersome to nurse. She eagerly reached for the swollen nipple of my other breast, while I wiped myself with a cloth diaper that I carried on my shoulder.

"I've been losing weight for a while now," Alma continued, placing her silverware on her plate and pushing the plate forward. "Everytime I look in the mirror, I see fat. It seems my stomach is an inevitable fate." She pinched a thin line of skin where her stomach should have been through the fabric of her tailored blouse. "You know, I don't even have my periods any more. I love it."

"Alma, I'm worried about you."

"Don't be."

"How does Cal feel about this?"

"Oh Calvin. He's been a bit of a brute. But let's not talk about me, please."

And so I launched into a self-conscious monologue about my life, my life with baby, my life with David. The night feedings, the diapers, the baby edging herself around the coffee table like a plump duck, giggling and cooing one moment, engaged in a tirade the next. I talked at considerable length about my body, all round and sagging, laced with white ribbons of stretch marks, and how the heat made me feel like a swollen pear, all thick and ripe and miserable. I talked about David and the business, how he liked his shirts ironed, that he liked his phone messages written neatly in ink, and how he wrote me a little note every morning before he left for work, "Sylvia, stick to your diet." And then I talked of the baby again, the La Leche League, the parenting group meetings, how zinc oxide is better for diaper rash than anything commercial on the market, how I intended to nurse Jenny until she was two years old even though my mother-in-law thought the whole idea disgusting. And it struck me as I spoke that I had no idea what language I spoke before this Baby Talk. What could I have possibly thought or said before there was a David or a Jenny? My head was filled with every movement that Jenny made, every monosyllable that she uttered, every new and startling skill she mastered. And when I did not speak of Jenny, it was David and his business, David and his needs, his desires for the family. I vaguely remember a young woman, with long black hair and black eyes, a literature major at a small university, who romped in a woolen turtleneck and faded blue jeans, carried a Greek woven bag she had bought in Europe, laced leather sandals up her calves, who met friends in dark campus taverns, political rallies, and in the dormitory rooms late at night. I vaguely remember her speaking, but the language and tools of speech are alien to me now, and the faces and names of her cohorts are impossible to remember. And this woman adopted a new language, and spoke to a woman who politely listened, but who did not share the language either.

Alma once had told me she had graduated from Stephens College in Missouri when Stephens was a finishing school devoted solely to preparing each young woman for a life with a successful man. Alma had jokingly mentioned once there was a mini-course in "the art of pouring tea" and she laughed, "the art of wearing gloves." She had been waiting for Calvin when he came along, she said. She was attracted to his angular frame and Nordic coloring, and she was bored with Stephens and her courses, and she fell for him so passionately that she forgot who she was and why she had ever gone to college in the first place. She quit Stephens her junior year and married Cal in a large ceremony somewhere out East.

I managed to finish college, but I fell hard for David, much like

Alma did for Cal. David told me he didn't usually like literature majors because he found them flighty and unpredictable, but he thought he could handle me and mold me into the perfect wife. I remember tossing back my black hair and laughing at that remark, telling him, this abrasive young man I had only known for two weeks, that you can only mold gelatin and cheese, neither of which I remotely resembled. He roared at that one, and later he told me he had decided that night he wanted to marry me. Something about the anger in my eyes intrigued him.

As I rambled on, Alma sat composed, smooth like carved marble, smiling a thin line of a smile, her hands, a small child's hands, folded neatly in her lap. Jenny was asleep at my breast.

After Alma had left, and I had put Jenny in her crib, I remembered back to the time when I had first met Alma. It was the night she and her husband Cal had thrown a celebration party honoring his new partnership with my husband, David. She was much rounder then, her face a soft pink, her blonde hair like a child's doll, and she was open, receptive, not the frigid mannequin that measured every move, every bite of food. She laughed appreciatively at everything her husband said that night, as if his words were golden, or god inspired, and she sat with her tea, her lacquered nails tapping delicately on the porcelain cup, smiling, giggling, winking at the other guests. I remembered the earrings and the fine golden chains that dangled from her neck and fell into the crevice of her then fuller breasts. She dressed flamboyantly, in odd-glittered colors, and men crowded around her. These same men often congratulated Cal on how lucky he was to find such a fine hostess and a good wife, and the other wives in the room envied her, myself included, because she was many things we were not. I hadn't had Jenny yet, and I sat at the dinner table, my pregnant belly resting in folds, straining in a slanted position, my puffed legs sprawled beneath me. David kept laying his hand on my stomach saying things like "That better be my cake baking in this oven," and he patted my stretched flesh, as if I wasn't even there, merely a receptacle for some precious cargo. Alma laughed heartily at David's humor, along with the other men at the table who spat and choked and roared, and I sat back, grinning, pretending I enjoyed all this attention. I remembered at one point the baby gave a strong kick and David raised his hand with an almost religious gesticulation and shouted, "Goddamn, it's going to be a first-string linebacker, sure as hell." I remember sipping my mineral water, amidst the laughing, and wondered what exactly a first-string linebacker did.

Alma sought me out later in the evening. "I'm so glad our husbands are going to be partners. We're going to be fast friends, I can tell. I want to hear all about your baby." And before I had a chance to respond, she had flittered away, off to Cal's side, crawling into the folds of his arms, and he steadied her, positioned her, and her form became fluid as she melted into a cool liquid in his grasp.

Several months had passed after that summer lunch with Alma, and I did not think much about her. I was engrossed with Jenny and the house, and my diet, which was David's pet obsession as well as mine. David had devised a curious regimen he had found in an old Air Force manual. He had written down my instructions neatly on a legal pad, detailing the precise amount of sit-ups, leg lifts, arm twirls that I was to do each day. By each category, there was a box to be checked each time the prescribed exercises were completed. Every morning, next to his "Daily Notes for Sylvia" ("Don't touch that Jamoca Almond Fudge ice cream, Syl, I'll check the level when I get home"), he left the annoying Air Force regimen, with a newly sharpened pencil laid next to it. I often greeted the note with a half-eaten banana or toasted bagel hanging from my mouth, and in an act of silent defiance, I checked the little squares perfunctorily as I dipped my finger into the Jamoca Almond Fudge.

I decided to have Alma over for lunch again in November. She arrived promptly, dressed in a roomy t-shirt that swallowed her boyish frame. Her hair was shorter, swept back above her ears, and she had lost more weight. She seemed to be in even more control, her posture rigid, almost military, her hands tight and folded in her lap, the purplish veins transparent, like frozen rivers in her flesh. I stared at her face, the skin still yellowed, but now deep grey circles swelled around the eyes, and her smile, much tighter, stretched like a violet string across her face. I had fixed something rich and pasty, I wanted to fatten her up, but she no longer bothered to lift the food to her mouth. She neatly separated it and let it converge again with each mechanical movement of her fork.

"Alma," I began, "Is it possible that you could have lost more weight? You really didn't need to." I saw in her form the frozen pictures of war and famine that lay like a sheet of cellophane over my consciousness.

"When I look into the mirror all I see is fat. It's funny, but I find I can live quite nicely on some meat broth and a sliver of fruit."

"But that's not enough, Alma. You need more."

"No, you're wrong," she shook her head. "I need nothing. I'm in complete control now."

"What do you mean you're in control?"

"My body is my own."

"Has Cal said anything about this to you?"

She laughed, and said nothing for a moment, then straightened herself in the chair. "Oh he forces me to eat. He pinches the food between his fingers and forces it into my mouth. I swallow it alright, but I throw it up later." She laughed again. "You think I'm crazy, don't you?"

"No, I don't think that," I answered. "But you and Cal were always so close."

"Oh really? Is that what you thought?" I heard the faint stirrings of Jenny in the upstairs bedroom. She's probably hungry, I thought, and my breasts ached. "I think that's the baby, Sylvia," Alma said, and stood to leave.

"Alma, please stay. You just got here. Have dessert. I made it special."

"Sylvia, please don't worry about me."

"How can I help you?"

"You can't."

I noticed the bruise as she was putting on her overcoat. It lay under her arm, large, circular, the deep purple of a summer plum.

"Alma!" She jerked, I must have startled her. "What happened to you?" I heard Jenny wailing in the upstairs bedroom. My attention shifted in the direction of the bedroom door, then back to Alma, who was quickly buttoning up her overcoat.

"Oh, that. A gift from Calvin. He had a bad day at work."

She lifted the woolen hood over her head, opened the door, and walked rigidly into the brutal wind. I felt a chill as the wind crept into the open weave of my sweater. I folded my arms across my chest and hid my hands under each arm. I closed the door behind her and stood for a moment ignoring the persistent cries of my child.

"She's the joke of the office," David said that night at dinner. "Mort Kreiners calls her 'Alma from Auschwitz.'"

"That's so sick." I said. "I can't believe you can even repeat that."

"Alma used to be some broad," he continued, "Cal was considered lucky going home to that every night. Mort says you couldn't pay him to lay her now."

"Mort Kreiners is an asshole."

"Mort Kreiners sold three houses last week."

"How can you defend him?"

"Like I said, he sold three houses last week."

"Anyway, I tried to get her to eat. I made Lasagne. She just played with it. Wouldn't take a bite."

"I figure if you can't get her to eat, no one can," he smirked, patting the meat of my thighs. "You're always feeding everyone, including yourself." He reached for his coffee, and swirled the black brew with his spoon. He smiled. "Did you do your leg lifts today?"

"I didn't have time." He let that one slip in, I thought, he's a real professional, him and his little calculated doses of disapproval. I had covered my advancing weight that winter with oversized sweaters and pants, and had been careful to keep my arms covered and my legs hidden under large towels after a shower, and then safely lost under a lounging gown. Even though Jenny had several teeth and was increasingly mobile, I was still nursing her and my breasts were still huge and swollen and laced with purple veins. That's it I thought. No more nursing, Jenny, you're going cold turkey tomorrow. No more feeding off of Momma.

"I think Cal has been hitting Alma and I'm worried," I said, looking for some type of reaction in David's face. I folded my hands across my breasts hoping to minimize my misshapen body.

"He says he has to get tough with her to make her eat. It's none of your business, Syl. Now drop it." He got up from the table and turned, "Cal is my friend, my partner, and we get along fine. Just drop all of this."

I took David's advice, letting it go, hoping Alma could resolve what was troubling her on her own, after all, she herself said I couldn't help her. Months later in the spring, when I had all but forgotten about Alma, and David ceased to even mention her in conversation, I became absorbed with Jenny and her expanding vocabulary. I wrote down every new word she acquired and the day she uttered it into a little journal I had been keeping since her birth. Her newest phrase was "I want, I want," and she followed me around the house playfully reiterating her new sentence. David had left a note for me one morning in the spring, and instead of his usual "Stick to your diet, Syl!", there was a set of terse instructions: "Get a hold of Alma Winters. Invite her and Cal to dinner tonight. I'll explain later."

Alma was distant on the phone, and responded in short, brittle sentences: "Yes. That will be fine. We can make it. Thank you. Good-bye." Her voice was a bizarre parody of one of those computer toys that respond verbally to a child's persistant finger punches. I heard a grey undercurrent of pain, not the whinings of a hungry child that I was so used to responding to, but the low, hollow moans of the wounded. Her voice made me think of that morning when I lay in bed, startled by the imperiled quakings of a small bird trapped in our roof that the workman had finished repairing the day before. It was a sparrow or a Brewers blackbird, which often nests in the soffits and gutters of the neighborhood homes. I stared at the sloped ceiling, directing my attention to where the bird had been entombed between the rafters. The scratchings became more frantic as I envisioned the bird flapping its fragile wings in the darkness, in blind panic, buffeted only by the freshly laid insulation. I threw off my covers and stood on the mattress.

"What are you doing Sylvia?" David had asked, turning in a half sleep. I lifted my fingertips and grazed the ceiling.

"There's a bird trapped in the ceiling. Can't you hear him?"

"He'll die soon. Let it go."

"Can't we get it out?"

"Now, how are we going to get it out, Syl? We just paid eight hundred dollars to have the roof fixed, and you want to save some damn bird?"

"I can't stand listening to it die."

"Then go downstairs and fix me some coffee."

"How can you stand it, David?"

"It's easy," he had answered, sitting up in bed. He turned on the radio.

The dinner party was Cal's idea. He had hoped that if Alma was around familiar faces, she might eat. He admitted to David she was losing more weight, that he had found her vomiting several more times in the bathroom, and that he had to get physical with her. He had to watch her constantly now, following her to the bathroom and having to force-feed her in the mornings before he went to work and at night when he got home. He thought it was time to involve a doctor, but Alma had refused.

The dinner surprisingly went well. Alma made a visible effort to eat, not toying with the food, but actually scooping large amounts of food onto her fork and shoving them into her mouth. David and Cal made a deliberate attempt to not watch Alma, and were engaged in a raucous retelling of some more office antics of Mort Kreiners. He had, so they said, deliberately spilled coffee on Miss Kendall's bosom, in hopes of getting to wipe it away with his pocket hand-kerchief. Miss Kendall, the secretary, was noticeably upset when old Mort dropped his handkerchief down her cleavage and proceeded to retrieve it. David recounted that "Her jugs were just a jiggling" at the sight of Kreiners hand, and she poured another cup of coffee on his three piece pin-stripe. I often wondered how a man I could be mar-ried to could defend a man who had such an open contempt for women. It seemed to me that David and Cal, and all men for that matter, had a fierce camaraderie, impenetrable, a shared, personal knowledge, fraternity, partnership, that excluded women. It is a code, an unspoken devotion. I felt jealous of Cal and David and Mort, much like I felt in high school when I saw the male athletes on a football or basketball squad hug each other after a win, or pat each other on the rump, or fiercely defend each other on the field, while I enviously sat in the stands, surrounded by the other girls, yearning for that type of camaraderie. The girls would cheer and wave at the men hoping for some form of recognition or male attention. But we were all separate entities, failing to acknowledge each other, only in-terested in extrapolating a small fragment of this male fraternity.

Alma asked for seconds of the dessert after finishing two helpings of the main course, and Cal smiled appreciatively at me. David nod-ded. She smiled and took large chunks of the cheesecake onto her fork and dropped them into her mouth. I reached for a piece of the cheesecake for myself, hoping that David was so lost in his reverie with Cal that he would not notice, but, as if on cue, he tapped my elbow with the prongs of his fork and whispered so Cal and Alma could almost certainly hear, "Not tonight, Darling, you've had enough as it is." So I continued to minister the meal, monitoring everyone's plate, standing, then sitting, treating each portion of food as a personal gift to the taker.

After coffee, Alma excused herself and left the table. Calvin gave me a sour, pleading look, so I offered to walk her up to the bath-room using the excuse that I wanted to check on Jenny. David winked at me, letting me know I had done the right thing.

I stood by the closed bathroom door. I heard the low gutteral sounds, the heavings, the moans, and then the sudden flush of the toilet. I wondered if I should knock, and then the door opened. Alma stood in the doorway, not surprised to see me at all, her dull hair matted and wet, fresh yellow balls of sweat beading her forehead and the pronounced hair above her lip. "Please don't tell Cal, Sylvia." I felt as if we shared a small closet, suffocating in the dark, acrid smell of vomit, and I felt the sad, sick walls of enclosure. She lifted her sweater and showed me several side strips of surgical tape wrapped around her emaciated body. "He did this," she announced, and headed down the stairs, her form distinctly masculine in nature. Her body was propelled by some ethereal energy, giving her strength, and as she disappeared down the stairway, I knew I would say nothing.

Alma called three weeks later, her voice was different, not the clipped military sentences, but a series of unpunctuated fragments. She asked to see me. It was urgent. I remembered a doctor's appointment I had made that day for Jenny's inoculations, and the promise to pick up David's pinstripe at the cleaners, and my luncheon meeting with David's mother. "Yes, Alma. Please come. I'll be waiting here for you."

I suddenly felt the same fear I did the night I stood in the imaginary closet, the stale air that hung low around me, the feeling of hopeless enclosure. Jenny had tripped over a line of toys in front of her and held out her arms for solace, a green plastic frog lodged in one hand, the other tugging at the fabric of my shirt, pleading to nurse. I walked into the kitchen and poured her a cup of juice, she tagging behind me, at first resisting the cup, still tugging at the cloth of my shirt. "No, Jen, you use a cup now. Momma has no more milk."

Ten minutes later Alma stood in the doorway in a pair of denims and a bloodied white shirt. There was a large untended bruise, split and bleeding on her forehead. I ushered her in, her frail body quaking, her hands, like strings of bones, convulsing. She bit into her shaking hand, making small indentations in the skin, trying by the self-induced pain, to steady herself. She composed herself, transfixed by the tiny dots that filled with blood and steamed the hollows of her skin. "Let me take care of that cut, Alma. Please." I sat her in the living room and then ran for some disinfectant and some bandages. When I returned, Jenny was yelling, "Hurt, Momma, hurt!" Shaking, I spilled the bright orange Mercurochrome over the wound.

Jenny pummeled my legs, disturbed at my behavior, tugged demandingly at my slacks, and then sat curiously to watch the bright spectacle, the Mercurochrome spreading like ink on white paper, creating a Rorschach abstract on Alma's face. I took some tissue out of my pocket and gently wiped away the excess, placed some soft gauze over the wound, finishing with two strips of adhesive tape.

"I thought I was strong enough to kill him," she began. "I worked at being strong . . . in control . . . I thought I could do it this time, this time . . . I waited so long for just the right time . . . I thought I had the power . . . I had the power . . ."

"Alma, what are you saying?" I grabbed her fists that were wound tight like hoarded string.

"I thought he couldn't touch me anymore . . . I thought my body was my own . . . I felt strong . . . did everything, everything right . . ."

"Alma . . ."

"But oh oh that bastard that bastard he walks in on me in the bathroom I had to had to vomit that toast he made me eat that morning and he walked in that bastard and he grabbed me and he still can beat me he still can hurt me and it still hurts still hurts and I thought I had the power to make it stop. I yelled I was going to leave him and he said 'You skinny bitch, I'll kill you yet.'"

"Alma, please, calm down, slow down."

Her trembling ceased and I wrapped my arms around her. Jenny, surprised by the sudden silence, edged into our circle, and with a surge of compassion that young children often intuitively display, reached for both of us. We sat there a very long time, arms entwined, heads together, eyes closed, listening to the ancient rhythm of our blood. And in this human huddle, we shared a secret knowledge, a silent, undying bond, a communion that only females can share.

Later in the day, David walked into the kitchen and found Alma, quiet and contemplative, sitting at the kitchen table warming her hands around a cup of tea. Jenny was in her highchair fingerpainting with a jello salad, tossing bits of strawberry gelatin onto the linoleum floor. David grabbed me by the arm and led to outside to the living room.

"Get her out of here, Sylvia," he said.

"She's hurt, David. She needs help."

"Cal said she got hysterical this morning, trying to puke her breakfast into the toilet. He says he's having her committed."

"He's the one that should be committed. He's an animal."

"Can't you see she's fucking nuts?" he yelled, and then more quietly, "Listen honey. She's his wife. This is his business. You're my wife, and I want you to get her out of here."

"I can't."

"He's my friend, Sylvia. He's my partner. This is his mess. I'm calling him." He picked up the phone and began to dial.

"David, please, don't."

"Do what I say Sylvia. Get your daughter, clean up that fucking mess she's made in there, and then start dinner. I'm not coming home to this kind of thing. I mean it!"

I walked into the kitchen, went over to Jenny, and lifted her from the highchair and wiped her face and hands with a dishrag. I looked at the bowl of jello on the floor and the little strawberry hills that peppered the tiles. I looked up at Alma, whose flushed and bruised face registered nothing. She sipped her tea. "Come on, Alma. We're going." She looked up. "Come on, I'm getting you out of here. David is calling Cal. He'll be here soon." She didn't move. I felt as if my chest was exploding. My anger was so rich, so deep, surging like volcanic lava, a grit that burned my throat, enflamed my voice. God, I thought. It's not only Alma that had to get out of there.

As we drove off, all three of us in the front seat, huddled together again, as soldiers do in combat trenches, I looked through the rear view mirror to see David in the driveway, yelling, I suppose, my name. As we pulled further and further away, I saw our roof, still neatly repaired, and I thought of that lost sparrow, entombed in the darkness, shrouded with its broken wings.

LESLÉA NEWMAN

One Shabbos Evening

(1987)

*L*ESLÉA Newman (b. 1955) cred-
its her grandmother, Ruth Levin, who lived across the street from her as
she was growing up in Brooklyn, New York, with teaching her the importance of self-assurance and patience. Her grandmother was not surprised when Lesléa's first book came out (the novel *Good Enough to Eat,*
1986) and she predicted a successful career, a prognosis that has been
brightly accurate.

Lesléa's career as a writer began much earlier. As a child she used
black-and-white composition books as journals, filling them with hundreds of her own poems. Her parents encouraged what they regarded as a
suitable hobby, but would suggest that she could not make money from
writing. She was elated when *Seventeen* magazine bought two of her
poems when she was still a teenager and sent her a check for $150.

At the University of Vermont she designed her own major in creative
writing and human services. After college, she worked a few years in
various jobs—as a day-care teacher, retail salesperson, secretary, and
waitress. At one point she read and critiqued manuscripts for *Redbook*
and *Mademoiselle.* In 1979–80 she attended the Naropa Institute in
Boulder, Colorado, where Allen Ginsburg convinced her that poets lived
in the real world. Anne Waldman was Newman's role model of a strong
woman poet. Lesléa enrolled in graduate school in 1981, planning an
M.A. in creative writing, but she didn't like the big university atmosphere and left after one semester. Too, she disliked being taught that
writers and all artists are very special people as distinguished from
everyone else. She believes that each person, given the freedom to do
what she or he loves best, will flourish.

In 1984, unhappy with jobs that left her unfulfilled, Lesléa decided to use money that she had received in a settlement for a personal injury to support herself for six months while writing full-time. Scared and excited by this risk, she visited a psychic hoping to be talked out of it, but the psychic advised getting to work at what she wanted to do. Lesléa took the advice, went home, and wrote the first twenty pages of her first novel. She felt exhilarated and went on to finish the book in six months.

Newman recognized the importance of a daily schedule, though it wasn't long before she found the writing such a delight that she needed to schedule other work, such as laundry, to get it done. The novel, *Good Enough to Eat,* the story of a Jewish lesbian with an eating disorder, was accepted by Firebrand Books. Rather than go back to jobs she disliked, she started her own business in 1987, Write from the Heart: Writing Workshops for Women. She teaches in her home, and her classes are for women only. She teaches a basic writing workshop called "Write from the Heart"; a variation, "Poems from the Heart"; and "What Are You Eating/What's Eating You," a writing workshop for women focusing on body image and their relationship to food. For women who have known a lack of personal power, the writing often results in a revaluing of themselves. The workshop situation provides immediate validation for the women as they write, read aloud to others, and get other women's responses. Newman has recently finished a book called *What Are You Eating, What's Eating You?* that includes forty writing exercises. In her workshops she encourages women to make writing a daily part of their lives. She tells students that real writers have full wastebaskets and that the process is sometimes more important than the product.

Two sources of Lesléa Newman's strength, she recognizes, are her Jewish heritage and her lesbian identity. Her working-class parents descended from immigrants who came to America to escape raging anti-Semitism in their native Russia. Her grandmother's sentence structure still relies heavily on Yiddish, and Lesléa recalls that in younger days she worked hard not to talk like her grandmother.

When she wrote "A Letter to Harvey Milk," her first short story, she felt opened up to her past. She wrote the story after a four-day workshop with Grace Paley. Told from the point of view of Harry, a seventy-seven-year-old Jewish man who attends a writing class at the local senior citizen's center and develops a nurturing relationship with his young instructor. She assigns him to write a letter to someone from his past. Harry had known Harvey Milk briefly in San Francisco. Touched by Harry's letter to Harvey, the teacher confides that she is gay. In a later assignment, Harry writes "What I Never Told Anyone," a touching narrative including memories of the holocaust.

Newman's story, under the title, "Something to Pass the Time," was the second-place finalist in the 1987 Raymond Carver Short Story Competition. As "A Letter to Harvey Milk" it provided the name of her second book published by Firebrand, a collection of nine stories that explores the meaning of being a lesbian and a Jew. The present story comes from that collection.[1]

Another book of stories, *Secrets,* was published in 1990.[2] Newman has also edited a book of poetry: *Bubbe Meisehs by Shayneh Maidelehs: An Anthology of Poetry by Jewish Granddaughters About Our Grandmothers* (1989).[3] HerBooks published a book of Lesléa's poems, *Love Me Like You Mean It,* a journey to self-affirmation that leads to a deepening love for other women.

Lesléa Newman lives in New England. She writes in the daytime and teaches at night. She's found time in her busy schedule to perform her poetry at colleges, bookstores, and conferences. In 1989 she was awarded a Massachusetts Artists Fellowship in Poetry. She has been director of creative writing at a summer program at Mount Holyoke College from 1986–90, teaching high school women from around the country. Her magazine credits include work in *Sojourner, Common Lives/Lesbian Lives, Sinister Wisdom,* and *Lilith. The Writer* published her article "Writing as Self-Discovery" in 1988.

Gail Koplow quotes Lesléa Newman in a *Sojourner* interview: "Writing is definitely a wonderful way to sit and be quiet with yourself, to get to know yourself. The act of putting words on paper, acknowledging 'I have something to say,' empowers a lot of women."

"One *Shabbos* Evening" first appeared in *Conditions: 14* (1987). The story is a joyful exchange between best friends who are Jewish dykes. Integrating her lesbian and Jewish worlds is a precious challenge to Lesléa Newman. In this story we can share the good energy.

MARTHA FICKLEN

For A., with much love

Lydia had just finished setting the table with her only two matching plates and bowls when the doorbell rang. She glanced at the clock and smiled to herself as she hurried to open the door. Exactly 5:55. Emily was the only other dyke she knew who was compulsively early, just like herself. That's why they were best friends.

"Hi, *mameleh*," Lydia said, as she pulled open the door.

"Hi, *bubbeleh*," Emily answered, handing Lydia a white paper bag that was sitting on her lap. "Here, take these," she said, as Lydia stepped aside and Emily wheeled past her into the apartment.

Lydia followed Emily down the hallway back to the kitchen, opening the top of the paper bag and sticking her nose inside. "Quelle *shayna* bagels," she said, pulling out a fat whole-wheat and raisin bagel and placing it in the basket on the table. She pulled out two more, and frowned at Emily who was wiggling out of her coat.

"Emily, did you get all whole-wheat and raisin?"

Emily twisted around in her wheelchair to get a small brown bag out of the blue pouch that was hanging behind her from two small straps looped over the handles of her chair. "I didn't want you to have a fit, so I went to Waldbaums and got you an onion bagel and some cream cheese." She opened the bag and put its contents on the table along with a stick of soy margarine. "I don't know why you insist on having white flour and dairy every Friday night when you know how bad it is for you."

"*Oy,* Emily, such a *goyishe kop* you have." Lydia bent down and kissed the top of Emily's head. "A whole-wheat and raisin bagel is like whole-wheat and raisin spaghetti. *Feh.*" She took Emily's coat from her and went to hang it in the hall closet. "Once a week I live a little," she called over her shoulder. "It didn't do my grandfather any harm, and he lived to be eighty-seven."

"I can't hear you," Emily called, as she wheeled over to the stove and lifted the lid off a big soup pot. A cloud of steam immediately enveloped her. "Umm. The soup smells great," Emily said, as Lydia came back into the room. "Let's light the candles and eat."

Lydia put two white candles into a pair of brass candlesticks and placed them on the table. She lit one, Emily lit the other, and both women made three wide circles in the air with their hands, bathing themselves in the *Shabbos* light. They sang the blessing and kissed each other on both cheeks, saying *Shabbot sholom*. Then Emily wheeled to her place at the table, and Lydia filled their bowls with chicken soup and sat down.

"So what's new?" Emily asked, dividing a *matzo* ball in half with the edge of her spoon.

"Well, Em, I've got a completely fabulous idea." Lydia reached across Emily's bowl for a bottle of seltzer. "You know that *klezmer* band we saw a few weeks ago, the one with that great singer, the blonde, what's-her-name?"

"Judy, I think it is."

"Yeah, Judy." Lydia filled her glass with seltzer. "Well, I've been thinking that we should have a lesbian *klezmer* band. Wouldn't that be great? And I've got the perfect name for it, too." Lydia's eyes twinkled in the light of the *Shabbos* candles as she looked up at Emily. "Are you ready?"

"No, let me guess." Emily reached for a whole wheat bagel, put it on her plate, and began slicing it in half. "The *Yentes?*"

"No." Lydia shook her head vigorously. "You'll never guess."

Emily put down her knife and fingered the maroon scarf she was wearing around her neck. "The Dyke Kikes?" she asked.

"Emily, that's gross." Lydia shook her head again, slowly this time. "It's a good thing you're Jewish, otherwise I'd give you such a *zetz*. . . ."

Emily laughed. "You sound just like my mother."

"Essen in gezunt, meyn klayne kind." Lydia put another bagel on Emily's plate, which Emily promptly removed. "So, do you give up?" she asked hopefully.

"I guess so."

Lydia put down the chicken wing she was gnawing on and executed a drum roll on the table with the tips of her fingers. "Ladies and jellybeans, may I present . . . the fabulous . . . Klezbians!"

"The Klezbians?" Emily repeated.

"Yeah, Emily, don't you get it? *Klezmer* plus lesbian equals . . ."

"Yeah, I get it, I get it. But who's going to be in it?"

"Well, let's see." Lydia stared for a moment at her curved reflection on the back of her silver soup spoon. Her face flattened out behind a huge nose and she flared her nostrils at herself a few times before turning her spoon around and dipping it back into her soup. "We'll need a horn player, a few fiddles, a drummer maybe, a flute. . . ."

"How about a triangle? I used to play the triangle in second grade."

"Great, Emily. I was counting on you to be in it." Lydia put her spoon down, picked up her bowl with both hands, and raised it to her lips, noisily slurping down the rest of her soup.

"Aren't you forgetting something?" Emily asked, as Lydia's face reappeared from behind her bowl.

"What?"

"Who's going to sing? Not that Judy girl, uness you know something I don't."

"I wish." Lydia sighed and unbuttoned the top two buttons of her purple velour pullover. The chicken soup was making her hot. "Did you ever see such a pair of gorgeous arms in your whole life? *Oy,* when she walked out on stage in that sleeveless blue sequin top, I almost *plotzed.*" A faraway look came into Lydia's eyes for a moment. Then she sighed again, bringing herself to the present. "Oh well. I never did like blondes much anyway." Lydia took her onion bagel from the basket, cut it in half and spread some cream cheese on it. "Maybe she'll teach me how to sing, though."

"You're going to sing?" Emily rolled her eyes.

"Yeah. What are you making such a *punim* for?" Lydia gestured at Emily with the knife in her hand.

"Lydia, in the first place, much as I love you, you can't carry a tune. And in the second place, you don't know Yiddish."

"So." Lydia's lower lip began to pout. "I can learn, you know. Besides, I do so know a *bisseleh* Yiddish." She jumped up from her seat and pointed at the table. *"Dos iz meyn tish, und dos iz meyn tush."* She put her hands on her hips, turned around and wiggled her behind. Emily laughed. Then Lydia crossed the room and took something out of the freezer. *"Dos iz meyn fish,"* she said, holding up a piece of frozen haddock, *"und dos iz meyn fus."* She lifted her left foot and pointed. Then she put the haddock back in the freezer and sat down again, smiling broadly at Emily. "See?"

"I'm impressed. You're practically fluent," Emily said, tilting her bowl toward her and pouring the last drop of soup into her spoon.

"I've even written a song already," Lydia informed her proudly.

"In Yiddish?" Emily's eyebrows rose.

"Partly."

"*Oy.* This I've got to hear. Are you going to sing it to me?"

"Maybe. If you're a good girl and finish the rest of your bagel."

"*Oy,* Lydia, you're sounding more and more like a Jewish mother everyday, you should pardon the expression."

"Well, I have to practice. I will be one someday, if I find the co-mother of my dreams." Lydia stood up and reached for Emily's bowl. "Want more soup?"

"No thanks. Well, yeah, give me another *knaydlach.*"

"*Knaydl,* Emily. *Knaydlach* is plural." Lydia went over to the stove and ladled some soup into Emily's bowl. Emily stared at her back. "You have been studying Yiddish," she said, with a note of surprise.

"Yeah, I'm serious," she said, setting Emily's bowl down in front of her. "I want to learn to speak the language of our grandmothers, Em. You know, language says so much about a culture. Like. . . ." she paused for a minute, "like, 'Will you sit over there?' sounds a lot different from '*zich zetzen dortn.*'"

"Where'd you learn that?" Emily asked.

"*Ich hob a buch.*" Lydia turned from the stove where she was filling her own bowl, and set her soup down on the table. Then she leaned over and picked up a book from the windowsill. "I have a book," she repeated, handing it to Emily and sitting down.

"*The Yiddish Teacher,*" Emily read aloud. She flipped through the book for a minute, staring at the Hebrew letters which were meaningless to her. She pushed the book over toward Lydia. "What gives with the Yiddish?" she asked.

Lydia stroked the cover of the book gently, as though it was a beloved cat. "I don't know, Em. That concert really moved me. You know, just hearing the sound of the words was like coming home. It must be in my genes or something." She stopped stroking the book and looked up at Emily. "And no, I don't mean in my pants."

"You read my mind." Emily grinned.

"I know. So anyway," Lydia continued, "I bought a *klezmer* tape, and I've been listening to it in my car every day on my way to work. It's like a private twenty-minute total immersion class. And then I got this book, and I've taught myself the alphabet and now I can even pick out a few words in the songs," Lydia said proudly.

"*Mazel tov.*" Emily picked up a black and white salt shaker shaped like a penguin and shook it over her soup. "I still don't see what the point of all this is."

"The point is. . . ." Lydia paused again, knowing that words couldn't explain this passion that had suddenly emerged in her. "The point is, Emily, that English is a foreign language to me. To you, too, you know. I want to speak to my grandmother in her own language, in our own language, just once before she dies."

Lydia looked at Emily intently. "I don't know. Maybe I'm a little *meshugeh.* But I have this mad yearning to learn Yiddish. You know, I'm really good at languages, like that summer I lived in Mexico, I picked up Spanish really fast. The trouble is, there's no place left to go to be totally immersed in Yiddish anymore."

Emily took a bite of her bagel and chewed thoughtfully. "How about Miami Beach?" she asked.

"Oh Emily, I'm serious."

"So am I."

"Well, I'm not going to Miami Beach. I'm going to work with my book and then take a course at the university and probably go to New York next summer. Columbia has a six-week Yiddish program that's supposed to be terrific."

Emily wrinkled up her nose. "New York in the summer? Lydia, are you out of your mind? You wouldn't last a week."

"Emily, why are you being so unsupportive?" Lydia looked directly in Emily's eyes, which were a dark liquid brown that always reminded her of milk chocolate.

"I don't know. I just don't understand why you want to learn Yiddish. You speak with your grandmother perfectly well in English. Yiddish is a dead language." She stared back into Lydia's eyes which were also brown, though lighter than her own, and flecked with bits of gold.

"Emily, that's a rotten thing to say." Lydia reached across the table for the penguin saltshaker, and rolled it back and forth between her hands. "You know, when I lived in Mexico I met this Spanish woman, and we talked a little in English. It was when I first got there. Then she turned away to talk to some of her friends and then she turned back to me. 'I'm sorry,' she said, 'I understand English, but when I speak in my own language, I understand in brighter colors.' I never forgot that, Emily. I want to understand the brighter colors of my grandmother's life."

"I'm sorry." Emily took the penguin peppershaker off the table and stared at it. It was wearing a red bowtie. "I'm just worried where all this Jewish stuff is taking you, Lydia. I'm scared I'll show up here one Friday night and you'll answer the door with a shaved head and a *sheytl* and seventeen kids and a husband off in *shul* and then you'll move to Israel and then . . ."

"Emily, are you serious?" Lydia set the saltshaker down on the table with a thump. "Em, going straight is the farthest thing from my mind, believe me. That's not what this is all about." She shook her head in disbelief. "Can you imagine me with a guy, Emily? Me? The woman who'd be happy if she never saw a man naked from the neck down again?" Lydia leaned forward in her chair. "Emily, I've been listening to that tape in my car every morning now for three weeks, and every single day it makes me cry. Really. I've had to tell them at work I've suddenly developed these strange allergies, so they don't think I'm losing my mind. I come in and my eyes are always full of tears." Lydia put her hand on Emily's arm. "It pulls at my heart-strings, Emily, and I just have to go with it."

"Well, don't go too far," Emily said, covering Lydia's hand with her own. "Judaism is just so entrenched with heterosexism. I can't even get near it for two seconds before I start feeling guilty for not perpetuating the race."

"I know what you mean." Lydia nodded her head. "But there are some gay synagogues. And I'm going to have a Jewish baby, even if it is with a turkey blaster. You just have to find your own balance." Lydia paused for a minute as she stood up and started clearing the table. "Like having *Shabbos* dinner with me every Friday night, Em. That's perpetuating the culture at least." She carried the dishes over to the sink. "Anyway, you shaved your head at Michigan last summer."

"But that was different." Emily ran her fingers through her thick black hair, which was still quite short.

"Don't worry, Emily. I'm not going to desert you for the wonderful world of heterosexuality." Lydia returned to the table and began wiping it with a sponge.

"I certainly hope not," Emily said, leaning down and pulling back the two levers that released her rear wheels. She backed up her chair and then moved forward, picking up the cream cheese and soy margarine and putting them into the refrigerator.

"I'll sing you my song, then you'll feel better," Lydia said, letting the water run in the sink. "Want some coffee or tea?" she asked Emily.

"No, let's go sit in the living room," Emily wheeled through the kitchen doorway and Lydia followed.

"I'll be right in," Lydia called, as she ducked into her bedroom for a minute. Then, carrying a blue spiral notebook, she entered the living room, to find Emily picking dead leaves off her philodendron plant.

"Lyd, you have to stop watering this plant so much. You're drowning the poor thing." Emily turned her chair and crossed the room, her lap full of withered yellow leaves. "Look at this."

"Oh, I thought I wasn't watering it enough and that's why it was dying." Lydia dropped her notebook onto the couch, bent over in front of the stereo, and started thumbing through some records, while Emily returned to the kitchen to get rid of the dead leaves. "I'm just going to play you a song or two, to get you in the mood," she said, as Emily came back.

Emily clasped her hands in front of her heart, and began to sing, in her best Perry Como imitation: "I'm in the mood for Jews. Simply because you're near me. Honey, but when you're near me, I'm in the mood for Jews."

"At least one of us can carry a tune," Lydia said as she turned the stereo on.

"Well, you can tune a fork but you can't tuna fish, har har har," Emily said, popping a wheely in the middle of the floor.

"Emily, don't do that. You know it gives me a heart attack." Lydia covered her eyes as Emily thrust herself forward and then leaned back, balancing herself up on her two rear wheels for a minute before coming back down.

"Can't a girl have any fun around here?" she asked, spinning around in a circle. "Alright, alright, I'll behave." She brought herself to a stop, right in front of Lydia. "What have you got there?"

"It's the *klezmer* band's second album. I got it at the library." Lydia handed her the cover and lowered the needle in the groove between the third and fourth songs. "This is called 'Mazel Tov Dances,'" she said, stepping back. Immediately, wild horn and fiddle music filled the room.

"Oh, let's dance," Emily put the album cover down and wheeled herself into the middle of the room. She pulled the small levers on either side of her chair forward, locking her rear wheels in place. Then she started clapping her hands, snapping her fingers, and moving her body in time to the music. Lydia joined her, doing a four-step grapevine back and forth in front of Emily.

"Hey, want to do a turn?" Emily asked.

"Sure. Wait a minute. "Lydia ran to push all the chairs back against the wall. She threw two big camel-colored pillows that had been lying on the floor out into the hallway. "Do you think there's enough room?"

Emily looked around, released her brakes, and moved her chair across the floor. "I think so," she said, grabbing Lydia's hand. Emily used her free hand to manipulate her wheelchair, and soon she was dipping under Lydia's arm and gliding around to her other side, while Lydia bent her knees and gracefully moved her body.

The song ended, and *"Rozinkes mit Mandlen,"* came on. Lydia went to turn the record off, but Emily said, "No, leave it," so Lydia flopped down on the couch instead. Emily wheeled over to sit next to her while they listened to the song. Lydia's eyes grew moist, and she wiped her tears with the back of her hand. *"Nu,* what did I tell you?" she whispered loudly, pointing to her face. Emily took one of Lydia's hands and listened intently to the music until the song was over.

"Did Judy sing that song at the concert?" she asked, as Lydia got up to turn off the stereo.

"'Raisins and Almonds'? I don't think so."

"It's really familiar. Maybe my grandmother used to sing it to me," Emily said as she watched Lydia slip the album back inside its cover. Lydia put the record away and returned to Emily's side.

"So, are you ready for my song?"

"As ready as I'll ever be."

Lydia opened her notebook and flipped through a few pages. "First I have to explain a few things," she said. "Number one, it's not really a song because I haven't written the music yet. I was kind of hoping Alix Dobkin would do it."

"Uh-huh." Emily nodded her head.

"Em-i-ly." Lydia exaggerated the syllables of Emily's name to illustrate her extreme annoyance.

"What? I didn't say anything."

"Yeah, but you were thinking it."

"What was I thinking, Miss Clairvoyant?"

"You were thinking, 'Alix Dobkin would never waste her time on something as stupid as Lydia Shapiro's Yiddish lesbian limericks."

"You wrote Yiddish lesbian limericks? This I gotta hear."

"Oh shit. Now you made me give it away." Lydia held her notebook up closer to her face. "Listen, they are kind of stupid. I was just trying to use all the Yiddish words I knew, and you know I have a warped sense of humor anyway."

"Yeah, so?"

"So, I was just trying to get the feel of the language. A lot of words rhyme, you know. Like *cheder* and *seder, maydl* and *draydl.* . . ."

"*Kichel* and pickle." Emily pronounced pickle with a guttural *ch,* making Lydia laugh.

"See what I mean?"

"Yeah." Emily thought for a minute. She loved word games. "How about *latke* and vodka? or *kvetch* and sketch? Or Etch-A-Sketch?"

"Very funny."

"Boy, are you touchy tonight." Emily scratched her chin and sighed.

"Well, I just don't want you to laugh at me. Someday I really do want to write in Yiddish, or maybe be a translator even. But this," she gestured with her notebook, "is just fooling around."

"Alright. I promise I won't laugh."

"But Emily, you have to laugh. It's funny."

"O.K., O.K. I'll laugh, I won't laugh. Quit stalling already."

"O.K." Lydia took a deep breath and let it out slowly. "It's in two parts, a mother and a daughter, O.K.? It starts with the mother." She held her notebook up in front of her face so she couldn't see Emily, and began to read:

Oy, Morris, have we got *tsuris.*
Vat can we do *mit* our *tochter* Doris?
    It's worse than a *Goy*
    It's not even a boy
She's in love *mit* the *maydl* Delores.

"Now this is Doris:"
Mama, Delores is such a *shayna maydl*
Her *punim's* as smooth as a *knaydl.*
    Such a *shayna shiksa*
    Makes me *kvell* in *meyn kishkas*
Oy, I'm spinning from love like a *draydl.*

Emily howled with delight, and thus encouraged, Lydia went on.

The Mama:
Oy, Doris come light the *menorah.*
We'll *zing* and we'll *tansig* the *hora.*
    I'll buy you some *tchotchkes*
    I'll fry you some *latkes*
If you don't see that Delores no more-a.

Doris:
Mama, I don't vant to say the *baruches.*
    I vant *meyn hentes* on Delores' *tuchus.*
    She makes me all *shvitzig*
    and soft like *gefilte* fishes
Oy, I'll love her from now until *Sukkoth.*

Lydia looked up, grinning wildly. "Now comes the responsive reading," she said.

The Mama:
Oy, Doris, you're worse than a *vildeh chaya*.
You think Delores is maybe the Messiah?

Doris:
But Mama, she makes me so *fraylach*.
Like I've just eaten forty-nine *knaydlach*.

Lydia shifted her weight and held the notebook so Emily could read along with her. "Now comes the 'Mama's Chorus'" she said, and both she and Emily began to read aloud:

"Oy, oy, oy, oy
She don't vant to know from a boy.

Oy vay iss mir
She won't even wear a brassière.

Oy, oy, oy vay
Why can't she be like Cousin Fay?

Oy, Gottenyu
What is the Mama to do?

Doris:
Oy, Mama don't make such a *futz*
Just because I don't vant me a *putz*.
Last night I had a *cholem*
The whole world had *sholom*
So you see I'm not really a *klutz*.

The Mama:
Oy, Doris, you got such a *shayna smeckle*.
Maybe you got just a *bisseleh seckle?*
Go get me some *lox*
I'm ready to *plotz*
I'm so *fahmished* I feel like a *yekl*.

Lydia turned another page. "*Oy*, there's more?" Emily asked. "*Shah*," Lydia said. "This is Doris."

Mama come sit down and *essen* a bagel.
Nice and fresh they are, from *Tante Raizl*.
I'll bring Delores to *Shabbos*
We'll all *shep* some *naches*
It'll be fine, you'll just be amazl.

"Amazl? What kind of *farshtunkeneh* Yiddish is that?" Emily asked.

"Keep *shtil*. Here's the responsive reading again." Lydia turned her head toward Emily to give her a dirty look, then turned back to the notebook again.

The Mama:
But what if the *Zayde* sits *shiva*?
Doris:
I'll bribe him *mit shmaltz* and chopped liver.
The Mama:
And *Bubbe* Esther and Minnie the *Yente*?
Doris:
Oy their faces like *borsht* so magenta!
The Mama:
It's the same from Miami Beach to Poughkeepsie.
The *maydls* go *mit maydls* just like gypsies.
Vot can we do but say *l'chaim*
And next year in *Yerushalayim*
We'll *trink* and we'll *tanse* till we're tipsy.

"I thought Jews didn't drink," Emily whispered loudly.
"Only Manischevitz," Lydia whispered back. "This is Doris:"

See Mama, I'm not such a *shlimazl*
I'm giving you double *tov-mazel*.
Instead of *ein tochter*
You now have *tsvey tichter*
It's even better than Harriet and Ozzl.

Emily cracked up. "Harriet and Ozzl? Oh my God, Lydia." Lydia glared at Emily. "This is the last verse."

The Mama:
Oy, vat will I do *mit meyn* Morris?
He vanted for you the tailor named Boris.
We won't have a *chuppa*
We'll have *kugel* for supper
And then we'll all *zing* in the chorus.

Lydia turned the notebook so Emily could see the words again, and together they read aloud the grand finale:

Oy, oy, oy, oy
Our cup is all filled up *mit* joy.

Oy vay iss mir
The *tochter's* a little bit queer.

Oy, oy, oy vay
The neighbors will give a *gershray.*

Oy, Gottenyu
The Mama will have to make do.

    La la!"

Lydia threw down her notebook triumphantly, jumped up and took a bow with one arm draped across her belly and the other behind her back. Emily applauded wildly, and then put two fingers in her mouth and whistled shrilly.

"Thank you, thank you," Lydia said, taking another bow and throwing kisses at Emily. "So what do you think, Em? Are we talking total fabulosity, or what?" Lydia knelt down in front of Emily and leaned her elbows on the arms of her wheelchair.

"I think you've finally flipped your lid, Lyd," Emily said, ruffling Lydia's short curly hair. "I can't believe my best friend is turning into the Allen Sherman of the lesbian community."

"Well, if not me, who?" Lydia asked.

"I think it's 'If not now, when?'" Emily said, correcting Lydia's misquotation of Rabbi Hillel, and still stroking Lydia's head. "It's great, Lydia, really. I love it. I think you should do it at the next lesbian talent show. The girls will go wild."

"Do you really think so?" Lydia sat up, clasped her hands together, turned them inside out and pulled, thus loudly cracking all eight of her knuckles at once, a gesture Emily hated. Emily responded by working up a good supply of saliva with her tongue, opening her mouth wide, and letting a bit spit bubble form between her lips.

"Emily, gross!" Lydia looked away.

"Well, you started with your god-awful knuckles."

"Alright, alright, truce." Lydia spread her fingers wide and placed them on her thighs, and Emily closed her mouth. Lydia scooted up and leaned her elbows on Emily's knee.

"You know, Em, it's kind of ironic when you think about it," she said, running her fingers along the cold metal arm of Emily's wheelchair. "I mean, seventy years ago, my grandparents were taking English lessons, and here I am giving myself Yiddish lessons."

"Yeah, it is kind of funny." Emily picked up Lydia's notebook from

the couch and turned a few pagse, wondering for a minute if Lydia
had misspelled *shlimazl.*

Lydia let out a deep sigh. "Em?"

"Yeah?" Emily put the notebook down.

"I'm afraid my grandmother is going to die before I learn Yiddish
well enough to talk to her." Lydia got up from the floor, sat down on
the couch, and rested her head on Emily's shoulder. "She's really old,
you know. All her brothers and sisters are gone. Her whole culture is
gone. Just imagine what it would be like to not hear your own language for fifty years." A tear welled up in Lydia's eye.

"I think you should call her up, Lyd, and just talk to her," Emily
said softly, stroking Lydia's cheek.

"But what could I say? I can't read her my song."

"You certainly can't." Emily thought for a minute. "Do you know
how to say 'I love you, Grandma'?"

"Sure, that's easy. *Ich hob dir libe, Bubbe.*"

"Well, you could start with that."

"I guess." Lydia sighed again. "But what if she laughs at me, Emily? Or what if she doesn't understand?"

"She won't laugh, Lydia. And she'll understand. I'll bet you a
dozen whole-wheat bagels." Emily smiled. "She'll understand," she
repeated.

"You know what, Em?" Lydia took Emily's hand and started playing with her fingers. "What I really want to do is learn Yiddish, and
then raise my kid bilingually. Wouldn't that be something?"

"I'll say." Emily stretched her arms high over her head and arched
her back. "It just goes to show you, Lydia. The more things change,
the more they stay the same."

"Can I quote you on that, *Reb* Emily-*Bat*-Sylvia?"

"I expect you to, *Reb* Lydia-*Bat*-Harriet." Emily let out a yawn. "I
should get going."

"What, before dessert?"

"What dessert? I'm so full I'm *plotzing.*"

"I cooked a little rice pudding. It shouldn't be a total loss. C'mon,
I'll make some decaf." Lydia rose and started for the kitchen.

Emily followed, protesting. "I don't know, Lydia. I really don't
think I could eat another thing."

Lydia, who had already put two small bowls on the table, turned
around to face Emily, with two teaspoons in her hand.

"But Em, I made it special. I used brown rice and everything."

Emily stopped her chair in the middle of the floor. "Brown rice pudding? *Feh!*" She pretended to spit on the tips of her fingers and then shook her hand at the floor. "What, all of a sudden a health food nut you're turning into?"

Lydia finished filling the coffeemaker with water and then turned to face Emily, a look of astonishment on her face. "But Emily, I thought you wouldn't eat it if I used white rice."

"Hey, bagels are bagels, but rice pudding is rice pudding," Emily said, taking the two mugs Lydia was handing her and putting them on the table. Then Lydia took the big glass bowl of rice pudding out of the refrigerator and set it on the table. A minute later, the decaf gurgled. Lydia poured some into each mug and then sat down across from Emily. The *Shabbos* candles were almost out, but the wicks still flickered above the rim of the brass candlesticks.

"*L'chaim,*" Lydia said, lifting her cup.

"*L'chaim,*" Emily answered, raising her own cup and touching it to Lydia's with a clink. Then each woman dipped her spoon into the rice pudding, and first Lydia fed Emily and then Emily fed Lydia, so that they would both have a sweet week until they met again the following Friday night for *Shabbos*.

MADELYN ARNOLD

Let Me See

(1991)

*M*ADELYN Arnold (b. 1948) grew up in a working-class family as the eldest of nine. Her German-Jewish mother was a musician and an artist; her mixed-race father was a part-time labor organizer and played the violin. Besides the love of music and art and the knowledge of labor history that Arnold learned in her home, she attended an old-fashioned primary school in which students were taught to memorize and recite poetry. Some of her later education took place at Indiana University in Bloomington, where she earned a B.S. in microbiology and botany. At the age of eighteen she found, quite by chance, a copy of Richard Wright's *Native Son* in a Salvation Army bin of free books, a work she counts as an important literary influence. Out of college, she found at a garage sale an English major's entire library, bought it, and read it. She began at Z with Emile Zola's *Germinal;* by the time she reached Voltaire's *Candide,* she had "caught fire" and begun to write.

Arnold sang professionally for a while, went to art school where she studied portrait painting, and has worked as a laboratory technician, a racing driver, a mental hospital attendant, a printer, a cab driver, and a truck driver. She has also taught college classes in composition, creative writing, and literature, and has earned an M.A. in creative writing at the University of Washington. She has great faith in some of her writing students.

As of this writing Madelyn Arnold has entered her forties. She suffers from multiple disabilities, including severe asthma with a particular allergy to book dust. This latter sometimes upsets her the most as she loves libraries. In addition to these difficulties she has led a life marked by severe chronic poverty. As she herself says, "My income has not yet made it all the way up to the working class."

Arnold's art, her early, life-taught feminism, and her commitment to social change come out of conditions that tend to destroy or silence artists, especially female ones; nonetheless she continues to write. Much of her work, in her own words, shows "my love for the rhythm and discursiveness of my native Kentucky speech." She would love to live in a small town like the one in which she passed her childhood and early adolescence, but she is a lesbian and fears the homophobia and lack of anonymity to be found in such places.

She has published short stories and poems. In 1988 her first novel, *Bird-Eyes,* was published by the Seal Press, a small feminist press in Seattle, and received favorable reviews. A collection of her short stories, including "Let Me See" has been accepted by St. Martin's Press and will be out in the fall of 1991.

Although Arnold has spent a lifetime struggling with ill health and the constraints caused by homophobia and poverty, there is one way in which her life has been rich: her friendships, which have crossed the boundaries of class, age, color, and sexuality. As she says, "I have always been lucky in my friends."

She intends to keep writing as long as illness and poverty allow her to do so.

JOANNA RUSS

Every time I would walk into her cafe, Lela would tell me about plastic.

"We're gonna get rid of all this here," she'd tell me, working widening circles with her dishcloth on the chipped linoleum counter. "Set down, Honey. You're the onliest one understands this." She'd hand me the single sheet menu and fool with the ammonia water in the sink. "One of these days, you know what? We're gonna get some nice chairs, nice plastic ones, instead of this wooden kind.

"You want coffee?" she'd ask as she slopped molten liquid into a buff china cup. "Let me see . . . and we're gonna get some disposable stuff that I don't got to wash two hundred million times—"

"Now, I don't need any water," I'd say. "Save the glass."

"I bet I washed a set of dishes for every man woman and child in the U.S.A.!"

I'd always look at the menu, picking out words among the creases
—taped and retaped—and the splashes of coffee and ketchup. I
knew it by heart, but sometimes I'd make up my mind to order
something new, would take a breath to say so, and—

"How do you want your eggs?" she'd say; and something like: "We
don't have no sausage today. You want some fresh pie? Rhubarb," or
whatever it was, if there'd been some change from the day and the
week before.

She liked to talk to someone who liked to listen or anyway, didn't
mind it. Her voice was like that old song on the radio that you like
when you know the words. I'd reach for the cream and—

"When you gonna start that diet, honey?"—and she'd fix her eyes
on me. Usually I'd take cream anyway.

"Fried," I'd say sometimes, as she poured eggs onto the grill beaten
into water.

"This place is driving me nuts," she'd say. "We're gonna get a nice
counter too, not like this-here. Lookit this. It's splintered all to the
devil on the one side and one of these days some hill jack is gonna
run one of them through his hand and we're gonna be up seeing
your boss in front of the judge. And these kids . . ." Here she'd gesture to the booths and the handfull of tables. "Lookit what they do to
them chairs! Crash them around like they was crates. And carving
all over everything. I bet every idiot over the age of five got his initials in my tables somewhere. And the girls there, in the potty. Yeah,
we're gonna get these melamine kind, that don't stain. It's gonna be
real nice."

Stains almost made a pattern everywhere, like calico overlaid on a
checkerboard design. The floor was of tired, mottled fir, and nearest
the door it was lowest. Behind the counter, the walls were speckled
with grease from the grill. Everywhere else messy fingerprints, notices and yellowed tape from notices gone by, covered all the wall
space in high reach. The chairs were shaking and unsightly, no two
of the same kin.

Folks would come in and show their kids where they'd carved
their initials in something. Generally, chairbacks.

"You know," she'd say, scrubbing the pattern off the counter, "I
think I'll paint it all yella, nice and cheerful. I'll get some of them
pictures of kids on the wall, the big-eyed kind like you get at K-Mart.
This here color is pukaceous."

The place was a sort of olive drab, and it wasn't that pretty. I'd lift my cup and saucer as her grinding hand rounded the ketchup, creeping up on my plate. "Let me see . . . and put nice flowers out. Oh, I know you gotta wash em every so often, but all you need to do is dip them in a little ammonia water and there you are! fresh as a daisy!"

She'd be really pleased when she said that, and would stand up and stretch her cramped back a little and wipe her hands on her apron. "Well how is everything?" She meant the food.

I never had the heart to tell her I didn't always want my eggs that way. But on the other hand, maybe I liked having something taken completely out of my hands; something that didn't change. It was the closest thing in my life to a confirmed religious experience.

My fate was eggs because the first time I came into the diner some twenty years before, when she wore her hair up and she looked very good that way, I had been so confused. That was after my one employer, Mr. Meredith, passed away, and there aren't many places around here for my kind of training. I was so nervous about starting for Mr. Sams that I couldn't make any kind of decision. The cafe was crowded, and I had to sit at the counter which I wasn't raised to do. The menu was discouraging, and I simply ordered the first thing I saw: sausage and eggs. Now I don't care for sausage, actually. And that sausage, Lela's own, gave me the most amazing heartburn, but mornings after I ordered the same thing because at least I knew what that was like. After a time, I just didn't have the choice because she knew me. She would have been so mortified if I'd told her otherwise: she prided herself on knowing her customers' minds.

It seems like I only once tried somewhere else in all those years, and that was because of my sister. She wasn't well, so one time when I went over and fixed a little something for Forrest and the boys, I found myself running late. I had to take a taxi. I couldn't see me stopping for a breakfast in a taxicab, with Lela's questions and me running late as it was; so I just went on, and then later I went to the new Strand for an early lunch. Just go where it was quiet, I thought. It was made inside of pink stone, pink like the inside of a Virginia ham, and after being stuck behind a pillar forty-five minutes, you might just say I didn't go back. That is, I didn't go back except when Harrison Sams actually *won* a case and took everyone about to dinner. But that wasn't often. Down here, the defense attorney is what you might call a formality. I never went anywhere aside from Lela's, where you could get a little conversation. And she was always there.

You need things in your life like that, that don't change with the next election or them buying up that nice little woods next door . . . and you grieve. You and the birds.

That's why one already sticky summer Saturday, I was surprised to see her clean, grim young nephew, punishing the grill with a dish-rag, alone in the cafe. Years before he had worked with Lela in the summers. It hit me as an impossible thing to see, as if he had been scrubbing on the ceiling. He looked up at me, all business, and was surprised that I took a seat at the counter. That's not the usual thing for a lady to do, here.

"Why, where's Lela?" I said.

"Well . . ." he was polite. He was most always and truly polite. "Well, I'm going to be watching . . . well, for a while."

That alarmed me and I said I was a friend, and was she all right?

"Well . . . ," he said. It was plain how much he liked her. Lela had introduced him to me as "her jewel," once. "Well, she's been awork-ing too hard . . . needs a little rest. . . ."

She was getting it at Sacred Name Hospital in the state capital. A little trouble with her heart.

Of course, the place changed. Junior was an industrious young man who worked like some people play. He must have had her genes, but he didn't know how to handle them. He painted the place, threw out the chairs and the carvers as well with the selfsame energy and attitude.

He was polite to me, even nice in his way, because I was fond of his aunt and he was fond of her. But he was impatient, even though he never said anything; I hate to be hurried, especially with a meal. He'd stand and wait and twist his toothpick, and after a while he'd kind of twist his mouth. And day after day after day, I ordered the eggs and toast and grits (#1), and he never once remembered what I wanted.

It was just barely before Christmastime when he got in a lot of little counters to line the walls and got rid of the booths and tables. The walls were lemon yellow; the wooden floor had fake brick linoleum all over it. It was all as bright as an operation room, light reflecting off the shiny counters with the chrome stools in front, very nice for anyone who likes to eat facing a wall. But to each his own.

Each section had paper napkins in a large dispenser and pastel chrysanthemums tucked into a new square plastic box. There wasn't any ketchup or sugar, you had to ask for that, and sugar was extra.

"Want coffee Miss Heilmann?" he asked that morning, and he smiled automatically. That was one thing I didn't really care for in him. Lela never smiled unless she wanted to, but this young man smiled like the guest of honor at a funeral: a smile that was fixed to his office, not his pleasure.

Well I always wanted coffee, and while he coaxed it out of a big new machine into a white foam cup, what was the principal difference in the cafe sort of came to me. It was so cleanable.

"You going to get the pictures?" I said.

"Ma'am?" He looked surprised. "Say, pictures? What pictures you mean? I got a tree up."

And he did. With the morning crowd in there, I hadn't seen it, but over behind one of our high school teachers was a little metal tree with little winking lights.

I don't really like to draw attention to myself, but I had started this. It seemed like I should finish all my say, and I got his attention again. "Well, you know, I suppose, for decoration's sake. Just, well, pictures. Lela always said she was going to have flowers around and, well, pictures on the walls."

This was obviously some big news to him.

I went back to my stool to drink my coffee, and was just thinking about what I should get my sister's new girl when in popped Lela like a jack-in-the-box.

"Junior!" she exclaimed, and she looked wonderful. Her cheeks were pink and friendly with the cold. "Well Merry Christmas, Honey! And everyone!" She caught sight of me.

"Why Martha Ann, how in the world are you! It was so nice a you to come all the way up there and see me! And them was the nicest flowers!" She swooped down and grabbed my shoulder and shook it. "I got one as a book mark," she said, proud.

Junior smiled and recommenced bruising the counter.

"Merry Christmas, Honey," she said. "You been losing weight? Why, lookit what he's been doing here. Why . . ." She stopped, her eyes roving over the walls and floor, up to the grill with its new aluminum hood. "My," she said. "Just look."

It wasn't a complete shock of course. They had told her he was making some of her changes, but still. I thought of all those initials, and I wondered.

"Why, Junior, it's just beautiful," she said finally, shaking her head. "You know you're gonna work yourself to death? He was that way before he even went in the Army."

Junior smiled, this time for real. It made him look his own age more than mine.

He looked around for a word or two, and found himself a cup, a real cup. "Here, Honey," he said. "You want you some cream in your coffee?" She shook her head, taking the cup without looking. It was the new counters she was seeing, the flowers on the shelves.

"Merry Christmas," I said finally.

"It's just like, it's just like the Strand, only cheerier," she decided. "And look at this!" She said, floating over to that little tree. "Let me see . . . now isn't that cute. Needs a little red on it, though."

"They's ribbons in back. I was thinking to put them up, um . . ." said Junior.

"Well I'll make us some bows. Martha, come help me. . . . Onliest thing," she added low as we went back to the stockroom. "I do love a real tree, the smell and all. . . . The plastic's nice, only the real thing's so much prettier, don't you think?"

SUSAN KOPPELMAN

Afterword

The Ethics of Reciprocity

The emotional availability of one woman to another is not a *visible* element in our social arrangements, yet it is often reciprocal and as such, mutually enhancing and immensely rewarding.[1]

In the stories in this collection, friendship between two women or among three or more women is fundamental in their lives and central to the story. What I have come to call the ethics of reciprocity is essential to the relationship between the participants in each of the friendships; the testing or measuring of the dimensions or boundaries of those ethics is central to the plot and provides the locus of what literary critics traditionally refer to as the conflict. In each of the stories, the issue of reciprocity is engaged directly.

Friendship is a rich, complex, archetypal relationship. Although friendships can vary infinitely, certain things must be part of their content. One thing that must be there is a recognition of the need for reciprocity in the relationship. There must also be the opportunity for reciprocity. Finally, there must be a balance of power or privilege between or among the participants in the relationship. That is, the friends must be equally in and subject to each other's power.

If any of those things, in any combination or number, is absent from a relationship we can say three things about the relationship: (1) it is not a friendship, regardless of what it might have been in the past or had the potential to become; (2) it is something else rather than nothing; (3) we do not have to think about those other relationships in our attempt to understand what friendship is.

Reciprocity involves both giving and receiving. Each must be done equally. But reciprocity is not a simple exchange. If, for example, I hand you a quart of a brand-name drink and you hand back another quart of the same drink, we have made an equal exchange. Neither of us has benefited or suffered from the exchange. We might as well have saved the time and effort of that exchange. Nothing has been altered by it, including ourselves and our relationship. This kind of an exchange does not constitute reciprocity. But if I give you that drink when you are thirsty and have nothing of your own to drink and, a while later, when I am equally thirsty and as bereft of drink, you *then* give me a drink equivalent to the drink I gave you, then we have engaged in reciprocity. Even though what we gave was exactly the same as that which we received, the staggered timing—staggered in response to need—lifts the exchange from a meaningless act of mimicry into the realm of a meaningful exchange, into an act of reciprocity.

Although sometimes the reciprocities in a friendship are as simple as the staggered exchange of a thirst-quenching drink, more often what is exchanged is unlike rather than like. It is in understanding the equivalence of value, regardless of the unlikeness of what is offered, that the heart's imagination, or the will to friendship, is most deeply tested.

We must each expect reciprocity in our relationship. We must have the opportunity and the ability to give and receive reciprocally for the relationship to be, to become, or to remain a friendship. Without reciprocity or the opportunity for it in the imaginable future, a disequilibrium or inequality develops. When there is not or is no longer equality in a relationship, it is no longer a friendship.

Equality is measured along many axes: mutual giving of pleasure, nurturance, and other support; mutual vulnerability; and so forth. We must give each other what we need and want, and learn how to receive from each other. We must serve and be served by each other in our relationship. Further we must understand the difference between being served by and serving each other—and being served by the relationship. Friendship is *not* just mutual back scratching although, at a basic level, mutual relieving of discomfort and giving of pleasure is part of friendship.

Women living in the patriarchy (and where else has there been for women to live lately?) now have and traditionally have had little access to material goods or to the most accepted medium of exchange in the patriarchal economy—that is, money. All women have had the common experience of being exploited (although, like the archetype of friendship with its infinite variety of contents, exploitation is also infinitely variable), of having their personal resources claimed or rejected by agents of the patriarchy without recompense or reciprocity. Friends, therefore, must always take care to acknowledge the value of what is exchanged between or among them, what is given and what is received, if they are to have an honorable relationship in which each woman is allowed to transcend the ways in which she is (de)valued by and in her role as a female in the patriarchy.

In each story in this book, the issue of reciprocity is engaged directly. We are not interested, in this book, in what becomes of the relationships or the participants after friendship ends. We are interested here in the friendships—how reciprocal friendships start and are maintained, how they vary at different times in our lives, how they are threatened and are reinforced—and in the rituals and patterns of women's friendships.

Story Clusters

The great number of stories about women's friendships indicates the centrality of the subject in women's writing. Some of the stories in this collection, which have been selected from a preliminary collection of more than seventy-five stories, have survived through many years as minor classics of particular periods or genres, such as the often anthologized "Miss Tempy's Watchers" by Jewett. Others have not seen print since their original publication, such as Child's "The Neighbour-in-Law." But regardless of their publication history and the history of their literary critical reputation, it is clear that they are part of the same thematic tradition in women's literature.

These stories cluster in my memory and imagination. They serve as magnets to which other stories seem drawn, each elaborating aspects of the theme spotlighted or alluded to in the centering stories. Ultimately, in the process of choosing which stories to include from among the many I gathered, each centering story has become a representative of a number that I have not included but might have.

The story clusters in this collection overlap: many of the stories are part of more than one cluster of stories. Not only does each story exceed what we can know about it by thinking of it in the context of a small number of stories that are "like it" in some important way, each story is more than what we can know about it by its membership in more than one cluster of stories. Each story is rich enough to yield multiple readings. Each is unique and is also part of a rich tradition. So little time, so many stories. I am glad they are short and I can read so many.

> When Audre Lorde, speaking of racism, states: "I urge each one of us to reach down into that deep place of knowledge inside herself and touch that terror and loathing of any difference that lives there." I am driven to do so because of the passion for women that lives in my body. . . . Sometimes for me "that deep place of knowledge" Audre refers to seems like an endless reservoir of pain, where I must continually unravel damage done to me. It is a calculated system of damage, intended to ensure our separation from other women, but particularly those we learned to see as most different from ourselves and therefore, most fearful. The women whose pain we do not want to see as our own. Call it racism, class oppression, men, or dyke-baiting, the system thrives.
>
> I mourn the friends and lovers I have lost to this damage. I mourn the women whom I have betrayed with my own ignorance, my own fear.[2]

In "A Bed for the Night," by Yezierska, Repplier's "Sin," Bruno's "The Feeder," Phelps's "At Bay," and Wharton's "Friends," women extend helping hands to each other across the boundaries between "good" women and "bad" women[3] or "successful" women and "unsuccessful" women. In Patton's "A Nice Name" Josephine does not know she is crossing the color line in her friendship with the intellectually stimulating woman with the nice name; we read the story from the perspective of the white pen pal. We can only speculate about what or if Mrs. Hannah Lee Marshall might have known or guessed or wondered about Josephine, Josephine's color, and Josephine's ideas about race relations when she wrote her first letter. We *know* that it never crossed Josephine's mind that her correspondent might have been a woman of color. It is in our speculations about what Mrs. Hannah Lee Marshall might have been thinking that we learn the most about our own attitudes about racism. In "In the Laundry Room" Mildred reaches across the color line to extend a hand of friendship to a racist white woman. She understands not only the deadly implications of racism in *her* life, but also those in the *white* woman's life: she has been distracted by her racism from the ways in which she is exploited as a woman and a worker. Thereby, she has been distracted from building coalitions with her most natural allies. Reaching across the boundaries that conspire to separate women from each other is always a radical act; radical acts are costly. It seems from these seven stories that a cost of these radical acts can be the friendships themselves: they often don't last.

As in so many stories and so many of our lives, women recognize the lifesaving value of friendship: the absence of loving nurturance reduces the chance for survival; its presence enhances the likelihood.[4] Naylor's "Etta Mae Johnson," Paley's "Friends," Cooper's "A Jewel for a Friend," and Phelps's "At Bay" explore the ways in which heterosexual women sustain each other with their friendship through the ups and downs of their relationships with men. In "At Bay" and "Etta Mae Johnson" one woman helps another survive and maintain self-esteem within the traditional heterosexual, patriarchal framework in which one of the women does not question her need or impulse to give a man or men priority in her life and the other woman does not question her friend's priorities. None of these four stories challenges the social expectation that women will play the various roles assigned to them by patriarchal custom and law—they give themselves and give first priority to men—but each of these stories makes clear that the women know they cannot survive on what men give back. These are stories of mutually enabled survival, not stories of defiance or rebellion—except for the fact that survival under the conditions of these women's lives is an act of defiance.

Gale's "Nobody Sick, Nobody Poor," Patton's "A Nice Name," and Paley's "Friends" are all stories in which friendships are shared by groups of women. Each group has a long history that has meant many things to each of the participants as, over time, her own life, needs, and interests have changed. In each story, we are given some hint of at least some of those changes both in individual lives and in the friendship group.

In the "friendships among" stories, we can spot women in the different roles that sociologists and psychologists predict will populate any group: the leader, the dissident, the clown, the follower, the peacemaker, the comforter, and so forth. It is interesting to see women take on these different roles as the circumstances of their lives change and are rearranged. As we follow the women of Gale's Friendship Village through the stages of organizing for Thanksgiving—planning the meal, imagining the needs of the expected guests, preparing the food and the table—we watch them exchange the roles within the group with the same ease and facility borne of habit and understanding that they use in handing back and forth the platters.

"Miss Tempy's Watchers" enables us to see that women's friendships and the reciprocal nurturance they entail are "negotiable commodities": they can be "willed" or bequeathed. If we understand friendship and nurturance as negotiable commodities then our definition of personal wealth, intangible property, indeed, of gross national product must be expanded.

Patton's "A Nice Name" and Childress's "In the Laundry Room" each portray *two* kinds of women's friendships. Intrinsic to all friendships is mutual reflection for the friends of images of themselves they cherish, visions of their best selves. Because we are complex and multi-faceted beings, most of us have and need a variety of friends to reflect to us the best images of different facets of ourselves. That is certainly the case with Patton's central character. The physical comfort, shared memories, and social community or sense of belonging shared by the central character with her old friends provide her with one kind of positive self-image: a woman with a place and a role in her community, someone valued over time by people she values, a woman who is comfortable in and with the world she has always known. The intellectual and creative stimulation and support from her new friend provides another kind of positive self-image: a woman of intellectual and creative energy, a woman growing and coming into the fullness of her adult powers, a woman unafraid to soar into new worlds. Each kind of friendship provides her with an image of herself that she likes—but in this story those images conflict with each other. The conflict between the two types of friendship is highlighted by the contrast between the group of white women friends and the friendship between one Southern, white, presumably Anglo-Saxon, Protestant woman and one African-American woman. The racism operating on the surface is so blatant, shocking, painful, and ugly, and it is so obvious that the pen pals' friendship is violated by racism, that it is easy to overlook the conflict between the two types of friendship portrayed in this story: one supports the status quo and the other encourages change; one is rooted in the past, the other is growing in the present. Likewise, the friendship between Mildred and Marge frames Mildred's story of her encounter with a racist white houseworker with whom she has tried to establish a friendship in preference to "popping" her in the mouth. Both of these friendships, in Childress's and Patton's stories, evoke the issues of stability and change.

I was distracted during my first reading of Child's "Neighbour-in-Law" by the overlay of the language of Christian piety,[5] but I could not put the story out of my mind. I had never read a story like this.[6] There is no *reason* for these women to become friends—and realizing that there was no reason made me realize that with other friendships between and among women, there often *is* some reason relating either to the circumstances of the friendship's beginning or to the back-scratching dimension of the relationship.

When we say that there is a reason for a friendship to begin we are acknowledging an ulterior motive or a practical concern perhaps being joined to a spontaneous emotional response that, when examined, results in a feeling that this new friendship "makes sense." In "The Neighbour-in-Law" there is neither a reason for the friendship nor a spontaneous emotional attraction between the two women. It is the utter "apracticality," the complete absence of any of the usual motivations, that makes this story of the beginning of a friendship between two women so unusual—and forces us to reflect on the reasons behind our own friendships.

Life Stages

> My own friendships have been different at different stages of my life— and my desire for them as well. I have wanted/needed lesser or greater intimacy and fewer or more friends at different periods.[7]

Two categories of life stages exist: infancy, puberty, menarche, and menopause are *biological* life stages; childhood, adolescence, maturity, and middle and old age are *sociological, historically determined* life stages.

Although the study of the development of infants, children, and adolescents has been going on for generations, in recent years studies of the stages of *adult* development have burgeoned. Biologists have tried to understand how people change over their lifetimes.

Historians and sociologists have been investigating the relationships between what seem to be biologically determined life stages and the philosophical ideas and historical circumstances that influence "human nature."

Short fiction tends to focus on biological stages, although there are also many stories about characters whose "stage of development" can be described more accurately from sociological rather than the biological perspectives. It is revealing to look at how one particular theme or issue in fiction looks different or similar when that theme is portrayed in the lives of characters of different ages.

Are friendships between and among women different at different stages of our lives? If yes, how? Are the pressures to isolate or separate us from each other different at different times in our lives? Do the forces that draw women together, the kinds of activities, feelings, and bonds we are likely to share, differ at different stages in our lives? And if there are significant differences at different stages, how are those differences affected by racial, class, cultural, regional, physical ability, and appearance differences among us?

Stories about girlhood friendships are scarce.[8] Agnes Repplier's "Sin," written in 1938, looks at the youngest friends in this collection—preadolescent upper-middle-class convent girls at the turn of the century. Sui Sin Far's story, "The Heart's Desire," from 1912, which is really a parable, can also be looked at as a story of childhood friendship.

Several stories in this collection look at friendships between young women at puberty, seen as a crucial life stage throughout history and across cultures and classes.[9] Deloris Harrison's "A Friend for a Season" portrays both the intensity of friendship and the disruptions to which friendship is vulnerable. Paula Gunn Allen's "They Make Their Climb" explores fears the young women have internalized about intense friendships that threaten to seduce pubescent women from loyalty to the patriarchy.

There are fewer stories about adolescence than about pubescent women, but the adolescent stories are more varied. Historians tell us that unlike the biological life stage of puberty, adolescence—a socially defined period between the comparative freedom from responsibility and powerlessness of childhood to the comparative responsibility and power of adulthood—is a social invention that changes over time in one or both of two ways: its duration and the time when it is believed to begin and end.

The adolescent stories by Phelps, Parker, and Yezierska are about courtship, first jobs, dreams of the future, and the initial economic struggles to survive without family support. They are adolescent stories insofar as we equate adolescence with the teenage years, but they were written between 1840 and 1940 and are about activities not usually associated with adolescence in the 1990s. Instead, they are stories about young adulthood, about that period when a post-pubescent (i.e., sexually mature) young person begins adult life.

The choices made at this time in women's lives are of permanent importance. Their friendships are forged and tested as they examine and explore together the choices that seem to be open to them or the choices they dream about—choices that, once made, will amost inevitably lead them in separate directions, away from each other.

A large number of stories about this period are written by writers from racial and ethnic minorities and other marginal groups. The illusion cherished by young women of this age that real choices exist for them makes these stories especially poignant. The characters are optimistic, yet the authors infuse the narratives with their own sense of futility. They know that the choices aren't real or free, and so the tone tends to range from ironic to tragic.

A combination of the consequences of these choices and the often bitter knowledge of being trapped by them concerns the characters in the stories of adult life or middle age. These friendships often explore collegiality, coalition, confrontation, and assertion. And the stories about friendships between women in old age tell of reconciliation, evaluation, and, again, assertion.

It is often at this time of life that women recognize that in their early adult lives they were not making real choices, not truly *their* choices. For instance, the question was never "How shall I live my life?" or even "Shall I marry?" but "*Whom* shall I marry;" not "Shall I be a mother," but "How will I be a *good* mother?" Like cows being driven through chutes, each chute narrower than the one before, until they walk, single file, into the slaughterhouse, girls finally walk down the aisle toward adulthood.

Adolescent women often prove their friendship by helping each other "get" the men they want. They enable their friends to attract and hold desirable males without regard to whether or not the male will support or disrupt their friendship. In the early days of the women's liberation movement, there was much talk of how we had betrayed each other at the behest of men, with the encouragement of men, to get a man, and so on. Stories were exchanged about the last minute cancellations of plans with a girl friend because a date called. Stories were told of best friends whose "lifelong" friendships ended with the wedding day of one of them. It is of this life stage that Phelps writes in "At Bay"—and just think of the images that title calls forth!

Some Dimensions of Friendships

Duration

The durations of friendships are explored in these stories. We often romanticize and delimit friendship, imagining that it is "real" only if it lasts a lifetime. "Friends for a Season" is about two African-American adolescent girls who share a friendship for one summer. Although the relationship is of short duration, there is no question that it is an important and authentic friendship. In "Joint Owners in Spain" two old New England women negotiate a friendship that will last, presumably, for the rest of their lives. (And there is irony in that, because the friendship becomes the only way they *can* survive; it is a truce transformed, a prison made a sanctuary.) The story by Anzia Yezierska is about a friendship between two young women that lasts only for one night. There are stories by Agnes Repplier and Paula Gunn Allen about friendships between girls, begun in childhood and ended in one way or another by puberty. Alice Brown's story is about a friendship begun in old age, Child's about a friendship begun in middle age, and Paley's about a group of friendships begun in young adulthood that look to be lifetime commitments. And there are Jewett's and Cooper's wonderful stories about friendships begun early in life and carried beyond the grave. In "A Nice Name" a new, short-lived friendship transforms the meaning and value of a set of lifelong friendships. Clearly, the coupling of duration with the ultimate value of a friendship is inappropriate.

One of the classic homophobic remarks used to dismiss the authenticity or seriousness of relationships between members of lesbian or gay couples is that they don't last. The implication is, of course, that relationships that don't last don't have value.

Relationships between adolescents often don't last. Adolescence is considered "just a stage" in life on the way to some other, final stage that is more real and more serious. Lingering in this devalued stage of life is thought to be either sick or bad, and whatever suffering an adolescent experiences is neither to be pitied nor ameliorated lest such kindness encourage further lingering.

As an adolescent I suffered both chronic and acute emotional pain because relationships didn't last. I have never again suffered so terribly, not because my adult relationships have always lasted, or *should* always have lasted, but because I have learned to survive loss, I have learned that I can find and cultivate other relationships and other kinds of relationships when I am ready.

But the romances and the friendships of my adolescence still matter to me. The lessons, the wounds, the sense of joy and terror, the memory of sky-obscuring intensity—none of it goes away and I remain the person who was forged in those relationships.

Are the only factors affecting the duration of a relationship immanent in the couple? Unless we are sociologically inclined we often assume this, without considering such factors as joblessness, poverty, illness, family pressures, and other kinds of social stress. Unless we are politically conscious, we fail to consider heterosexism, racism, classism, looksism, ageism, ablism, anti-Semitism, and all the other forces that drive wedges between groups and between individuals.

For a relationship to continue, a balance between the centripetal forces holding people together and the centrifugal forces that force people apart must be achieved. Proscribed relationships experience no pressure from society to continue, to heal rifts, to grow and deepen, or to take pride through anniversary parties in their duration. People in socially valued relationships not only are rewarded for staying together, the partners are usually subject to negative consequences if their relationships end.

Intensity/Depth

Obviously, friendships vary in their intensity and depth. We cannot say a friendship is not a friendship because it is not like another friendship, not as intense, not as deep, or, conversely, so much deeper or more intense and satisfying than one has known before or been led to expect a friendship might be. Certainly the friendships in "A Nice Name" differ in these respects, as they differ in duration. The friendships among the women in "Nobody Poor, Nobody Sick" differ in intensity, depth, and the degree and kinds of satisfactions derived—just as there are differences in the duration of the friendships, the propinquity of the friends, the rhythm of their friendships, the frequency of their interactions, and so forth.

Settings

The settings for these stories vary in many ways. Settings include not only the regional or geographical environment, not only the urban, small town, or rural nature of the human and natural setting of the characters' lives, but also the cultural or ethnic, class, or racial circumstances.

In terms of regional environment, we move from the big city setting of Dorothy Parker's New York City story "The Standard of Living," to the small New England towns of Jewett's and Wharton's stories, to the midwestern suburb of Bruno's "The Feeder," to the southwestern hills of Allen's "They Make Their Climb," and from the palace of Eaton's story to the ghettos of Naylor's and Yezierska's. While variations in the setting of a friendship between women may influence the kinds of activities they share and affect the frequency with which they meet and the conditions under which those meetings occur, those different settings and the differences they produce in the outward circumstances of the relationship do not seem to have any detectable influence on the nature of the friendships.

Yezierska's, Bruno's, and Sui Sin Far's stories remind us that all American literature, except that by American Indians, is written by immigrants and their descendants, who came, willingly or not, from all over the world, bringing with them the diversity of their native cultures and the similarity of their experience as newcomers.[10]

Important Differences

The real differences between friendships seem most closely connected to life stages and to the relationship of the friends to the patriarchy. If what appears to be a friendship supports the status quo—that is, reinforces the power of the patriarchy—it is socially recognized and valuable. If the friendship enables two women to survive hard lives in the patriarchy without giving out, up, or in before their usefulness has ended, it is an invisible but permitted relationship. If the relationship is that of comrades to the death in a revolutionary struggle to achieve not just autonomy, survival, and some pleasure despite the racist heteropatriarchy, but also radical social change and an end to oppression, then it is a proscribed relationship.

Each friendship women enter has the potential to be any one of the three kinds of relationships and most partake of more than one of these kinds, regardlesss of duration—just a short exchange "In the Laundry Room" or the sharing of "A Bed for a Night," or if one is just "A Friend for a Season," or if the friendship survives as long as one of the friends survives, as in Paley's "Friends" or Cooper's "A Jewel for a Friend."

Friendship's Beginnings

How do some people have no friends? There are always wonderful people appearing on the horizon.[11]

The stories in this collection focus on different stages not only in the lives of the characters but also in the friendships. Some stories tell about friendships beginning: "The Neighbour-in-Law," "Joint Owners in Spain," "A Nice Name," and "In the Laundry Room" are some of these.

Traditionally many friendships begin because they reinforce the status quo, the patriarchy. Women often become friends with the wives of their husbands' friends and business associates[12] and with the women who are members of their husband's extended or immediate family.[13] "The Feeder," by Maria Bruno, represents those stories about women who have the opportunity to become friends because of a connection between their husbands.

In "The Neighbour-in-Law" two women become friends because, once the narrator settles into her half of the house (as in Alice Brown's "Joint Owners in Spain") they cannot avoid their proximity. Neither "belongs" to a man: one is a widow and the other is single. They aren't related by blood or by marriage. They live where they live because of their own choices.

If two women find themselves in that situation, they can choose freely to befried one another, they can ignore each other, or they can become enemies. Do they meet and see if they like each other? Wait for the electricity, a thunderbolt of recognition that tells them "there is something between us"?

In this story two women decide and learn to be friends without extenuating circumstances. They don't befriend each other to please

or benefit anyone other than themselves, and there are no thunder-
bolts. Each acts selfishly, although it seems on first reading that only
one acts selfishly. Each acts in her own best interests, without regard
to the patriarchy or anyone else's values, benefitting only herself in
her free choice of the other.

The Maintenance of Friendships

Nutritional Economics

> The personal is political: . . . Networks of love and support are crucial to
> our ability as women to work in a hostile world where we are not in fact
> expected to survive. . . . Frequently the networks of love and support
> that enable politically and professionally active women to function inde-
> pendently and intensively consist largely of other women.[14]

One consistent characteristic of women's friendships *always seen in
women's friendship stories* is mutuality, or reciprocity. Women friends
in women's stories are sensitive to the nuances of how we can and do
give to and take from each other. A constant, subtle system of exchange goes on all the time. Most women friends reciprocate when
and as they can and, even when they cannot reciprocate, recognize
the debt. They do not steal from each other, they do not plunder
each other's resources, and *they recognize honestly what constitutes
resources.*

In women's friendship stories, if one woman needs to take more
than she can give—whether she needs material help or the healing
of speaking to a sympathetic listener—she does not think she has
taken nothing from the woman who has given to her. That isn't always true in life,[15] but *the stories demonstrate over and over again
the ethical lesson that nurturance is learned behavior, is work, and is
negotiable.*

We see in one story after another that nurturance is a commodity.
Whether it is Miss Tempy bequeathing to her two friends each other
as nurturers or the nameless prostitute in "A Bed for a Night" literally feeding a starving woman or Parker's two women who fantasize
together about "The Standard of Living" they would like to achieve
and in so doing feed each other's fantasy lives. Women's friendships
often provide women with the necessary encouragement and the
strength to dream. The narrator in "Hunger" sharing what little she
has with an old friend who has never been able before to be quite a

friend because of the previous power imbalance between the two is yet another illustration of nurturance and the ethic of reciprocity.

In the economy created by women who do not have access to material wealth in the patriarchy, the system of exchange is a carefully worked out but undocumented reality. Women reinforce a sense of personal dignity and autonomy by giving to each other and taking from each other reciprocally.

Women's Friendships and Food

For women, the need and desire to nurture each other is not pathological but redemptive.[16]

When women feed each other and eat together, women affirm each other's right to live, to have appetites, and to take up space in the world. This most material and practical way of nurturing each other—feeding each other, sharing food—is so emblematic of women's friendships that it has elements of the ritualistic about it.

Most of the stories include food sharing and the offering of food: the staving off of literal starvation in "Hunger," "A Bed for the Night," and "The Feeder" and, indirectly, in Wharton's "Friends"; ritualistic celebrations of appetite in "Nobody Sick, Nobody Poor" and Newman's "One *Shabbos* Evening"; coffee klatching in Paley's "Friends" and "In the Laundry room"; the offering of pie in "The Neighbour-in-Law"; the repeated feeding and partaking ritual in Arnold's "Let Me See."

In "Let Me See" all three reciprocity requirements are met. However, what is exchanged is not what is wanted. Lela gives the narrator food she never really liked. In doing so, she gives her the gift of being known—although she is known ineptly. She is given the gift of being nurtured—although it is not the nurturance she would prefer. What kind of friendship is this? This is a friendship between emotionally clumsy but well-intentioned people. They are like two people who love the idea of dancing, feel the music in their bones, but always step on each other's feet because they are clumsy. Still, it's better to dance and tangle your feet than it is to sit alone, never to dance; and better every day to honor your friend by feeding her what you think is her favorite breakfast because it is what she ordered on the day you first met. It is better to honor that first meeting with this meal than not to honor and commemorate, not to value and respect, not to want to please. So it's the wrong meal. Too bad. Big deal.

On the other hand, isn't it important to be able to say to your lover, "The really sensitive spot is a little to the left"?

Friendship's Endings

I have been musing quite a bit on women's friendship and women friends breaking up—which is exactly like lovers breaking up, only the pain seems more deep, more complex.[17]

Death ends the friendships between the woman who dies and her friends, but the occasion of her dying reinforces the other women's friendships in Grace Paley's "Friends"; the death of one friend leads to the beginning of another friendship in "Miss Tempy's Watchers"; and the ritual attendance on the grave of one friend by another portrays the survival of friendship after death in "A Jewel for a Friend." In these stories, the dying or death is attended with rituals. When friendship ends with a death, the women's friendships are reaffirmed through rituals of mourning. So, the endings of friendships by death are the least conclusive endings; there is always the sense that friendship outlasts the friends themselves, and will continue.

But friendships *do* end as the result of social interventions, as in "A Nice Name," "A Bed for the Night," "They Make Their Climb," and "Sin." Conditions have remained the same for women during the period that separates these stories—women police themselves and other women to enforce the will of the heteropatriarchy. The fear of lesbian love, the proscription of relationships that exclude men, associations between women across the divisions between us that undergird the patriarchal social order—race, class, age, and so forth—all these friendships are stressed to death by women, but it is patriarchal property values that are being reinforced.

In stories where unilateral nonreciprocal sacrifice is required to save a friend from a dire immediate future, the friendships end: "The Sin," Edith Wharton's "Friends," and "A Bed for the Night." Only the friendship in "At Bay" survives this threat. Friendships end because there can no longer be reciprocity: the cost paid by one for the other's safety or survival is too great. Friendships cannot be maintained between women where there is not the potential for future reciprocity.

That doesn't mean that there aren't times when one of the friends gives more nurturance or support—either or both material and emotional—than the other, as in "The Feeder," but the imbalance is temporary and is never one that cannot in time be righted.

Friendships between women often end because patriarchal ideas about propriety and status result in social inequality between women. Women often seem unable to sustain a friendship when one of them is "in" and the other is "out," or one "good" and the other "bad," or one "special" and the other "normal": the prostitute and the virtuous woman; the daughter of an apparently successfully married mother and the daughter of a divorced and therefore deviant mother; the woman who is "successful" as a woman (does well at a "woman's job" such as teaching, has a man's stamp of approval—an engagement ring) and the woman who is a "failure" as a woman (poor, jobless, unmarried); the woman with a "bad" reputation and the one with an unsullied reputation; the woman with a disability and the temporarily able-bodied woman.

"At Bay" is unusual in that both issues that often end friendships arise—nonreciprocity and unequal status—and yet the relationship does not end. When a woman is compromised by a man and by rumors, the social code dictates that her women friends abandon her or suffer her fate—dishonor and social isolation. The narrator, instead of abandoning her friend, both continues in the public role of her friend, thereby jeopardizing her own reputation, and further risks her personal reputation by confronting the man. The nonreciprocity in this story has led more than one reader to suggest that perhaps it is a covert lesbian story, a story of unrequited, sacrificial, romantic love rather than a friendship story. What do you think?

Occasional and Ritual Stories

The body is the image relator. In ritual, we *embody* and activate images of the archetypal, the eternal feminine, the Goddess. Images of power, of transformation, of harmony, and of duality. One woman empowering another. The crucial exchange of gifts. I cross the circle to give you something; you cross the circle to give her something. And so on until we have all changed places. Power held is powerless; power given is power for all. In feminist ritual we maintain a center of which we are all aware. It is our collective heart which beats there. We hold together, our center endures. Even the most painful separation, the dispersal which is feared but necessary, cannot disconnect us from that ritual circle. Once that circle is created and affirmed, chaos is subdued. We survive. We thrive.[18]

Certain themes are written about so frequently by women writers that it is as if the writing of these stories is a ritual—something that women have to write in order to be writers. These are ritual stories in two ways: the writing of them is a literary woman's ritual, and what is portrayed in the stories are the rituals of women's lives. If we look at these women's stories as ritual stories, we are alerted to look for those interchanges and transformations that Kay Turner describes as essential to women's rituals.

Some rituals of friendship described in these stories most readers will recognize as rituals from their own lives. What are these rituals? Are they the same across time and in spite as the differences among us? How much of the difference in these rituals can be accounted for by the cultural, racial, or generational differences among us and how much can be accounted for by our individuality and our individual relationships?

When popular culture scholars look at a genre work, they ask themselves how much of what is there is typical of the genre (that is, what are the *conventions* of the genre) and how much is attributable to the creativity of the artist (that is, what are the *inventions* in the work). When feminist scholars look at women's literature, they might ask themselves how much of what they are reading is the writer's portrayal of women's reality in the patriarchy and how much reflects the author's own imagination. Traditionally, literary critics look at what is unique in a work of art as if that were the primary measure of its right to be considered meritorious and the major element of interest to a critic. But if we overlook what is typical in order to concentrate entirely or primarily on what is unique, then we miss at least half of what is important about the work. We must understand what is alike among works of art and also understand how those similarities are similar to our lived experience as individuals and as women.

If we look at these stories with the above questions in mind, we see certain elements—certain actions, exchanges, and crises—recurring. It is in those recurring elements that we find the typical rituals of women's friendships.

Native writers write out of tribal traditions, and into them. They, like oral storytellers, work within a literary tradition that is at base connected to ritual and beyond that to tribal metaphysics or mysticism. What has been experienced over the ages mystically and communally—with individual experiences fitting within that overarching pattern—forms the basis for tribal aesthetics and therefore of tribal literatures.[19]

In Western literary history, the writing that is composed out of the tradition connected to community rituals is called occasional literature. Although there is a history of cultural critics taking seriously the visual, musical, and even poetic artworks composed out of this tradition, occasional short stories have been given short shrift. Nevertheless, there is an enormous body of short stories known as occasional stories and these stories have much to tell us about who we are and how we live.

Occasional stories celebrate or commemorate an event or a holiday designated on a regularly repeating basis. Such days include the beginning of a new phase of the lunar year, such as the vernal equinox; historically significant days, such as Thanksgiving or the Wounded Knee massacre; the beginning of the season of harvest, such as Succoth; a major transition in the life of a group, such as Memorial Day or the anniversary of the ratification of the Women's Suffrage Amendment; the birthday or the day of death of a cultural or political hero or a mythical or religious figure, such as Martin Luther King, Jr., Day or Susan B. Anthony Day or Christmas.

The celebrations of these occasions have developed a commercial component. These occasions also offer the opportunity for the creating and sharing of public art. Often, the commercial and the artistic elements merge, resulting in commissions for and the creation of important and lasting works of art—such as an Easter mass or illustrations for a Pesach Hagadah. There has always been a great demand for occasional writing in the popular periodicals. More May magazines will be bought if the issue has a good Mother's Day story. Even more issues are sold if that occasional story is written by a famous and beloved writer. The most famous writers are paid more than usual for occasional stories, even if they are mediocre. But even with relaxed standards, there are still never enough occasional stories or poems by famous writers, so the occasional story market is open to new, unknown writers.

Because women have had so few opportunities to earn an adequate living, the few jobs open to women that offer the chance to strike it rich, to work in pleasant and safe circumstances, and to have flex-time have been eagerly pursued by a great many women.

Writing was and is one of these good jobs. Although many writing women might be first attracted to the profession of letters by romantic myths about being an artist, those who stick with it are usually writing out of economic motivation at least as much as any other.

So, since there have always been many women writing out of economic motivation and since the market for occasional literature has always been both large and lucrative, women have written an enormous amount of occasional literature. They have, in fact, been chief among those who developed the occasional story as we have come to know it in this country.

Stories about Thanksgiving are second only to those about Christmas in terms of the welcome offered them by the literary marketplace. It also seems to be an especially favored occasion for women to write about. "Nobody Sick, Nobody Poor" is among the most provocative Thanksgiving stories ever written and yet it is also typical. Women's Thanksgiving stories are seldom patriotic or connected in any way with the historical first Thanksgiving; most often the emphasis is on assessing or counting blessings and the expression of gratitude for those blessings. There is usually an ironic twist.

In occasional stories, the occasion may be either in the foreground or in the background. In the best such stories, the occasion seems to be in the background, but it is inextricably interwoven with the foreground story. In other words, what happens could only have happened in the atmosphere generated by that particular occasion.

Occasional stories offer writers the opportunity to be more philosophical, didactic, moralistic, or fabulous than they can be at other more ordinary, nonritualistic times. It is often in the occasional stories that we find the clearest statements of a writer's beliefs, attitudes, hopes, and vision, the clearest focus on their major social or moral concerns.

The three stories about death—Paley's "Friends," "Miss Tempy's Watchers," and "A Jewel for a Friend"—are also occasional stories: they are mourning stories. In each there is a summing up of the past, a sort of concluding assessment (it was good, that friendship, that woman, us together), and a commitment by the living to keep on living. A mourning of loss, a reaffirmation of life.

"One *Shabbos* Evening" is an occasional story about two friends sharing the single most important ritual of Judaism, the weekly welcoming and celebrating of the Sabbath. This ritual is traditionally centered in and the focus of family life; and these Jewish lesbians who do not live in traditional heterosexual nuclear families expand the dimensions of friendship by centering their friendship in the sharing and transformation of this traditional ritual.

Women have written many occasional stories because of the reasons enumerated above. They have also written innumerable women's ritual stories. Among the most interesting stories are the stories that are both. In this collection, all of the stories are ritual stories; five of the stories are occasional stories. *All* of the occasional stories are ritual stories.

Conclusion

It is by now evident to most feminist theorists that female bonding and friendship are at the heart of any transformation of the patriarchy.[20]

In early April 1988, I finished my work on *"May Your Days Be Merry and Bright" and Other Christmas Stories by Women.* After I mailed the manuscript I drove off to Lexington, Kentucky, to the Women Writers' Tenth Annual Conference, where I joined Janet Palmer Mullaney, the founder and editor of *Belles Lettres: A Review of Books by Women.*

At the conference a woman we met invited us for dinner the night that the conference ended. Two others had also been invited, so there were five of us.

The evening was one of celebration—our hostess's thesis had been accepted; it was another woman's birthday; I had completed my new collection of stories; Janet had received a grant to help bring *Belles Lettres* to new readers. Janet and I were also celebrating our new friendship, although we didn't talk about that until the next day.

On the kitchen wall was a framed poster. It read,

Friendship is the comfort, the inexpressible comfort of feeling safe with a person having neither to weigh thoughts nor measure words, but pouring all right out just as they are, chaff and grain together, certain that a faithful hand will take and sift them, keep what is worth keeping, and with a breath of comfort, blow the rest away.

George Eliot

Our hostess had prepared a wonderful meal: barbecued country ribs, fresh asparagus with lemon butter, homemade corn bread, cooked carrots and turnips, and potatoes stewed with tomatoes and basil. We five spent our first hour together in the kitchen, exchanging life histories. We talked about work, love, politics, our favorite books, and our favorite food. We admired our hostess's competence as she prepared our meal. We shared memories of other meals, of other times of food preparation, other recipes.

Then we moved into the dining room and sat down around the table. We ate, the food was wonderful, and our conversation flowed.

By the end of the meal we realized that we could have stayed together and continued talking for a very, very long time. There seemed to be no end to our conversations, but we were tired and so we parted.

We may never see each other again, certainly not in the same configuration. On that night, however, we were friends. We enacted certain ritual exchanges that we all recognized as acts of friendship. We shared personal histories, stories of our work (and we are each passionately engaged in work that we hope will improve the world), laughter, memories, ambitions, and food. During our evening together, we were intense, we were hilarious, we were sensual, we were sentimental, we were vulnerable, we were strong. We shared our worry and anger about all the kinds of oppression. We amused and admired each other; we nurtured each other. We each knew what friendship meant, although we did not attempt to define it. That night we befriended each other; we all knew how to be friends together.

Reliving that experience later, I realized that everything that happened that evening is in one of these stories; and each one of these stories is about what went on that evening.

I want us all to be friends. I congratulate us on knowing how to be friends. I applaud us for recovering women's stories about women's friendships.

NOTES

Preface
1. Carol P. Christ, *Diving Deep and Surfacing: Women Writers on Spiritual Quest* (Boston: Beacon Press, 1980).
2. London: Methuen, Pandora Press.

Introduction
1. Betty Burnett, letter to the author, June 1988.

Carolyn L. Karcher, "The Neighbour-in-Law" by Lydia Maria Child
1. Lydia Maria Child, *Lydia Maria Child: Selected Letters, 1817–1880,* ed. Milton Meltzer and Patricia G. Holland (Amherst: University of Massachusetts Press, 1982), 443.
2. Ibid., 426.
3. Ibid., 13.
4. Ibid., 506.

Carol Farley Kessler, "At Bay" by Elizabeth Stuart Phelps
1. "At Bay" first appeared in *Harper's New Monthly Magazine* 34 (May 1867), 780–87.
2. *Atlantic Monthly* 7 (April 1861).
3. *Atlantic Monthly* 5 (May–July 1863), 11–12.
4. Some additional information may be helpful in understanding the story. A "horse-car" was like a horse-drawn bus. The war referred to in the story is the Civil War; the story is set in the early 1860s. "The car" into which Dan puts Sarah is not a bus or trolley, but more likely a railroad car, her "check" being for her luggage.
5. *Atlantic Monthly* 21 (March 1868).

Barbara A. White, "Joint Owners in Spain" by Alice Brown
1. For references to Maria G. Reed, see especially Brown's letters in the collections of the American Antiquarian Society, Pennsylvania State University, the University of New Hampshire, and the Beinecke Library, Yale University.

2. *Alice Brown: Author of the New Novel, "The Prisoner"* (New York: Macmillan, 1916): 8.

3. A copy of Brown's will may be found at the library of the Boston Athenaeum.

4. Alice Brown, p. 2, 4. Alice Brown, *The Author of "Dear Old Templeton" Interviews Herself* (New York: Macmillan, 1927): 2. Subsequent short quotations from Brown are taken from the latter work.

5. Nancy Sahli, "Smashing: Women's Relationships Before the Fall," *Chrysalis* 8 (Summer 1979): 25. The letter referred to is quoted in Dorothea Walker, *Alice Brown* (Boston: Twayne, 1974): 163.

6. See especially three articles by Susan A. Toth: "Alice Brown (1857–1948)," *American Literary Realism* 5 (Spring 1972): 134–43; "Sarah Orne Jewett and Friends: A Community of Interest," *Studies in Short Fiction* 9 (1972): 233–41; and "A Forgotten View from Beacon Hill: Alice Brown's New England Short Stories," *Colby Library Quarterly* 10 (March 1973): 1–17. Dorothea Walker's full-length study *Alice Brown* appeared in 1974 but is very general and introductory.

7. Bobby Ellen Kimbel, ed. (Detroit: Gale Research, 1989): 21–31.

Leah Hackleman, "Friends" by Edith Wharton

1. For a discussion of the Wharton-Norton correspondence, see chapter 2 in Susan Goodman's *Edith Wharton's Women: Friends and Rivals* (Hanover: University Press of New England, 1990): 29–47. Wharton's friendships with lively, intellectual women have yet to be fully examined by critics or biographers. Two important biographies are R. W. B. Lewis, *Edith Wharton: A Biography* (New York: Fromm International, 1975) and Cynthia Griffin Woolf, *A Feast of Words: The Triumph of Edith Wharton* (Oxford: Oxford University Press, 1977). For feminist approaches to Wharton's work and life, see Elizabeth Ammons, *Edith Wharton's Argument with America* (Athens: University of Georgia Press, 1980) and Shari Benstock, *Women of the Left Bank: Paris, 1900–1940* (Austin: University of Texas Press, 1988).

2. Cited in Lewis, *Edith Wharton*, 527.

3. *Youth's Companion* 74 (August 23, 30, 1900).

Virginia Cox, "Nobody Sick, Nobody Poor" by Zona Gale

1. In preparing this headnote I have consulted the following works: *Notable American Women*, Vol. 1; *American Women Writers*, Vol. 2: 97–98; August Derleth, *A Still Small Voice* (New York: D. Appleton Co., 1940); Harold Simonson, *Zona Gale* (New York: Twayne U.S. Artist Series, 1960). Zona Gale's collections of short stories, none of which is in print, include these volumes: *Friendship Village* (New York: Macmillan, 1908); *Friendship Village Love Stories* (New York: Macmillan, 1914); *Peace in Friendship Village* (New York: D. Appleton-Century Co., 1919); *Yellow Gentians and Blue* (New York: D. Appleton & Co., 1927); *Bridal Pond* (New York: Alfred Knopf, 1930); *Old-Fashioned Tales* (New York: D. Appleton-Century Co., 1935).

Amy Ling, "The Heart's Desire" by Sui Sin Far

1. Sui Sin Far [pseud. of Edith Eaton], *Mrs. Spring Fragrance* (Chicago: McClurg, 1912).

2. Sui Sin Far [pseud. of Edith Eaton], "Leaves from the Mental Portfolio of an Eurasian," *Independent* 66 (January 21, 1909): 125–32.

3. [Winnifred Eaton], *Me, a Book of Remembrance* (New York: Century, 1915).

4. [Winnifred Eaton and Sara Eaton Bosse], *Marion, the Story of an Artist's Model* (New York: Watt, 1916).

5. Rooney, Paul B. [Winnifred Eaton's grandson], a series of letters dating from August 12, 1981, to March 2, 1984 (Toronto, Ontario).

6. Linda Di Biase, "*Mrs. Spring Fragrance* and Seattle's Springtime," *Weekly* (September 10, 1986): 24–26.

7. Other works consulted in preparing this headnote include the following: Sui Sin Far, *Mrs. Spring Fragrance*; S. E. Solberg, "Sui Sin Far/Edith Eaton: First Chinese-American Fictionist," *MELUS* 8, no. 1 (1981): 27–39; Onoto Watanna [pseud. of Winnifred Eaton], *A Japanese Nightingale* (New York: Harper, 1901). Other works by Amy Ling: "Edith Eaton: Pioneer Chinamerican Writer and Feminist," *American Literary Realism* 16, no. 2 (1983): 287–98; "Winnifred Eaton: Ethnic Chameleon and Popular Success," *MELUS* 11, no. 3 (1984): 5–15; "Writers with a Cause: Sui Sin Far and Han Suyin," *Women's Studies International Forum* 9, no. 4 (1986): 411–19.

Sally Ann Drucker, "A Bed for the Night" by Anzia Yezierska

1. *Hungry Hearts* (Salem, N.H.: Arno Press, 1975); *Bread Givers* (New York: Persea Books, 1975); *The Open Cage* (New York: Persea Books, 1979); *Red Ribbon on a White Horse* (New York: Persea Books, 1981); *Hungry Hearts and Other Stories* (New York: Persea Books, 1985).

2. Carol B. Schoen, *Anzia Yezierska* (Schenectady, N.Y.: New College and University Press, Twayne, 1982); Louise Levitas Henriksen, *Anzia Yezierska: A Writer's Life* (New Brunswick, N.J.: Rutgers University Press, 1988).

Lucy M. Freibert, "Sin" by Agnes Repplier

1. Agnes Repplier, *Eight Decades* (Boston: Houghton Mifflin Co., 1937): 7.

2. George S. Stokes, *Agnes Repplier: Lady of Letters* (Philadelphia: University of Pennsylvania Press, 1949): 6.

3. The following are works I consulted in preparing this headnote: Emma Repplier, *Agnes Repplier: A Memoir by Her Niece* (Philadelphia: Dorrance and Co., 1957); Velma Bourgeois Richmond, "Agnes Repplier" in *American Women Writers* 3 (New York: Frederick Unger, 1981): 457–59; John T. Flanagan, "A Distinguished American Essayist," *South Atlantic Quarterly* 44 (April 1945): 162–69. An extensive bibliography of Repplier's writings, along with reviews and criticism of her works, may be found at the University of Pennyslvania Library. Two of her diaries are also located at this library.

Betty Burnett, "Hunger" by Marjorie Worthington

1. Marjorie Worthington, *The Strange World of Willie Seabrook* (New York: Harcourt, Brace & World, 1966): 190.

Trudier Harris, "In the Laundry Room" by Alice Childress

1. 1956; reprinted in 1986 (Boston: Beacon Press) with an introduction by Trudier Harris.

2. Quotations throughout are taken from an interview I conducted with Childress on October 2, 1988.

3. Rosemary Curb, "An Unfashionable Tragedy of American Racism: Alice Childress' *Wedding Band*," *MELUS* 7 (Winter 1980): 57–68.

4. Philadelphia, Penn.: Temple University Press.

Margaret W. Merrill, "A Friend for a Season" by Deloris Harrison

1. "A Friend for a Season" first appeared in *Redbook* 133, no. 4 (August 1969). It was later reprinted in *Out of Our Lives: A Collection of Contemporary Black Fiction,* ed. Quandra Prettyman Stadler (Washington, D.C.: Howard University Press, 1975).

Patricia Clark Smith, "They Make Their Climb" by Paula Gunn Allen

1. Brian Swann and Arnold Krupat, eds., *I Tell You Now: Autobiographical Essays by Native American Writers* (Lincoln: University of Nebraska Press, 1987).

2. San Francisco: Spinsters Ink.

3. *Survival This Way: Interviews with American Indian Poets* (Tucson: University of Arizona Press, 1987).

4. New York: Harper & Row.

5. See, for example, her collection of essays *The Sacred Hoop: Recovering the Feminine in American Indian Traditions* (Boston: Beacon Press, 1986).

Judith Arcana, "Friends" by Grace Paley

1. Reginald Gibbons, ed., *The Writer in Our World: A Triquarterly Symposium* (New York: Atlantic Monthly, 1986).

Carol Taylor, "Etta Mae Johnson" by Gloria Naylor

1. Gloria Naylor, "Until Death Do Us Part," *Essence* (May 1985): 133.

2. New York: Penguin Books.

3. Bronwyn Mills, "Gloria Naylor: Dreaming the Dream," *Sojourner* (May 1988): 17.

4. "'Three Cheers for Good Marks': Writers on Their Prizes," *New York Times Book Review* (November 16, 1986): 46.

5. New York: Pocket Books, 1972.

6. "Gloria Naylor and Toni Morrison: A Conversation," *Southern Review* (Summer 1985): 567–93, 568.

7. William Goldstein, "A Talk with Gloria Naylor About the Black Female Experience in America," *Publishers Weekly* (September 9, 1983): 36.

Linda Wagner-Martin, "The Feeder" by Maria Bruno.

1. "The Feeder" first appeared in the Michigan State University *Women's Studies Newsletter* (Spring 1985).

Martha Ficklen, "One *Shabbos* Evening" by Lesléa Newman

1. *A Letter to Harvey Milk* (Ithaca, N.Y.: Firebrand, 1988).

2. Norwich, Vt.: New Victoria.

3. Santa Cruz, Calif.: HerBooks.

Afterword

1. Dale Spender, *Women of Ideas (and What Men Have Done to Them)* (London: Routledge & Kegan Paul, 1982), 2.

2. Cherrie Moraga, "Preface," in *This Bridge Called My Back: Writings by Radical Women of Color,* ed. Cherrie Moraga and Gloria Anzaldua (Watertown, Mass.: Persephone Press, 1981), xvi–xvii.

3. For further explorations of the relationships between women who earn their living doing sex work and women who earn their living doing other kinds of work, see the novel by W. L. George, *A Bed of Roses* (New York: Brentano's, 1911); Frederique Delacoste and Priscilla Alexander, eds., *Sex Work: Writings by Women in the Sex Industry* (San Francisco: Cleis Press, 1987); and Gail Pheterson, ed., *A Vindication of the Rights of Whores* (Seattle: Seal Press, 1989).

4. A powerful story about the practical utility of friendship—and the sad truth that by itself it is not always enough to ensure survival—is told in Marge Piercy's *Gone to Soldiers* (New York: Summit Books, 1987).

5. I now realize that for many nineteenth-century gentile writers the use of this language was a convention as much as or more than a conviction. I do not think it necessarily means anything about the characters' spiritual lives or belief systems. It is instead phatic communication ("phatic" is defined in Webster's as "revealing or sharing feelings or establishing an atmosphere of sociability rather than communicating ideas"). It was their way of saying, "I'm respectable."

6. Of course, it is always true about each of Lydia Maria Child's stories that I have never read one like it before, or, if I have, the story was written later than a similar story by Child. Child, as one of the creators of the American short story, was one of the first to define subject matter for women's short stories. Each of her stories is ground-breaking. Each is an important story because she was writing so early, making so many "first" choices, and establishing so many traditions.

7. Judith Arcana, letter to the author, n.d.

8. There are many stories about girlhood in women's autobiographies, memoirs, and novels. In those stories (see the works of Alice Cary, Louisa May Alcott, Mary E. Wilkins Freeman, Nancy Hale, and Rita Mae Brown for a sampler from the 1850s to the 1970s), the children have close friendships. But the friendships, which often include groups of children of both sexes, are rarely the focus of the stories. Instead, the friendship groups are usually part of the structure—the way plans are made and carried out, the way the reader is given information, and so on. In addition to this, the friends are often siblings, having become friends because of proximity. In fact, the less urban the setting, the more likely the friends are to be siblings.

9. On this stage of life, I recommend the excellent multi-generic, multi-national collection *I'm on My Way Running: Women Speak on Coming of Age,* edited by Lyn Reese, Jean Wilkinson, and Phyllis Sheon Koppelman (no relation that we know of; New York: Avon Books, 1983).

10. Although these stories are written by writers and about characters who can be described as "marginal"—as women, as writers, as members of particular ethnic, racial, generational, geographical, class, and caste groups—I do not want to suggest that this literature and these writers belong outside the mainstream of literature.

In her introduction to *The Dream Book: An Anthology of Writings by Italian American Women* (New York: Schocken Books, 1985) editor Helen Barolini puts it this way: "It is not as a separation from the mainstream of literature, but for purposes of historical and cultural perspective, that the writers in [The Dream Book] are identified as having some connection with *italianita,* for I am always aware that as individual writers, each transcends the limitations of qualifiers." p. xi.

11. Susan Hauser, letter to the author, July 28, 1989.

12. Many women's friendships based on this kind of proximity become genuine friendships because the women recognize that friendships are necessary for mental and emotional health and survival and so they reciprocate the acts and the trust that are the components of friendship in an effort to choose healthy lives.

13. An interesting aside about women's involvement with their husband's worlds: three librarians (from the St. Louis Public Library, the Missouri Historical Society Library, and the Saul Brodsky Jewish Community Center library) have told me that most people who come to their libraries to do genealogical research are women; most of the women are researching the history of their *husband's* family.

14. Blanche Wiesen Cook, "Female Support Networks and Political Activism: Lillian Wald, Crystal Eastman, Emma Goldman, and Jane Addams," *Chrysalis* 3 (Autumn 1977), reprinted in Blanche Wiesen Cook, *Women and Support Networks* (Brooklyn: Out and Out Books, 1979).

15. One of the most common complaints I hear from women about other women is this: "I listened to her pour out her troubles for hours, I held her hand and gave her my best advice, and then—when *he* called/came back/got sober/got a job/promotion/ended his affair, she just disappeared from my life." Most often, but not always, it is heterosexual romances or love relationships that tempt women to exploit their friendships with other women.

Another variety of this exploitation of women by women is the experience of single heterosexual women who are expected to "be there" for their friends when neither has a date, but to release the friend from any obligation or commitment if a man makes a later bid for the woman friend's time or attention. It used to be that women condemned themselves for selfishness if they resented this system and were accused of jealousy if they demanded more respectful treatment, but feminist analysis explains how divisive, woman hating, and unethical such behavior and the values that underlie it are.

Although I know that this unconscionable theft of nurturance still goes on, awareness and reciprocal nurturance among women seems to be increasing. These are formally modeled in the rape crisis center movement, often staffed by women who are themselves rape survivors and have been counseled in such a center. The same reciprocity of care can be seen in the battered women's rescue movement, the incest survivors movement, and in services for women recovering from various addictions.

16. Audre Lorde, "The Master's Tools Will Never Dismantle the Master's House," in *This Bridge Called My Back,* ed. Moraga and Anzaldua, 98.

17. Susie Rogers, letter to the author, September 10, 1990.

18. Kay Turner, "Contemporary Feminist Rituals," in *The Politics of Women's Spirituality: Essays on the Rise of Spiritual Power Within the Feminist Movement,* Charlene Spretnak, ed. (Garden City, N.Y.: Doubleday, Anchor, 1982), 219.

19. Paula Gunn Allen, "Introduction," in *Spider Woman's Granddaughters: Traditional Tales and Contemporary Writing by Native American Women* (Boston: Beacon Press, 1989): 4.

20. Carolyn G. Heilbrun, "The Future of Friendship," *Women's Review of Books* 3, no. 9 (June 1986): 1.

SELECT BIBLIOGRAPHY

Abel, Elizabeth. "Merging Identities: The Dynamics of Female Friendship in Contemporary Fiction by Women." *Signs* 6, no. 3 (1981): 413–33. Response by Gardiner with reply by Abel.

Alger, William Rounseville. *The Friendships of Women*. 1867. 9th ed. Boston: Roberts Brothers, 1879.

Armstrong, M. Jocelyn. "Women's Friendships under Urbanization: A Malaysian Study." *Women's Studies International Forum* 10, no. 6 (1987): 623–33.

Ascher, Carol. "It's All Right to Be Honest: How One Friendship Survived an Incurable Illness." *Ms.* (April 1985): 86.

Auerbach, Nina. *Communities of Women: An Idea in Fiction*. Cambridge, Mass.: Harvard University Press, 1978.

Bernikow, Louise. *Among Women*. New York: Harper & Row, Harper Colophone Book, 1980.

Brittain, Vera. *Testament of Friendship: The Story Of Winifred Holtby*. London: Macmillan, 1940. Reprint. London: Virago, 1981.

Broner, E. M. "Blessing the Ties that Bind." *Ms.* (December 1986).

Carr, Glynis. "The Female World of Love and Racism: Interracial Friendship in African American and White U.S. Women's Fiction, 1840–1940." Ph.D. diss., The Ohio State University, 1989.

Cole, Diane. "The Responsibility to Respond: What One Friend Owes Another." *Ms.* (December 1986).

Conlon, Faith, Rachel da Silva, and Barbara Wilson, eds. *The Things that Divide Us*. Seattle: Seal Press, 1985.

Cook, Blanche Wiesen. "Female Support Networks and Political Activism:

Lillian Wald, Crystal Eastman, Emma Goldman, and Jane Addams." *Chrysalis* 3 (Autumn 1977): 43.

Cosslett, Tess. *Woman to Woman: Female Friendships in Victorian Fiction.* Atlantic Highlands, N.J.: Humanities Press International, 1988.

Ehrenreich, Barbara. "In Praise of 'Best Friends': The Revival of a Fine Old Institution." *Ms.* (January 1987).

Ehrenreich, Barbara, and Jane O'Reilly. "No Jiggles. No Scheming. Just Real Women as Friends." *T.V. Guide* (November 24, 1984): 6–10.

Fite, Karen, and Nikola Trumbo. "Betrayals Among Women: Barriers to a Common Language." *Lesbian Ethics* 1, no. 1 (1984).

Gillespie, Marcia Ann. "Sister Friends." *Ms.* (July–August 1987): 130.

Goldenberg, Myrna. "Different Horrors, Same Hell: Women Remembering the Holocaust." Lecture, April 3, 1990, George Mason University "About Women" Series.

Gordon, Mary. "Women's Friendships." *Redbook* (July 1979).

Harris, D. J. "Women/Friends." *Sojourner* (April 1987): 7–8.

Hauser, Tina. "If There's Anything I Can Do . . ." *Athritis Today* (January–February 1990): 31–33.

Heineman, Helen. *Restless Angels: The Friendship of Six Victorian Women.* Athens: Ohio University Press, 1983.

Ives, Alice E. "Friendship Among Women." In *What Can a Woman Do: Or, Her Position in the Business and Literary World,* edited by Mrs. M. L. Rayne, 407–15. Petersburgh, N.Y.: Eagle Publishing Co., 1893.

Jeffreys, Sheila. "Women's Friendships and Lesbianism." In *The Spinster and Her Enemies: Feminism and Sexuality 1880–1930,* 102–27. London: Methuen, Pandora Press, 1985.

Komaiko, Leah. *Annie Bananie.* Illustrated by Laura Cornell. New York: Harper & Row, Harper Trophy Edition, 1987.

Lamb, Patricia Frazer, and Kathryn Joyce Hohlwein. *Touchstones: Letters Between Two Women, 1953–1964.* New York: Harper & Row, 1983.

Lee, Anna. "Therapy: The Evil Within." *Trivia: A Journal of Ideas* (Fall 1986): 34–45.

Margolies, Eva. *The Best of Friends, The Worst of Enemies: Women's Hidden Power over Women.* New York: Dial Press, 1985.

Myerhoff, Barbara. "After Fifteen Years of Feminism, Where Is Women's Friendship?" *Ms.* (June 1985).

Naylor, Gloria. "Until Death Do Us Part." *Essence* (May 1985): 133.

Nestor, Pauline. *Female Friendships and Communities: Charlotte Bronte, George Eliot, Elizabeth Gaskell.* New York: Oxford University Press, 1986.

Oliker, Stacey J. *Best Friends and Marriage: Exchange Among Women.* Berkeley: University of California Press, 1989.

Oosthuizen, Ann. *Stepping Out: Short Stories on Friendship Between Women.* London: Methuen, Pandora Press, 1986.

Pogrebin, Letty Cottin. *Among Friends: Who We Like, Why We Like Them, and What We Do with Them.* New York: McGraw Hill, 1986.

Raymond, Janice G. *A Passion for Friends: Toward a Philosophy of Female Affection.* Boston: Beacon Press, 1986.

Rubin, Lillian B. *Just Friends: The Role of Friendship in Our Lives.* New York: Harper & Row, 1985.

Sahli, Nancy. "Smashing: Women's Relationships Before the Fall." *Chrysalis* 8 (Summer 1979): 18.

Schultz, Elizabeth. "Out of the Woods and into the World: A Study of Inter-racial Friendships Between Women in American Novels." In *Conjuring: Black Women, Fiction, and Literary Tradition,* edited by Marjorie Pryse and Hortense J. Spillers. Bloomington: Indiana University Press, 1985.

Sinister Wisdom [special issue]. "On Friendship." 40 (April 1990).

Smith-Rosenberg, Carroll. "The Female World of Love and Ritual: Relations Between Women in Nineteenth Century America." *Signs* 1 (Autumn 1975). Reprinted in N. F. Cott and E. H. Pleck, eds., *A Heritage of Her Own.* New York: Simon & Schuster, Touchstone Books, 1979.

Spangler, Lynn C. "A Historical Overview of Female Friendships on Prime-Time Television." *Journal of Popular Culture* 22, no. 4 (Spring 1989): 13–23.

Tobin, Jean. "Narrative Uses of Friendship in the Novels of Marge Piercy." Presented at session 34, Women's Lives in Literature, Midwest Popular Culture Conference, St. Louis, Oct. 18, 1988.

Todd, Janet. *Women's Friendship in Literature.* New York: Columbia University Press, 1980.

Nonprint Media

"Sisters in the Name of Love." Home Box Office special. Based on the individual talents of and the long friendship shared by Patti LaBelle, Gladys Knight, and Dionne Warwick.

"Just Between Friends: Oprah Explores the Bonds of Friendship." Special program, aired June 4, 1989, Oprah Winfrey, producer.

THE CONTRIBUTORS

Compiled by Susan Koppelman

Judith Arcana, Director of the Center for Women at the Union Institute, is the author of *Our Mothers' Daughters, Every Mother's Son, Celebrating Nelly,* and *Cultural Dreamer: Grace Paley's Life Stories.* She has recently published articles about D. H. Lawrence, Keats, *Beowulf*, Sherwood Anderson, and Grace Paley. Her poetry has appeared recently in *Women and Language, Rhino,* and *Bridges.*

Lynn Z. Bloom (B.A., M.A., Ph.D., University of Michigan) is Professor of English and first holder of the Aetna Chair of Writing at the University of Connecticut. Her numerous publications include *Doctor Spock* (1972), *Fact and Artifact: Writing Nonfiction* (1985), and *Forbidden Family* (1989). Much of her research centers on families and the friendships they engender or destroy.

Betty Burnett, senior editor of the Patrice Press, holds a Ph.D. in American studies from St. Louis University. She has written *One Hundred Years of Caring: The History of Missouri Baptist Hospital* (1985), *St. Louis at War: The Story of a City 1941–45* (1987), *A Time of Favor: The Story of the Catholic Family of Southern Illinois* (1987), *St. Louis: Gateway to Tomorrow* (1989), and coauthored *St. Louis: Its Neighbors and Neighborhoods* (1986) and *Missouri: Mother of the American West* (1988). Her work focuses on the ways in which groups of people define and achieve goals within the context of social institutions—the practical uses of friendship.

Glynis Carr, Assistant Professor of English at Bucknell University, is writing a book about friendships between black and white women in U.S. literature by women since the 1840s. With Susan Koppelman, she is co-editing an anthology of women's short fiction on this topic. She first taught Frances Gray Patton's "A Nice Name" in her and her friends' women's studies classes at The Ohio State University, always finding the story to be an effective tool for exploring the psychopathology of racism in women's everyday lives. Carr has published articles on Virginia Woolf, Zora Neale Hurston, and Caribbean women writers. She believes that feminist literary scholarship should be engaged with significant issues in women's lives. Her research topics include friendship, creativity, family, and work—but the greatest of these is friendship.

Virginia Cox is Professor of English at the University of Wisconsin, Oshkosh, where she teaches in the Women's Studies Program. She is currently working on a biography of Zona Gale.

Sally Ann Drucker currently teaches in the Department of English at North Carolina State University. She received her Ph.D. from the State University of New York at Buffalo; her dissertation was entitled "Anzia Yezierska: An Immigrant Cinderella." An article by Drucker on Yezierska has appeared in *Modern Jewish Studies* and one on immigrant Jewish women in *American Jewish History*. A book of her poems, *Walking the Desert Lion,* was published by Ena Press in Tulsa.

Martha Ficklen is a radical dyke at heart and a public school teacher by trade. She is book review editor for *The Lesbian and Gay News Telegraph* in St. Louis.

Lucy M. Freibert teaches English at the University of Louisville where she also directs the English Honors Program. With Barbara A. White, she co-edited *Hidden Hands: An Anthology of American Women Writers, 1790–1870,* which received the first Susan Koppelman Award for Excellence in Feminist Studies from the Popular Culture Association/American Culture Association Women's Caucus. She enjoys reading and writing about women, and credits her mother, the women religious who taught her, and her feminist friends with empowering her.

Leah Hackleman received her A.B. from Washington University and her M.A. from Miami University. She is currently resting up before enrolling in in doctoral studies in 1991. Her literary interests include cultural theory and women's writing; and she teaches composition at Miami University–Hamilton. She and four friends—including cats Boo, Maggie, and Fannie—live in Oxford, Ohio, as active feminists.

Trudier Harris is J. Carlyle Sitterson Professor of English and Chair of the Curriculum in African and Afro-American Studies at the University of

North Carolina at Chapel Hill, where she has taught courses in African-American literature and folklore since she joined the faculty in 1979. She is author, coeditor, or editor of eleven volumes; her most recent critical work is *Fiction and Folklore: The Novels of Toni Morrison* (1991). She is self-appointed "president for life" of the Chapel Hill branch of the Alice Childress Fan Club.

Carolyn L. Karcher is Associate Professor of English at Temple University, author of *Shadow over the Promised Land: Slavery, Race, and Violence in Melville's America,* and editor of *Hobomok and Other Writings on Indians* by Lydia Maria Child. Through her book in progress on Child, to be titled *The Woman of Letters as Political Activist,* she hopes to restore to the present generation the empowering legacy of a writer who devoted her life to fighting for racial and sexual equality.

Abigail Keegan is an Assistant Professor at Oklahoma City University. She is the author of a collection of poetry, *The Feast of the Assumptions,* and co-editor of a women's poetry journal, *Piecework.* The chosen obsessions of her poetry and criticism are women, gardens, food, spirituality, incest, and friends. She believes that the seeds of cultural transformation lie in the study and cultivation of women's friendships, the relationships most potentially free of the dominance syndrome.

Carol Farley Kessler is an Associate Professor of English, American studies, and women's studies at Penn State Delaware County Campus; she teaches composition from remedial to technical writing, as well as folklife, popular culture, and women's literature. Professor Kessler received a B.A. in English literature from Swarthmore College, an A.M.T. from Radcliffe College, and a Ph.D. from the University of Pennsylvania. In 1981 and 1988, she was awarded year-long fellowships from the National Endowment for the Humanities for her study of United States women's utopian fiction, 1836 to the present. In addition to numerous articles, she has published *Elizabeth Stuart Phelps* (1982), *Daring to Dream: Utopian Stories by United States Women, 1836-1919* (1984), and *The Story of Avis* by Elizabeth Stuart Phelps (1877; rpt. 1985, 1988). Currently she is completing a bio-critical study of the utopian writing of Charlotte Perkins Gilman, and revising and enlarging *Daring to Dream.*

Susan Koppelman, a chronically ill radical feminist, a second-generation American Jew, and an independent scholar, began teaching women's studies in 1967 at an adult education program she founded in Boston. After editing the 1972 anthology *Images of Women in Fiction: Feminist Perspectives,* she began working to recover U.S. women's short stories. Her publications in that field include *Old Maids: Short Stories by Nineteenth Century U.S. Women*

Writers (1984), *The Other Woman: Stories of Two Women and a Man* (1984), *Between Mothers and Daughters: Stories Across a Generation* (1985), *"May Your Days Be Merry and Bright" and Other Christmas Stories by Women* (1988, 1989), and the *Signet Classic Book of Southern Short Stories* (with Dorothy Abbott, 1991). More thematic and historical collections of short stories by U.S. women writers, including a selection of stories by Fannie Hurst, are forthcoming.

Born in Beijing, China, *Amy Ling* was brought to the United States at age six. She attended American schools from first grade in Allentown, Pennsylvania, through a Ph.D. in comparative literature from New York University, but was rarely assigned a book by a woman and never by a writer of color. She made it her life's purpose to complete her education and that of others by researching, reading, and writing about the work of ethnic minority American writers and of women. In 1984 she published a chapbook of her poems and painting, *Chinamerican Reflections,* and in 1990 her historical/ critical study *Between Worlds: Women Writers of Chinese Ancestry* was published by Pergamon Press. She has taught at numerous colleges and universities, including City College of New York, Brooklyn College, Rutgers, and Georgetown. In 1989–90 she was a Rockefeller Fellow in Humanities at the Asian/American Center at Queens College. In 1990–91 she was a visiting professor at Harvard and Trinity College, Hartford, initiating Asian American literature courses. She is presently associate professor in the English Department at the University of Wisconsin, Madison, and director of the Asian American Studies Program.

Margaret W. Merrill lives on a farm in Woodstock, Vermont, and teaches creative writing at Johnson State College. She has served as a writer in residence in high schools for the Vermont Council of the Arts. She and Deloris Harrison, who could not have come from more dissimilar backgrounds, became friends after Peggy took a class in American literature from Deloris.

Janet Palmer Mullaney publishes *Belles Lettres: A Review of Books by Women,* a limitless source of literary friendships and an activity infinitely more satisfying than doctoral courses barren of women looked in the late 1970s. She concurs with Gloria Naylor, who once remarked, "My own career would have still been assigned to the hinterlands of 'maybe' had it not been for my discovery of a single text by a woman writer who reflected my existence."

Joanna Russ is a novelist and short story writer whose recent publications include *The Hidden Side of the Moon* (a collection of short stories), *Magic Mommas, Trembling Sisters, Puritans and Perverts* (feminist essays), and *How*

To Suppress Women's Writing. She is the author of two other short-story collections and eight books. She is fifty-three (and cannot believe it yet) and teaches fiction writing at the University of Washington, Seattle. She is disabled, has no time, and is trying to write a book putting together (some) socialist and (some) feminist theory.

Patricia Clark Smith grew up in Massachusetts and Maine. Her first son was born on the eve of her Ph.D. orals at Yale. Her second arrived one week after her dissertation was completed. Since 1971 she has taught in the English Department at the University of New Mexico at Albuquerque. Her second book of poems is *Changing Your Story* (1991). Most of her scholarly work centers on contemporary American Indian women's writing. She and her friend Paula Gunn Allen coauthored a chapter on American Indian women and landscape in *The Desert Is No Lady* (1987).

Carol Taylor is an Assistant Professor at The Ohio State University – Mansfield. She teaches literature, composition, and black studies courses in the Department of English. Her work is in areas of black literature and African-American folklore. She is currently doing research on the folk traditions of the Gullah-speaking blacks along the coastal areas of South Carolina and Georgia.

Linda Wagner-Martin is Hanes Professor of English at the University of North Carolina, Chapel Hill. Recent books are *The Modern American Novel, 1914–1945, Denise Levertov: Critical Essays,* and the paperback edition of *Sylvia Plath, A Biography.* She is presently working on a revisionist biography of Gertrude Stein and her family. She relies heavily on the friendships of her women colleagues.

Barbara A. White teaches women's studies at the University of New Hampshire and writes about our literary foremothers. She is the author of *American Women Writers* (1977), *Hidden Hands: An Anthology of American Women Writers, 1790–1870* (1985, with her friend Lucy Freibert), *Growing Up Female: Adolescent Girlhood in American Fiction* (1985), and, most recently, *American Women's Fiction, 1790–1870: A Reference Guide.* Like her friend Susan Koppelman, Barbara is dedicated to retrieving the works of forgotten writers such as Alice Brown.